BAD KiTTY
SUPERCAT

NICK BRUEL

ROARING BROOK PRESS
NEW YORK

To Big Jim, Little Jim, Lynda, Catherine,
John, and all the iconic Infantinos including—
of course—Carmine, for all the comic book
inspiration you've given me over the years.

Published by Roaring Brook Press
Roaring Brook Press is a division of Holtzbrinck Publishing Holdings Limited Partnership
120 Broadway, New York, NY 10271 • mackids.com

Our books may be purchased in bulk for promotional, educational, or business use.
Please contact your local bookseller or the Macmillan Corporate and Premium Sales
Department at (800) 221-7945 ext. 5442 or by email at
MacmillanSpecialMarkets@macmillan.com.

Library of Congress Cataloging-in-Publication Data is available.

First edition, 2022 • Book design by Veronica Mang • Coloring by Saba Illustrations
Printed in China by RR Donnelley Asia Printing Solutions Ltd.,
Dongguan City, Guangdong Province

ISBN 978-1-250-74998-7 (hardcover)

1 3 5 7 9 10 8 6 4 2

• CONTENTS •

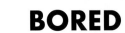

• CHAPTER ONE •

BORED

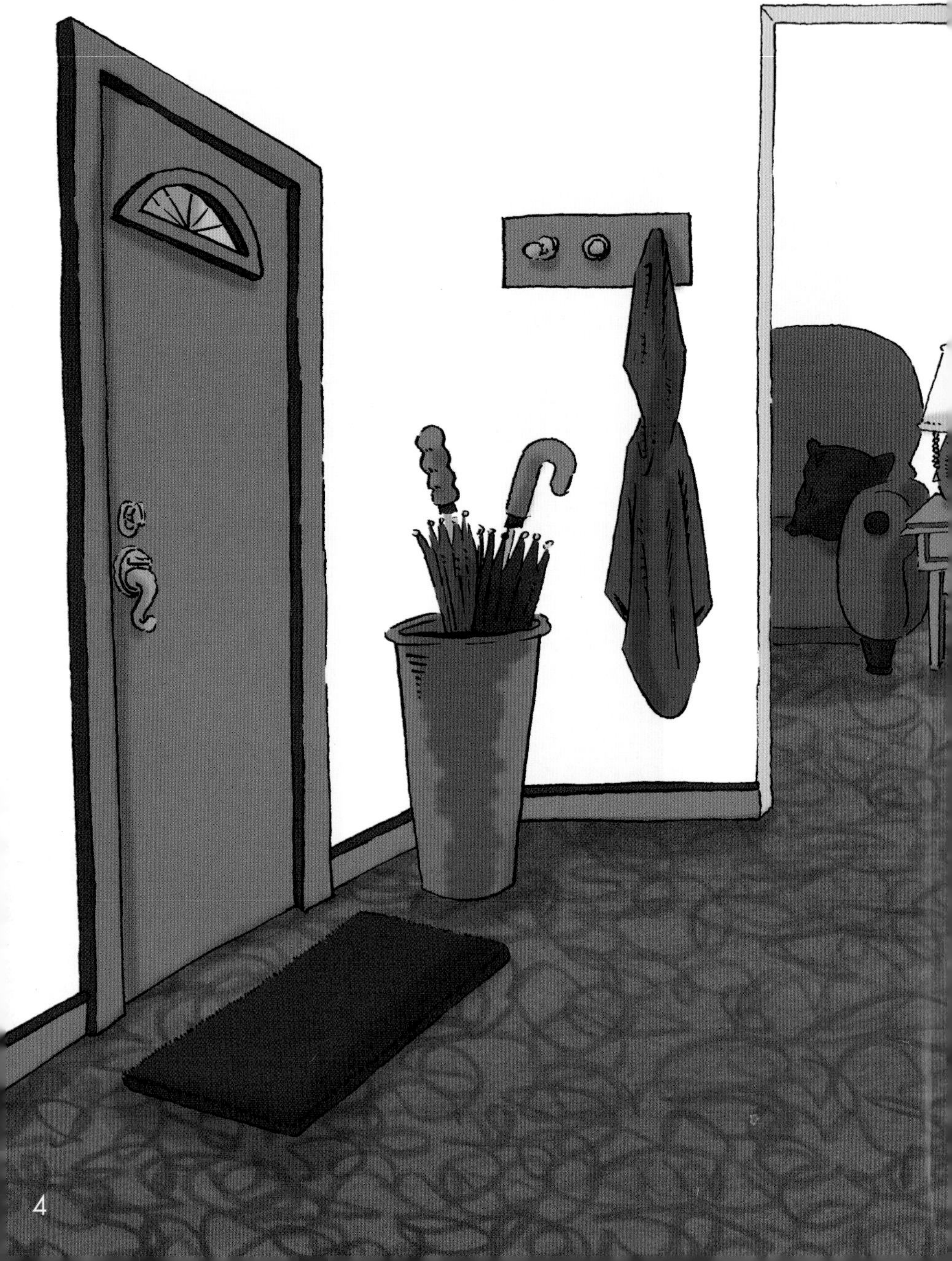

Kitty
is

bored.

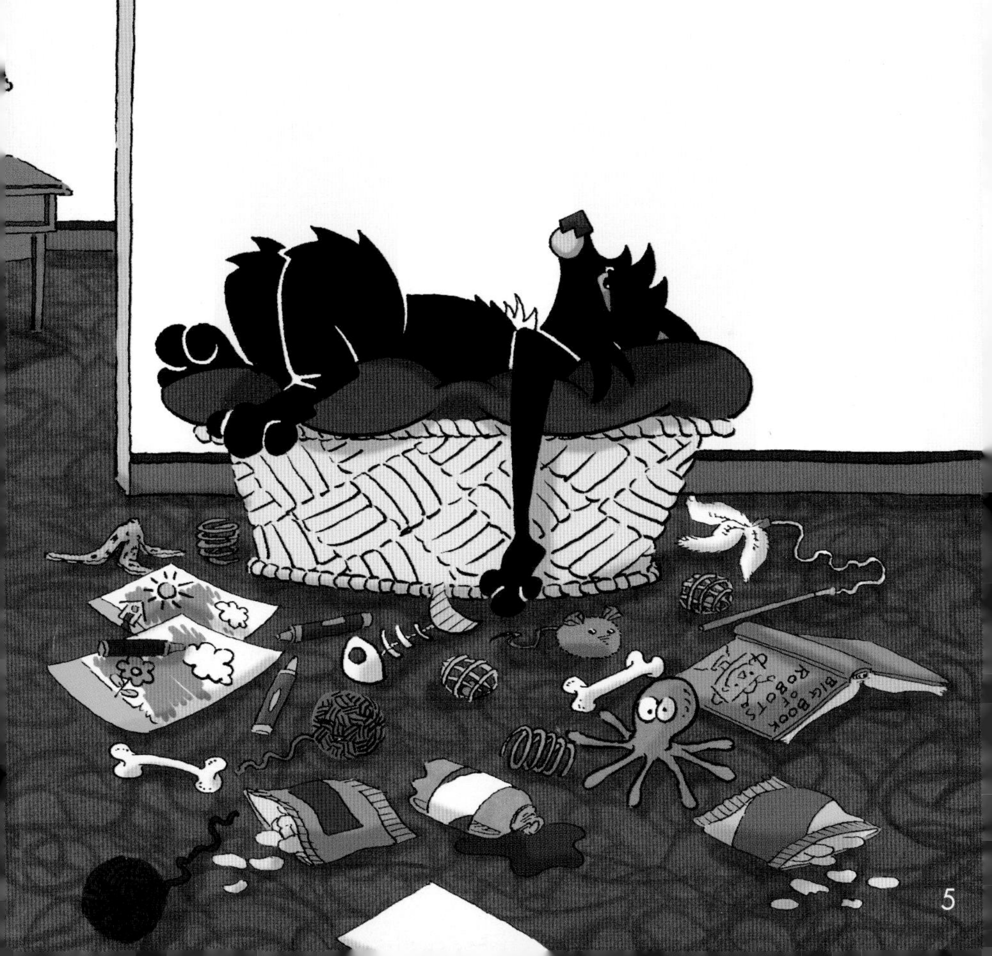
BIG BOOK of ROBOTS

BORED BORED BORED BORED BORED BORED
BORED BORED BORED BORED BORED BORED
BORED BORED BORED BORED BORED BORED
BORED BORED BORED BORED BORED BORED
BORED BORED BORED BORED BORED BORED
BORED BORED BORED BORED BORED BORED
BORED BORED BORED BORED BORED BORED
BORED BORED BORED BORED BORED BORED

Bored.

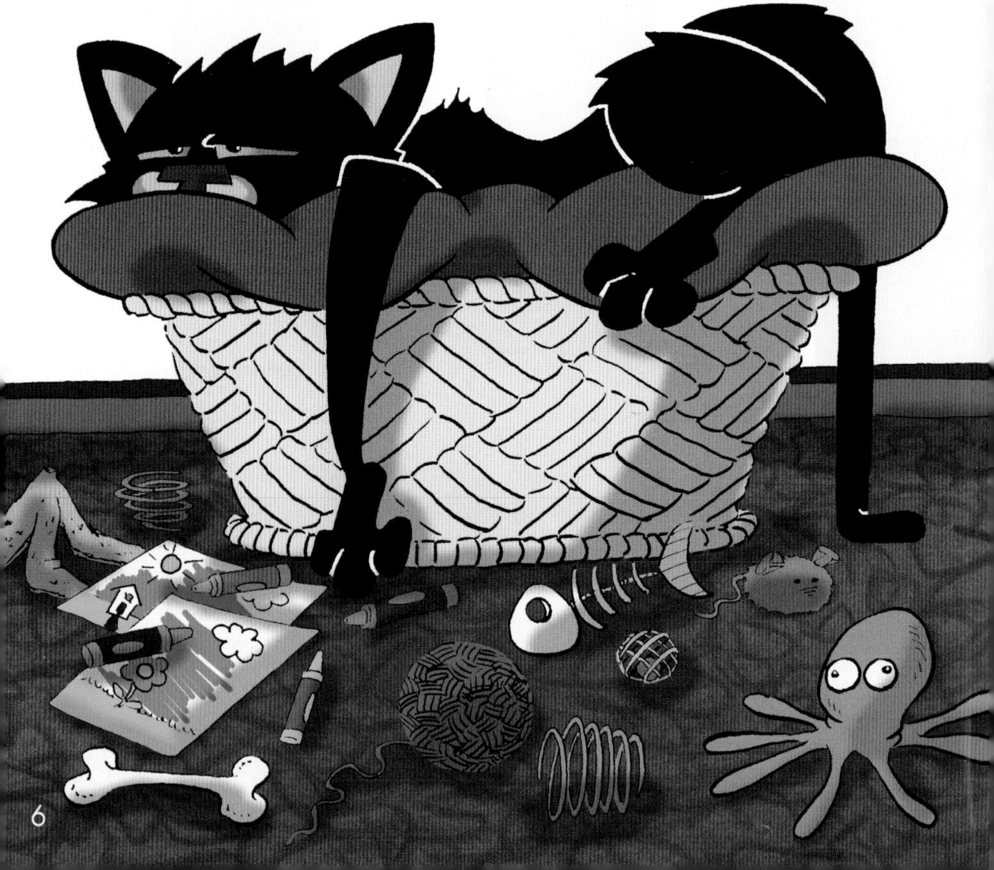

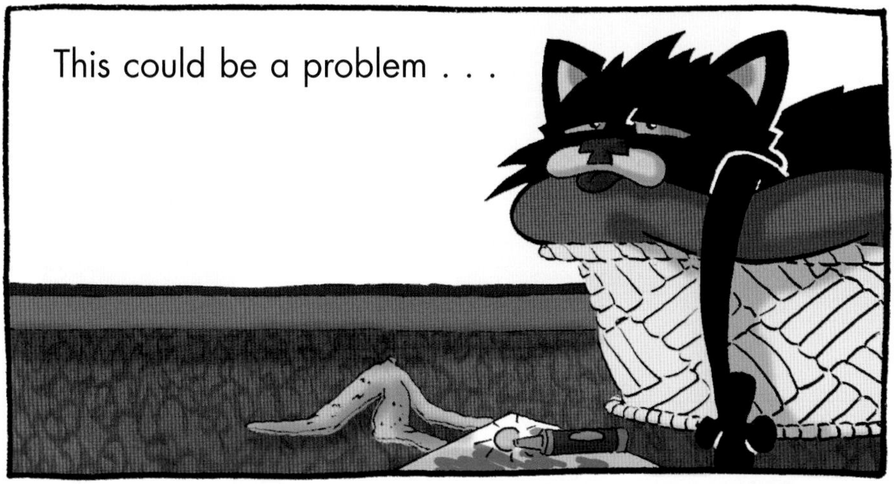
This could be a problem . . .

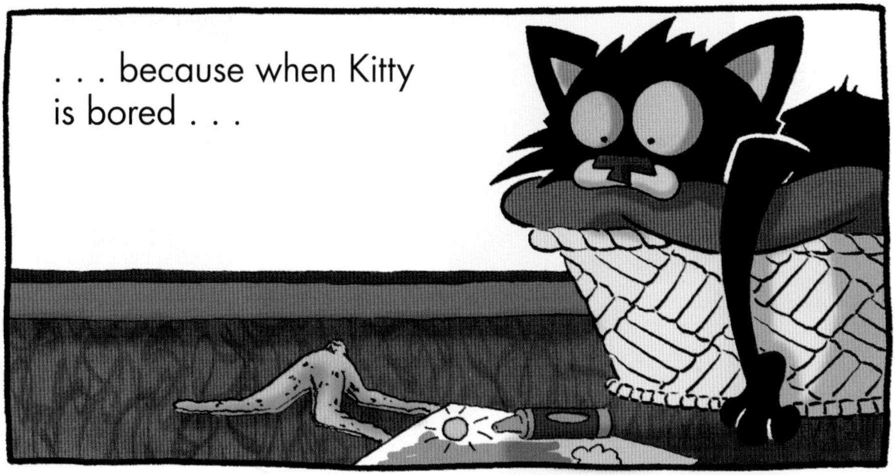
. . . because when Kitty is bored . . .

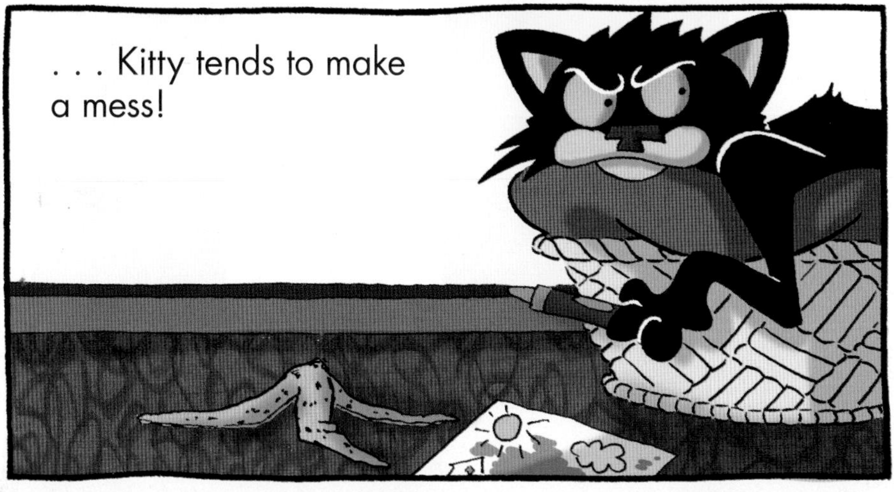
. . . Kitty tends to make a mess!

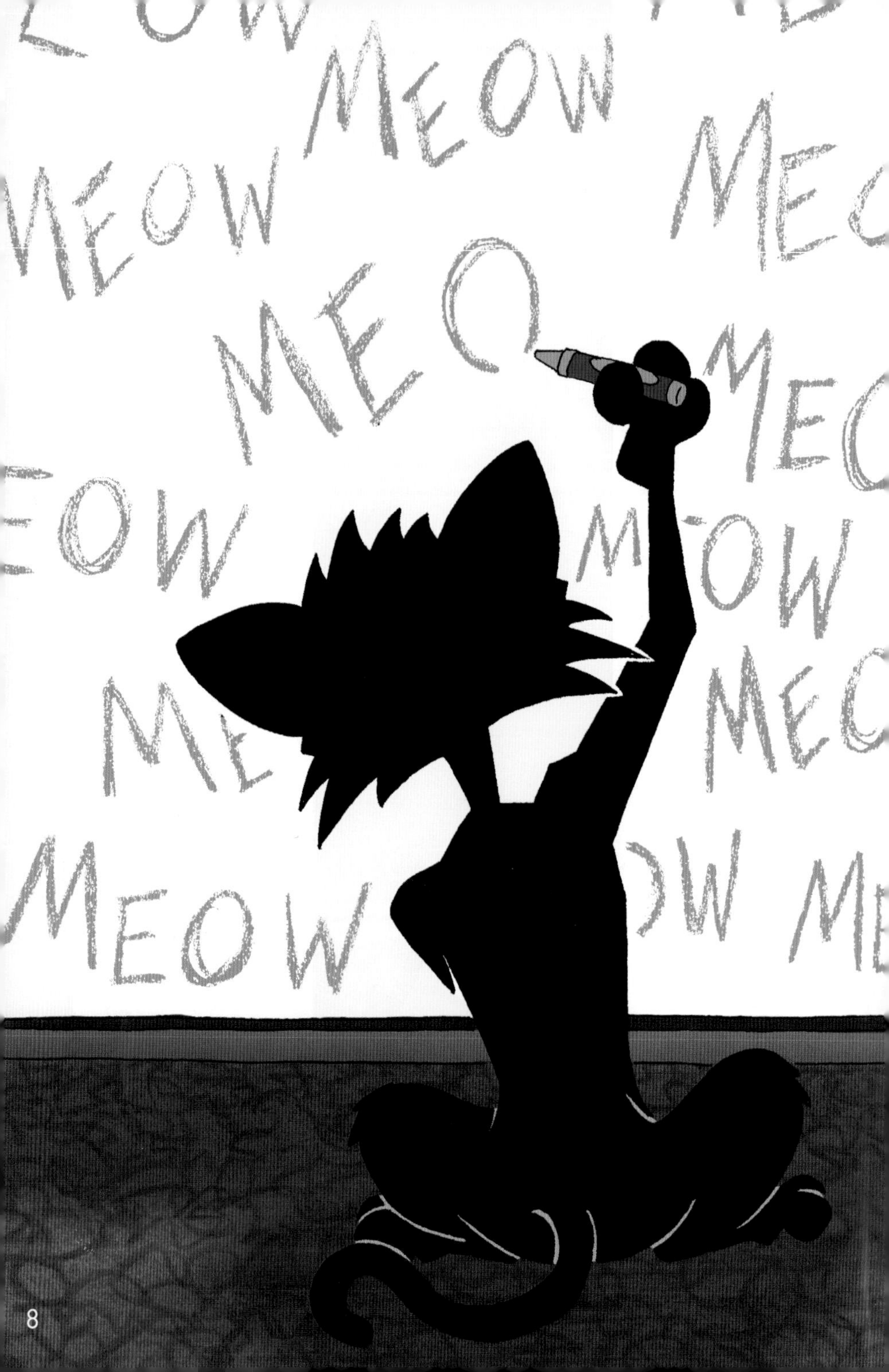
MEOW
MEOW
MEOW

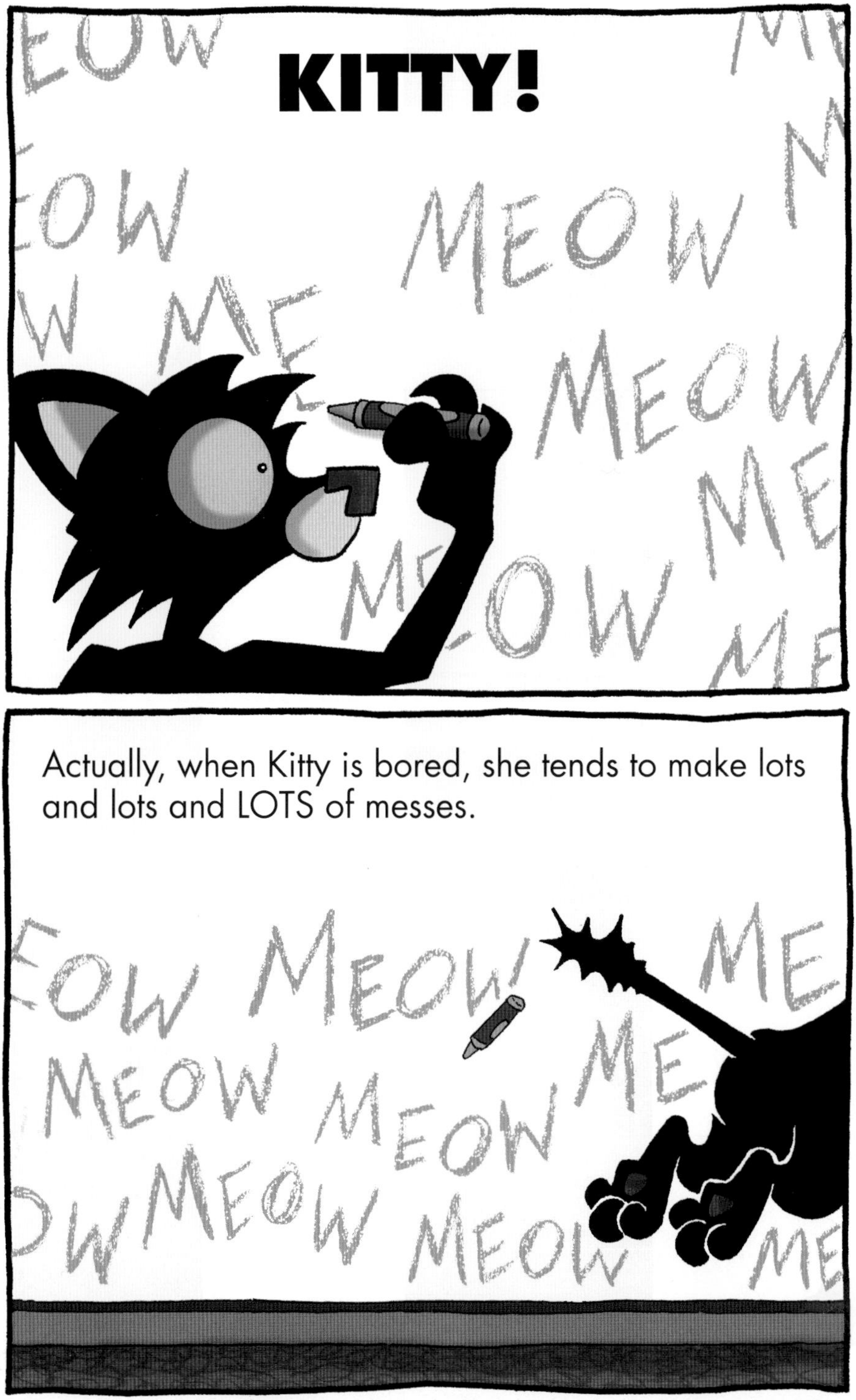
KITTY!
Actually, when Kitty is bored, she tends to make lots and lots and LOTS of messes.

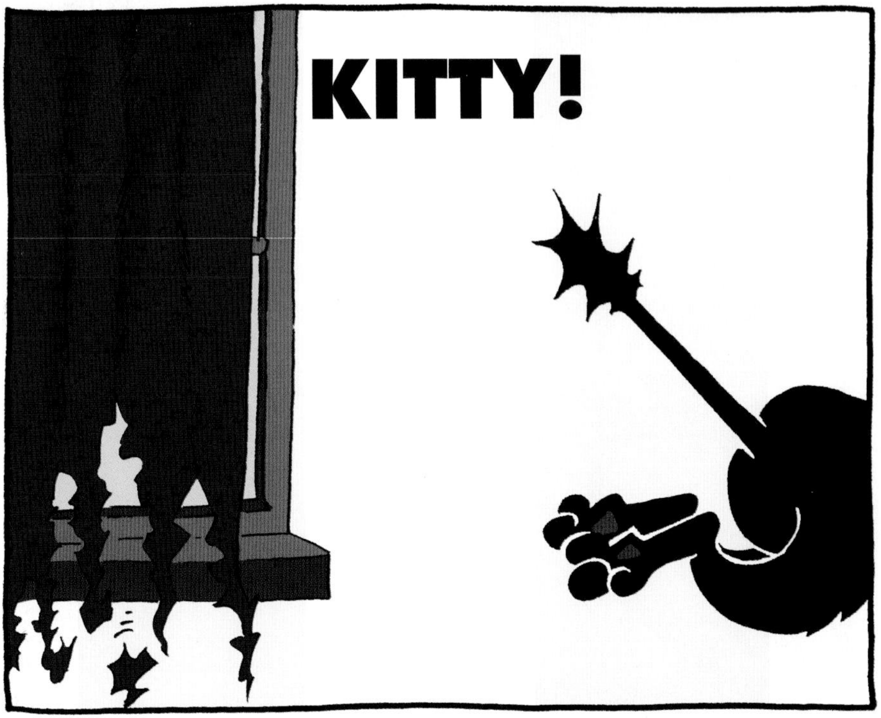
KITTY!

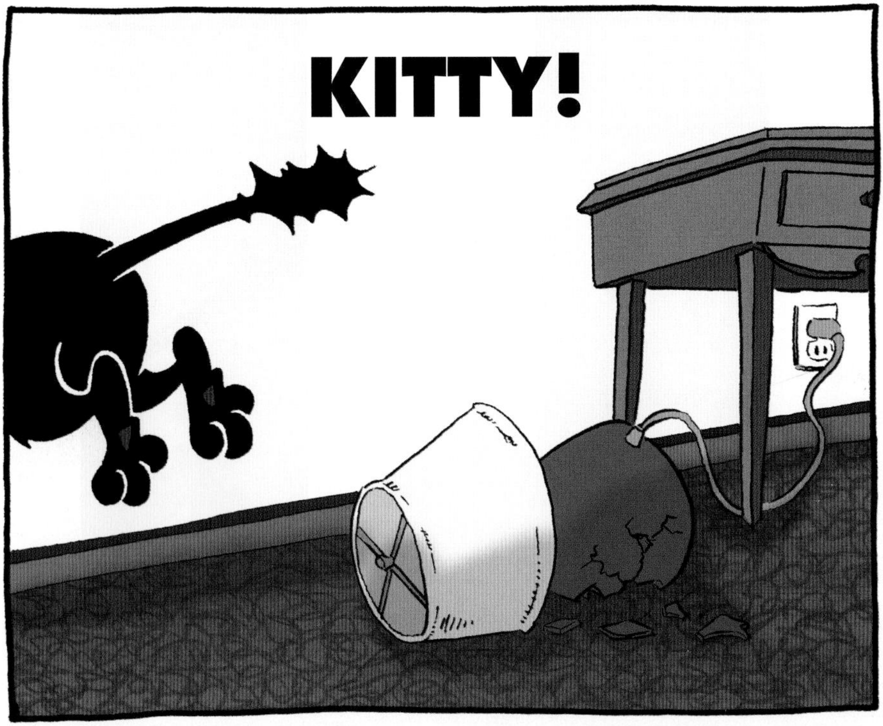
KITTY!

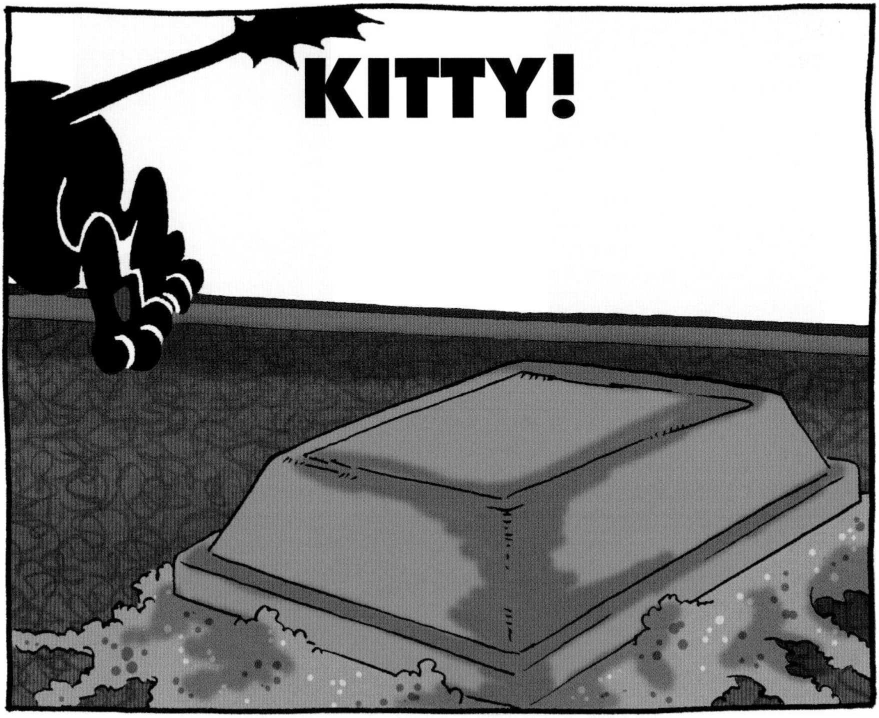
KITTY!

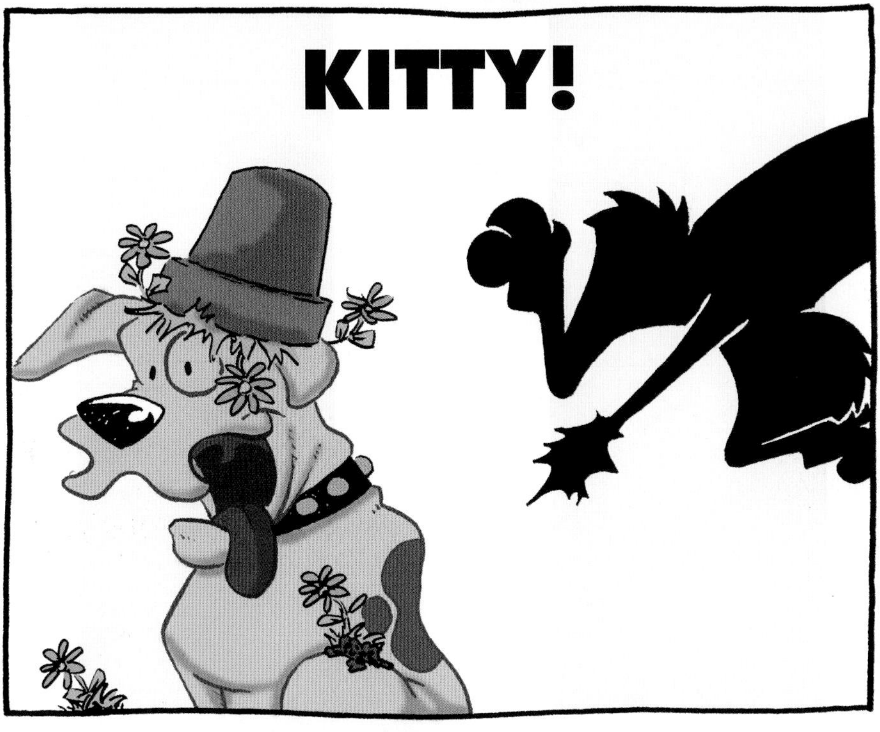
KITTY!

Look at the huge mess you've made all over the house, Kitty! Yes, I'm talking to you. Don't pretend like you had nothing to do with this.

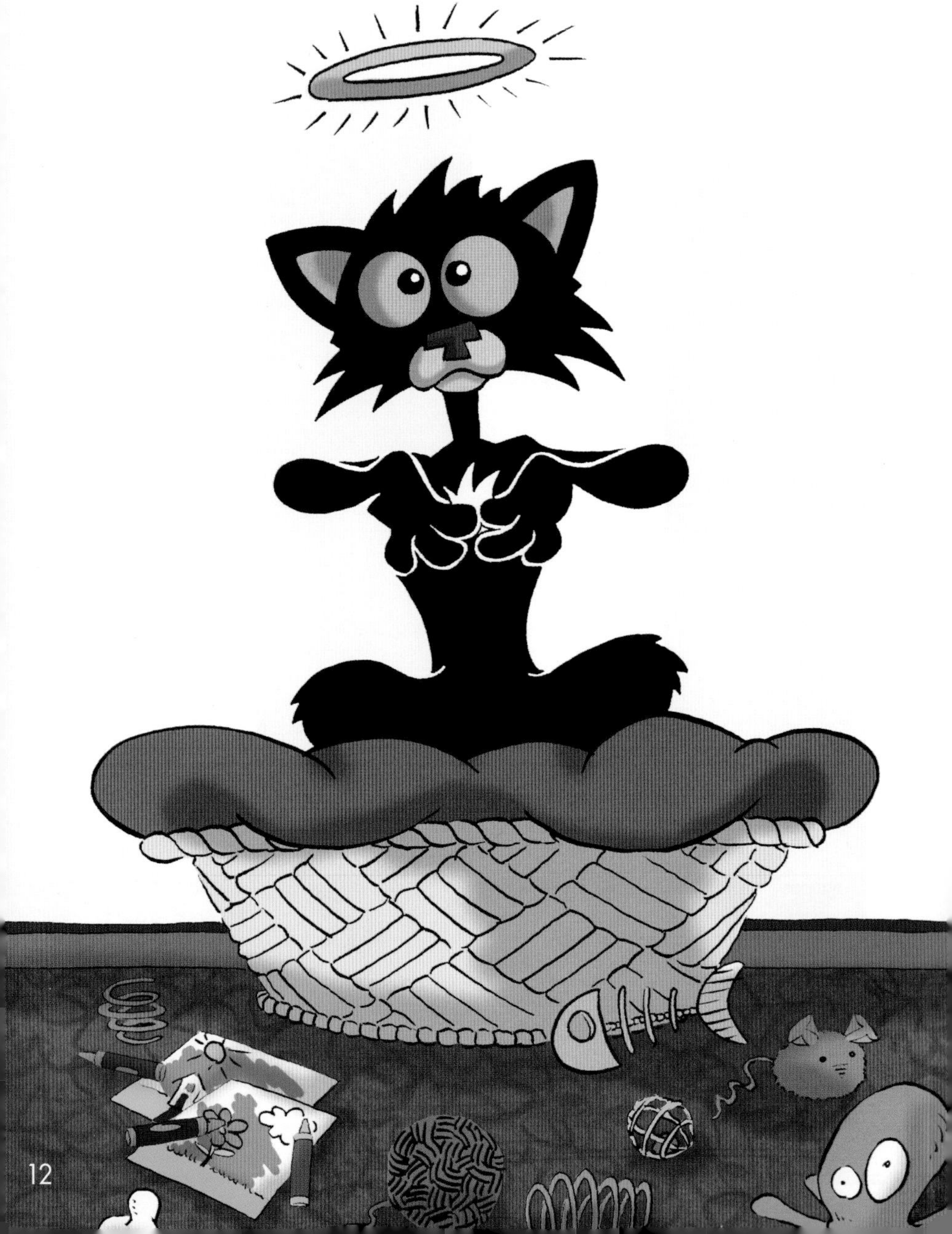

I don't know if you've made any plans for the rest of the day, but you're going to spend it helping me clean this place up!

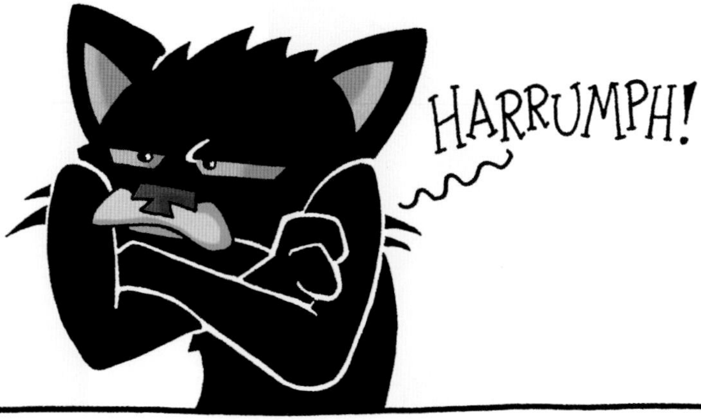
HARRUMPH!

This means that we have to wash the windows, scrub the walls, mop the floors, vacuum the curtains, do the laundry, rinse the dishes, change the sheets, mow the lawn, and clean the bathroom!

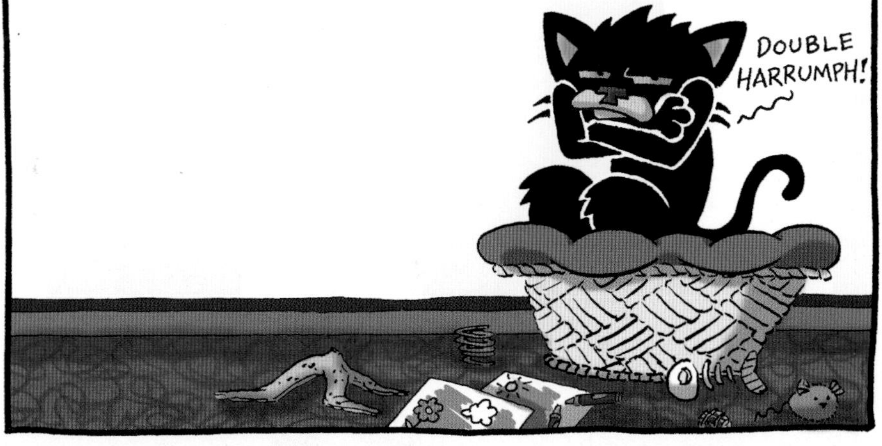
DOUBLE HARRUMPH!

You can start by picking up all the trash that's lying around your bed. Either put it away or throw it out! Okay?

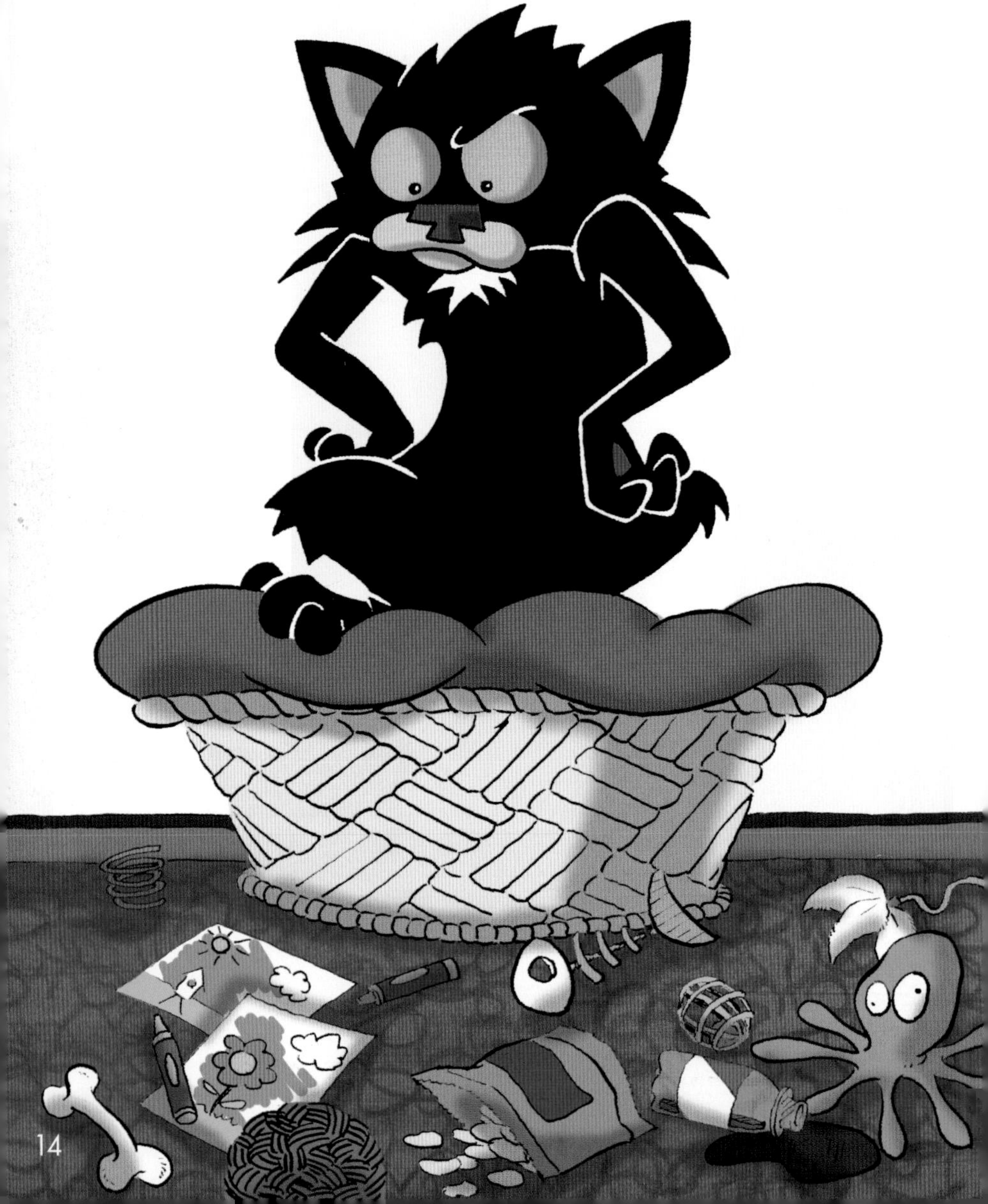

Here's a trash bin for all the garbage.

LET'S GO, KITTY!

LET'S GO!

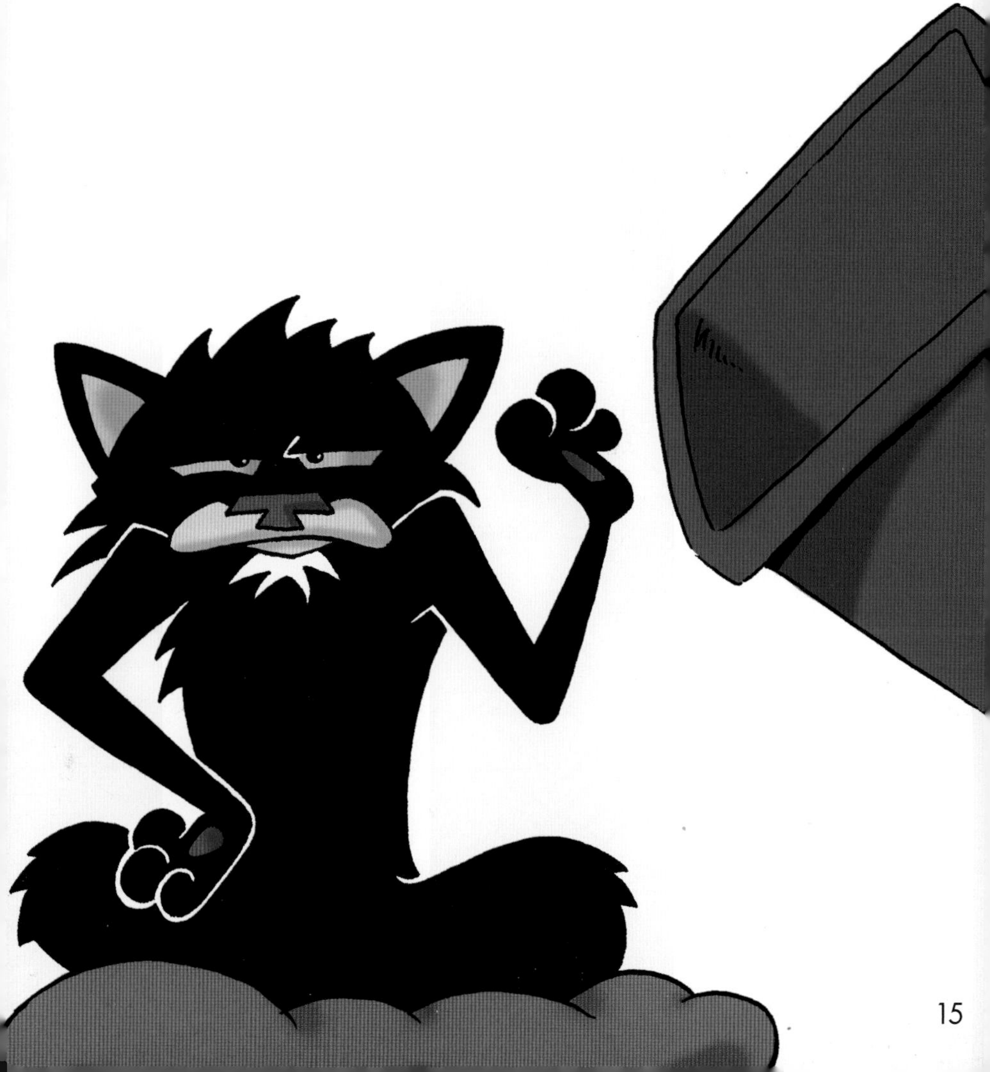

FOUR HOURS LATER . . .

WHEW!

Well, Kitty, I washed the windows, scrubbed the walls, mopped the floors, vacuumed the curtains, did the laundry, rinsed the dishes, changed the sheets, mowed the lawn, and cleaned the bathroom. It was a lot of work, but I'm glad it's done. And now the house is nice and clean!

What did you do, Kitty?

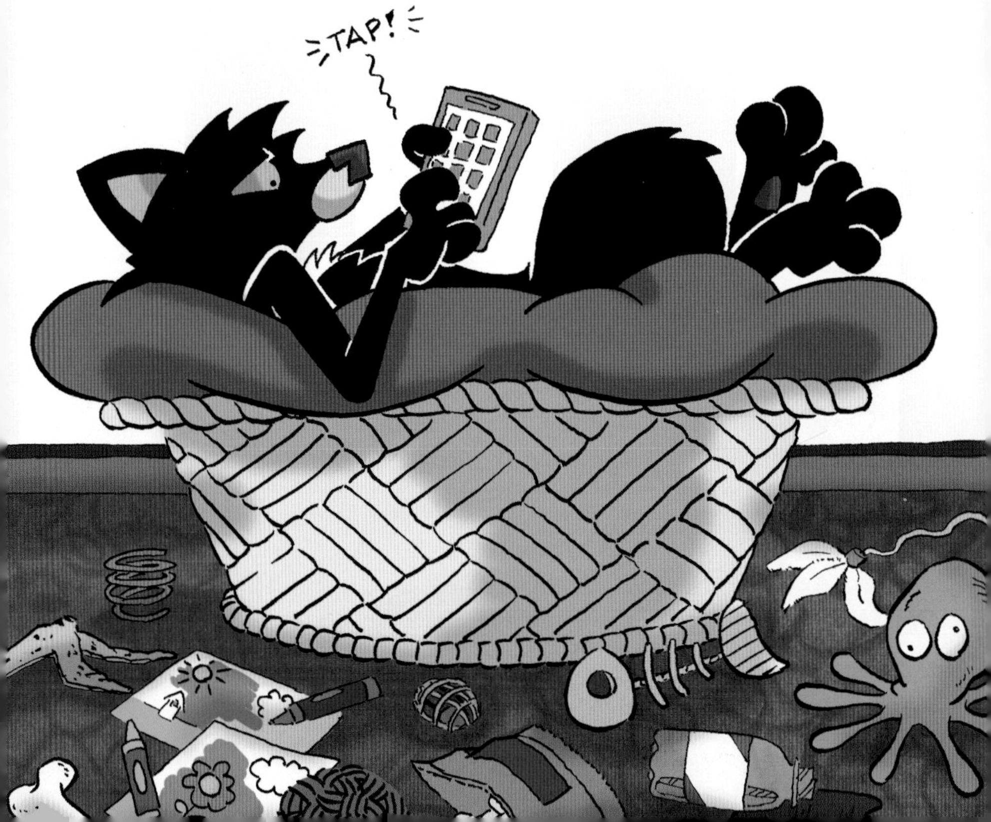
TAP!

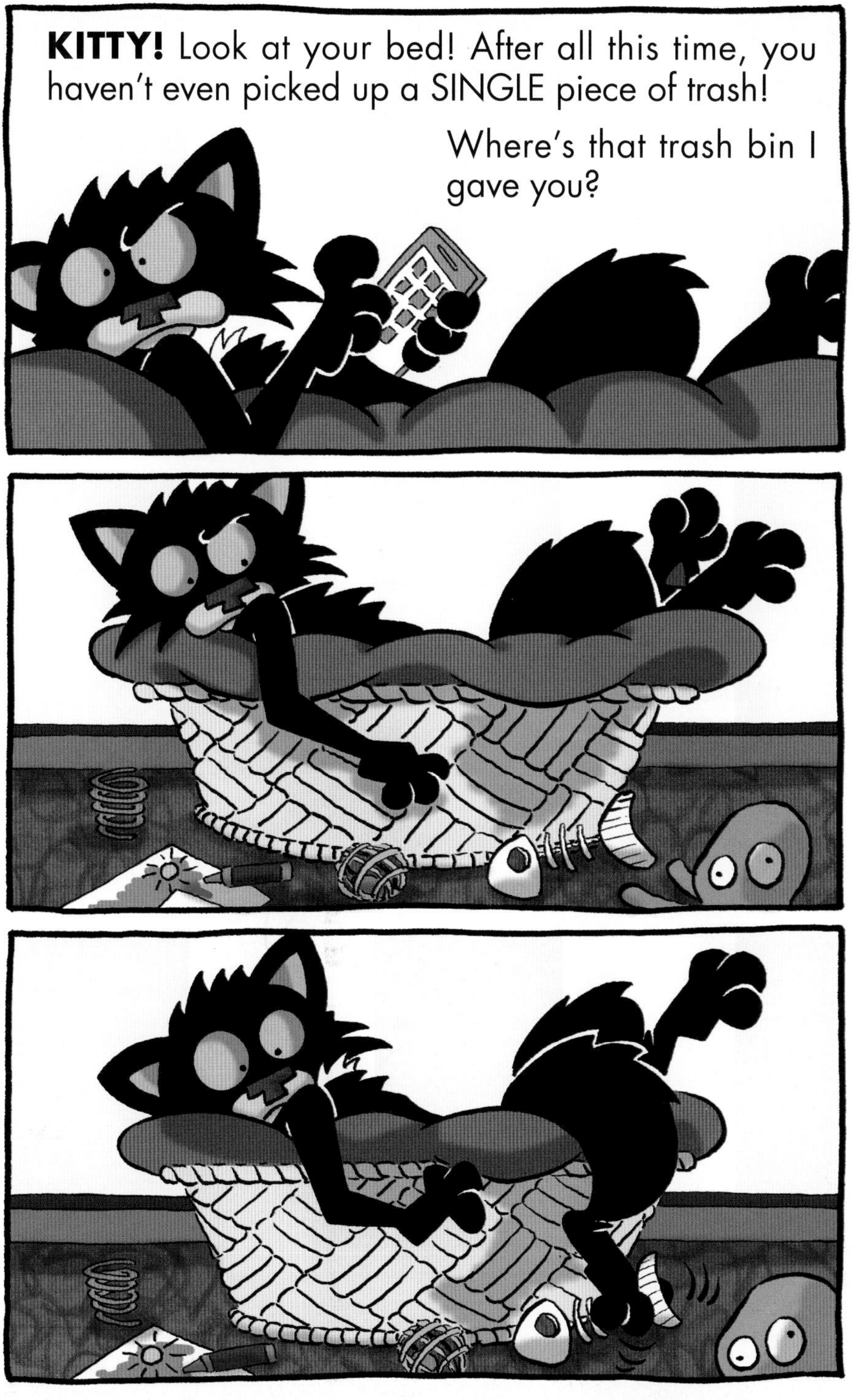
KITTY! Look at your bed! After all this time, you haven't even picked up a SINGLE piece of trash!
Where's that trash bin I gave you?

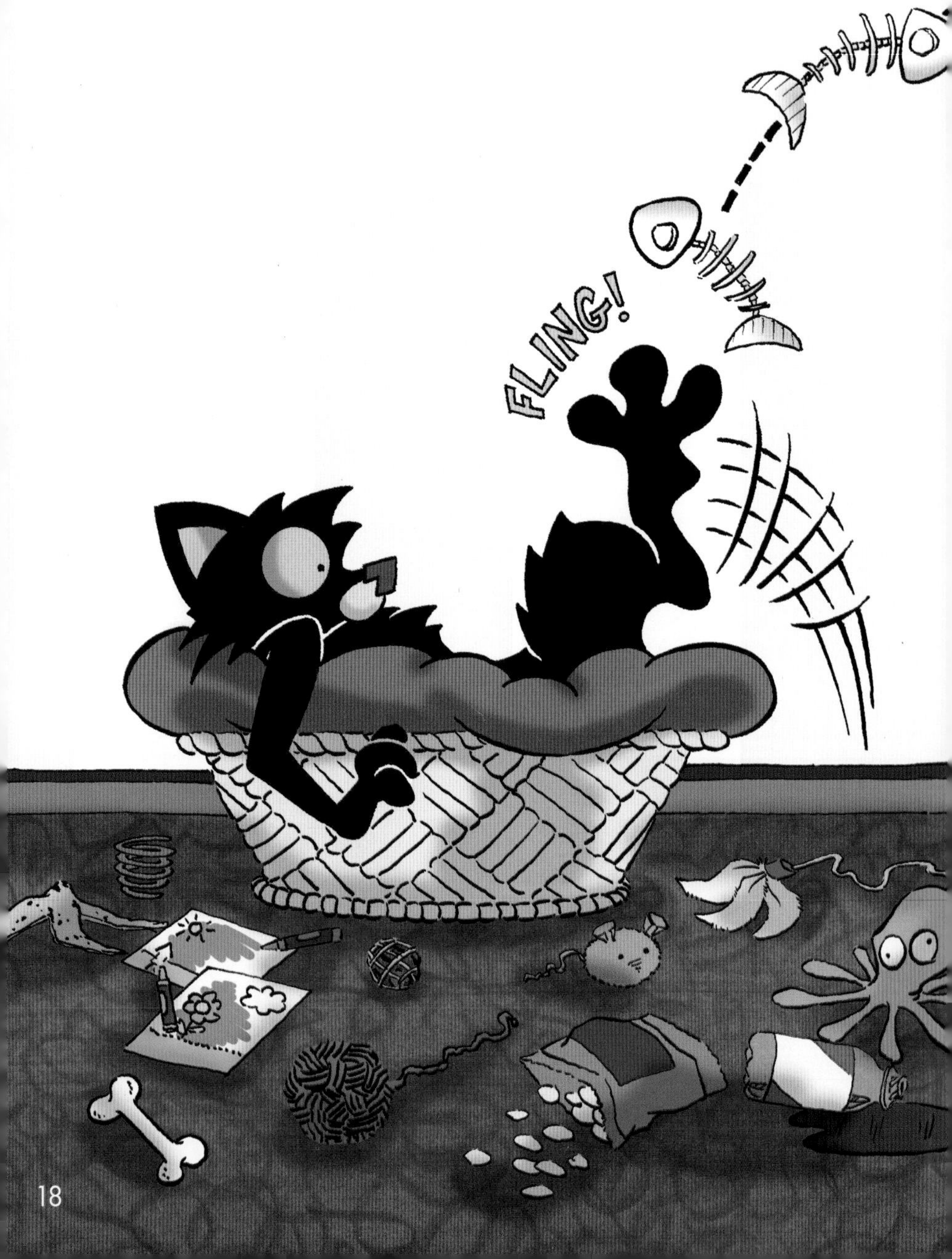
FLING!

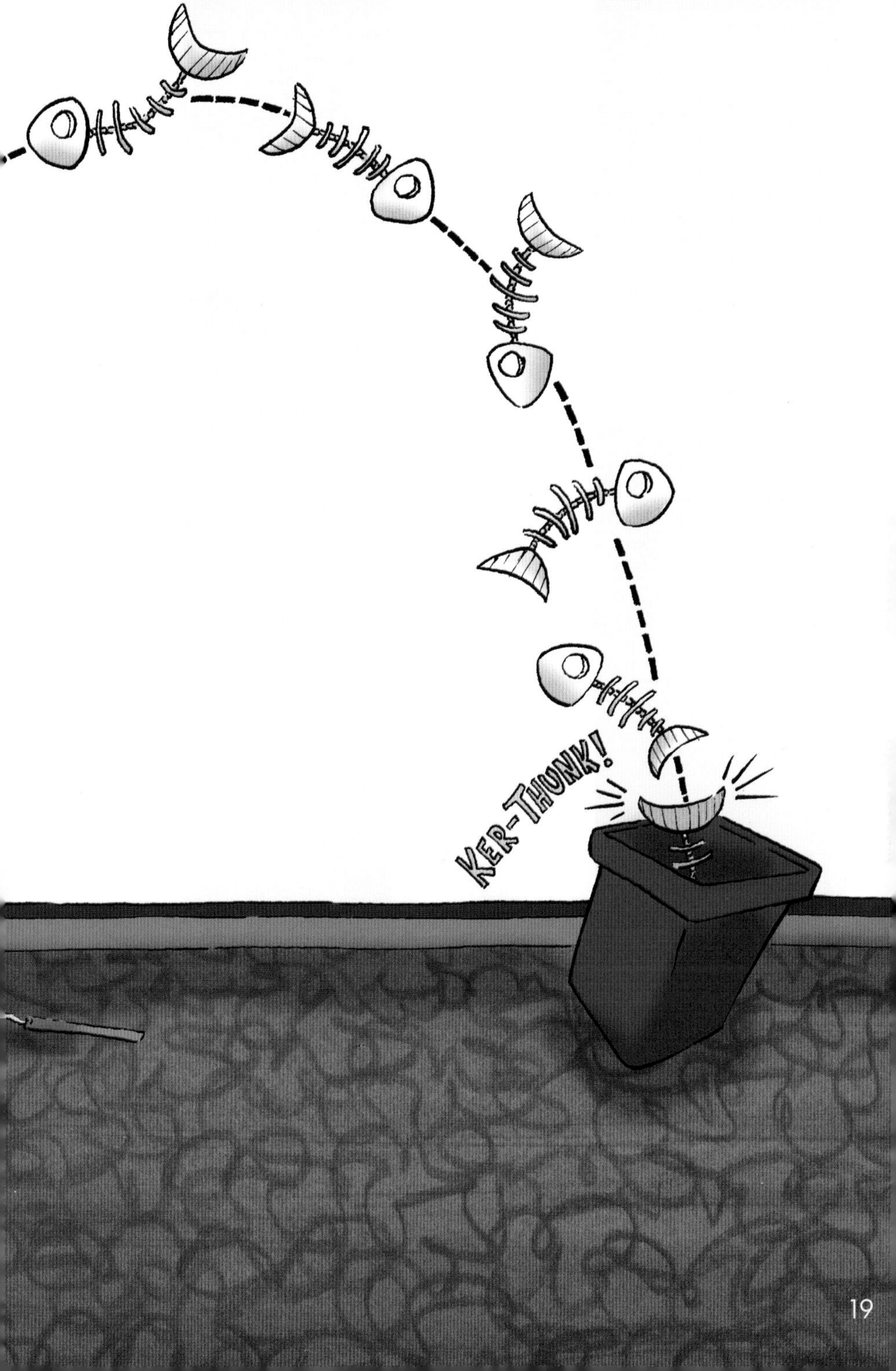
KER-THUNK!

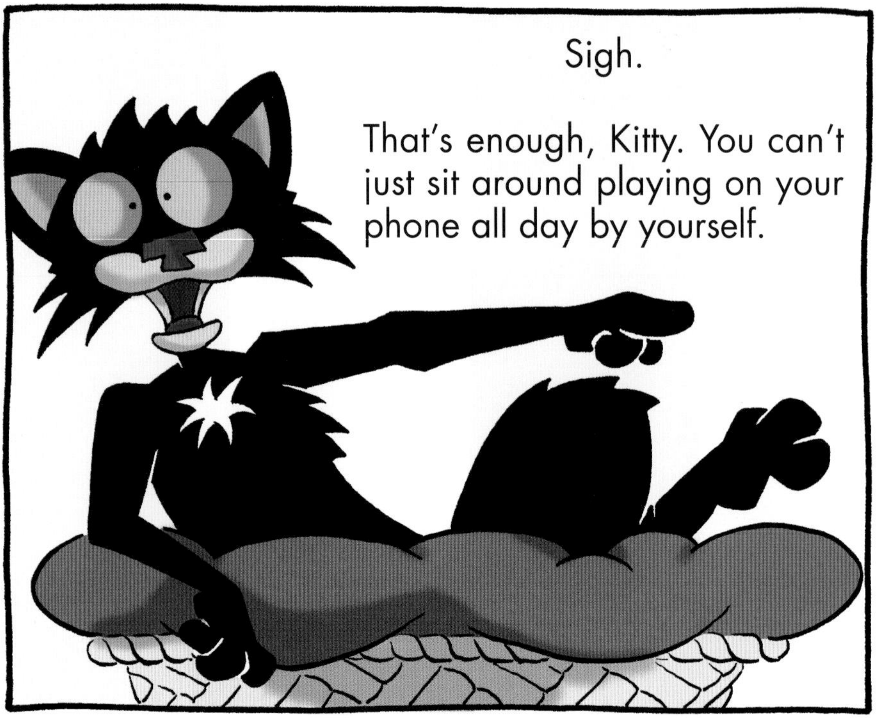
Sigh.
That's enough, Kitty. You can't just sit around playing on your phone all day by yourself.

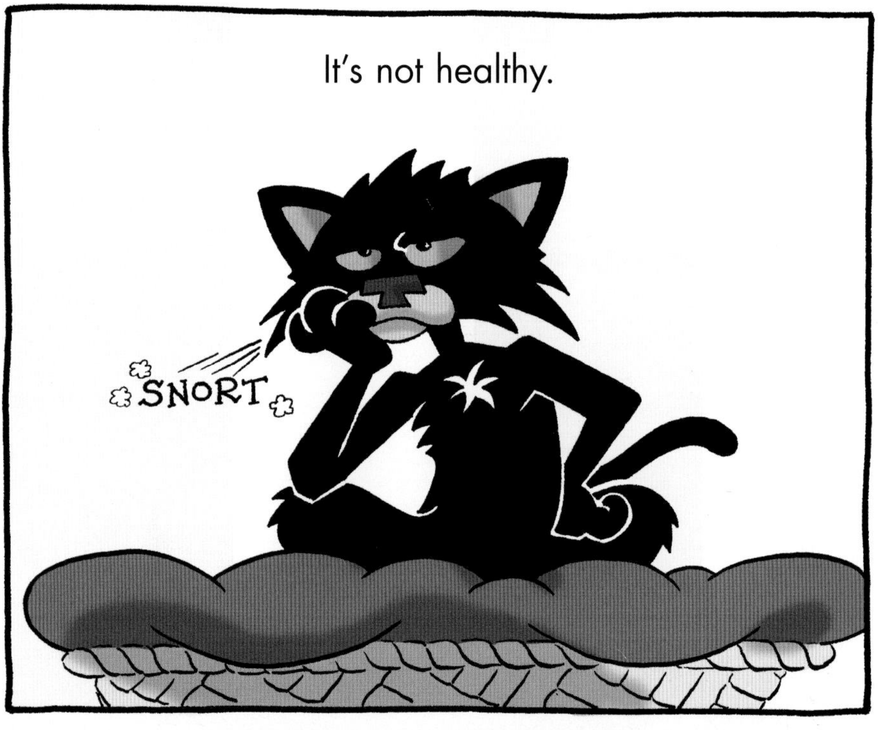
It's not healthy.
SNORT

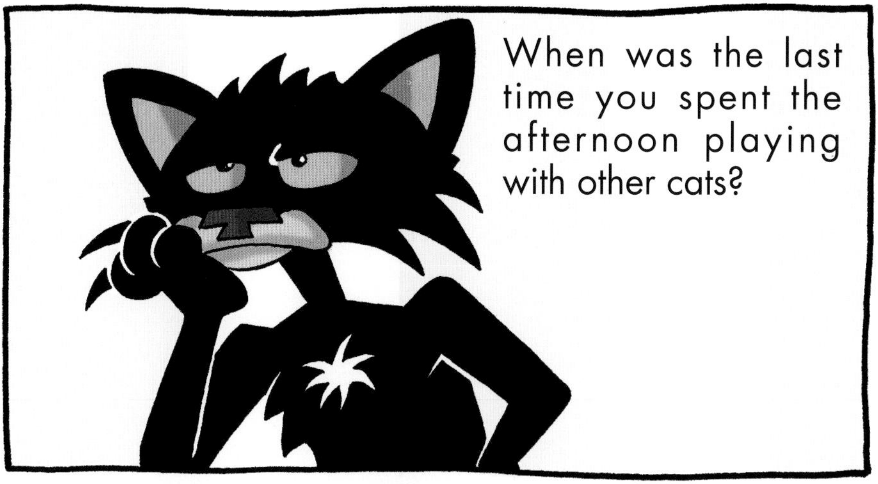
When was the last time you spent the afternoon playing with other cats?

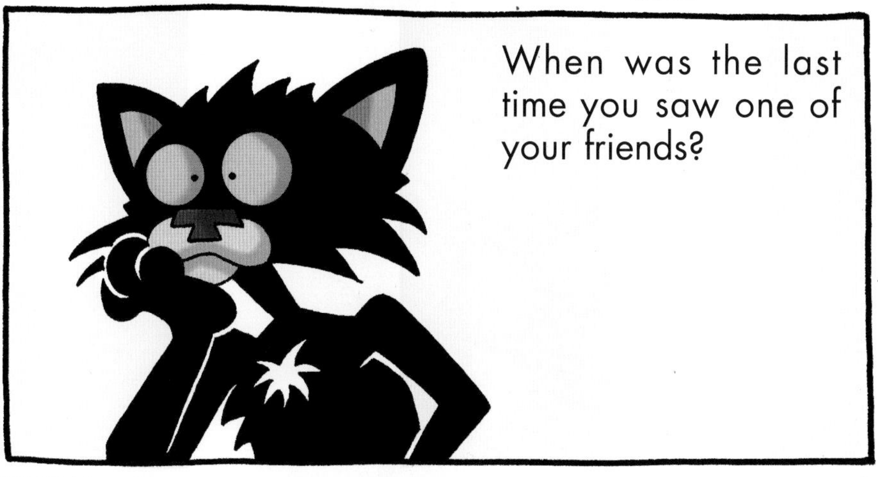
When was the last time you saw one of your friends?

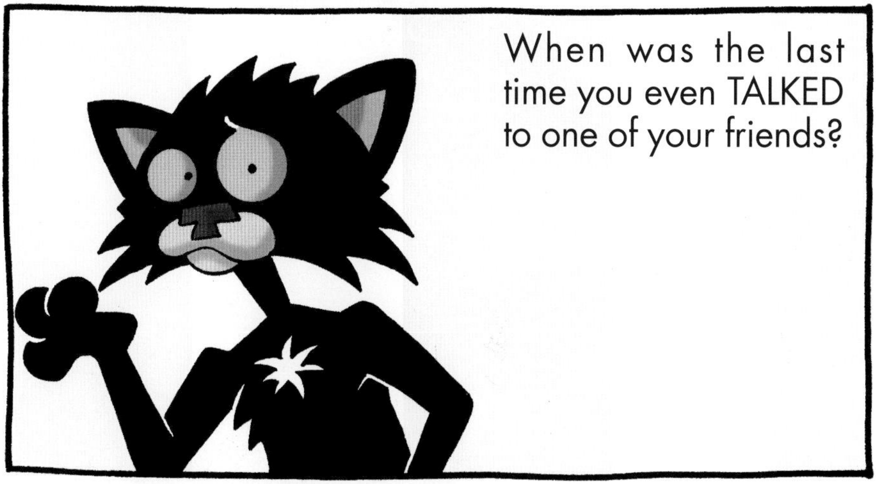
When was the last time you even TALKED to one of your friends?

That settles it, Kitty. It's been much too long since you spent any time with one of your friends. I think today is the day that we schedule a . . .

PLAYDATE!

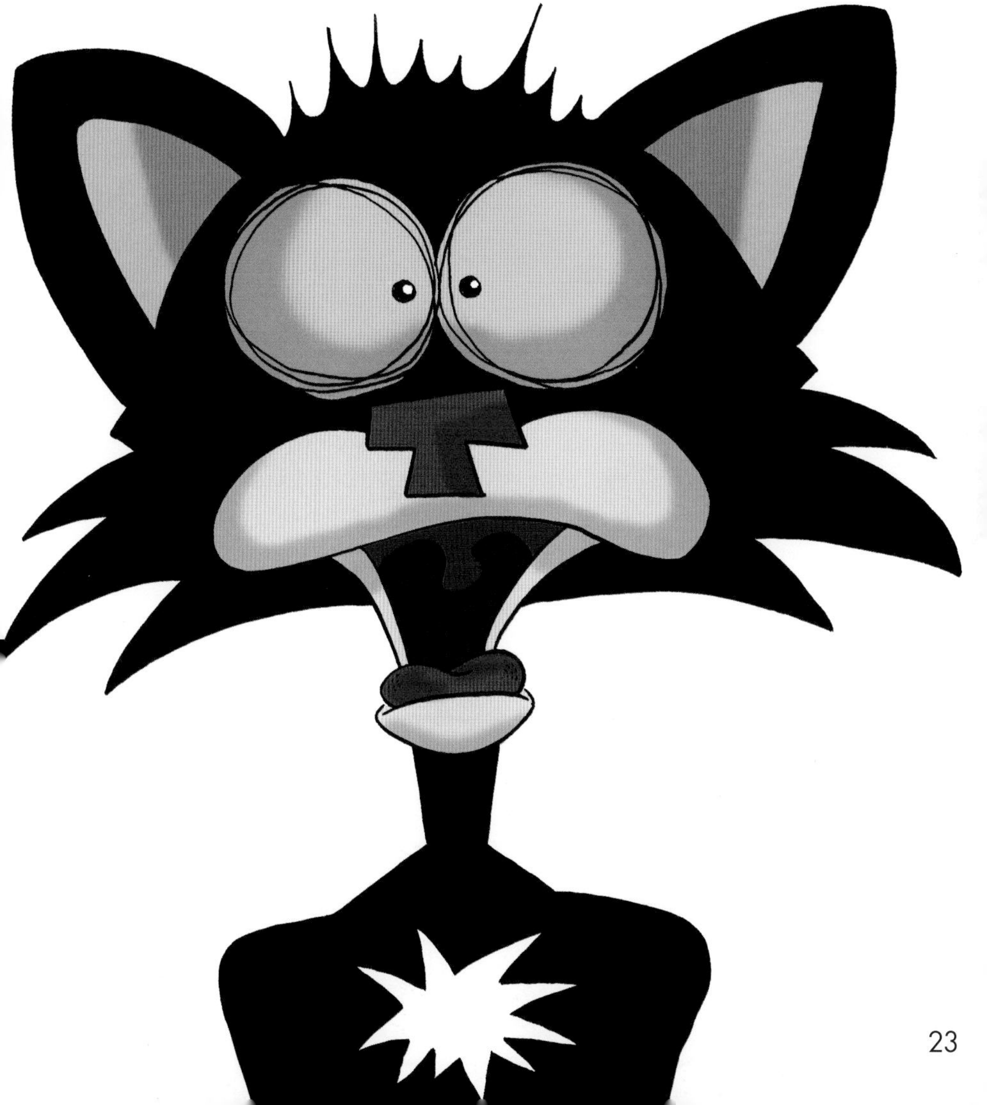

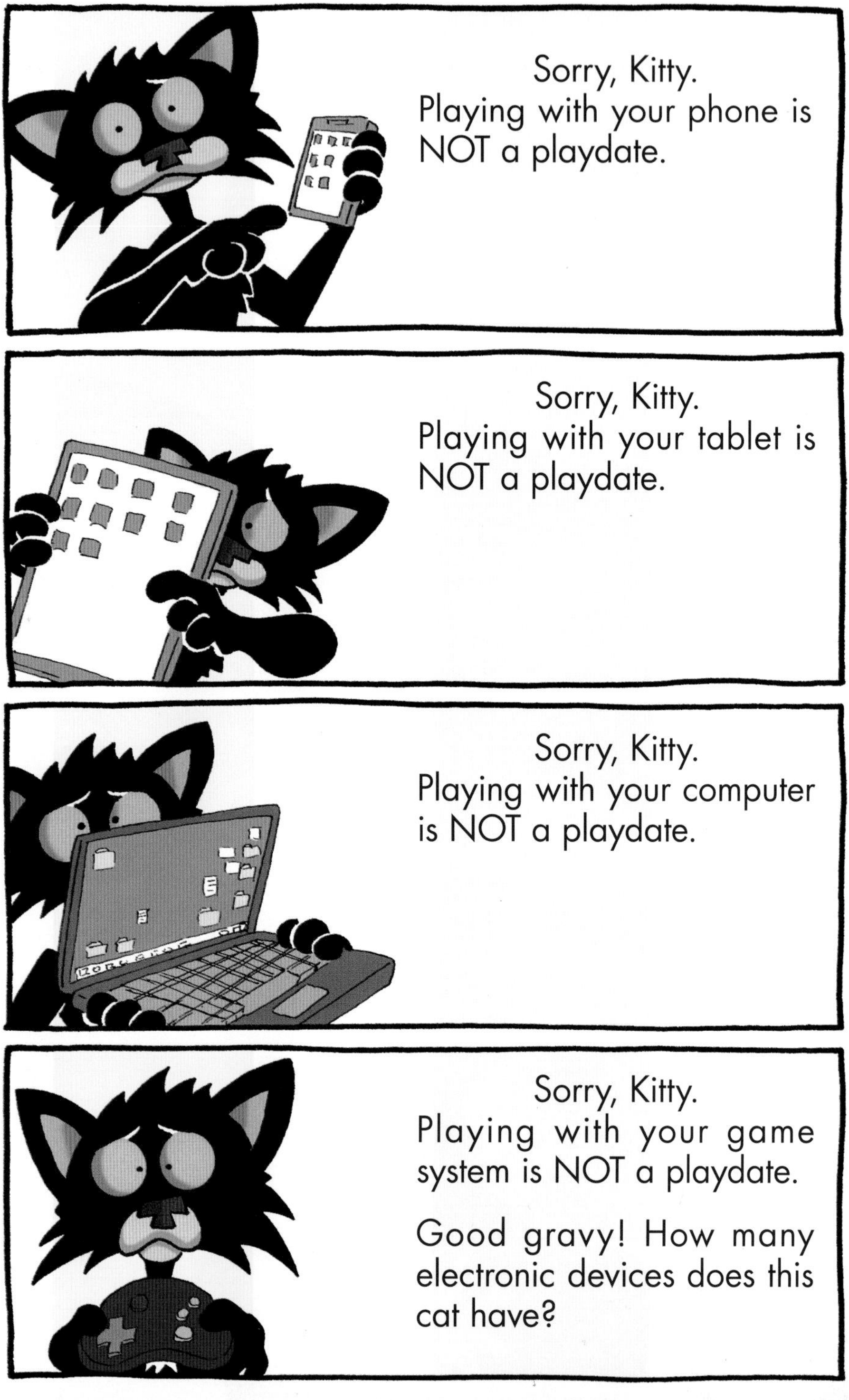
Sorry, Kitty.
Playing with your phone is NOT a playdate.
Sorry, Kitty.
Playing with your tablet is NOT a playdate.
Sorry, Kitty.
Playing with your computer is NOT a playdate.
Sorry, Kitty.
Playing with your game system is NOT a playdate.
Good gravy! How many electronic devices does this cat have?

The whole point of a playdate is that playing with someone else is good for your well-being. I'm going to start making some phone calls to see if any of your friends are free to come over.

And by the way, if someone comes over to play with you, there will be . . .

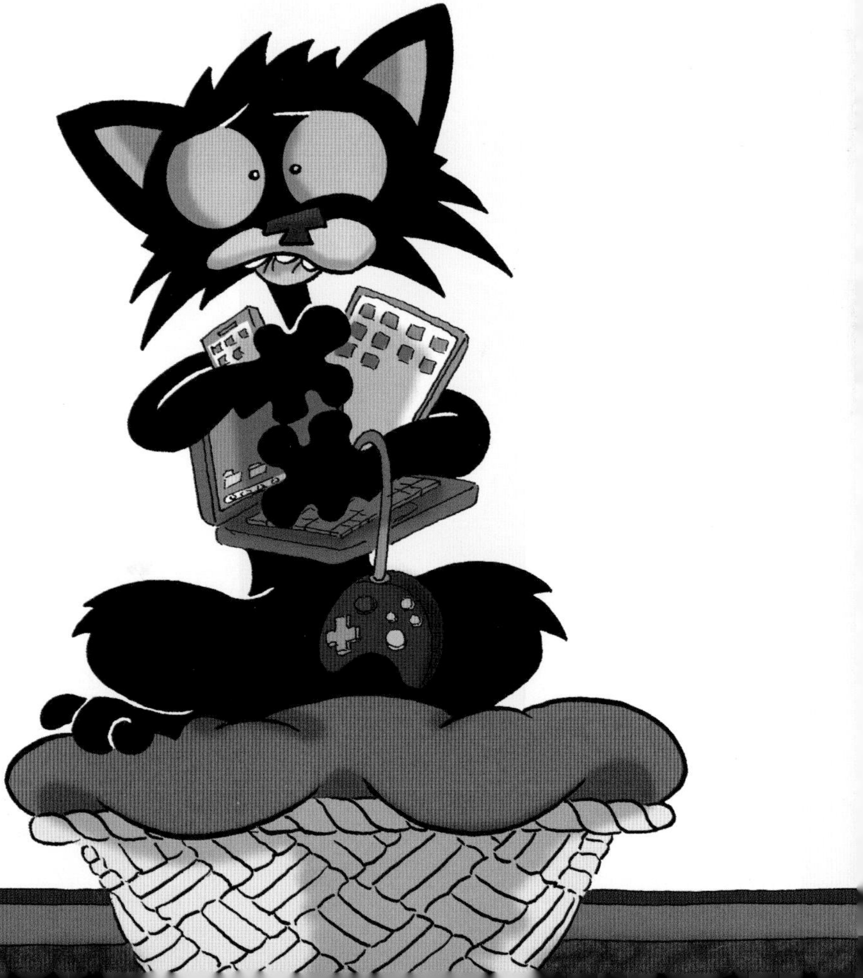

NO ELECTRONICS DURING YOUR PLAYDATE!

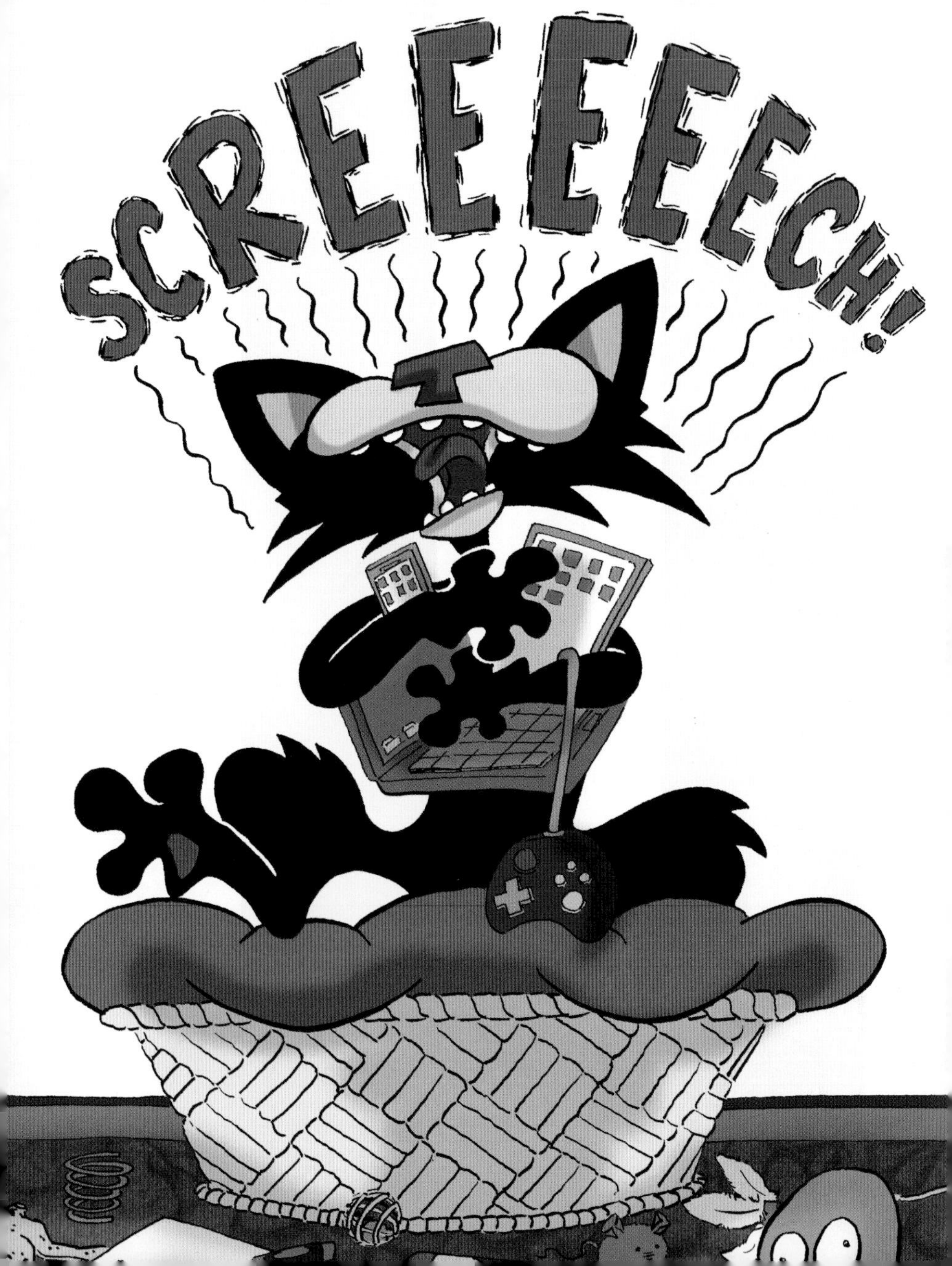
SCREEEEEECH!

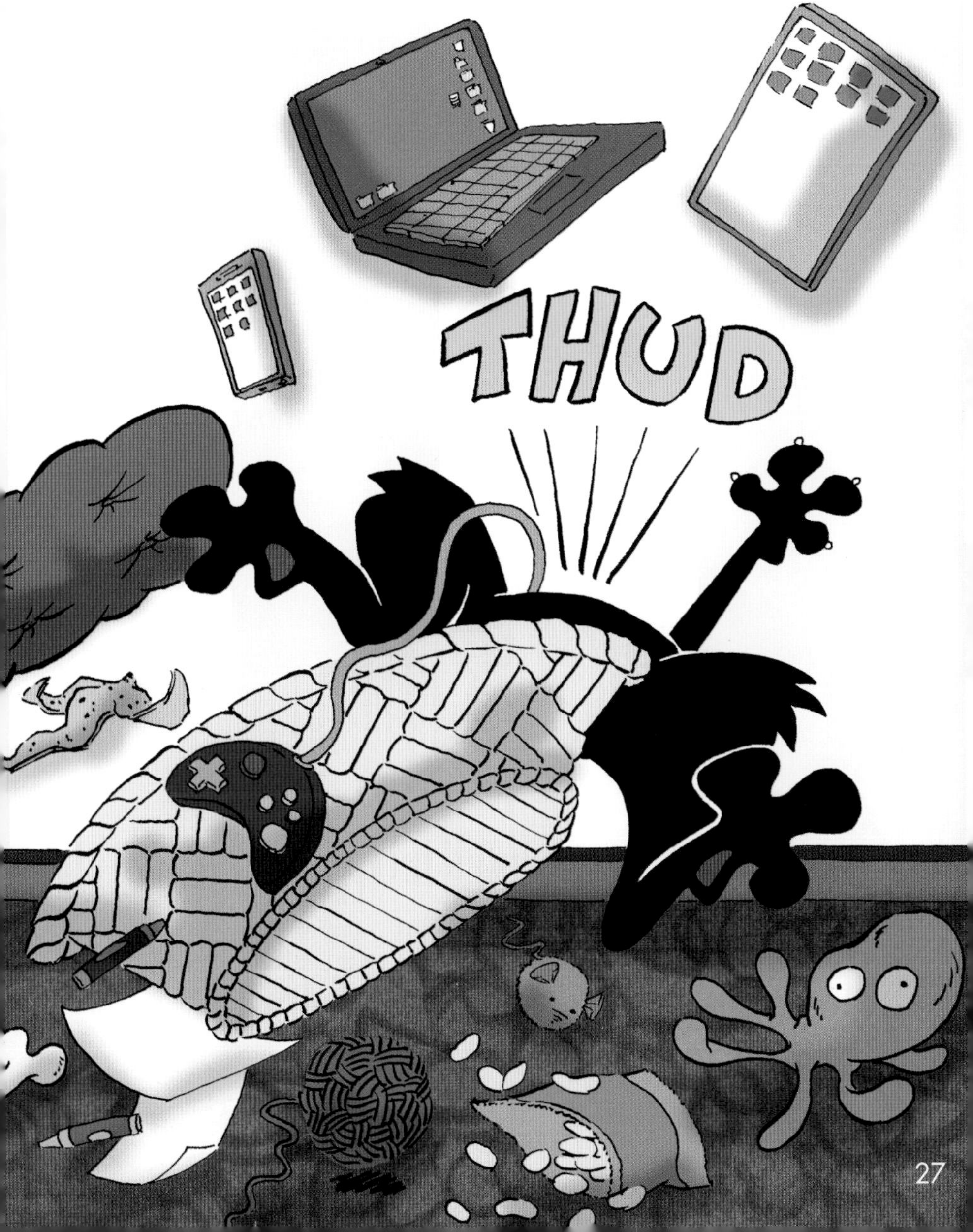
THUD

•CHAPTER TWO•

KITTY'S VIEW

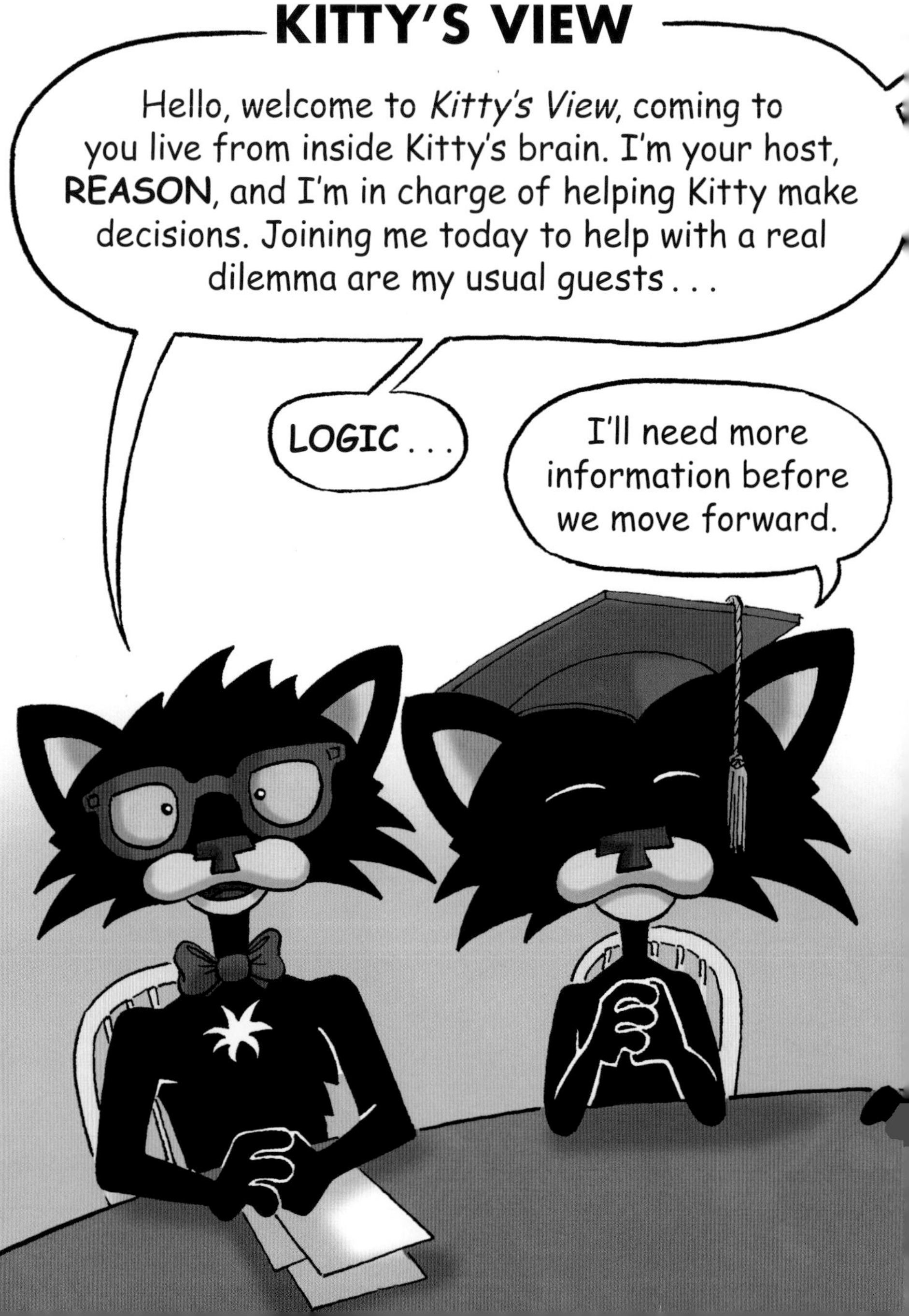
Hello, welcome to *Kitty's View*, coming to you live from inside Kitty's brain. I'm your host, **REASON**, and I'm in charge of helping Kitty make decisions. Joining me today to help with a real dilemma are my usual guests . . .
LOGIC . . .
I'll need more information before we move forward.

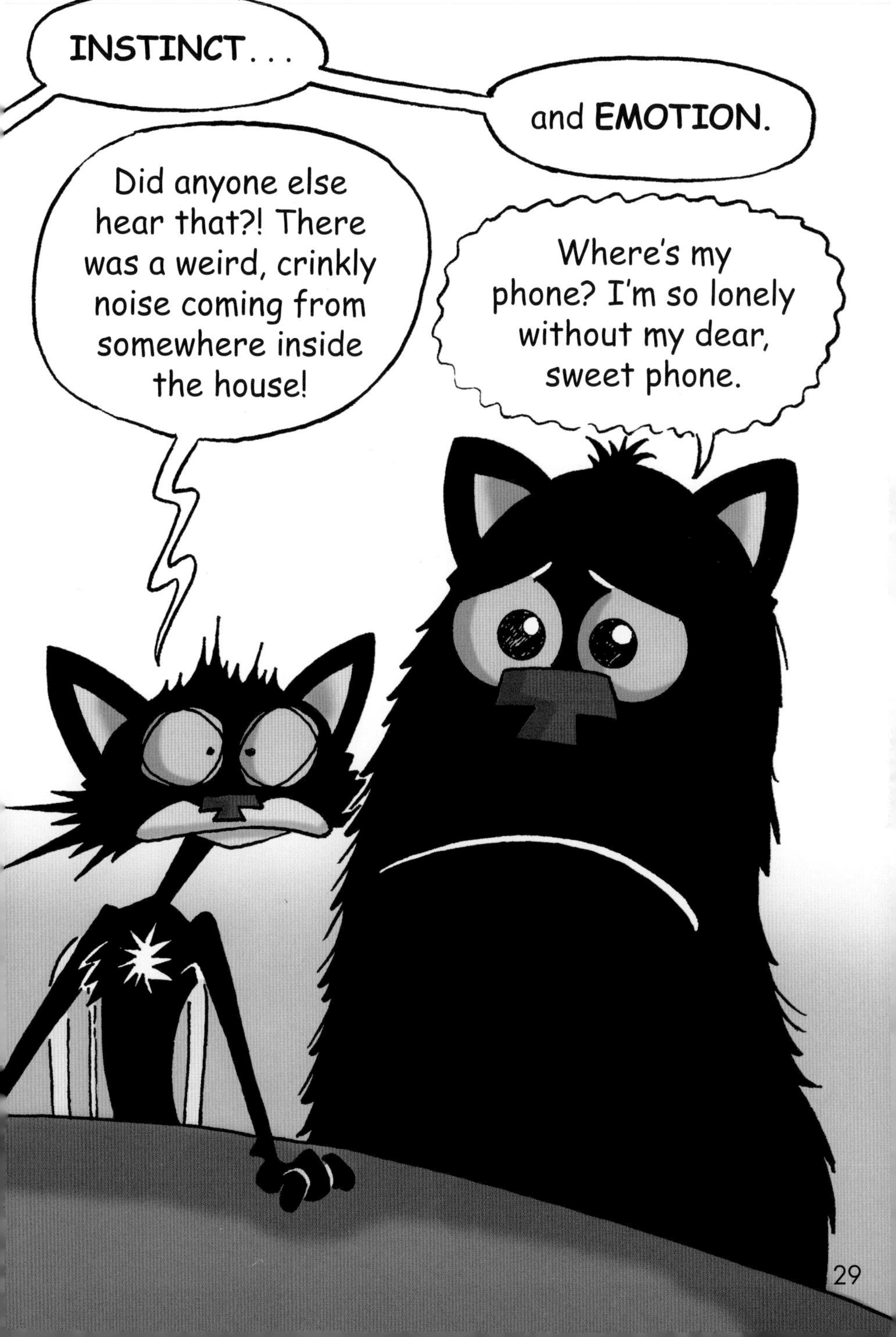
INSTINCT . . .
and EMOTION.
Did anyone else hear that?! There was a weird, crinkly noise coming from somewhere inside the house!
Where's my phone? I'm so lonely without my dear, sweet phone.

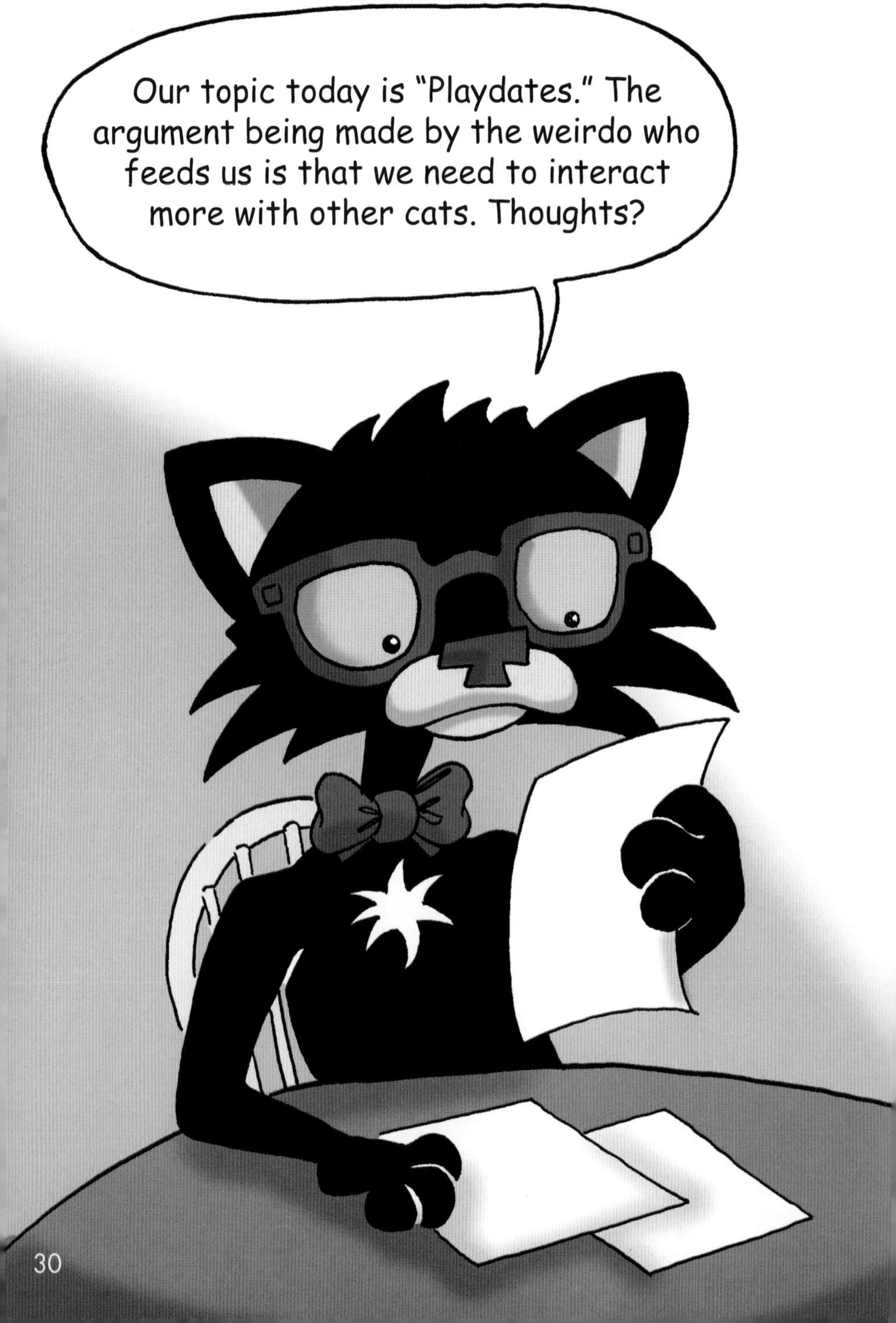
Our topic today is "Playdates." The argument being made by the weirdo who feeds us is that we need to interact more with other cats. Thoughts?

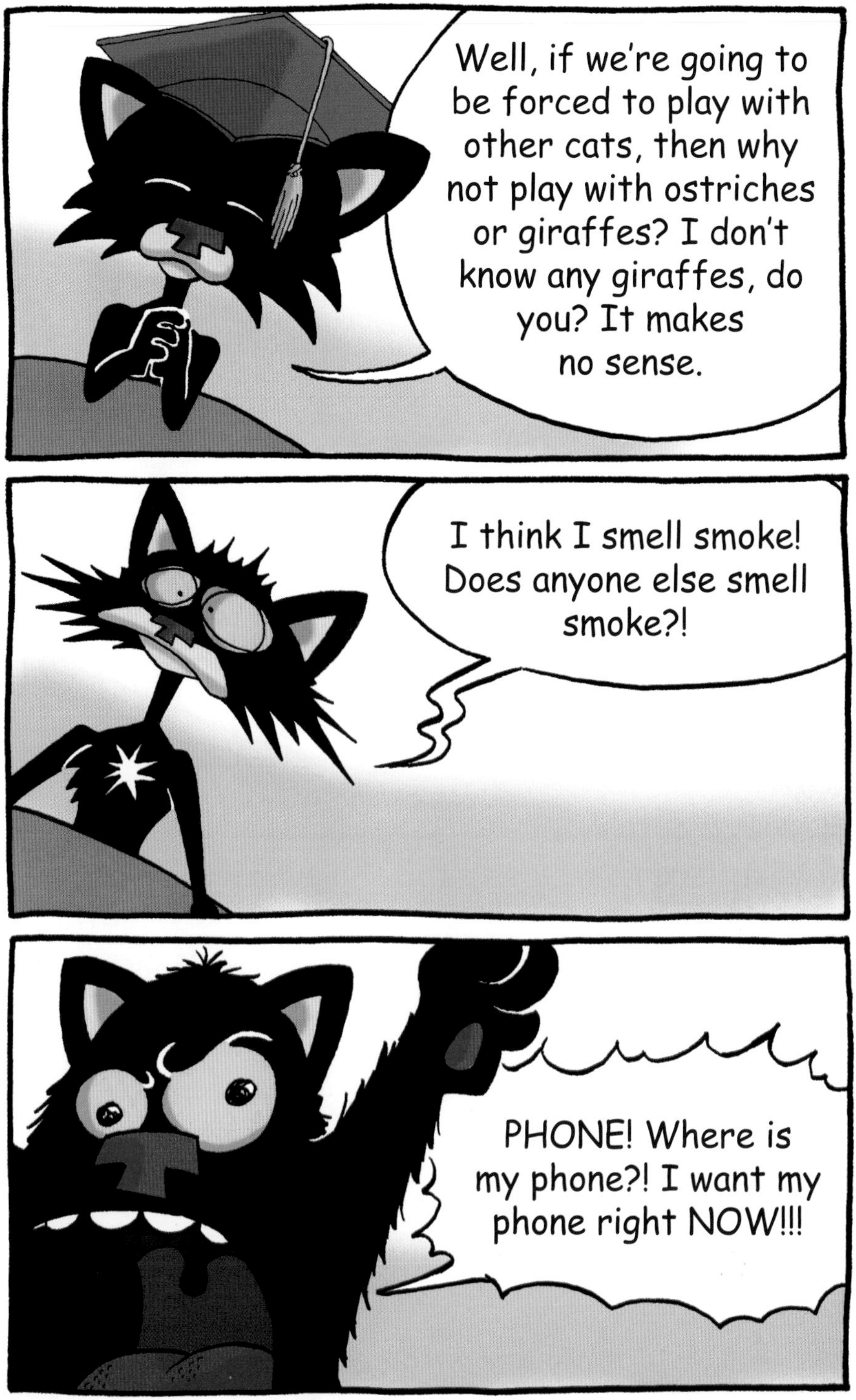
Well, if we're going to be forced to play with other cats, then why not play with ostriches or giraffes? I don't know any giraffes, do you? It makes no sense.
I think I smell smoke! Does anyone else smell smoke?!
PHONE! Where is my phone?! I want my phone right NOW!!!

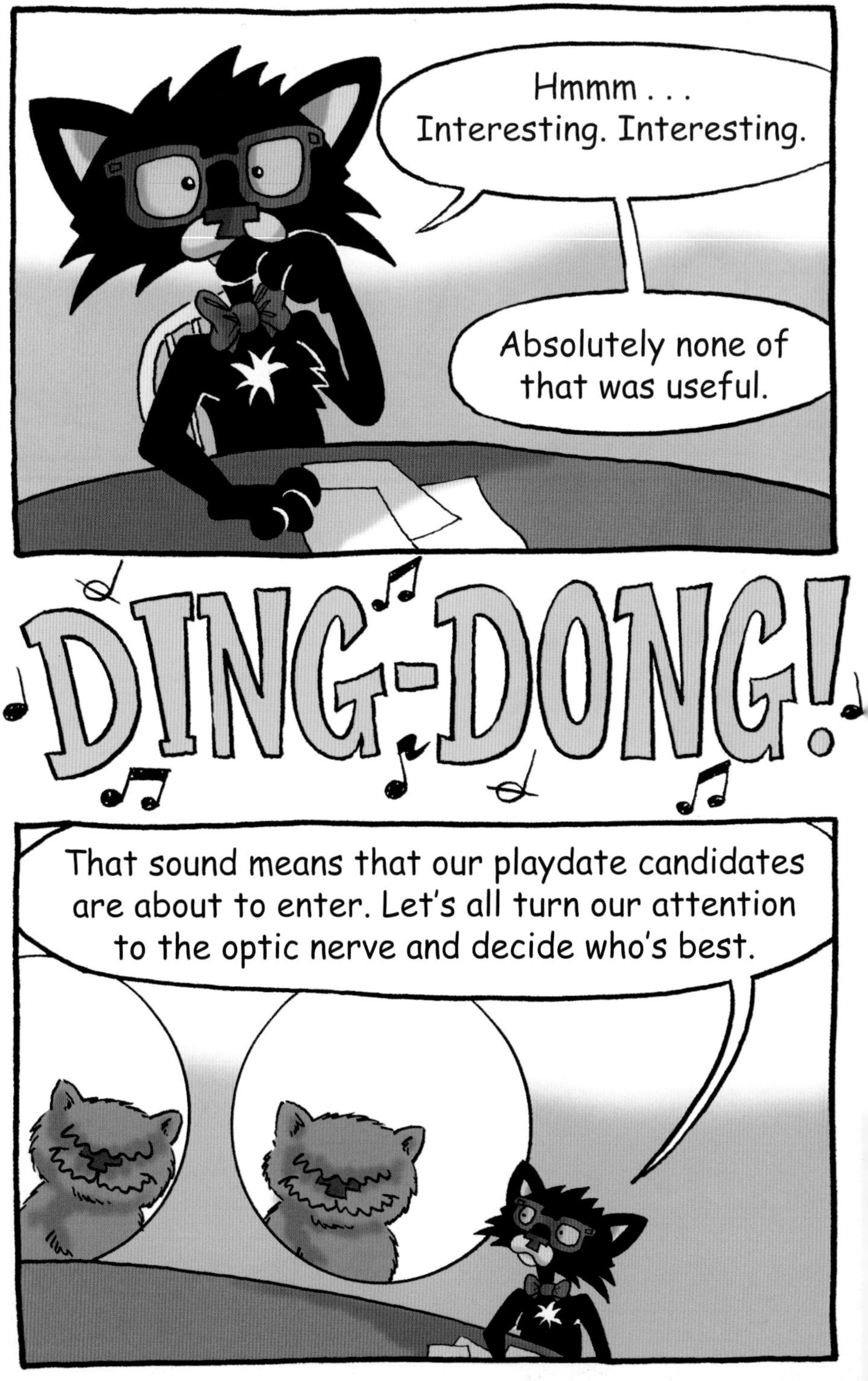
Hmmm . . .
Interesting. Interesting.
Absolutely none of
that was useful.
DING-DONG!
That sound means that our playdate candidates are about to enter. Let's all turn our attention to the optic nerve and decide who's best.

PLAYDATE CANDIDATE #1: STINKY KITTY

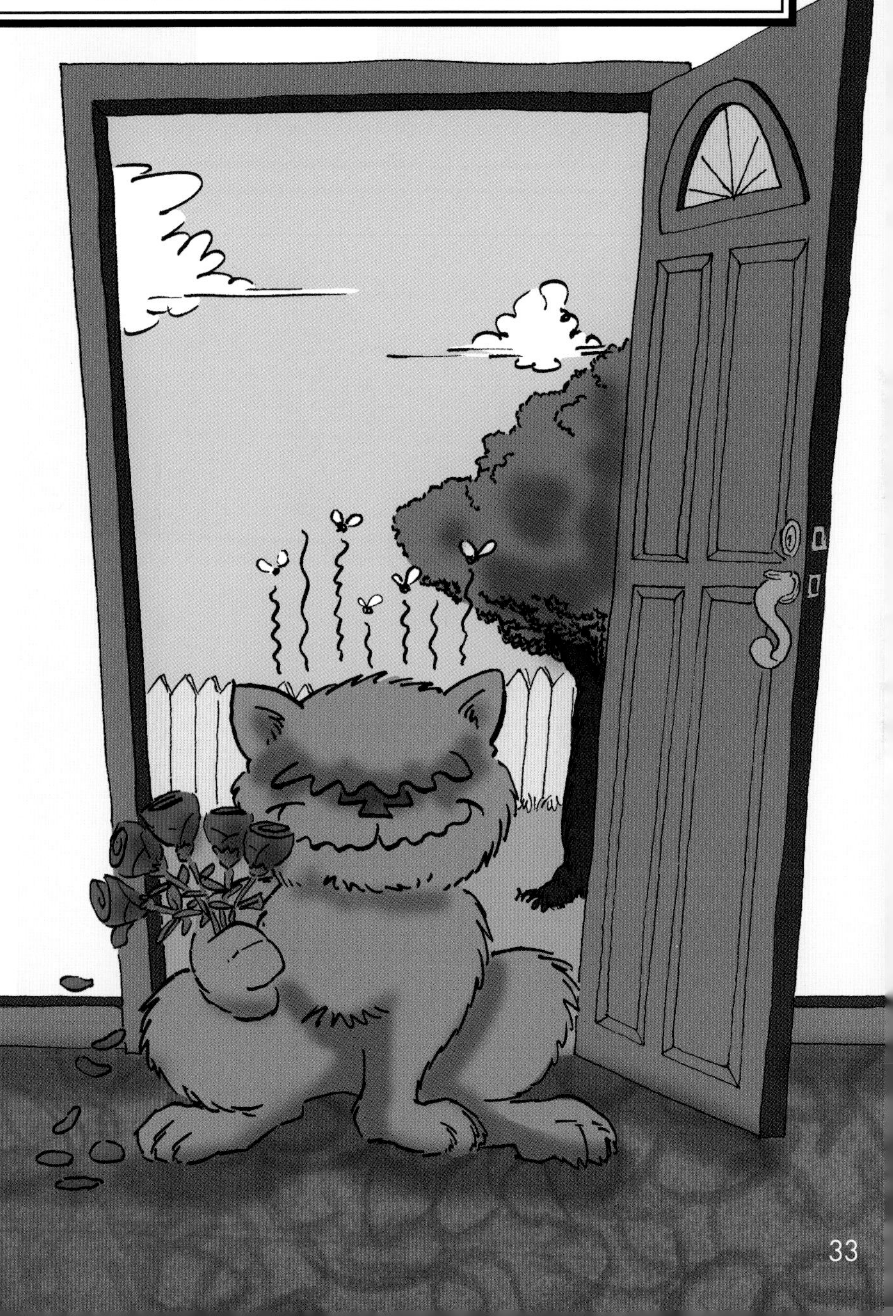

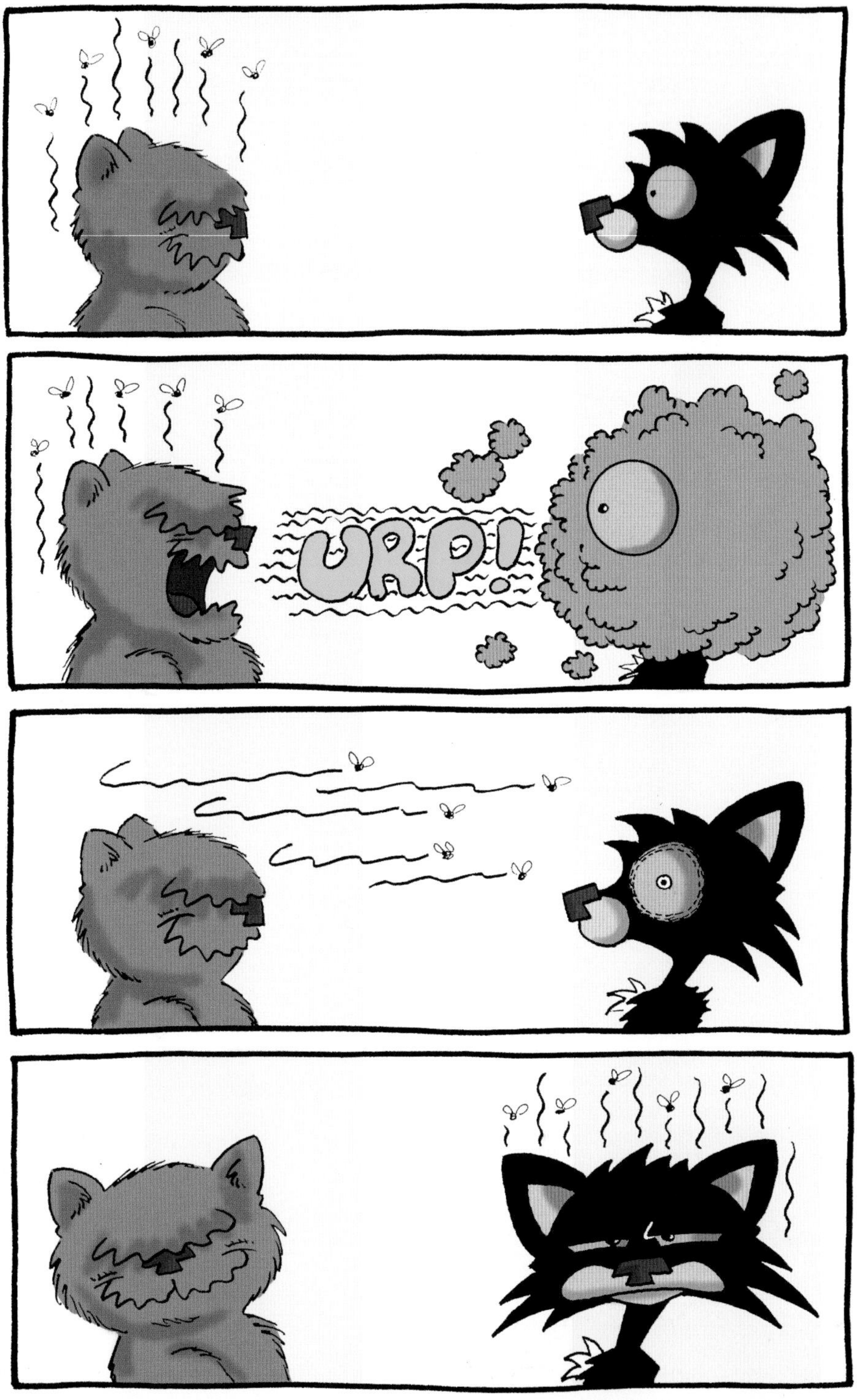
URP!

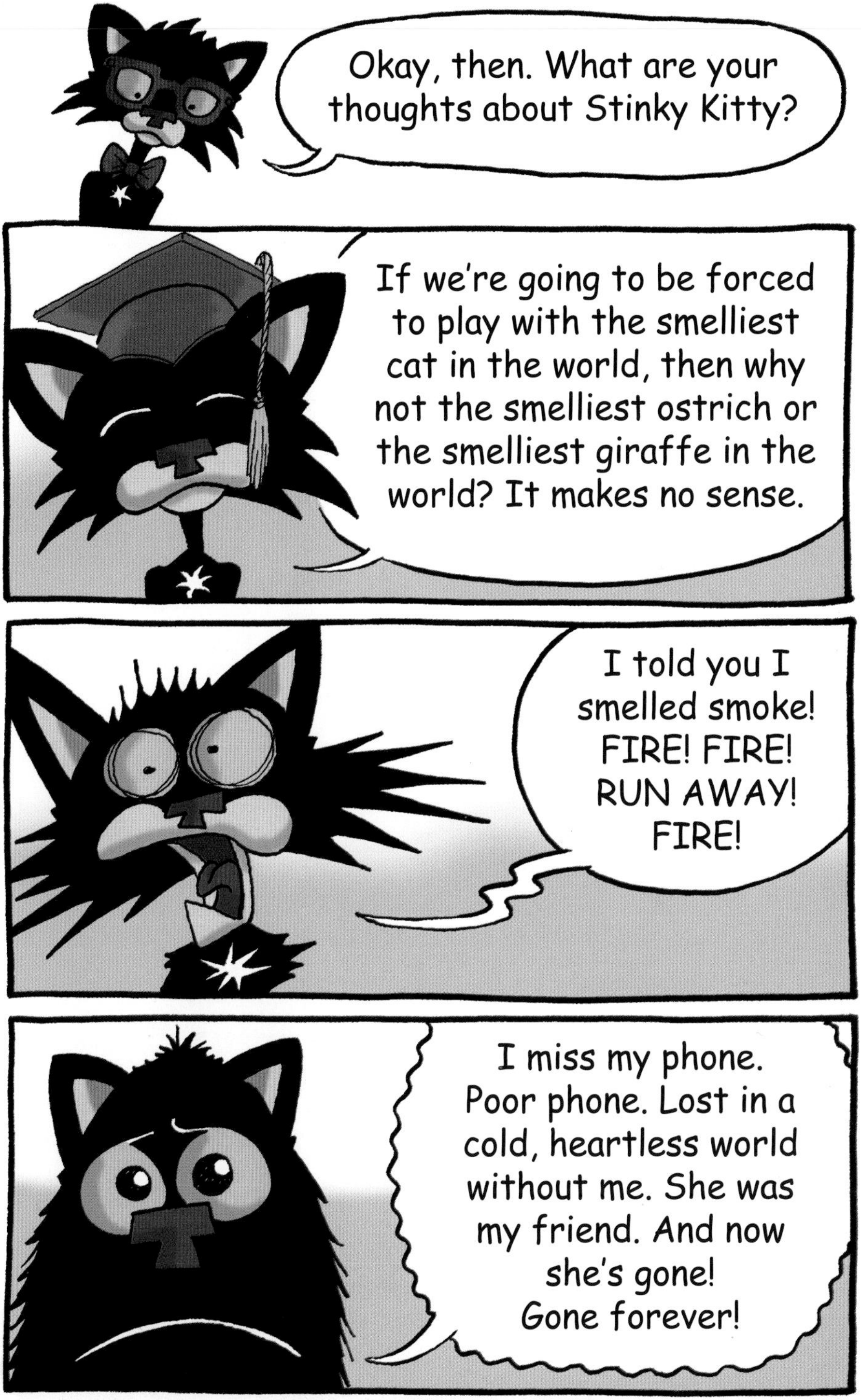
Okay, then. What are your thoughts about Stinky Kitty?
If we're going to be forced to play with the smelliest cat in the world, then why not the smelliest ostrich or the smelliest giraffe in the world? It makes no sense.
I told you I smelled smoke! FIRE! FIRE! RUN AWAY! FIRE!
I miss my phone. Poor phone. Lost in a cold, heartless world without me. She was my friend. And now she's gone! Gone forever!

PLAYDATE CANDIDATE #2:
CHATTY KITTY

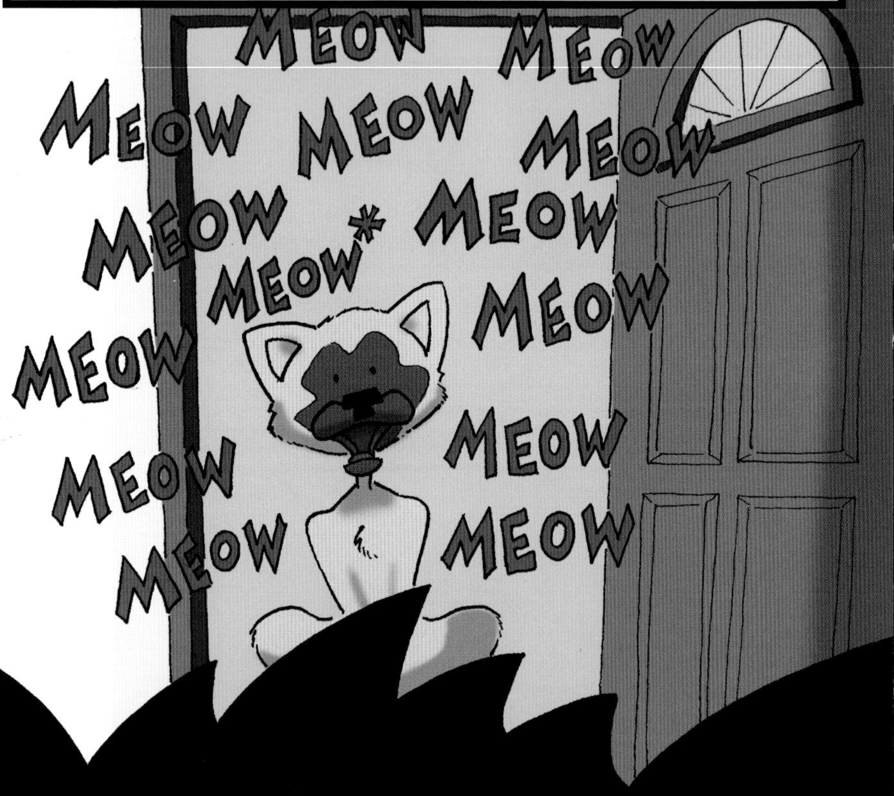
MEOW MEOW
MEOW MEOW MEOW
MEOW* MEOW
MEOW
MEOW MEOW
MEOW MEOW
MEOW MEOW

*Hi, Kitty! I was thinking about some of the things we could do together. At first I thought we could do a jigsaw puzzle, but then I realized that it was missing some pieces. In fact, it's missing all of its pieces. I can't even find the box. So then I thought we could play something outside like Red Light, Green Light. But then I remembered that cats are practically color-blind and we can't tell the difference between a red light and a green light. So then I thought that someone could just yell "LIGHT," and we can decide for ourselves if we want to run or stop or do whatever we feel like, which could be fun but confusing. So then I thought that we could watch a movie. But I don't like scary movies. Do you like scary movies? I like movies about cats. The only problem is that a lot of movies about cats are really scary. Like, there's that one about cats who look like people, or maybe it's the other way around, and they're all inside this old abandoned theater, singing and dancing and being generally weird. I had nightmares for weeks.

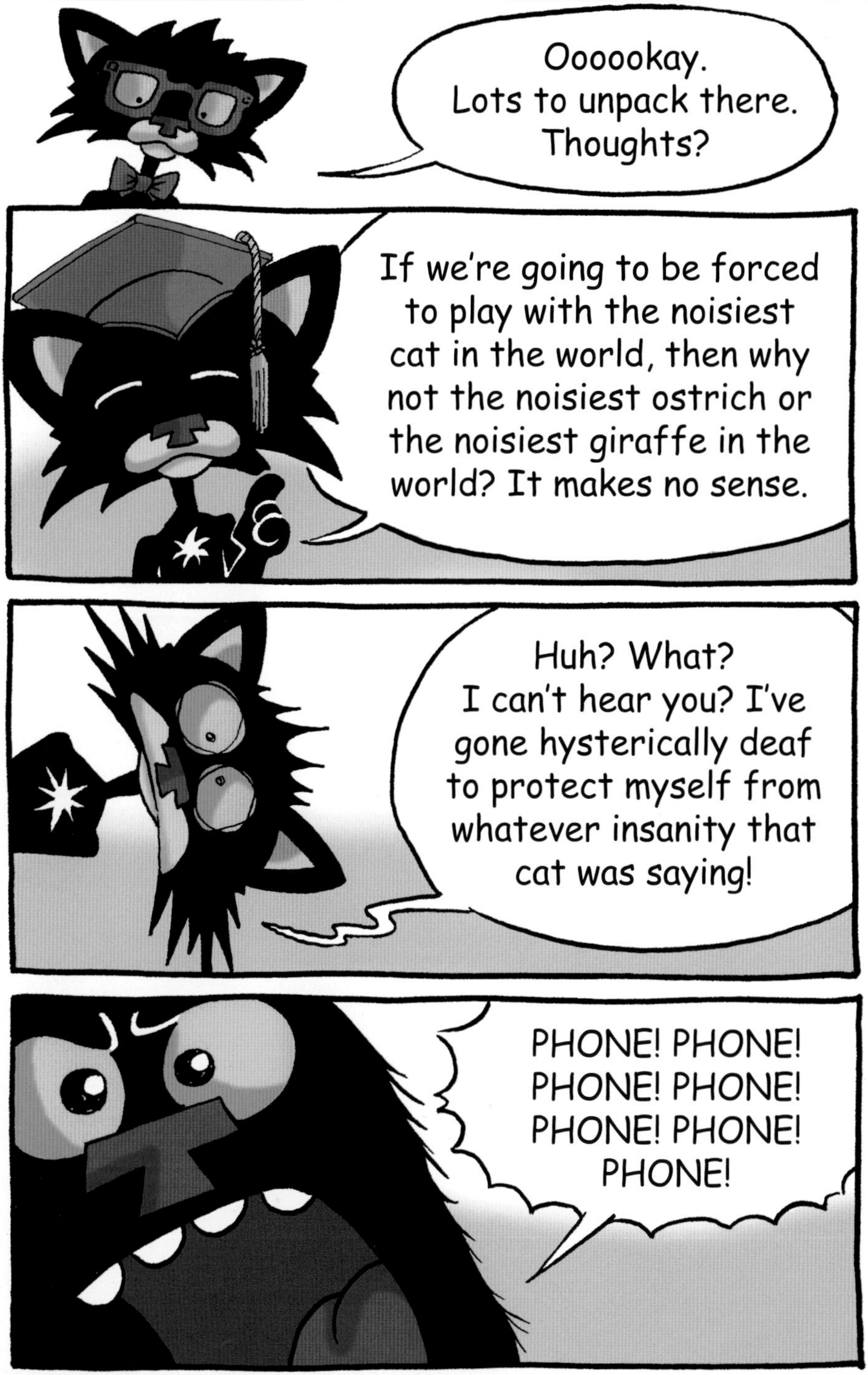
Oooookay. Lots to unpack there. Thoughts?
If we're going to be forced to play with the noisiest cat in the world, then why not the noisiest ostrich or the noisiest giraffe in the world? It makes no sense.
Huh? What? I can't hear you? I've gone hysterically deaf to protect myself from whatever insanity that cat was saying!
PHONE! PHONE! PHONE! PHONE! PHONE! PHONE! PHONE!

PLAYDATE CANDIDATE #3:
PETUNIA

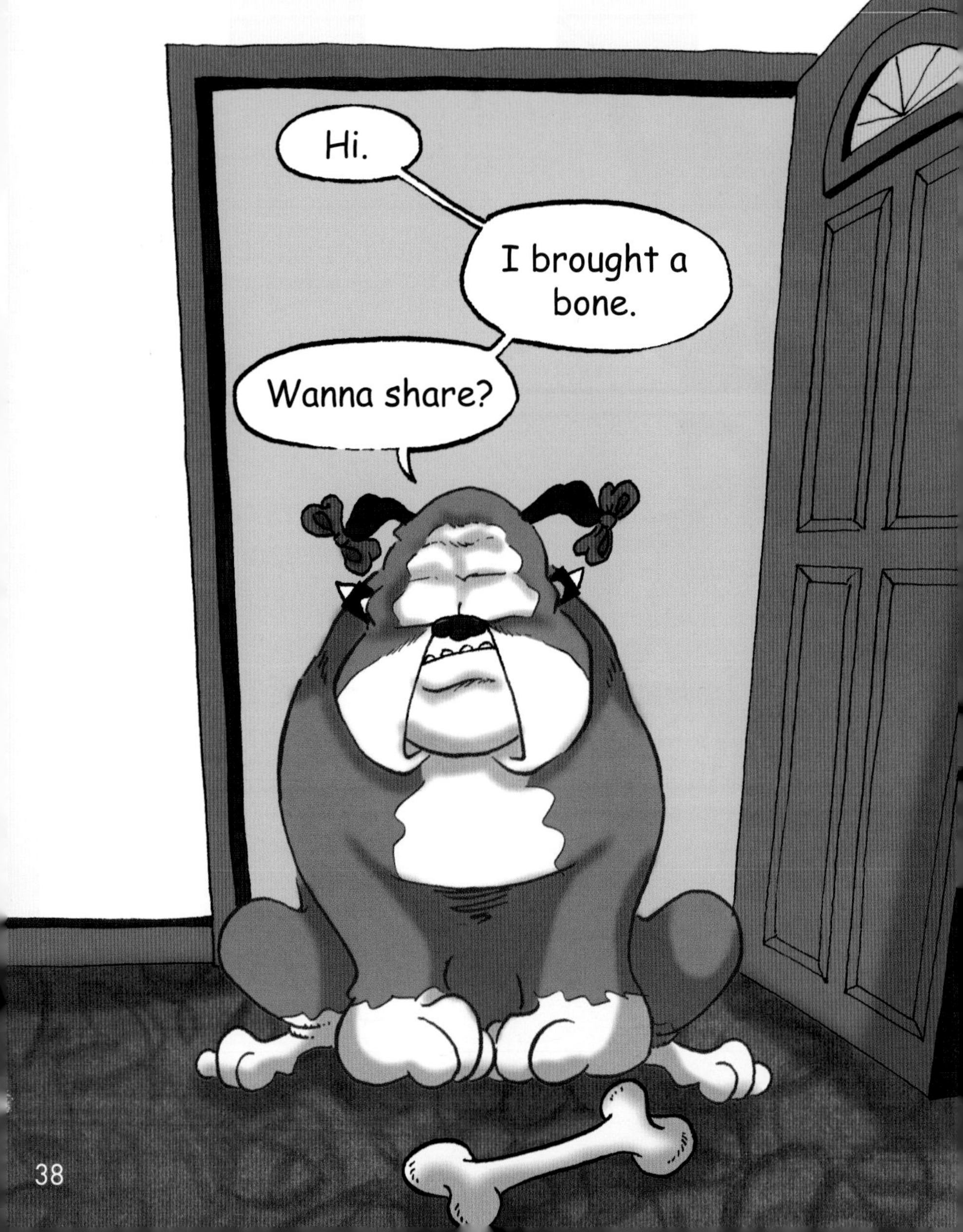
Hi.
I brought a bone.
Wanna share?

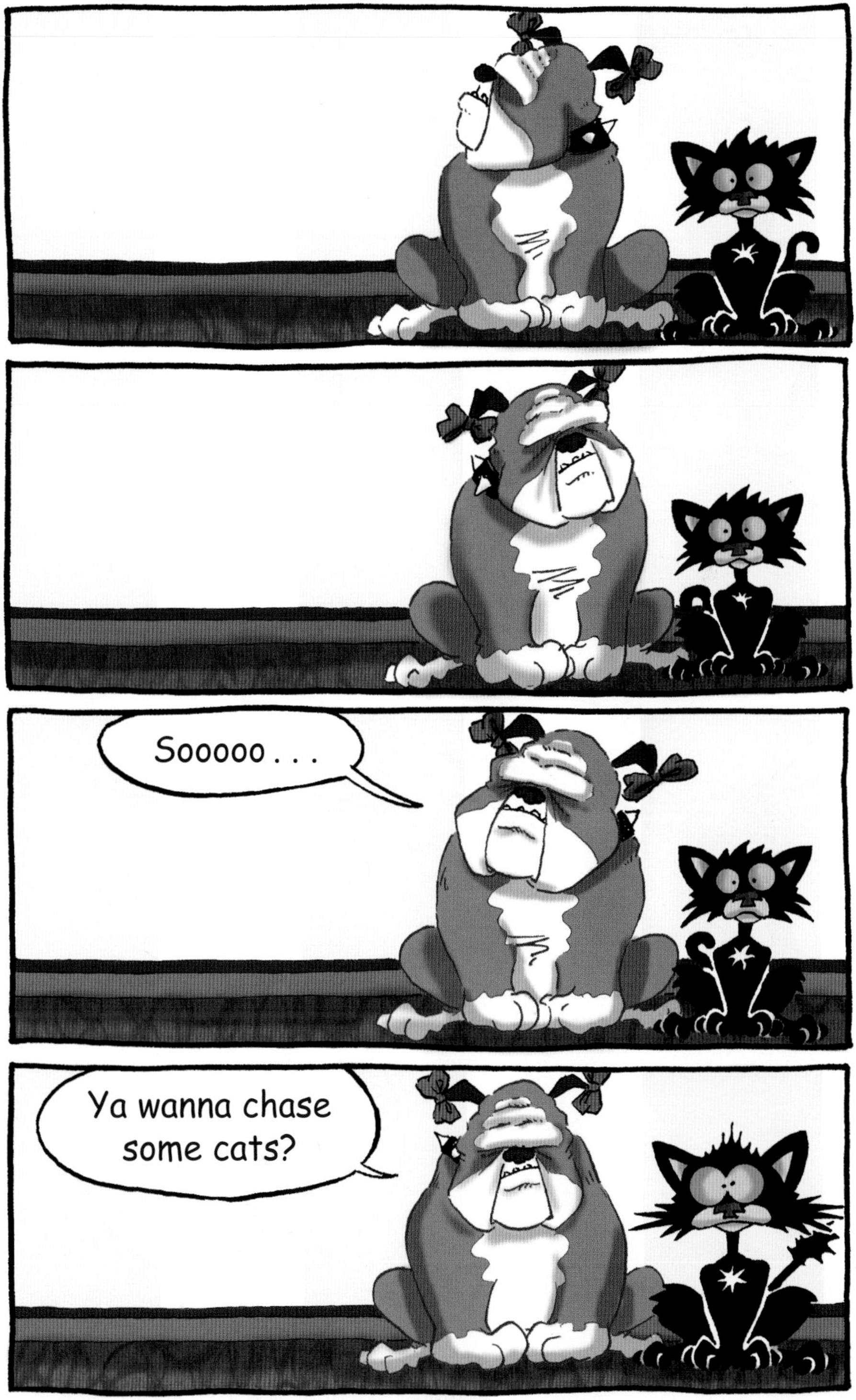
Sooooo . . .
Ya wanna chase some cats?

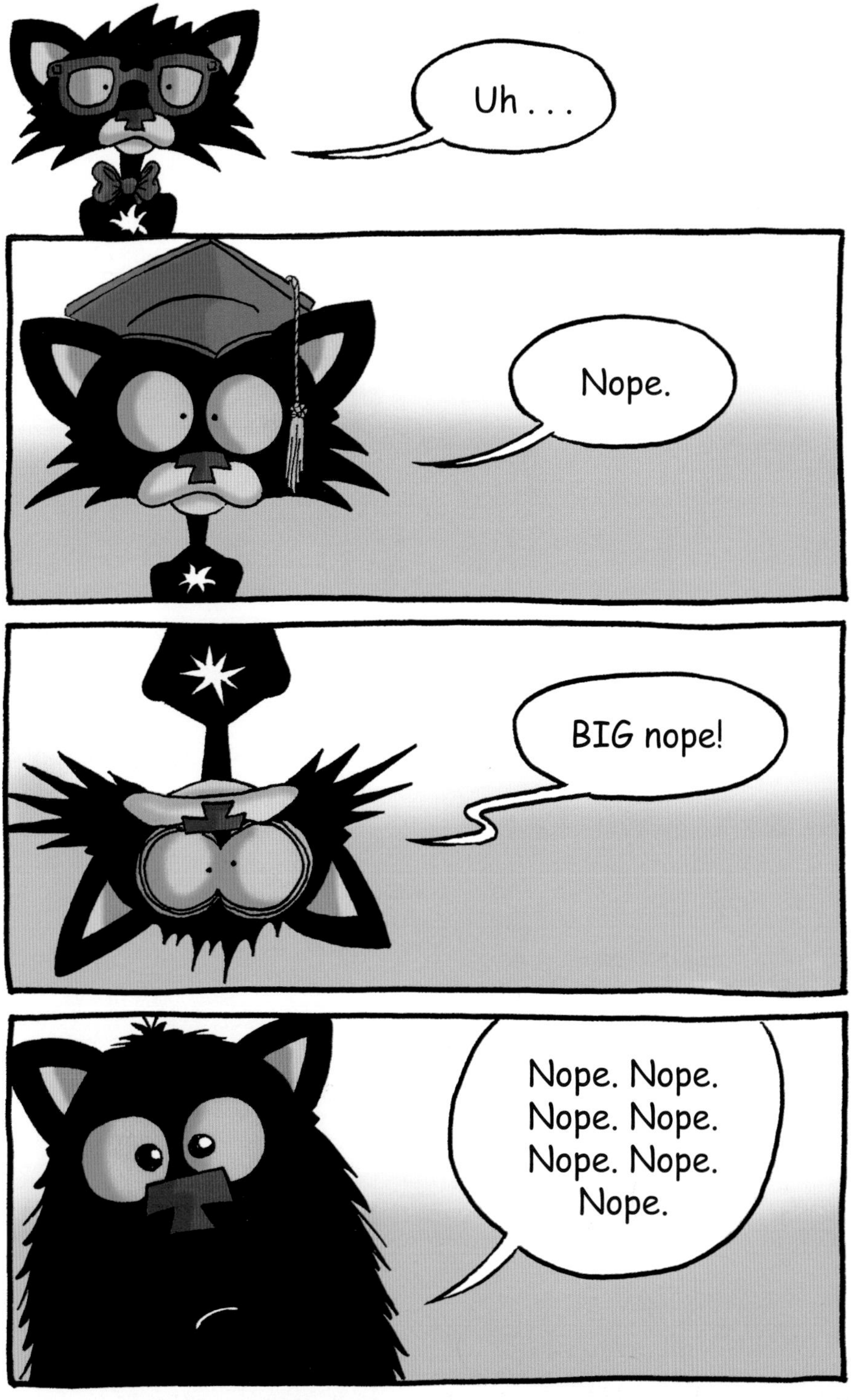
Uh . . .
Nope.
BIG nope!
Nope. Nope. Nope. Nope. Nope. Nope. Nope.

PLAYDATE CANDIDATE #4:
STRANGE KITTY

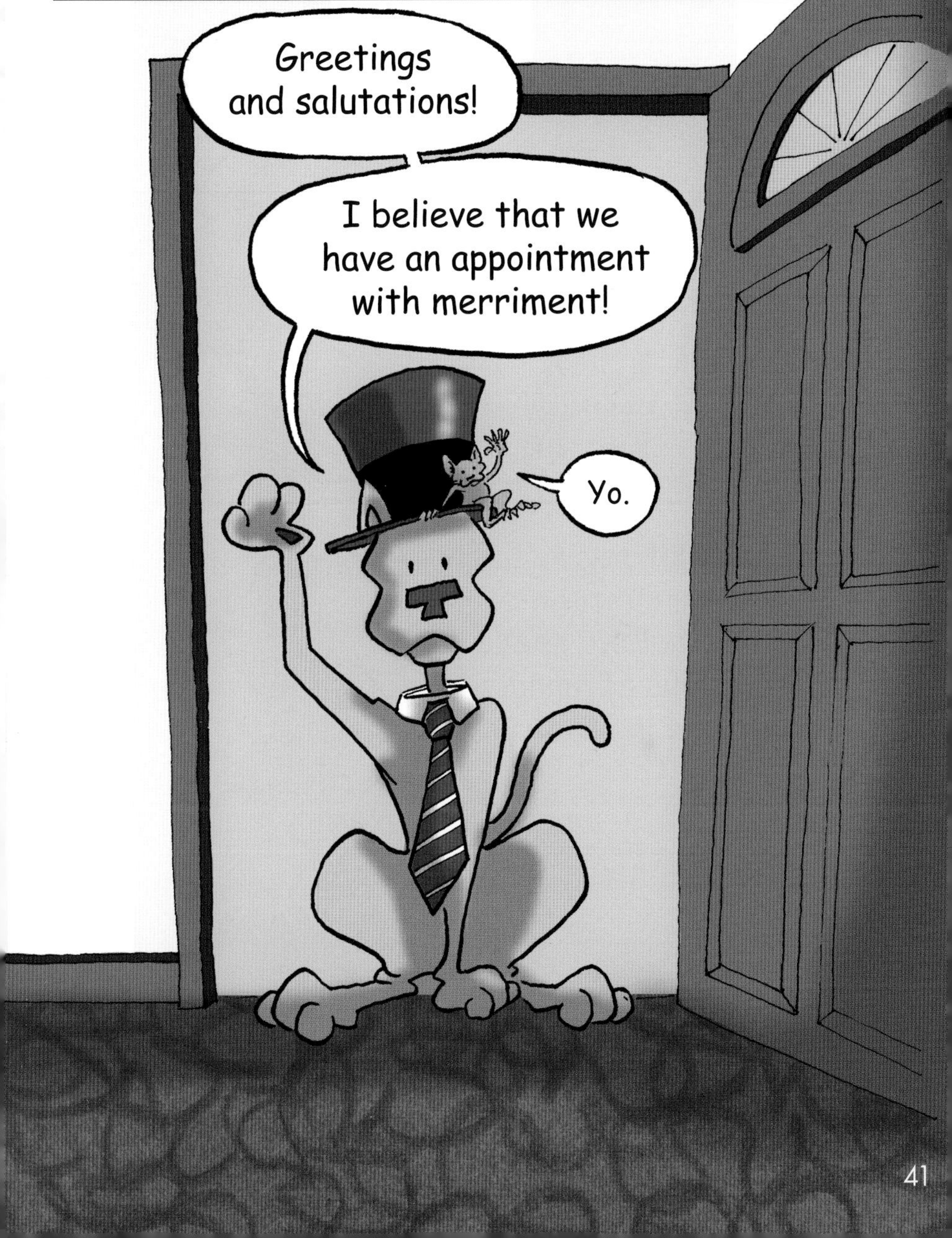
Greetings and salutations!
I believe that we have an appointment with merriment!
Yo.

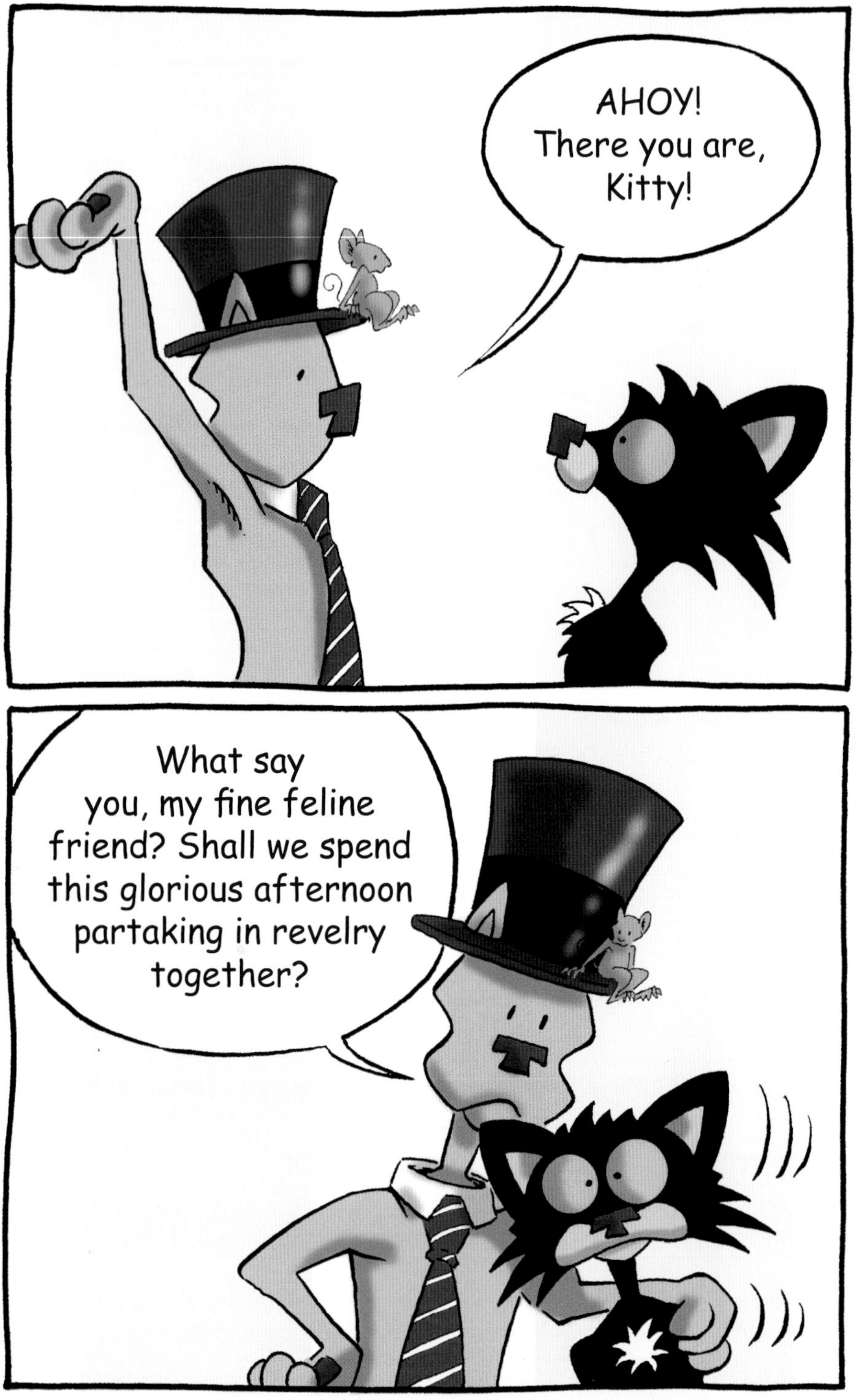
AHOY! There you are, Kitty!
What say you, my fine feline friend? Shall we spend this glorious afternoon partaking in revelry together?

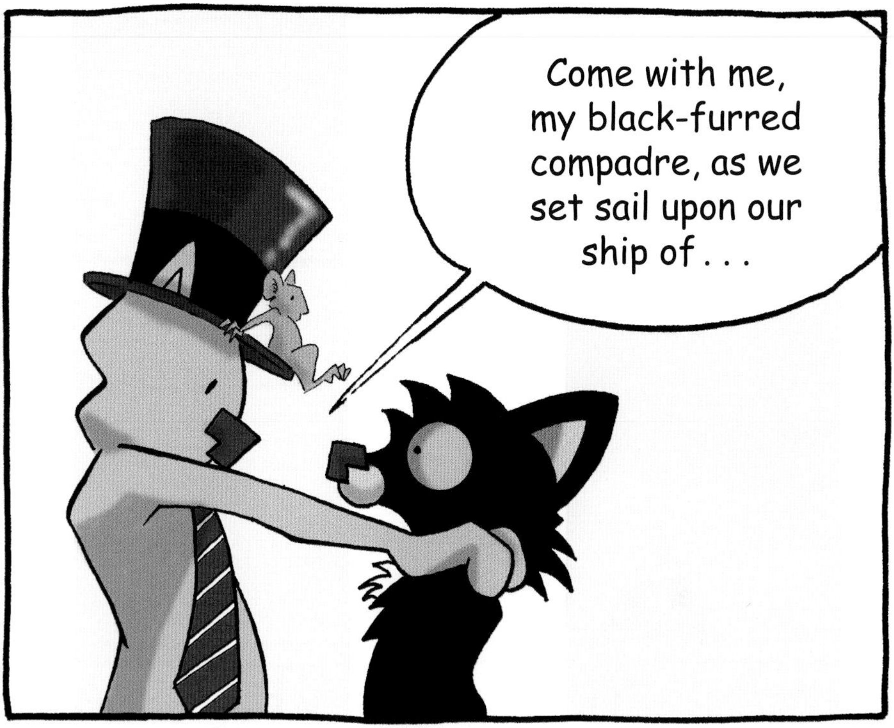
Come with me, my black-furred compadre, as we set sail upon our ship of . . .

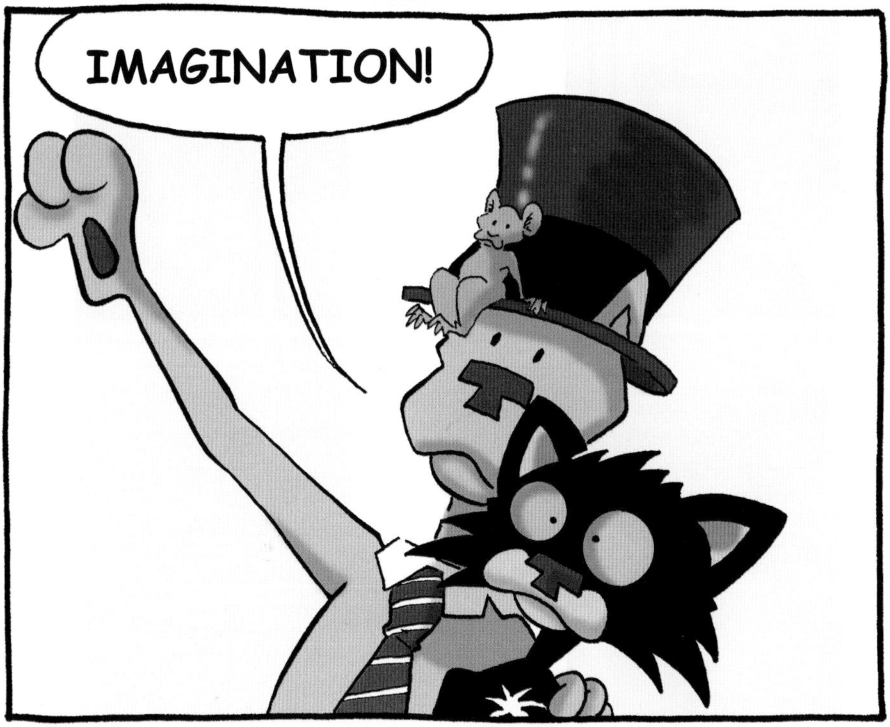
IMAGINATION!

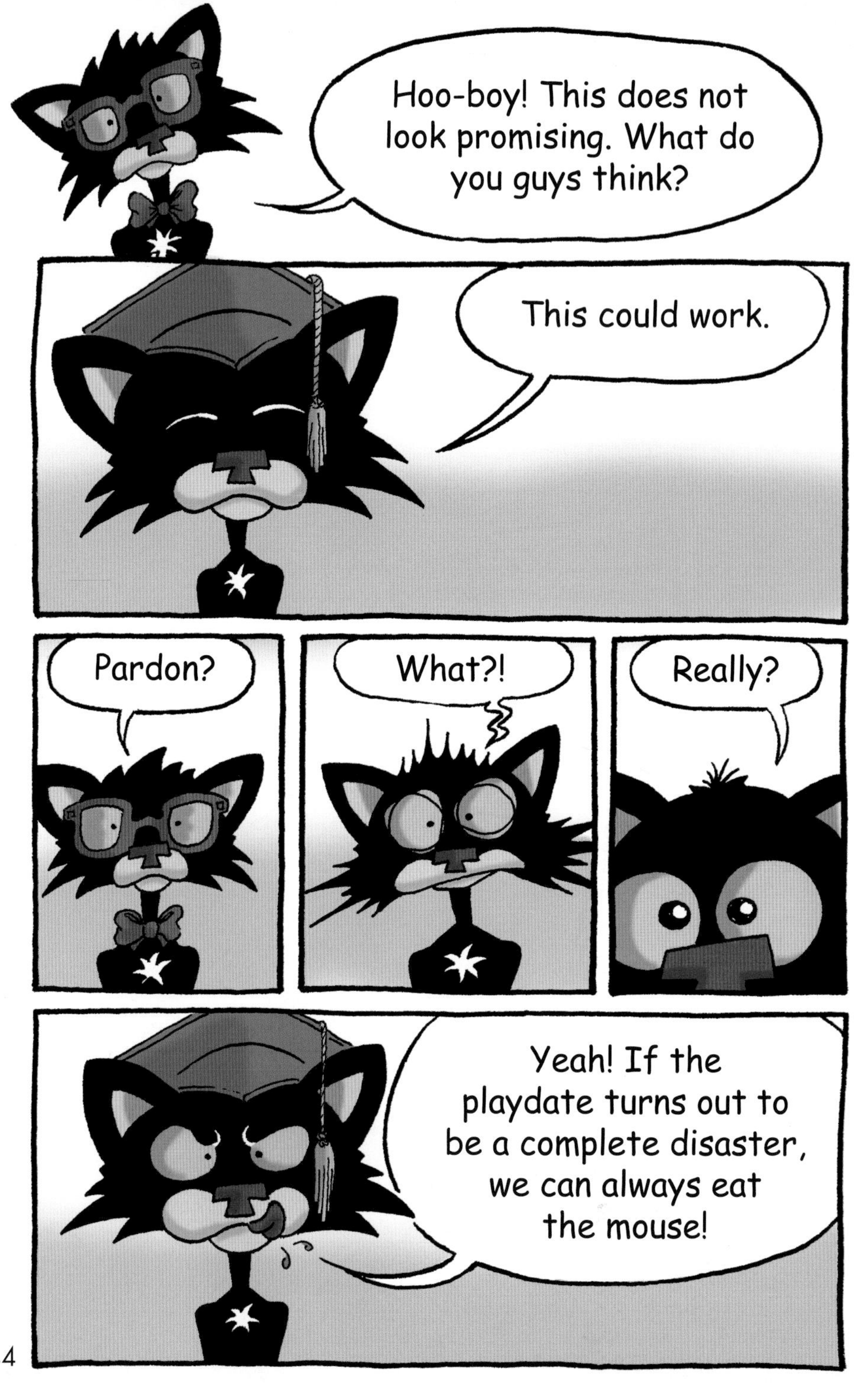
Hoo-boy! This does not look promising. What do you guys think?
This could work.
Pardon?
What?!
Really?
Yeah! If the playdate turns out to be a complete disaster, we can always eat the mouse!

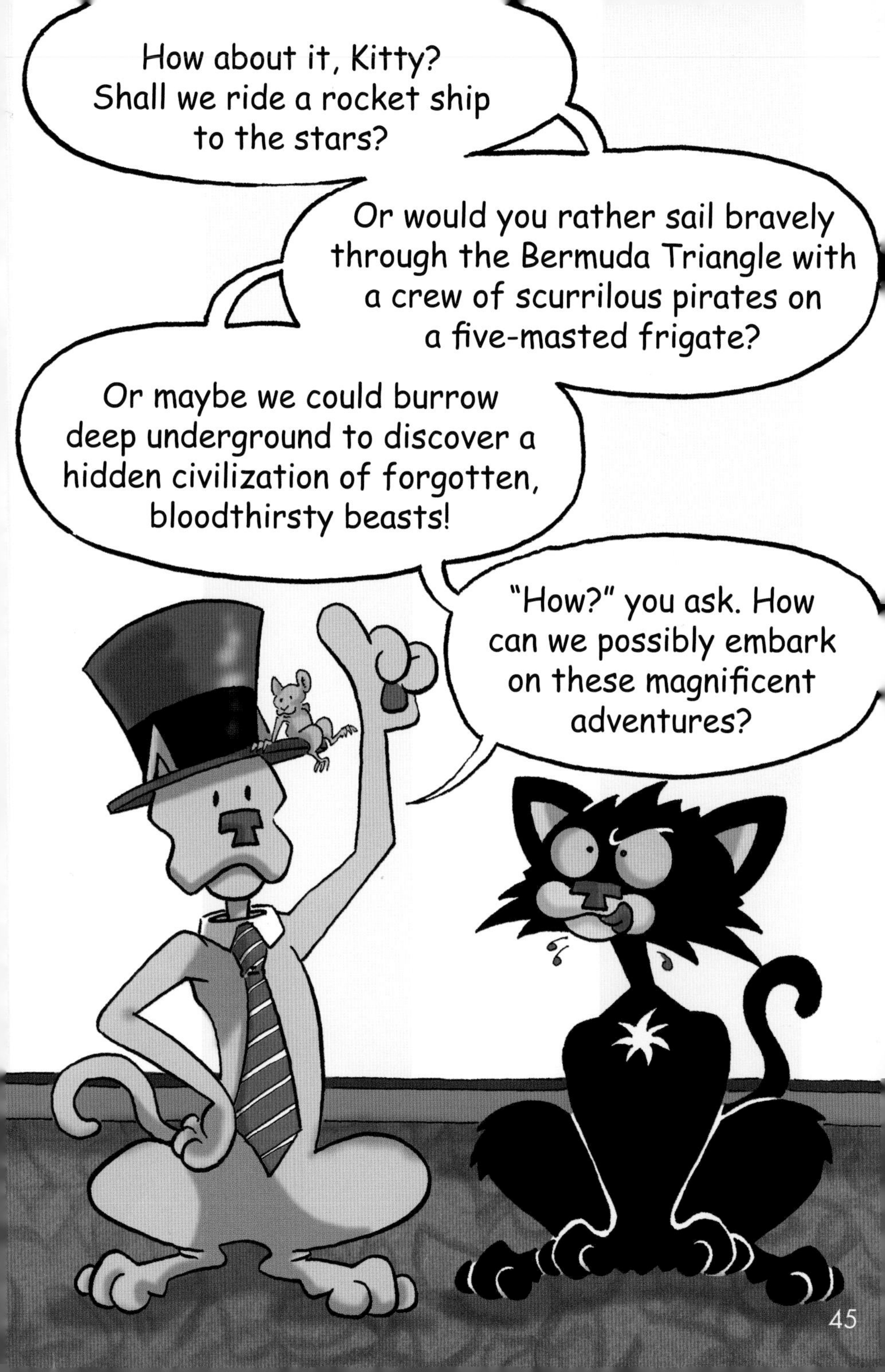
How about it, Kitty? Shall we ride a rocket ship to the stars?
Or would you rather sail bravely through the Bermuda Triangle with a crew of scurrilous pirates on a five-masted frigate?
Or maybe we could burrow deep underground to discover a hidden civilization of forgotten, bloodthirsty beasts!
"How?" you ask. How can we possibly embark on these magnificent adventures?

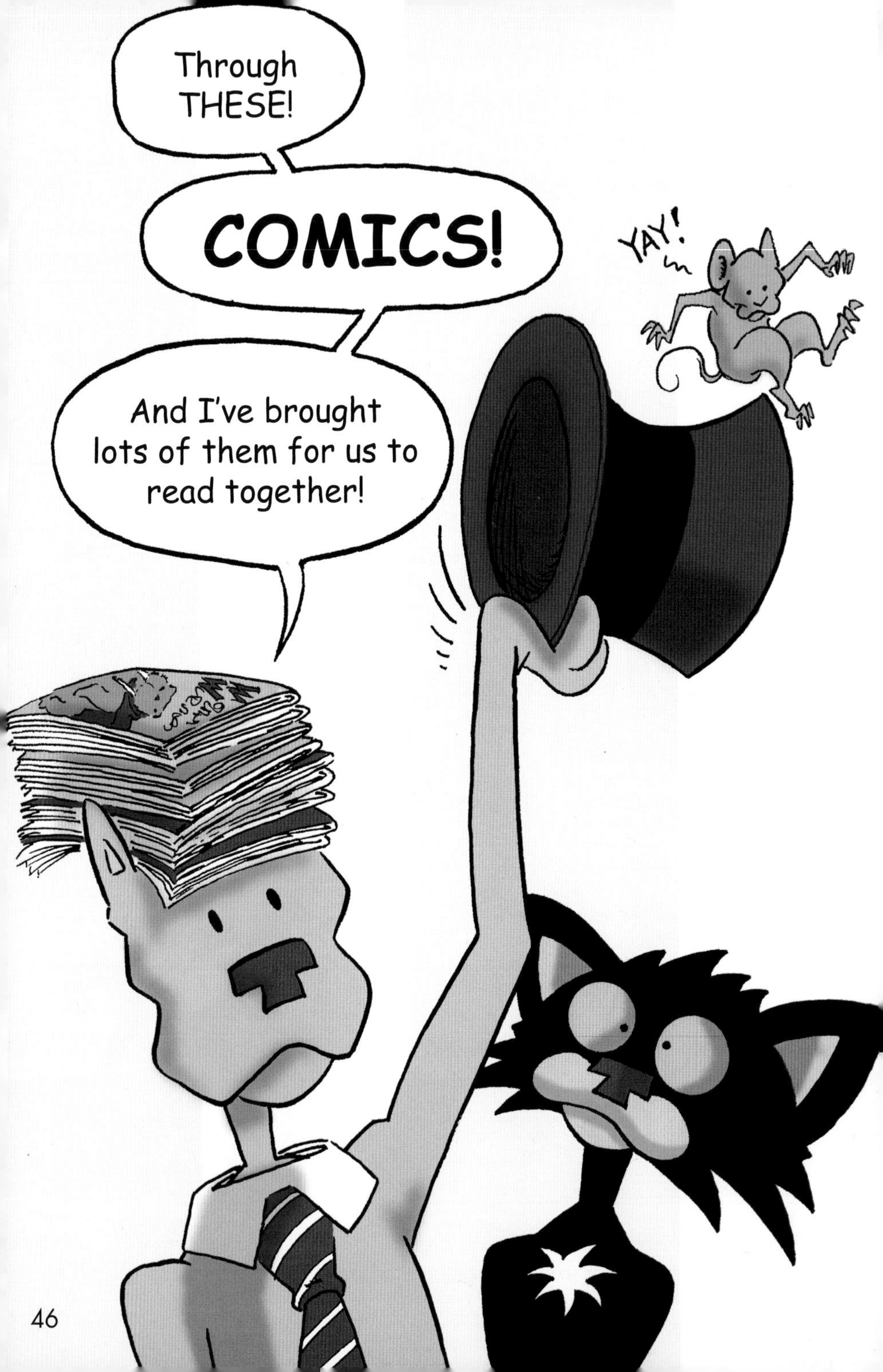
Through THESE!
COMICS!
And I've brought lots of them for us to read together!
YAY!

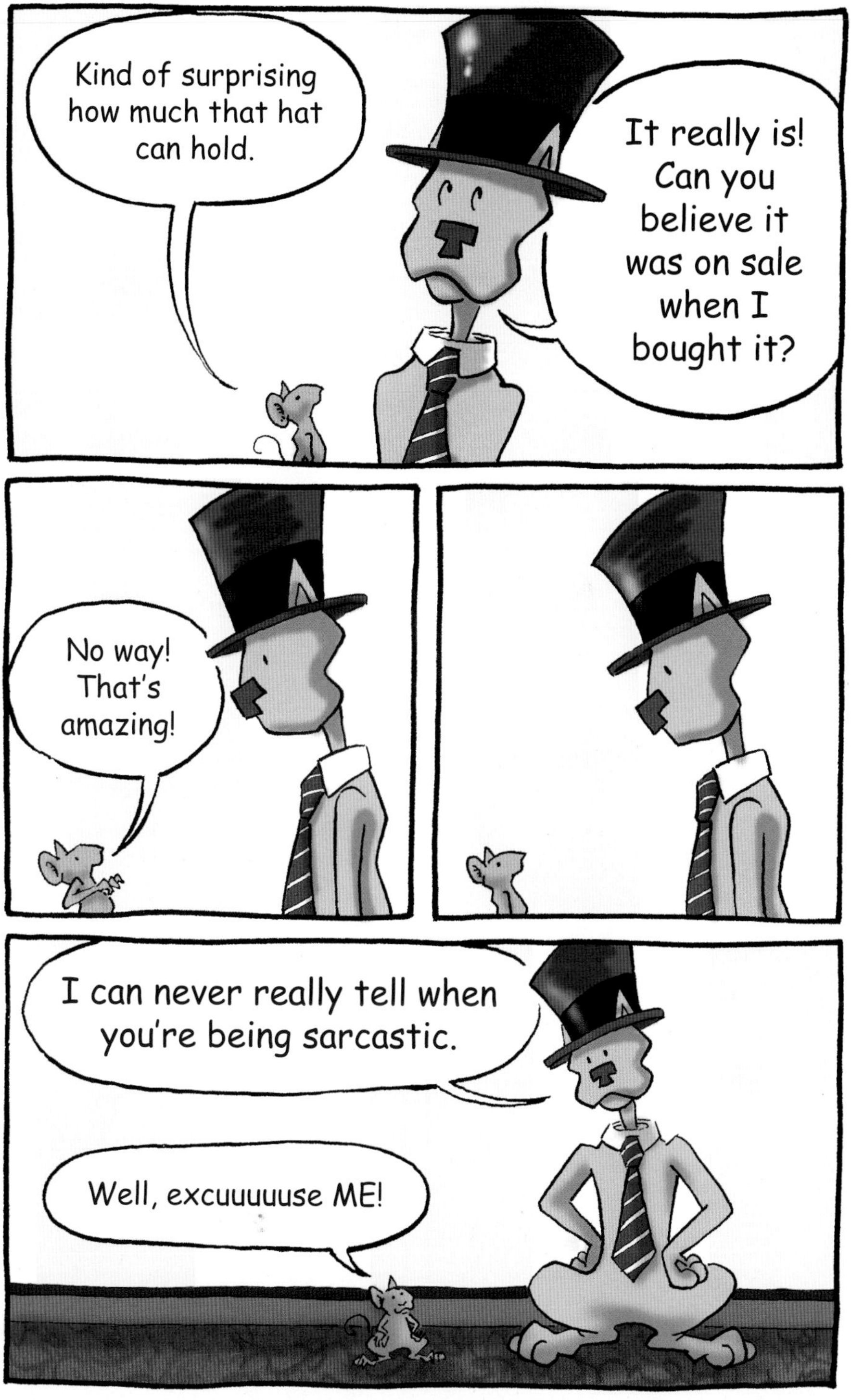
Kind of surprising how much that hat can hold.
It really is! Can you believe it was on sale when I bought it?
No way! That's amazing!
I can never really tell when you're being sarcastic.
Well, excuuuuuse ME!

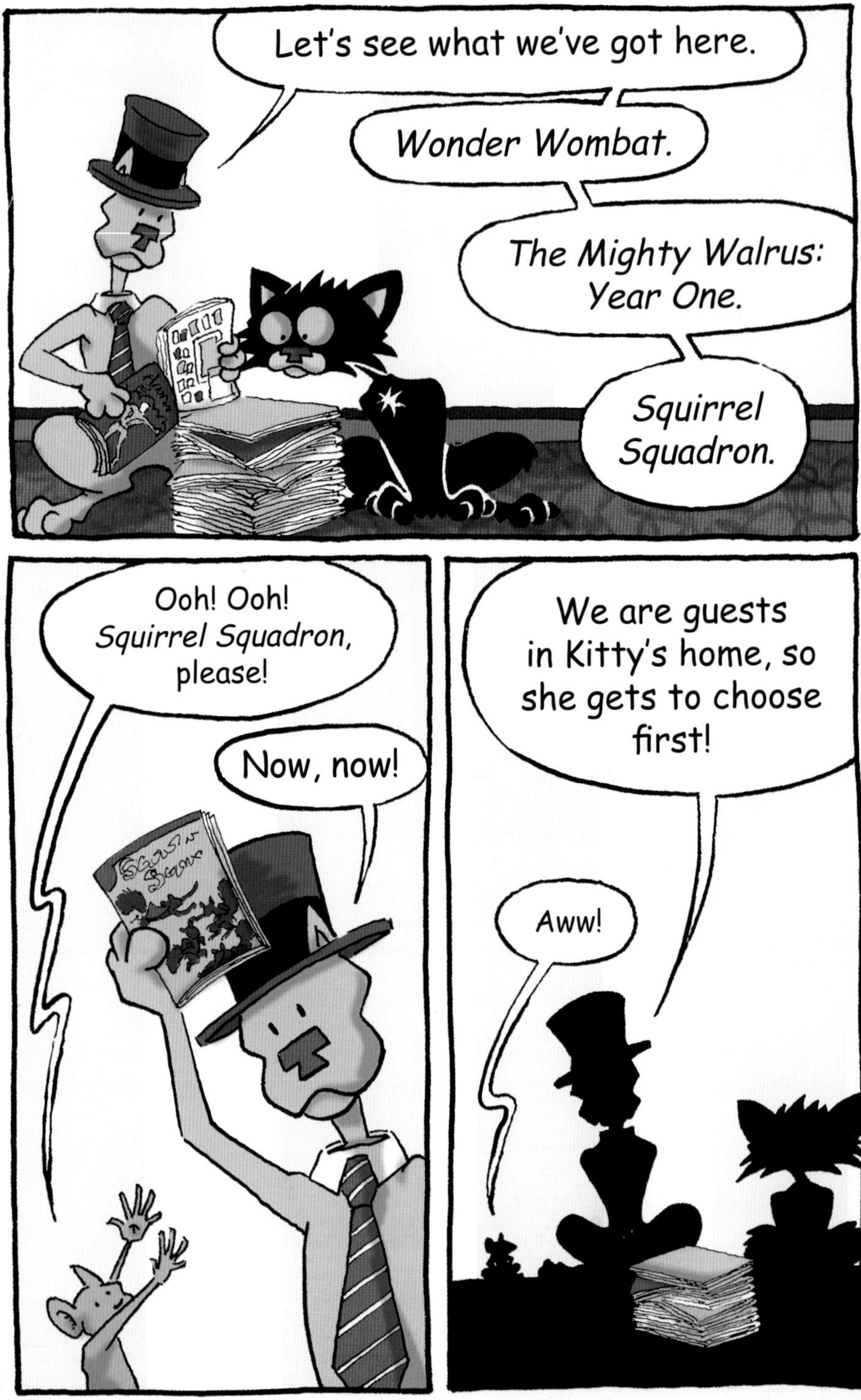
Let's see what we've got here.
Wonder Wombat.
The Mighty Walrus: Year One.
Squirrel Squadron.
Ooh! Ooh! *Squirrel Squadron,* please!
Now, now!
We are guests in Kitty's home, so she gets to choose first!
Aww!

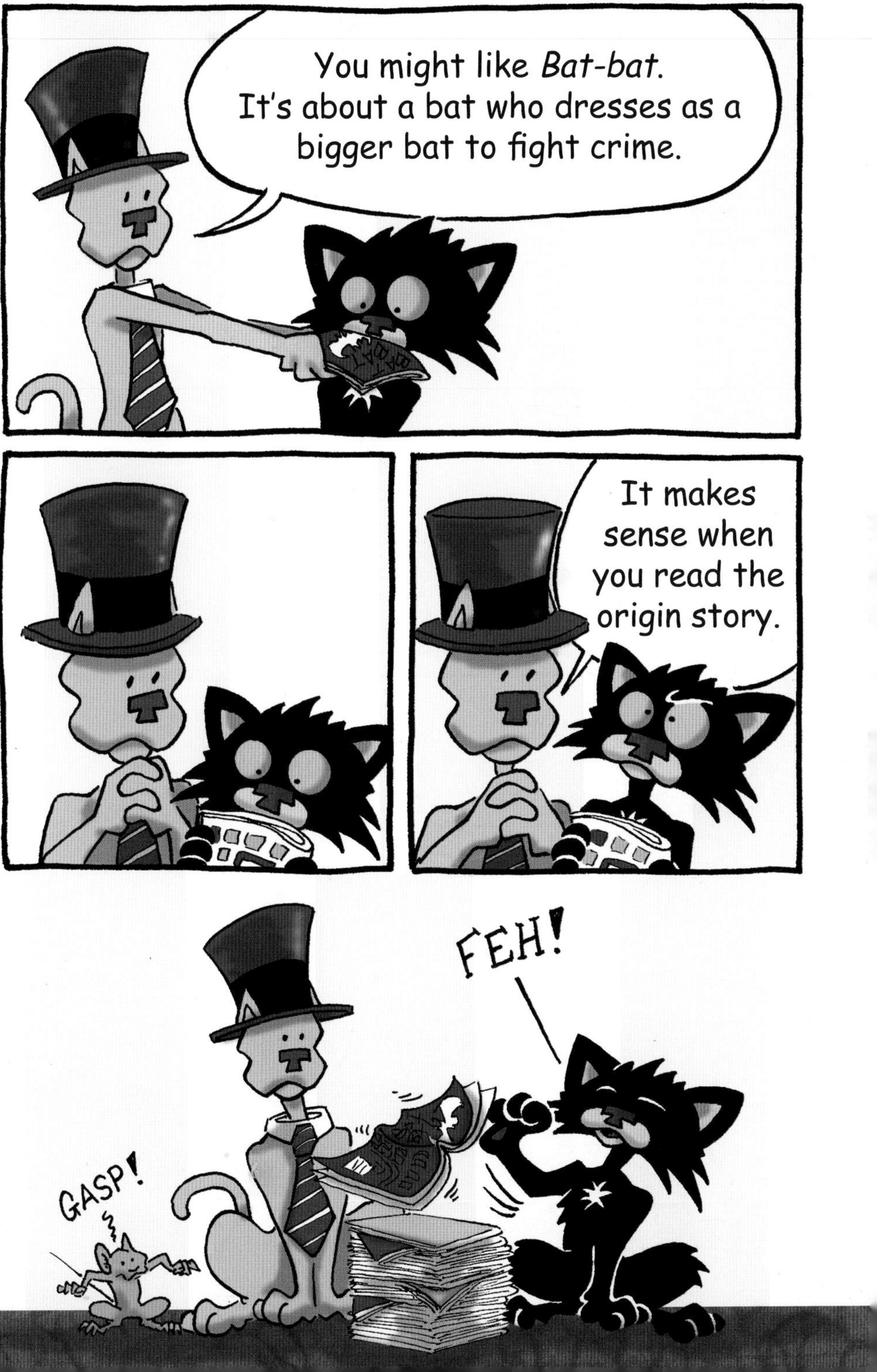
You might like *Bat-bat*. It's about a bat who dresses as a bigger bat to fight crime.
It makes sense when you read the origin story.
FEH!
GASP!

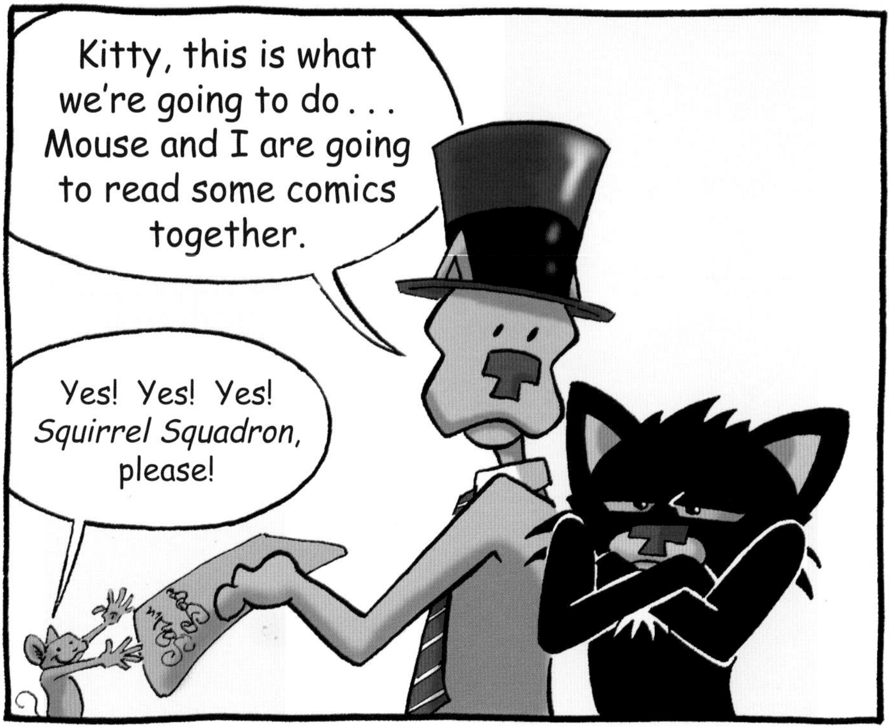
Kitty, this is what we're going to do . . . Mouse and I are going to read some comics together.
Yes! Yes! Yes! *Squirrel Squadron*, please!

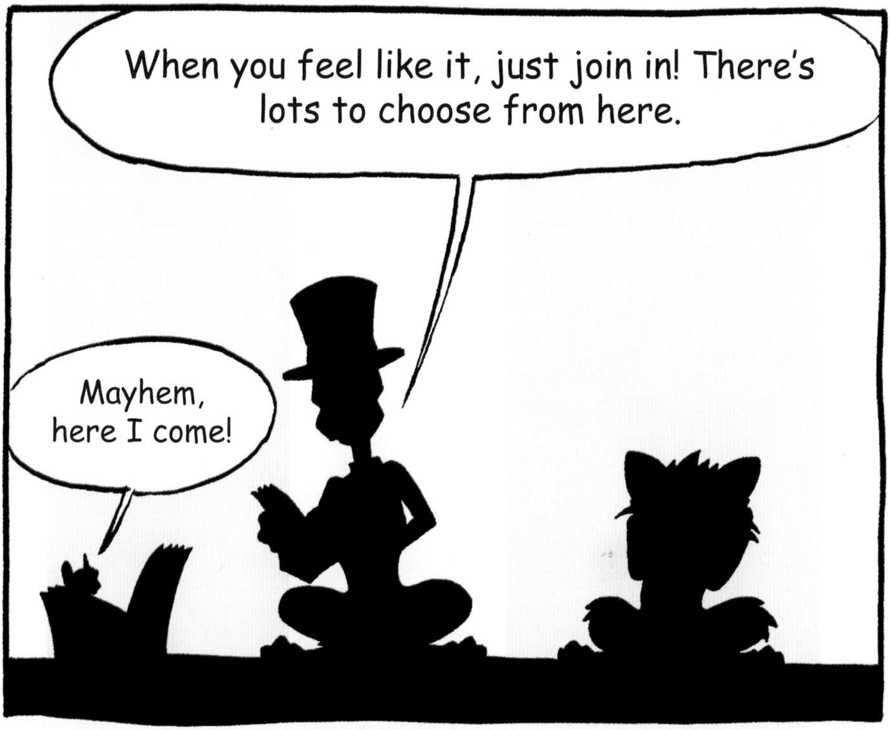
When you feel like it, just join in! There's lots to choose from here.
Mayhem, here I come!

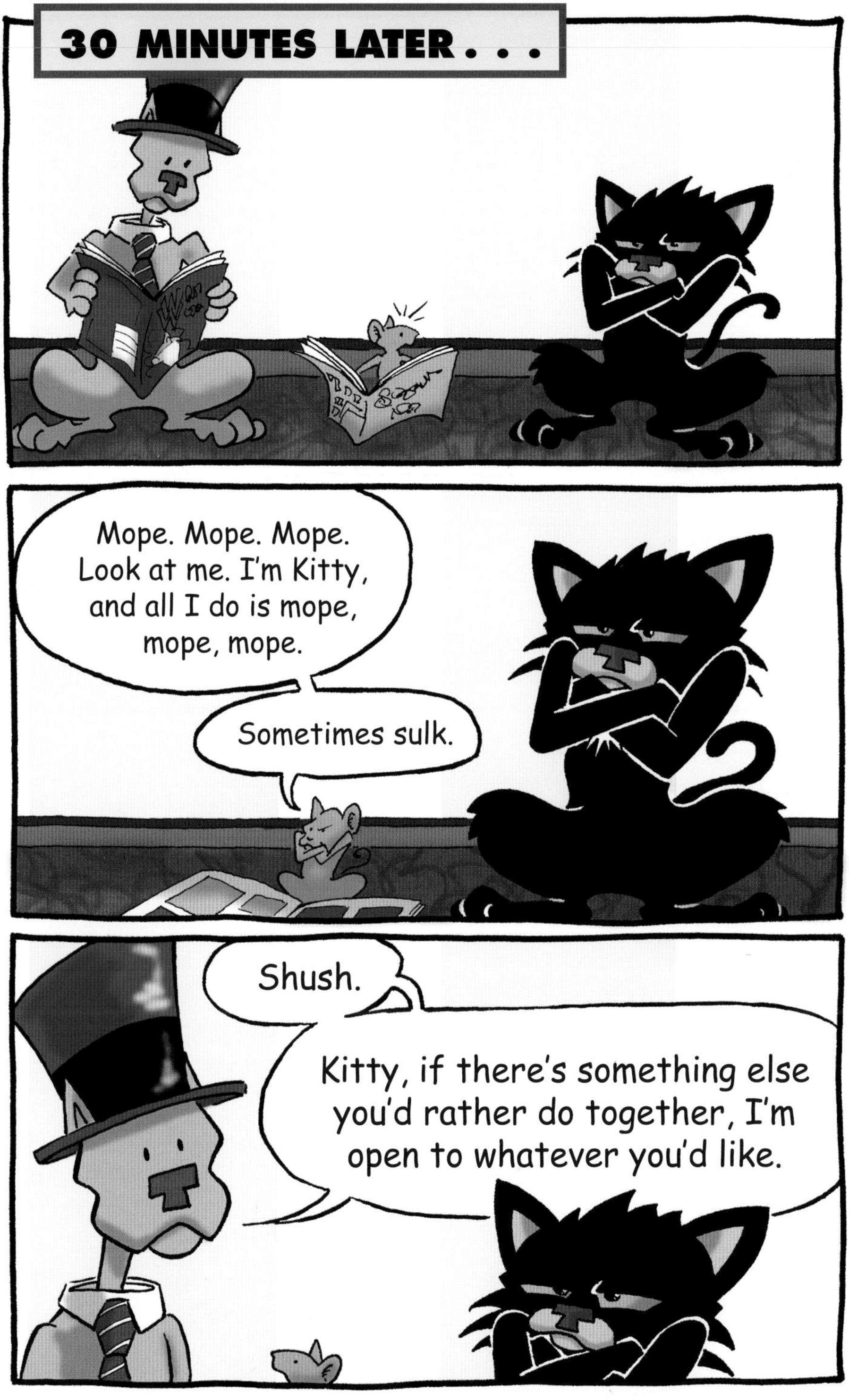
30 MINUTES LATER . . .
Mope. Mope. Mope. Look at me. I'm Kitty, and all I do is mope, mope, mope.
Sometimes sulk.
Shush.
Kitty, if there's something else you'd rather do together, I'm open to whatever you'd like.

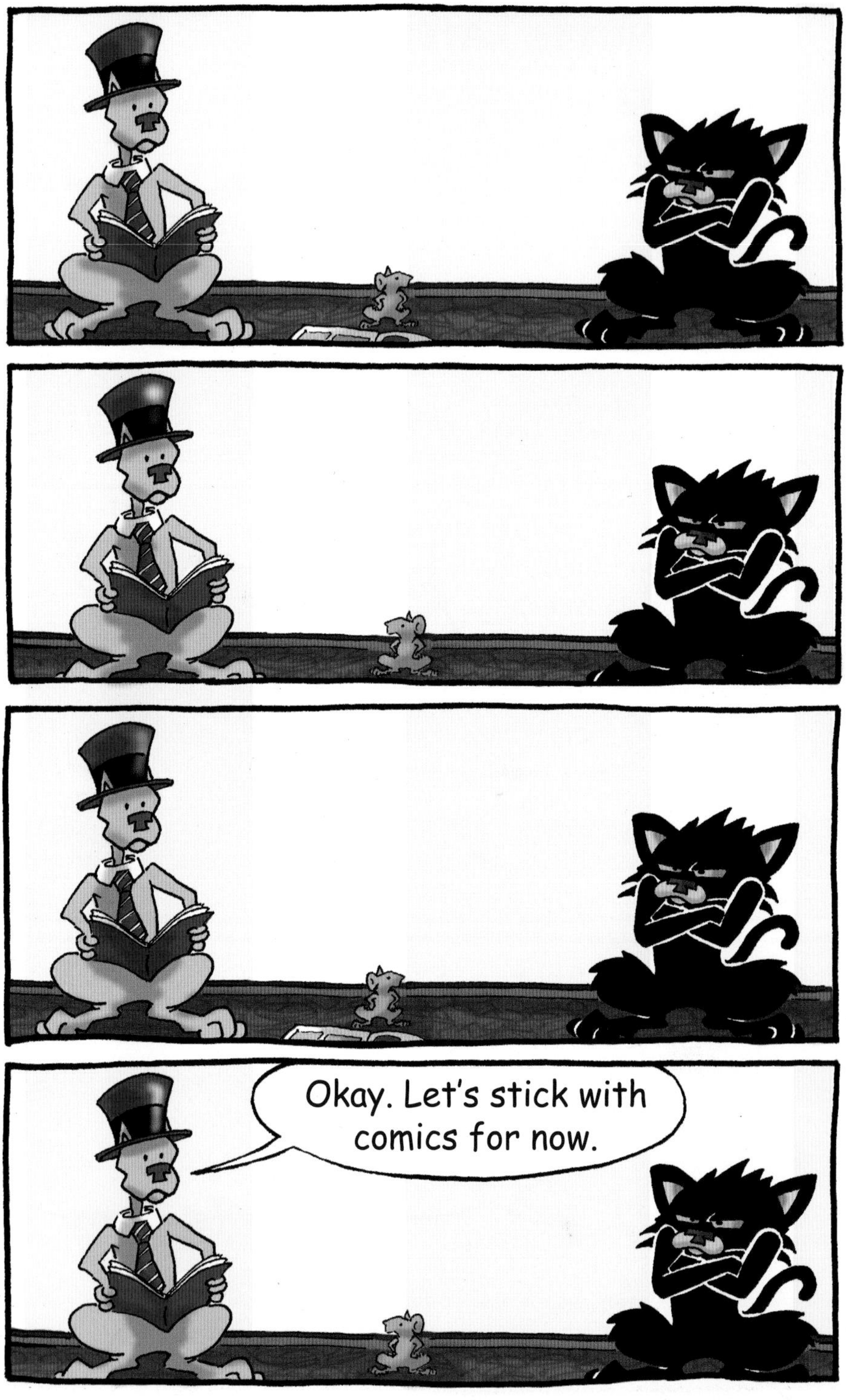
Okay. Let's stick with comics for now.

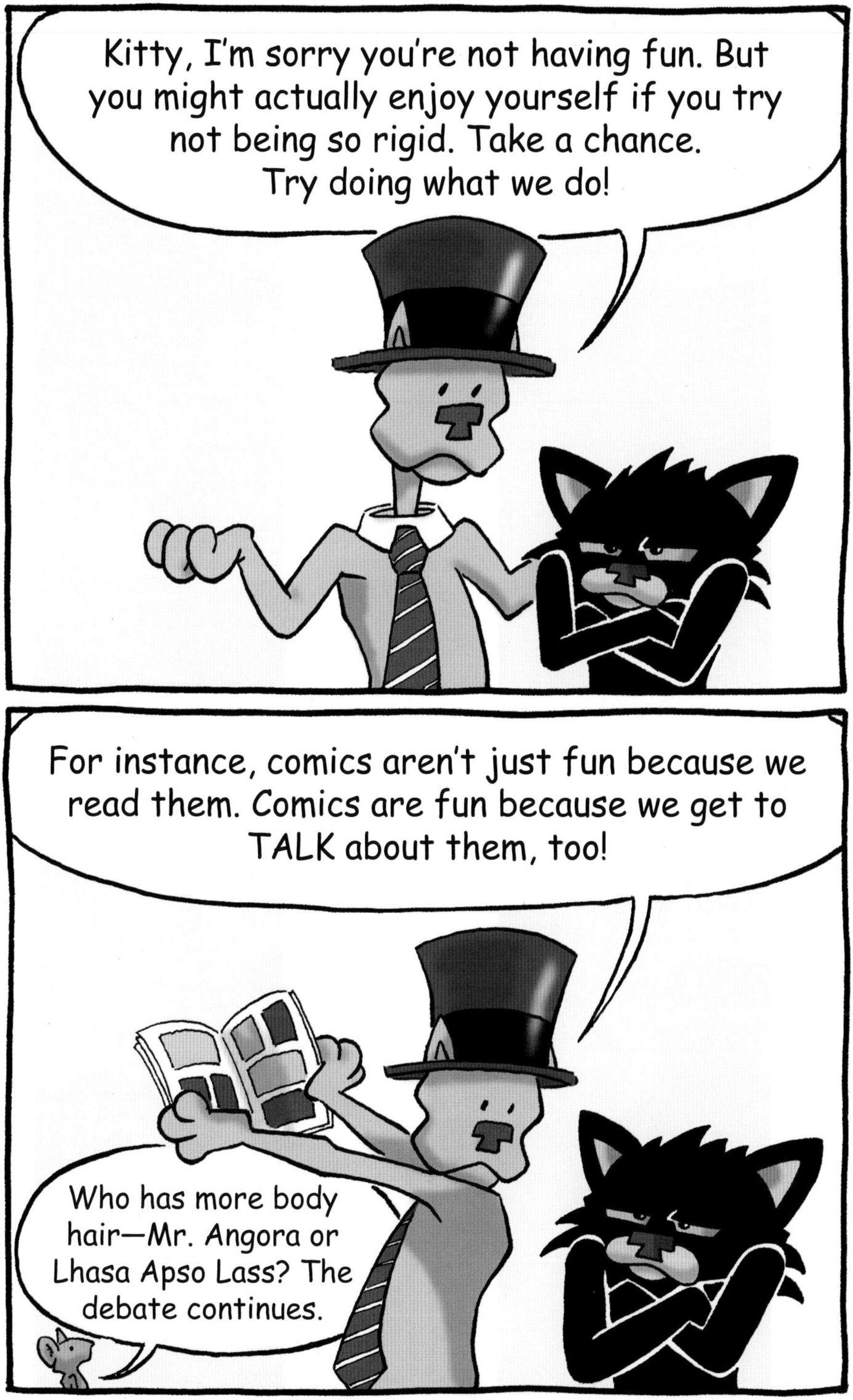
Kitty, I'm sorry you're not having fun. But you might actually enjoy yourself if you try not being so rigid. Take a chance. Try doing what we do!
For instance, comics aren't just fun because we read them. Comics are fun because we get to TALK about them, too!
Who has more body hair—Mr. Angora or Lhasa Apso Lass? The debate continues.

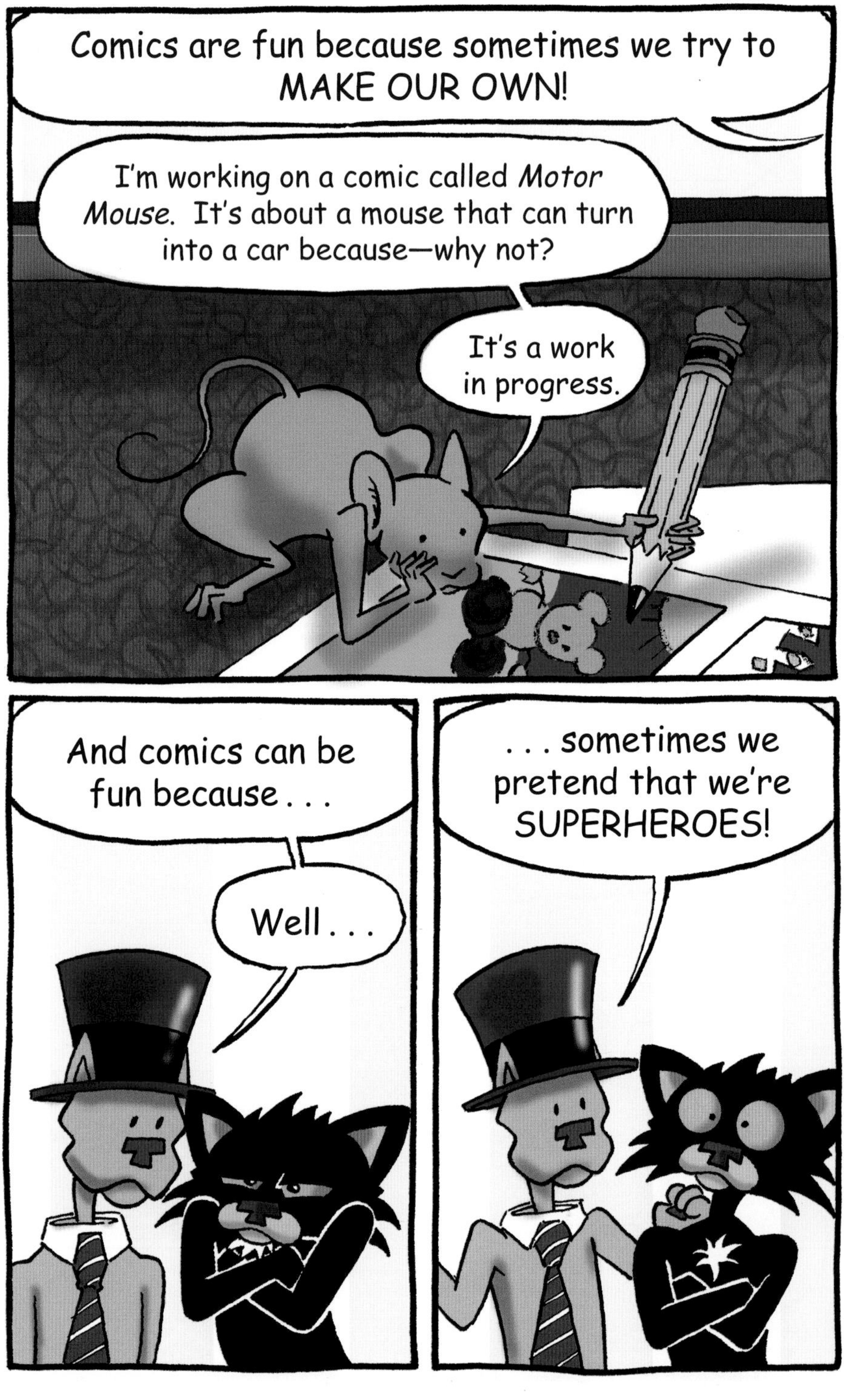

Comics are fun because sometimes we try to MAKE OUR OWN!
I'm working on a comic called *Motor Mouse*. It's about a mouse that can turn into a car because—why not?
It's a work in progress.
And comics can be fun because . . .
Well . . .
. . . sometimes we pretend that we're SUPERHEROES!

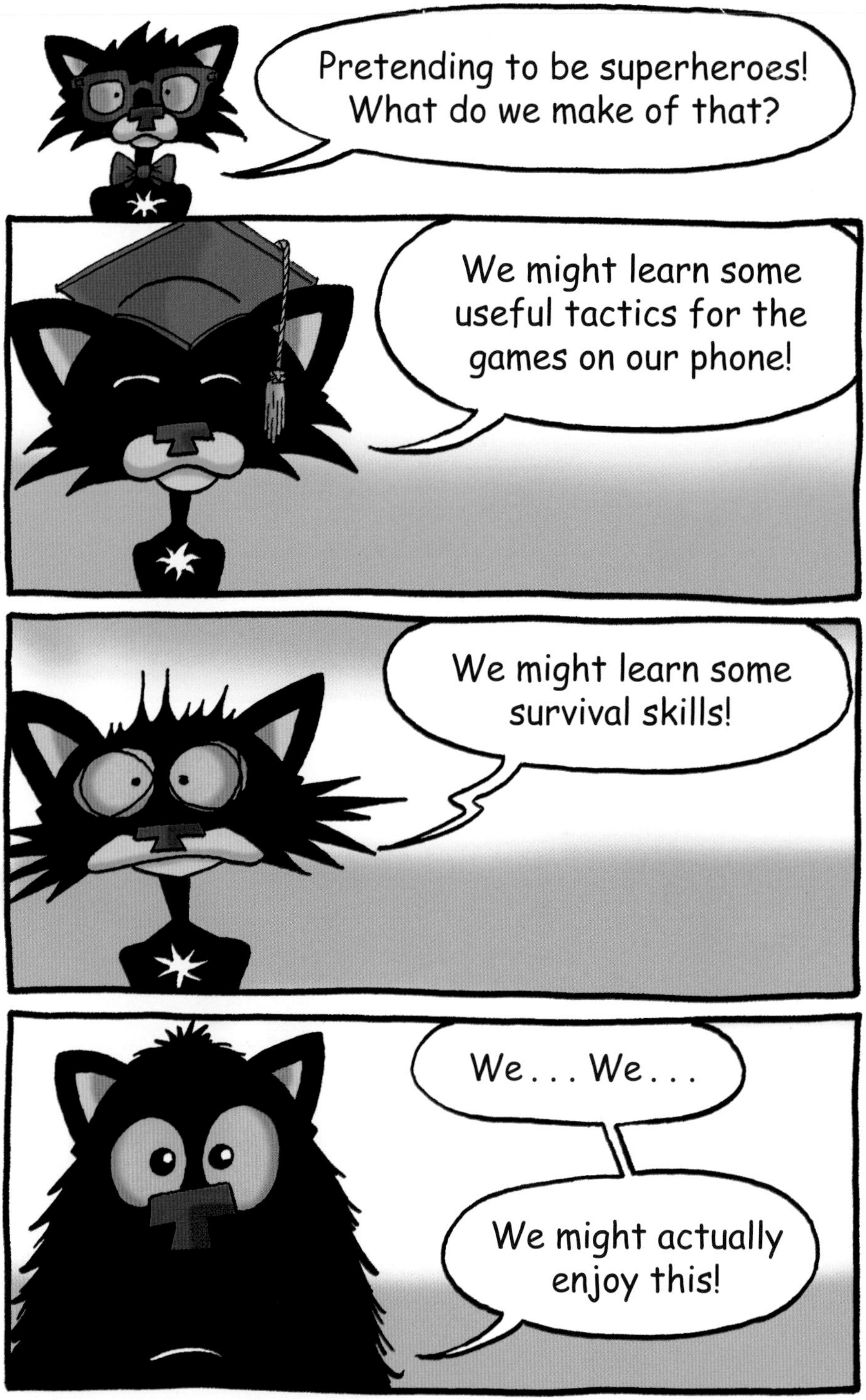
Pretending to be superheroes! What do we make of that?
We might learn some useful tactics for the games on our phone!
We might learn some survival skills!
We... We...
We might actually enjoy this!

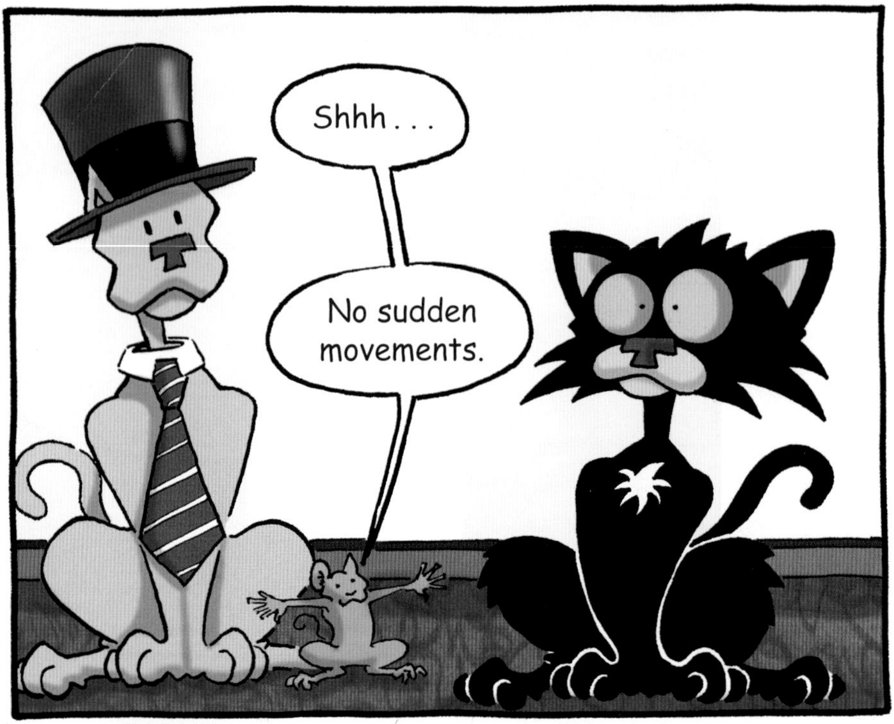
Shhh . . .
No sudden movements.

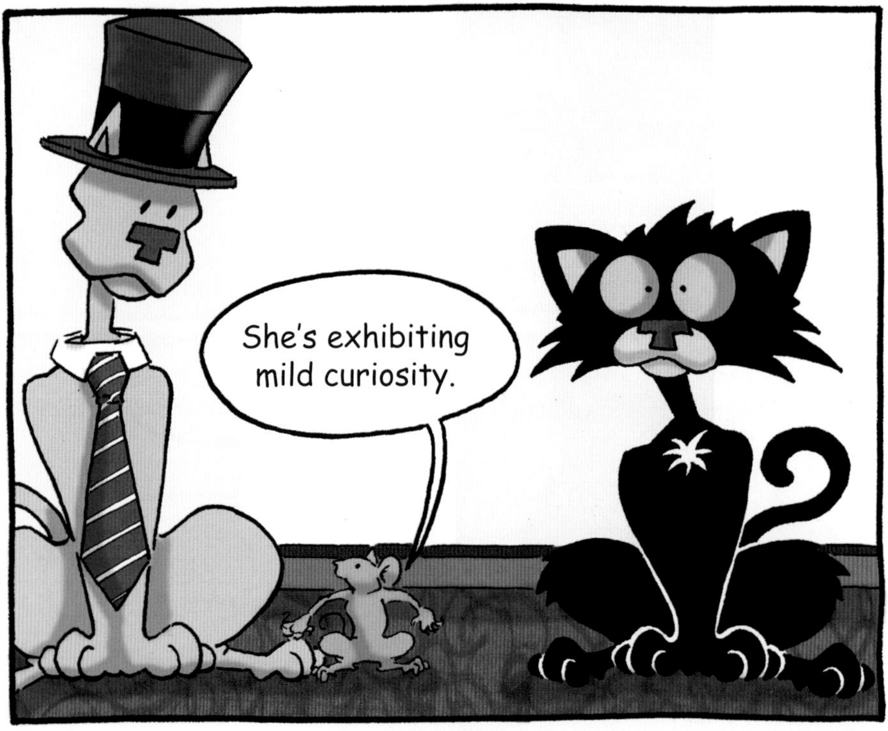
She's exhibiting mild curiosity.

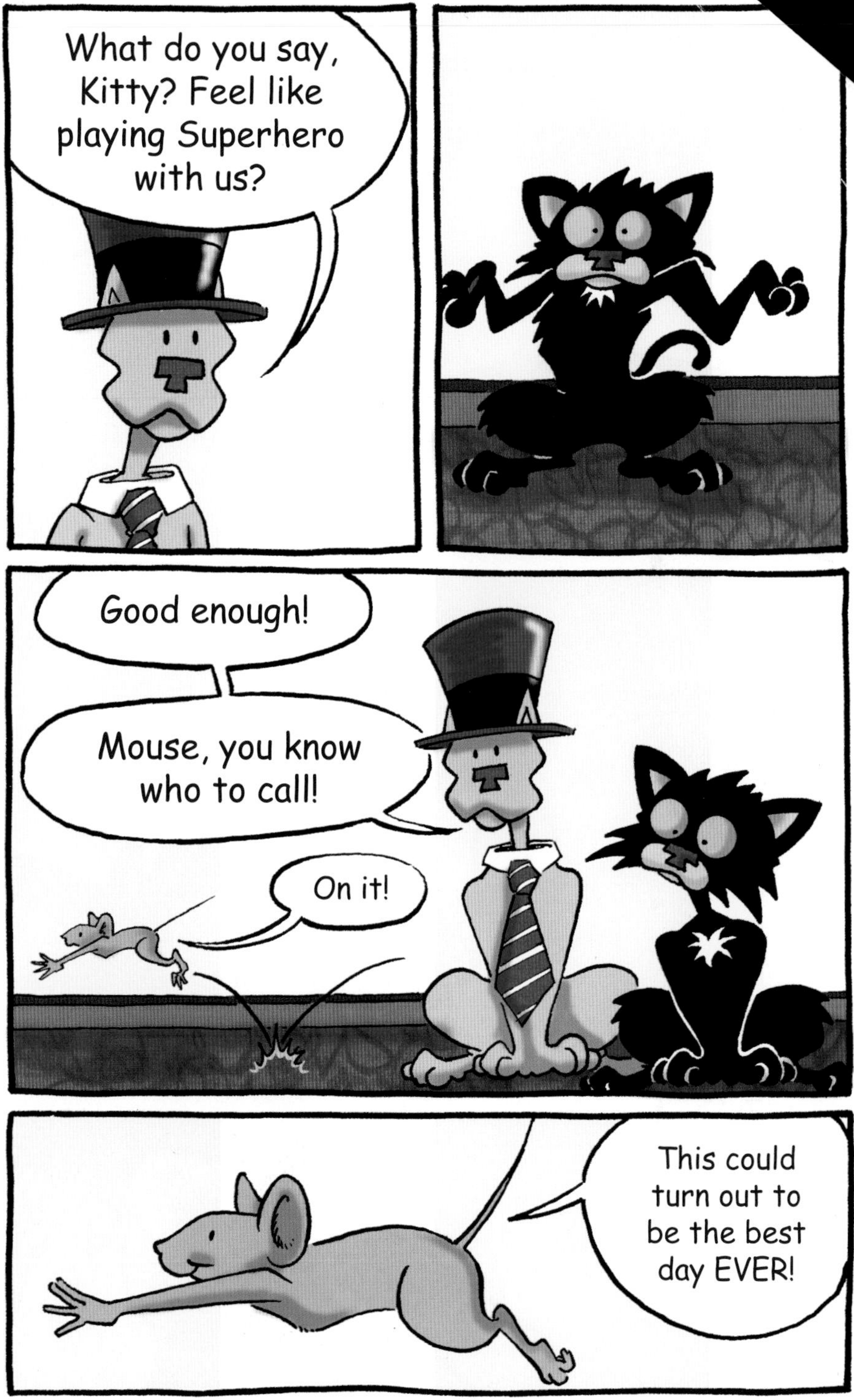
What do you say, Kitty? Feel like playing Superhero with us?
Good enough!
Mouse, you know who to call!
On it!
This could turn out to be the best day EVER!

•CHAPTER THREE•

MAKING A SUPERHERO

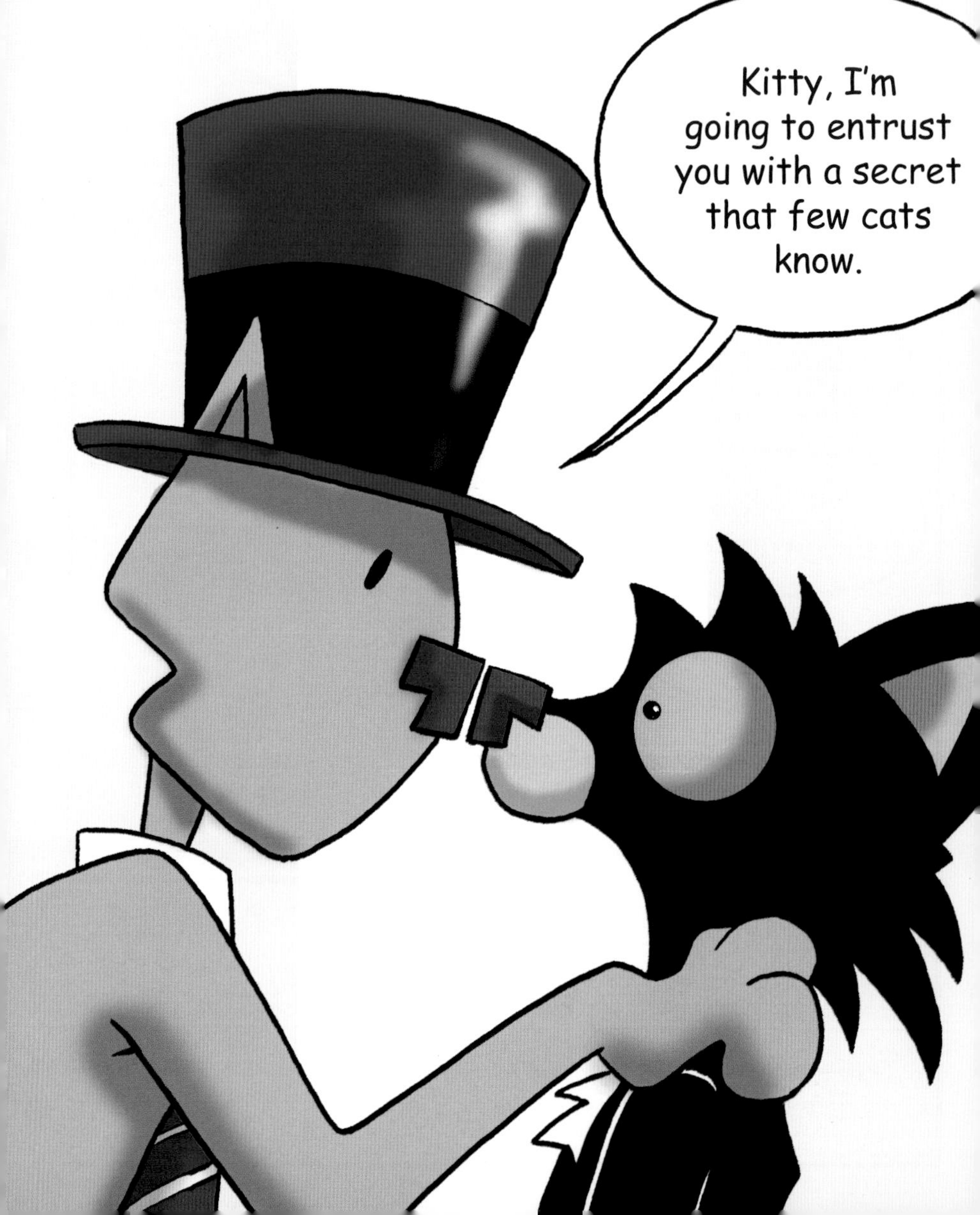
Kitty, I'm going to entrust you with a secret that few cats know.

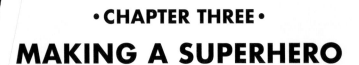

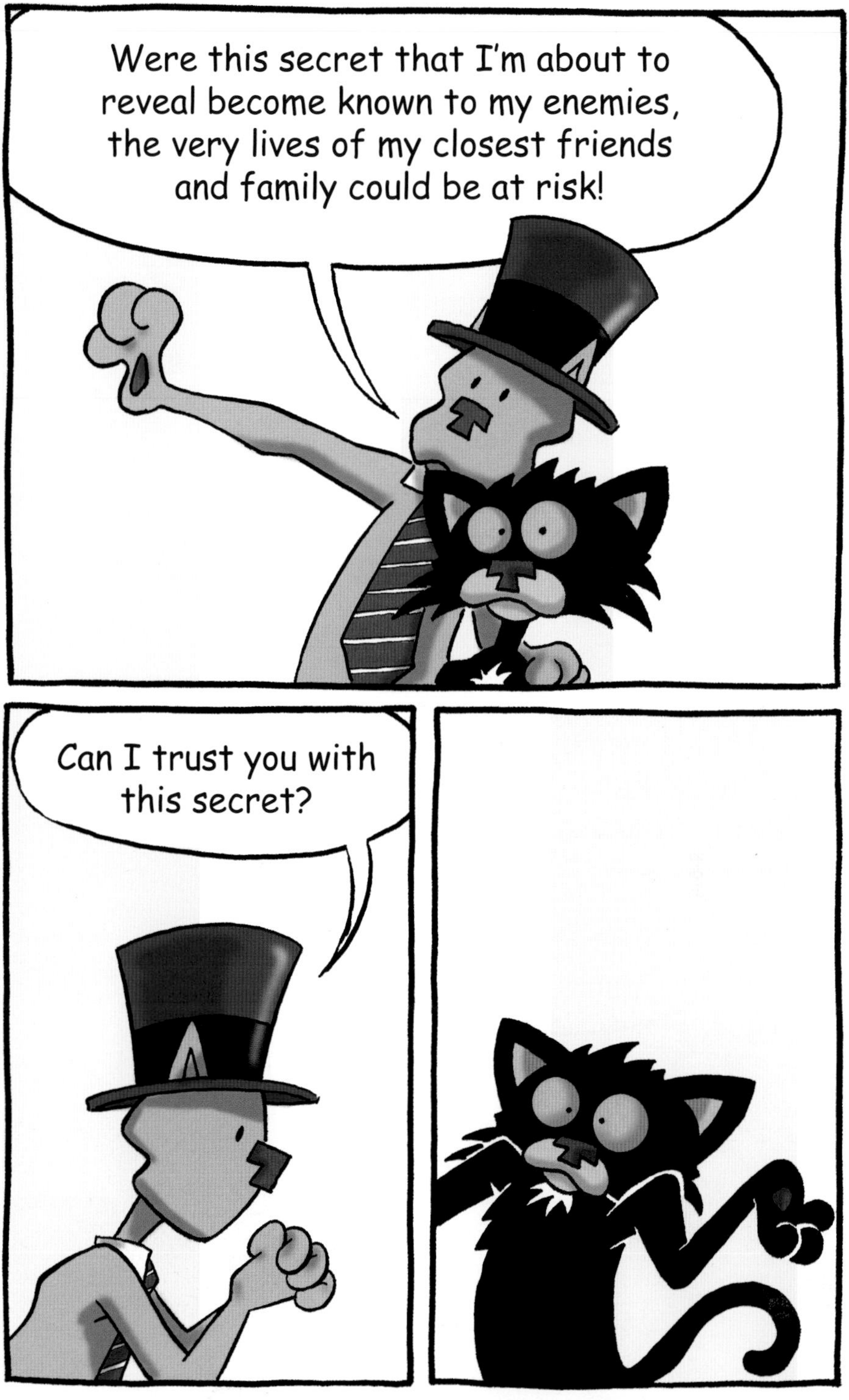
Were this secret that I'm about to reveal become known to my enemies, the very lives of my closest friends and family could be at risk!
Can I trust you with this secret?

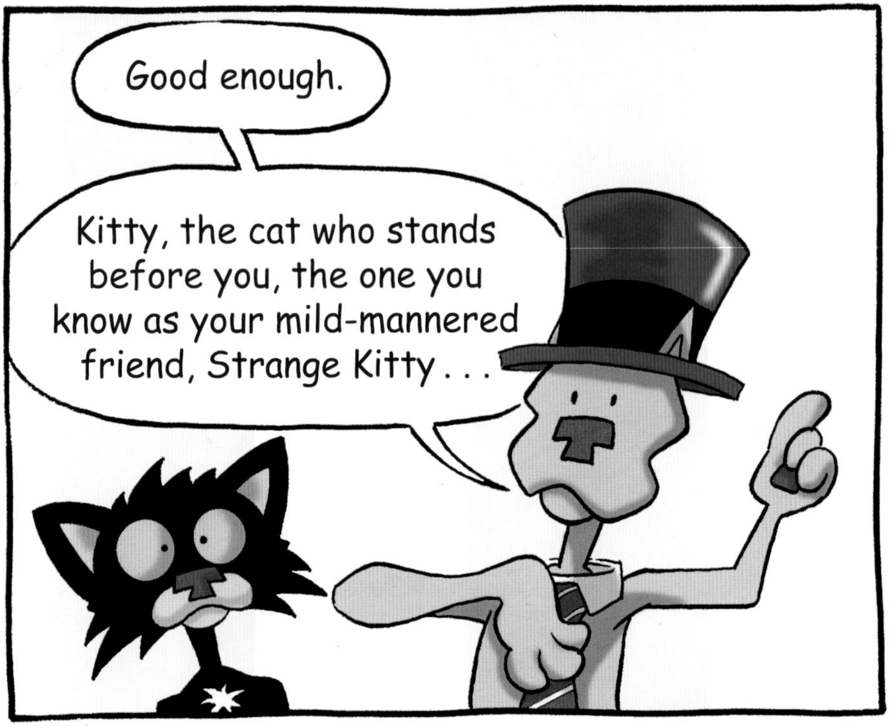
Good enough.
Kitty, the cat who stands before you, the one you know as your mild-mannered friend, Strange Kitty . . .

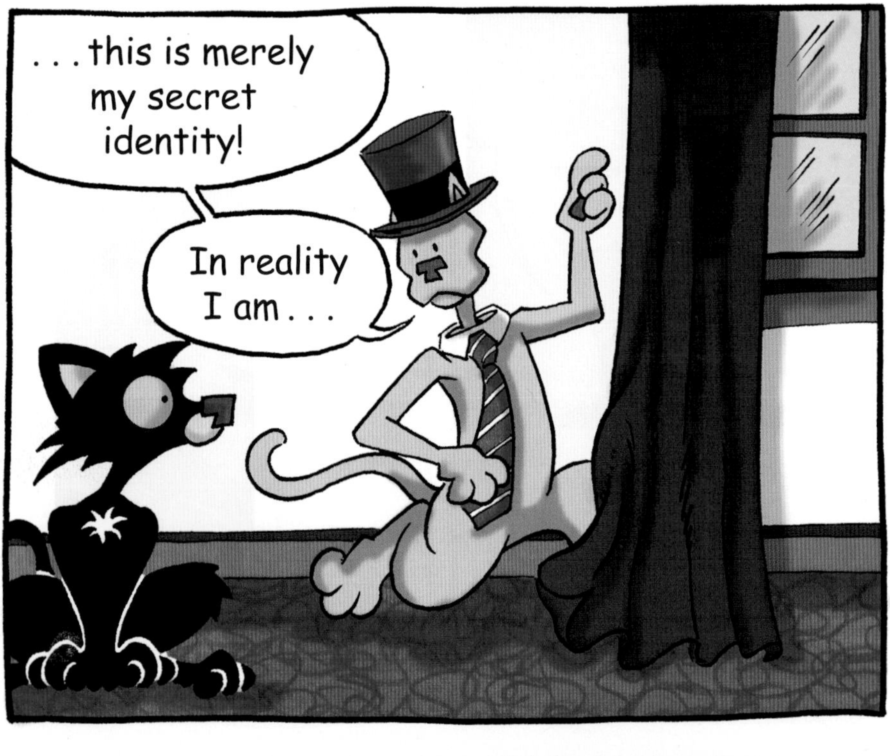
. . . this is merely my secret identity!
In reality I am . . .

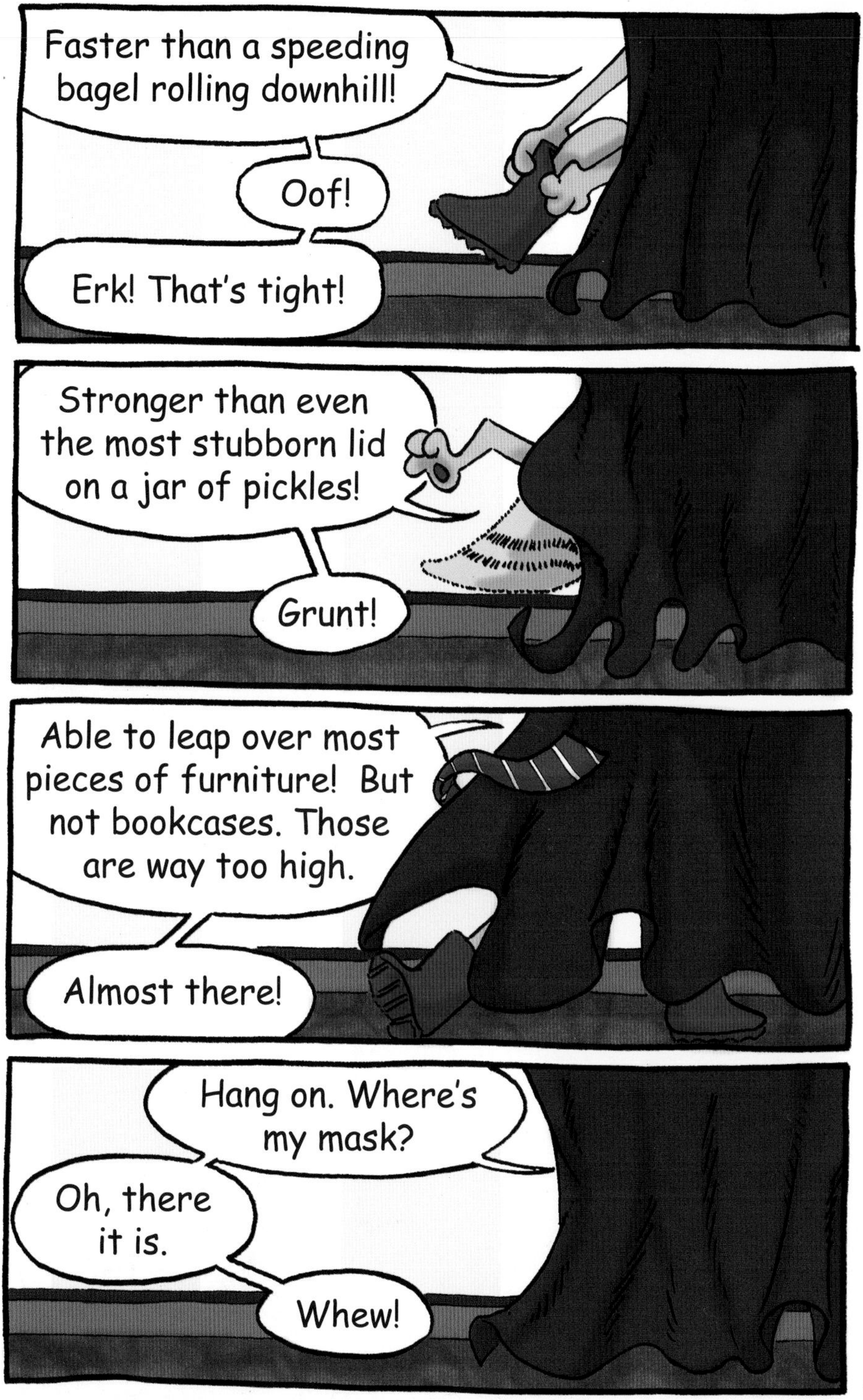
Faster than a speeding bagel rolling downhill!
Oof!
Erk! That's tight!
Stronger than even the most stubborn lid on a jar of pickles!
Grunt!
Able to leap over most pieces of furniture! But not bookcases. Those are way too high.
Almost there!
Hang on. Where's my mask?
Oh, there it is.
Whew!

CAPTAIN FANTASTICAT

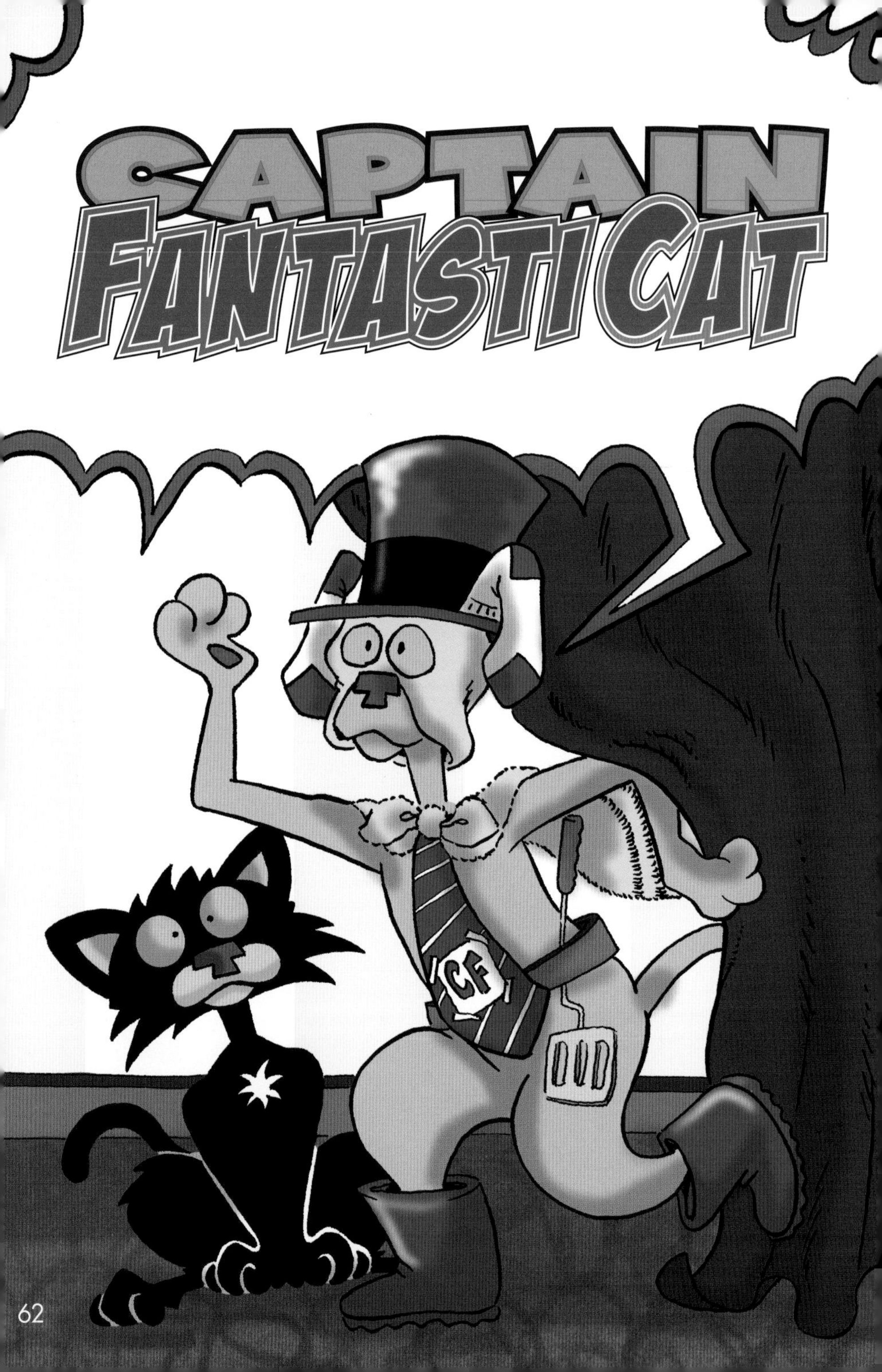
CF

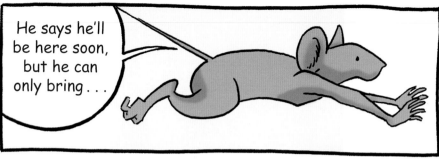

He says he'll be here soon, but he can only bring . . .

Oh, wow! You're in costume already!

Yup!

Give me a second.

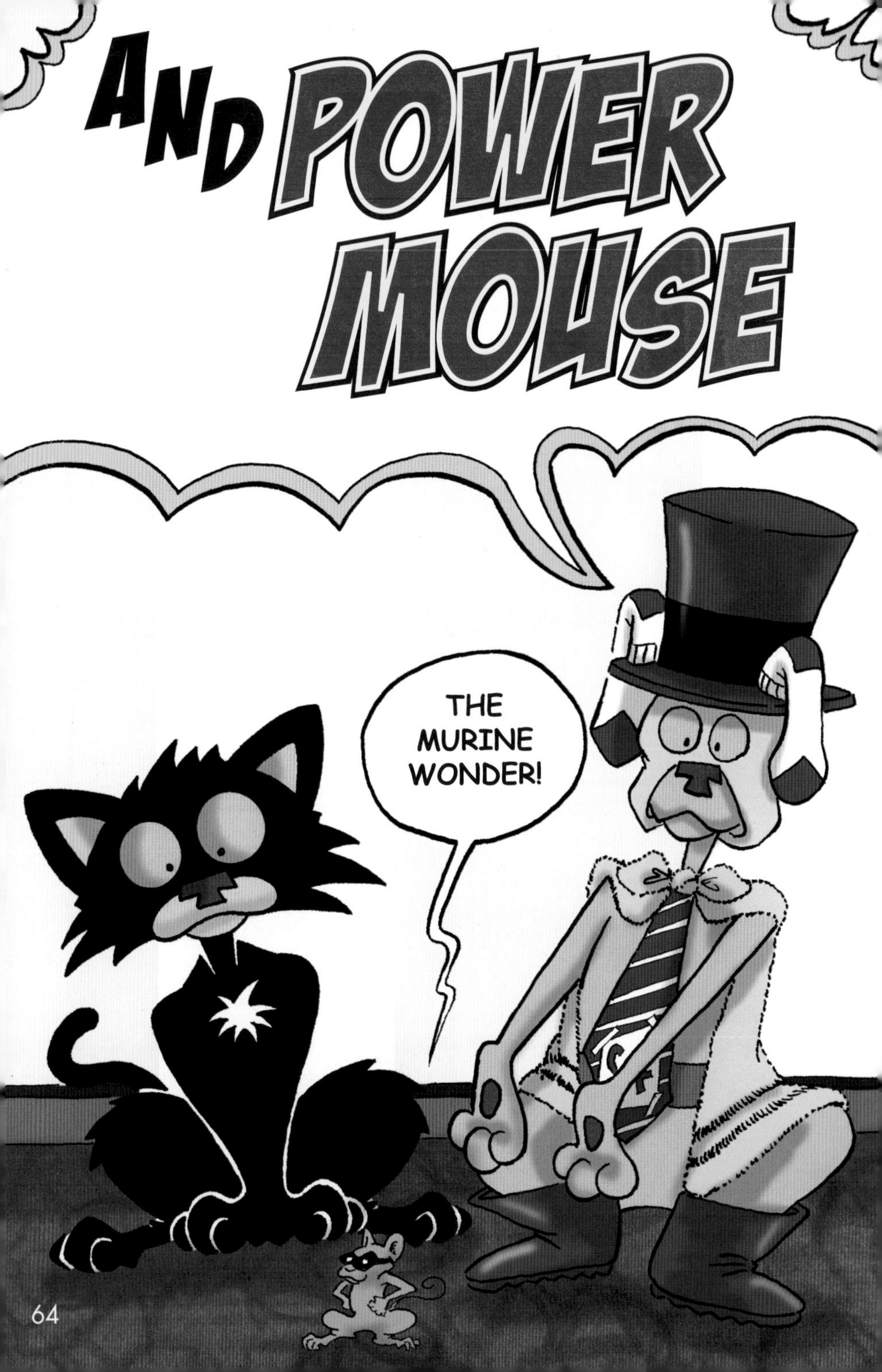
AND POWER MOUSE
THE MURINE WONDER!

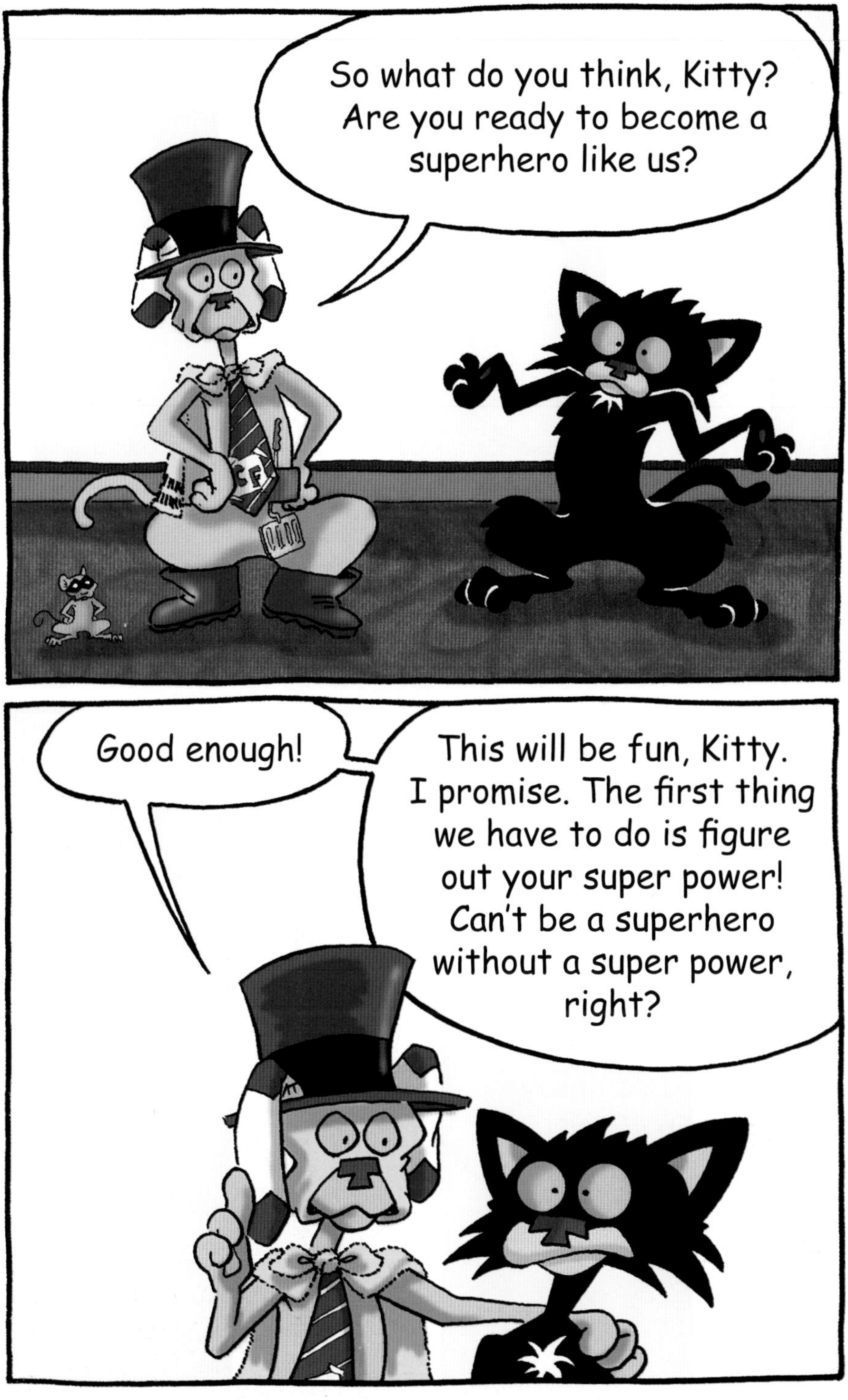
So what do you think, Kitty? Are you ready to become a superhero like us?
Good enough!
This will be fun, Kitty. I promise. The first thing we have to do is figure out your super power! Can't be a superhero without a super power, right?

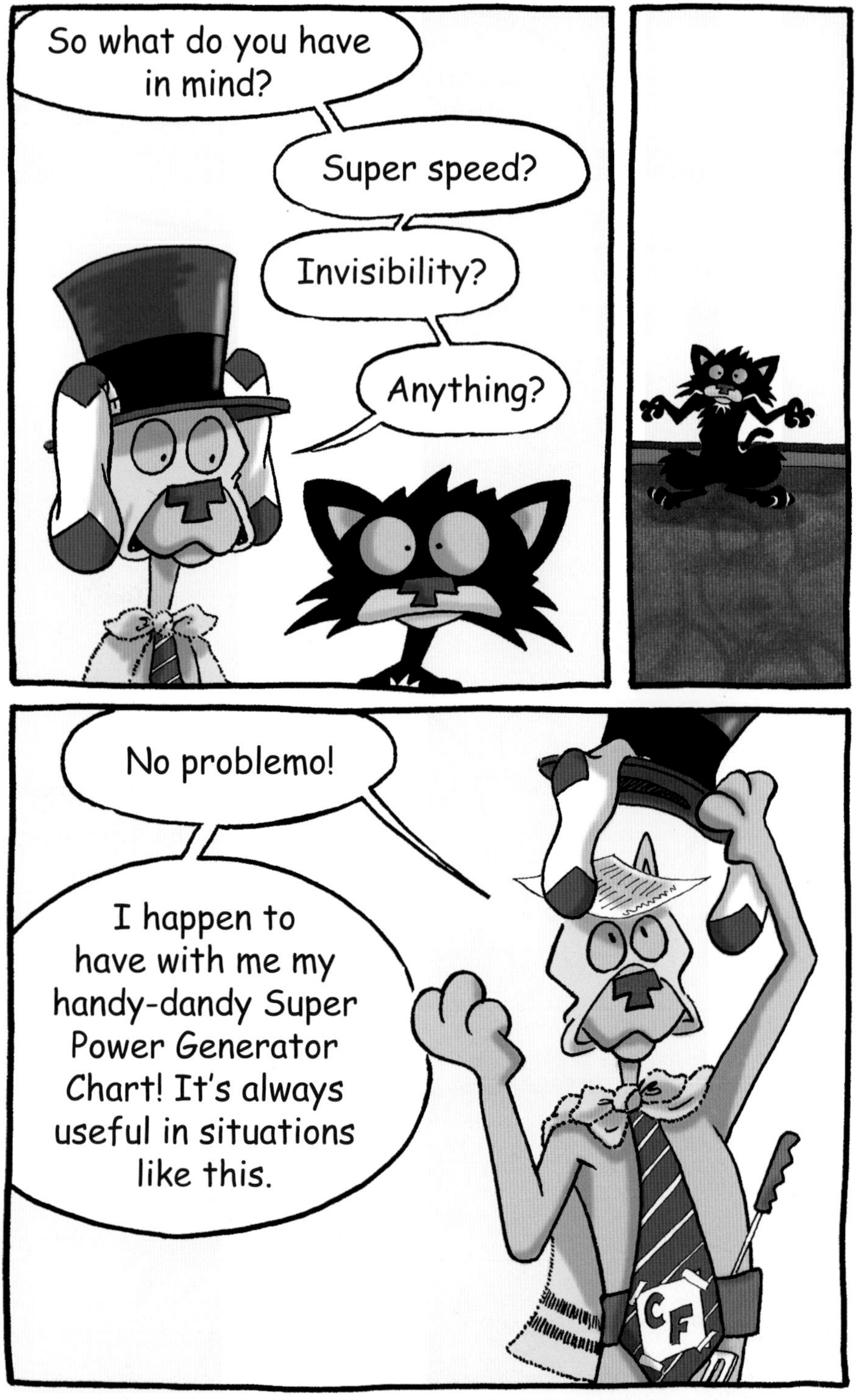
So what do you have in mind?
Super speed?
Invisibility?
Anything?
No problemo!
I happen to have with me my handy-dandy Super Power Generator Chart! It's always useful in situations like this.
CF

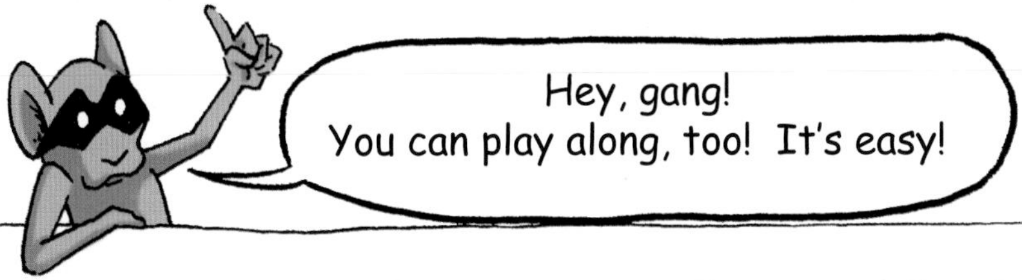
Hey, gang!
You can play along, too! It's easy!

SUPER POWER GENERATOR

THE FIRST LETTER OF YOUR FIRST NAME IS YOUR SUPER POWER!

A—Super speed

B—Shape-shifting

C—Laser-beam eyes

D—Ability to control animals

E—Mind control

F—Ability to control weather

G—Teleportation

H—Super stretching powers

I—Impenetrable armor

J—Super martial arts powers

K—Super strength

L—Invisibility

M—Can grow to any height

N—Flight

O—Ability to control metal

P—Can eat anything. Seriously. ANYTHING.

Q—Can shrink to any size

R—Super intelligence

S—Incredibly awesome spatula skills

T—Robot arms

U—Ability to control electricity

V—Ability to control time

W—Ability to control plants

X—Ability to predict future

Y—Create energy blasts

Z—Ability to create invisible force fields

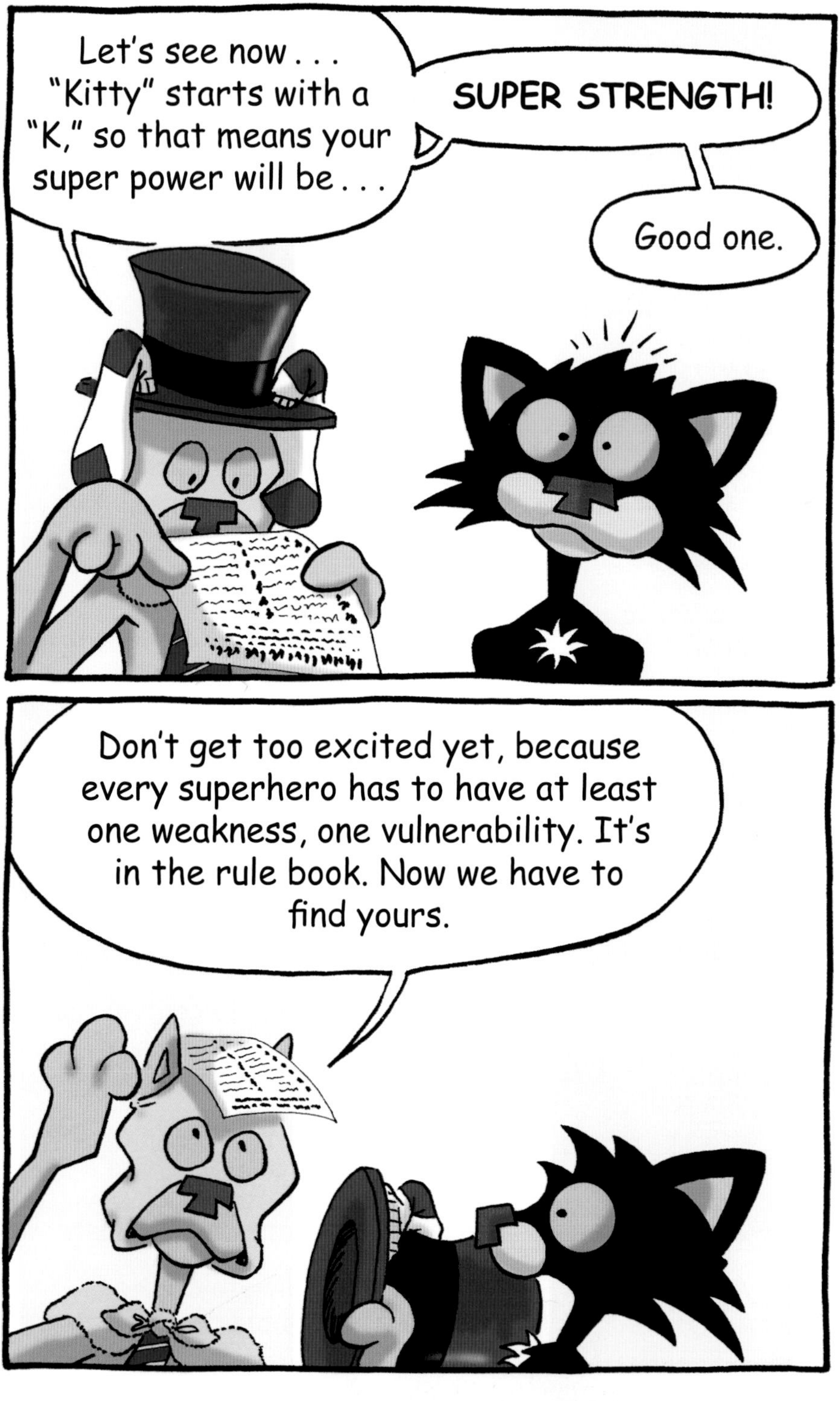
Let's see now . . . "Kitty" starts with a "K," so that means your super power will be . . .
SUPER STRENGTH!
Good one.
Don't get too excited yet, because every superhero has to have at least one weakness, one vulnerability. It's in the rule book. Now we have to find yours.

You know what to do.

SUPER WEAKNESS GENERATOR

THE SECOND LETTER OF YOUR FIRST NAME IS YOUR SUPERHERO VULNERABILITY!

A — Loud noises

B — Pollen

C — The color yellow

D — A rock from your home planet

E — Sand

F — Anything electronic

G — Anything sticky

H — The color red

I — Water

J — Coins

K — Plants

L — Feathers

M — Anything made of wood

N — Fruit

O — Bright lights

P — The color blue

Q — Anything that starts with the letter "Q"

R — Grass

S — Anything made of metal

T — Anything cold

U — Anything hot

V — The color black

W — Anything that's fuzzy

X — Gluten

Y — Anything made of plastic

Z — Bad smells

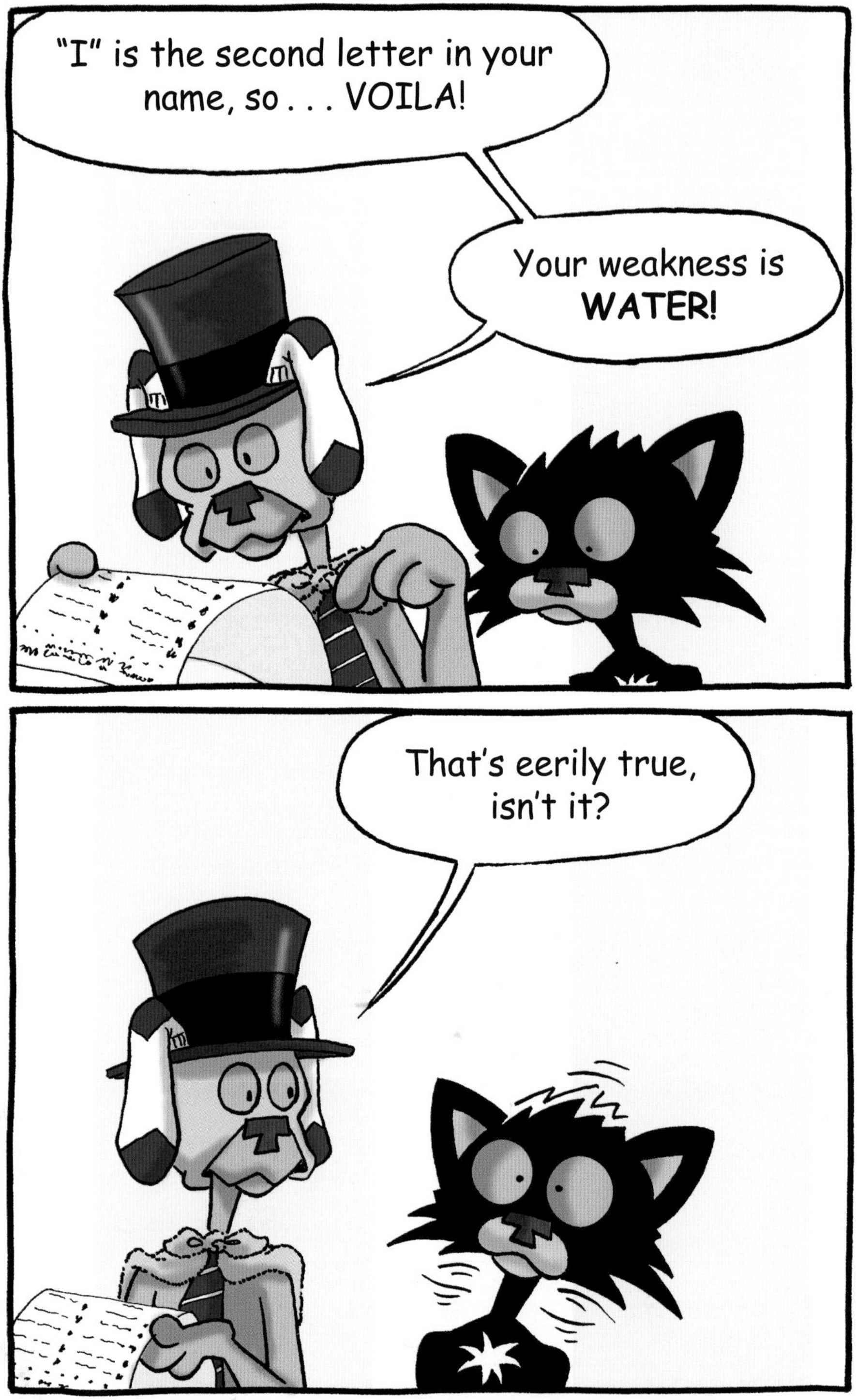
"I" is the second letter in your name, so . . . VOILA!
Your weakness is WATER!
That's eerily true, isn't it?

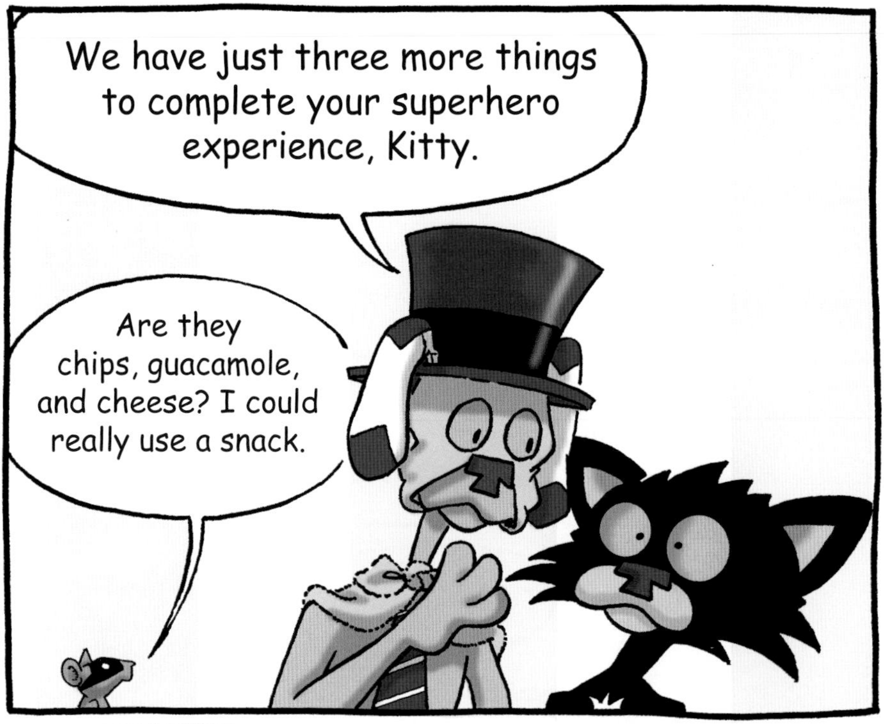
We have just three more things to complete your superhero experience, Kitty.
Are they chips, guacamole, and cheese? I could really use a snack.

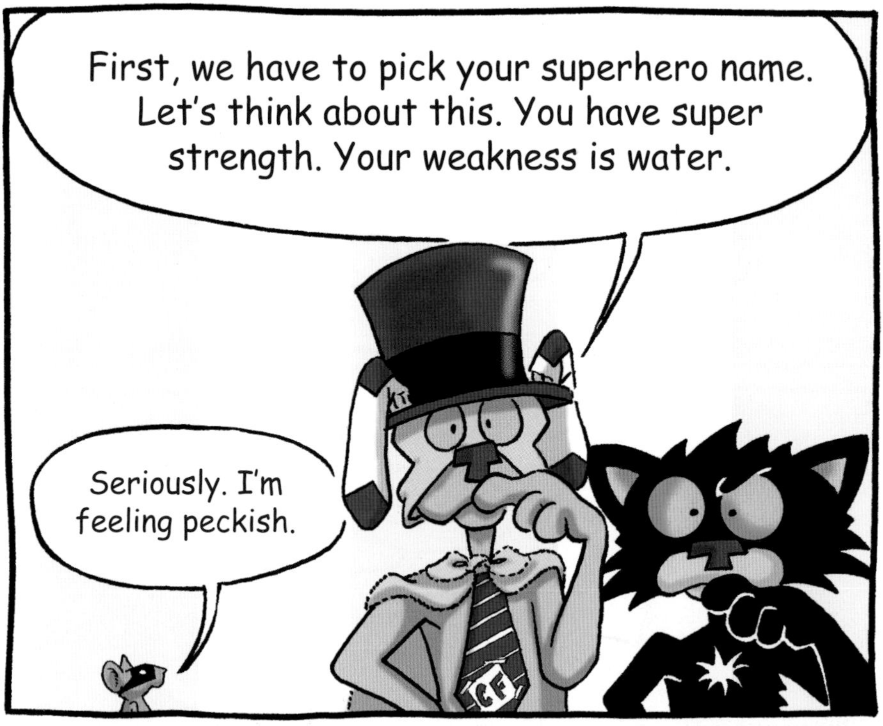
First, we have to pick your superhero name. Let's think about this. You have super strength. Your weakness is water.
Seriously. I'm feeling peckish.

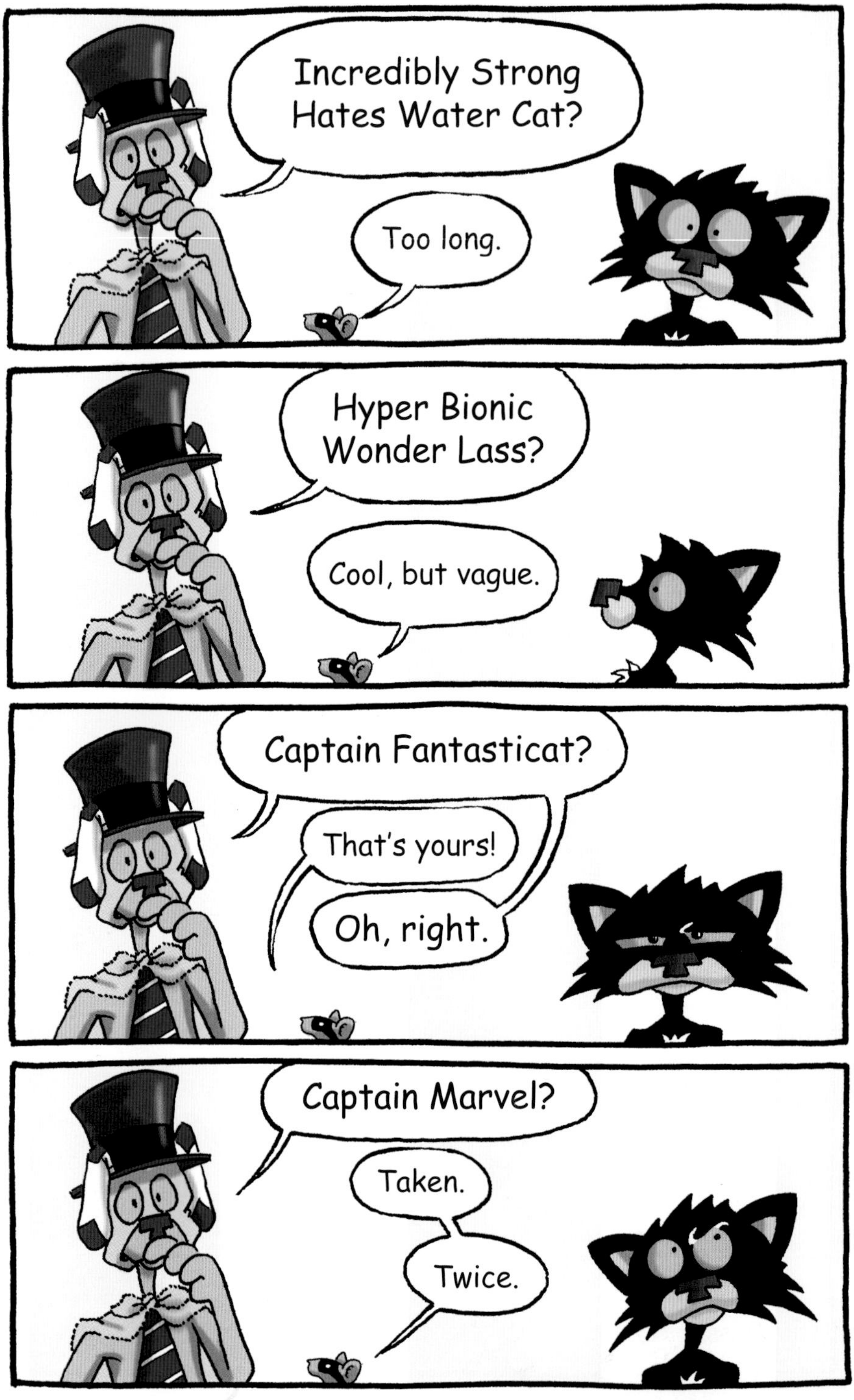
Incredibly Strong Hates Water Cat?
Too long.
Hyper Bionic Wonder Lass?
Cool, but vague.
Captain Fantasticat?
That's yours!
Oh, right.
Captain Marvel?
Taken.
Twice.

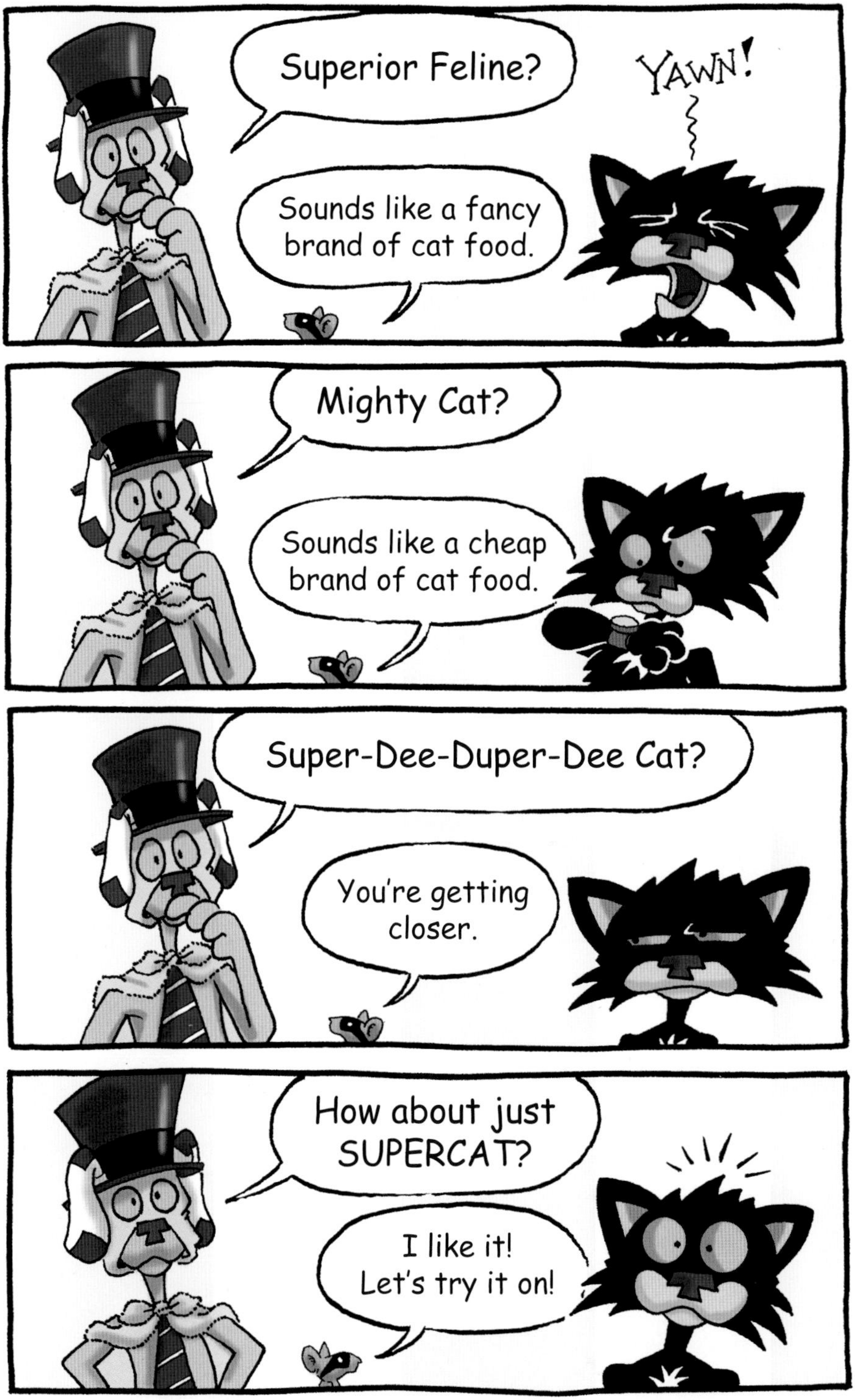
Superior Feline?
YAWN!
Sounds like a fancy brand of cat food.
Mighty Cat?
Sounds like a cheap brand of cat food.
Super-Dee-Duper-Dee Cat?
You're getting closer.
How about just SUPERCAT?
I like it! Let's try it on!

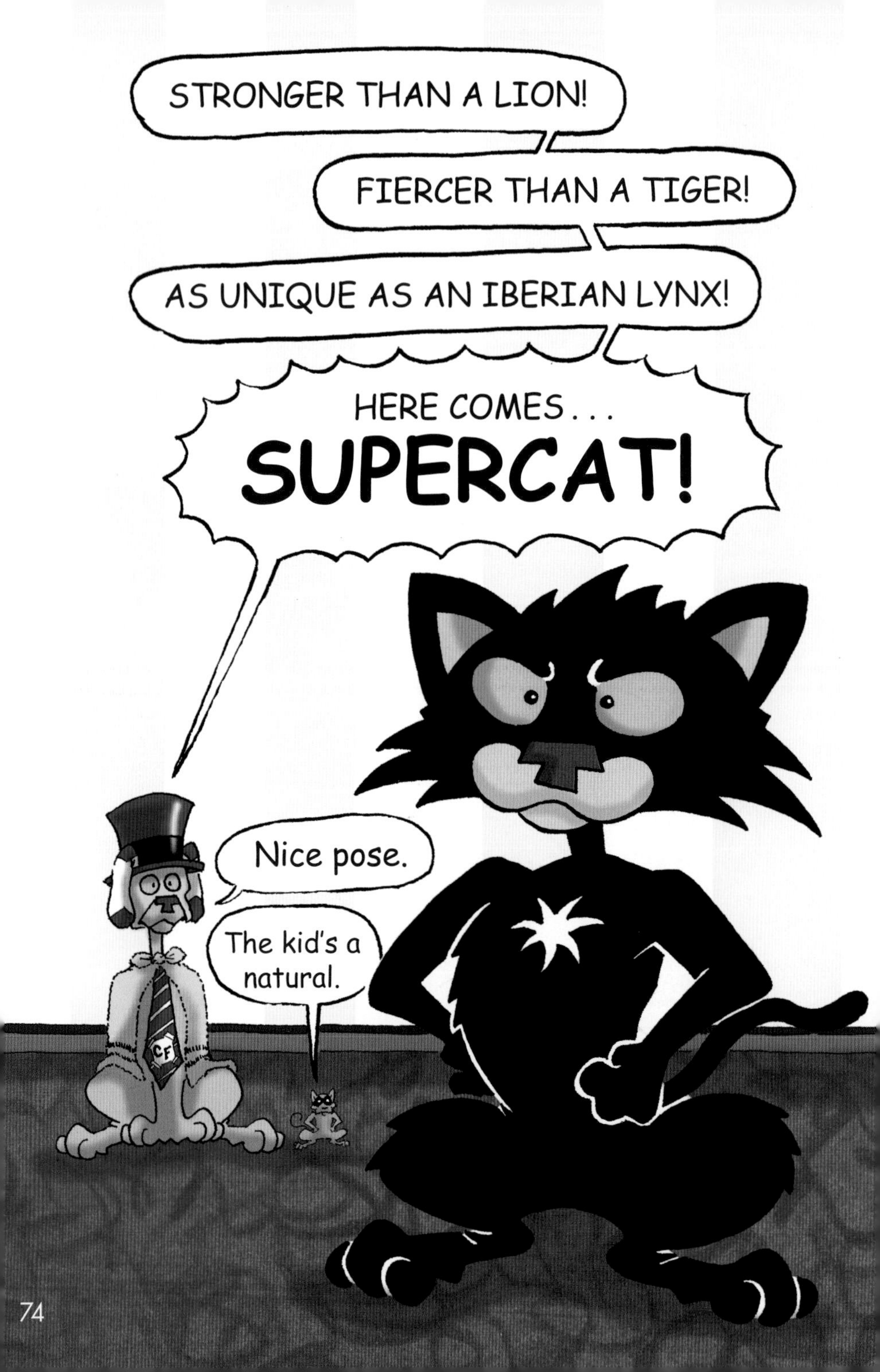
STRONGER THAN A LION!
FIERCER THAN A TIGER!
AS UNIQUE AS AN IBERIAN LYNX!
HERE COMES . . . SUPERCAT!
Nice pose.
The kid's a natural.
CF

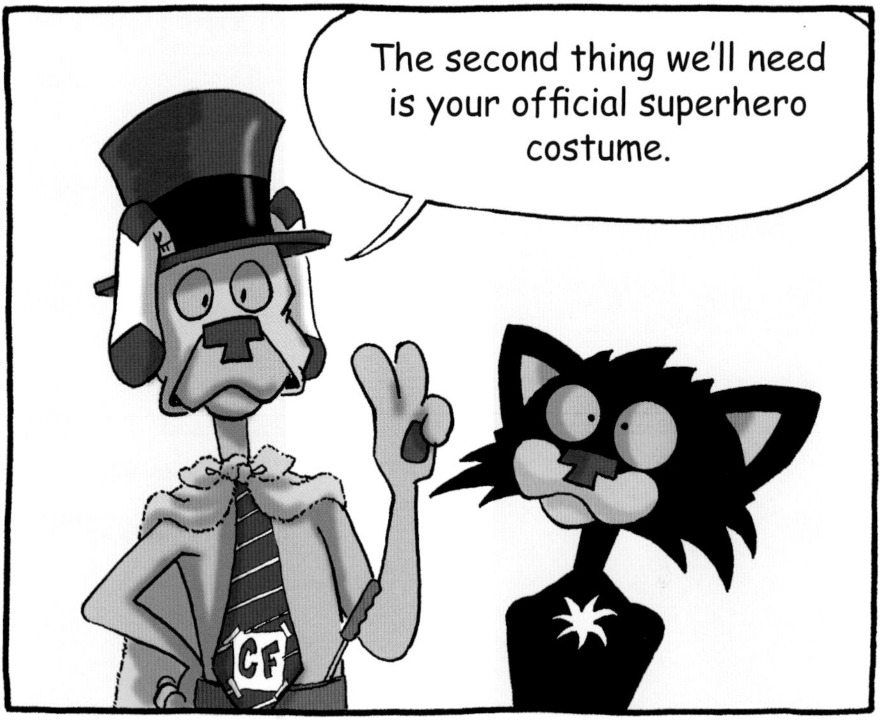
The second thing we'll need is your official superhero costume.

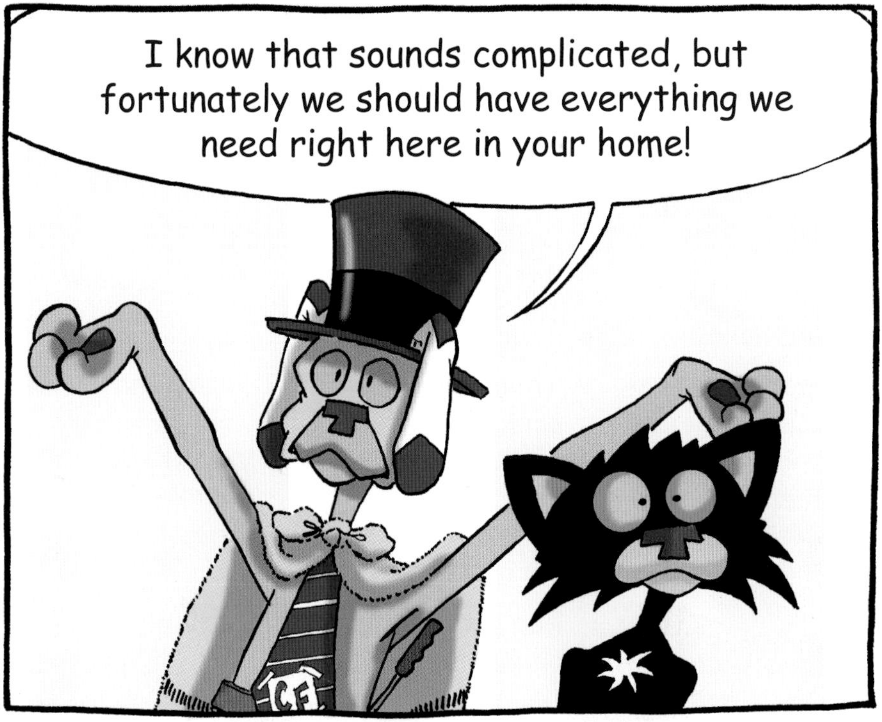
I know that sounds complicated, but fortunately we should have everything we need right here in your home!

HOW TO MAKE A COOL SUPERHERO HELMET

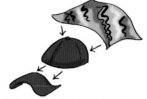

Carefully cut the brim off an old baseball cap. Cover the cap with tinfoil or duct tape. Add your logo.

HOW TO MAKE A COOL SUPERHERO CAPE

Take a T-shirt and cut away everything below the collar EXCEPT for the back. Add your logo.

HOW TO MAKE A COOL SUPERHERO MASK

Take a clean sock and cut away equal measurements of each end.

This is what your sock will look like without the two ends.

Fold the sock over lengthwise and make two "U" shaped cuts on the fold.

Run a string, elastic, or shoelace through the mask to tie.

HOW TO MAKE A COOL SUPERHERO LOGO

Take two or more sheets of paper, felt, or fabric. Draw and cut out your logo on one sheet. Glue your cutout logo over another sheet and trim away the edges. Glue your logo onto a T-shirt or anything else.

HOW TO MAKE COOL SUPERHERO ARM BRACELETS

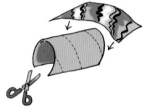

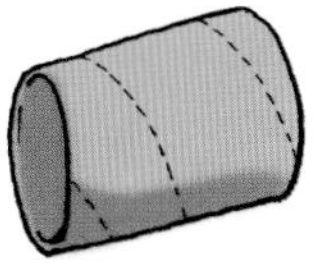

Take two toilet paper rolls.

Cut lengthwise and cover with tinfoil or duct tape.

Glue on a logo if you'd like.

Supplement your costume with shorts or boots or whatever else you like.

Hey, gang! These are all things you can do yourself! Just make sure there's an adult around to help. You'll need scissors and glue, and that's it!

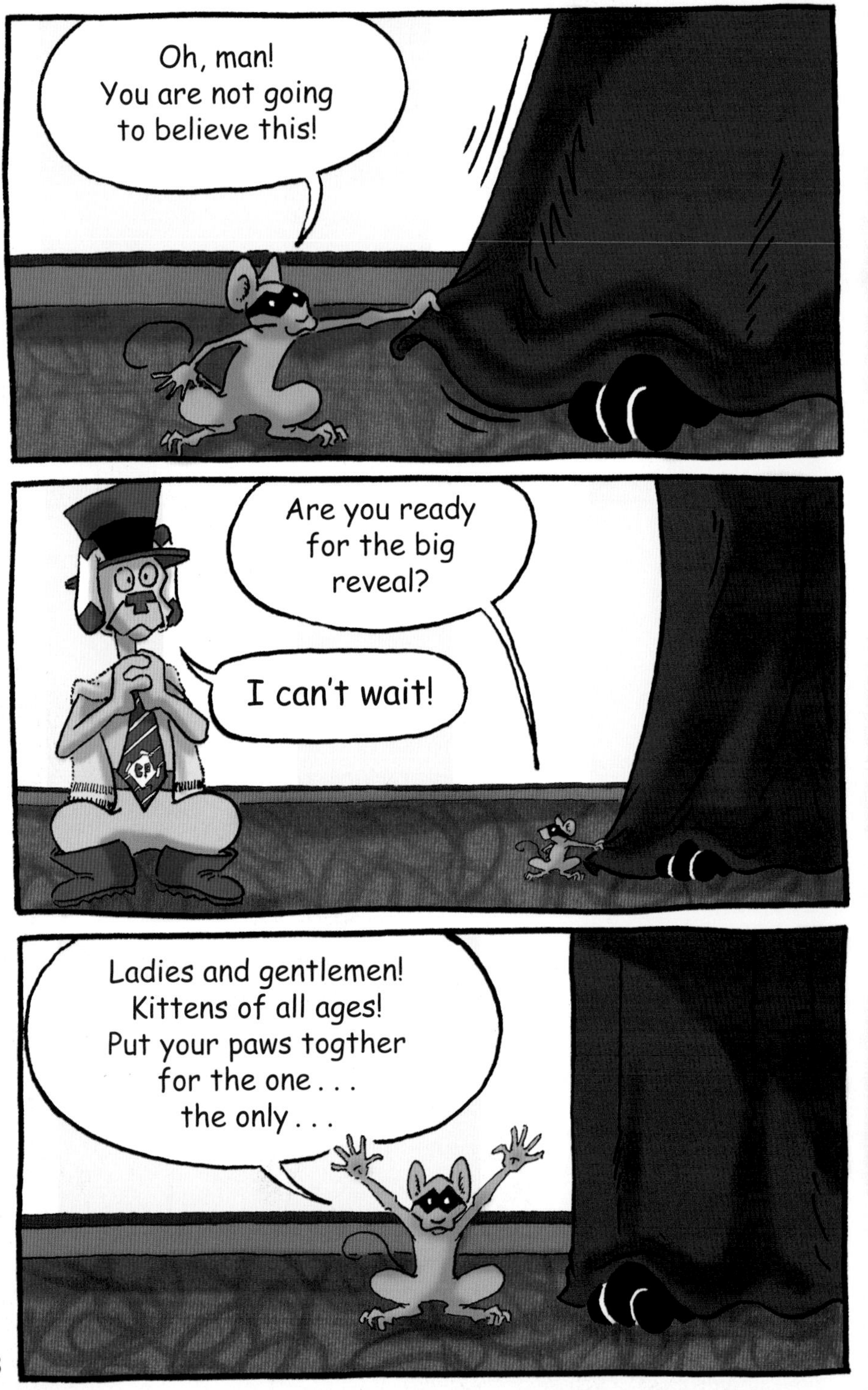
Oh, man! You are not going to believe this!
Are you ready for the big reveal?
I can't wait!
Ladies and gentlemen! Kittens of all ages! Put your paws togther for the one . . . the only . . .

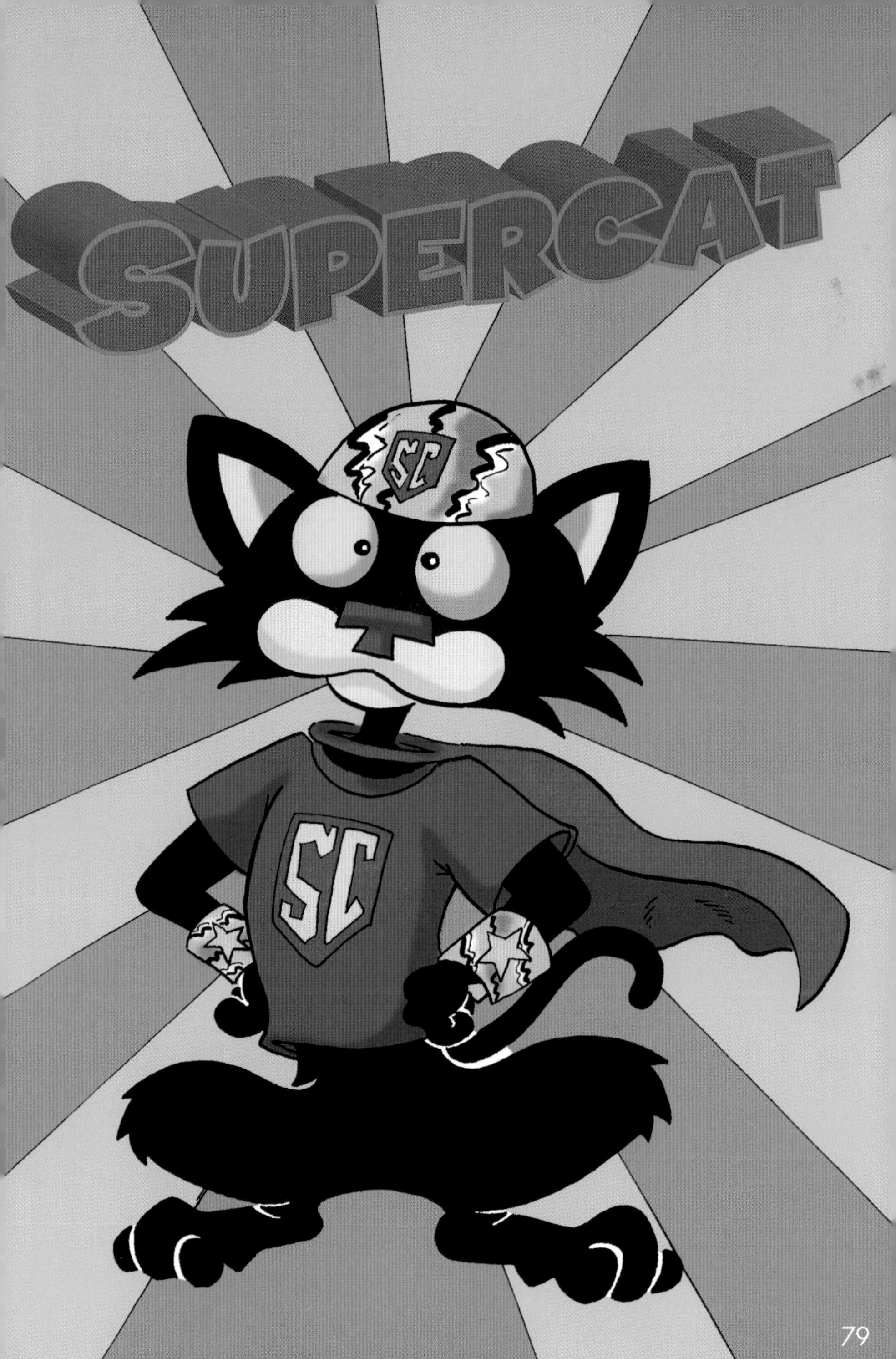
SUPERCAT
SC
SC

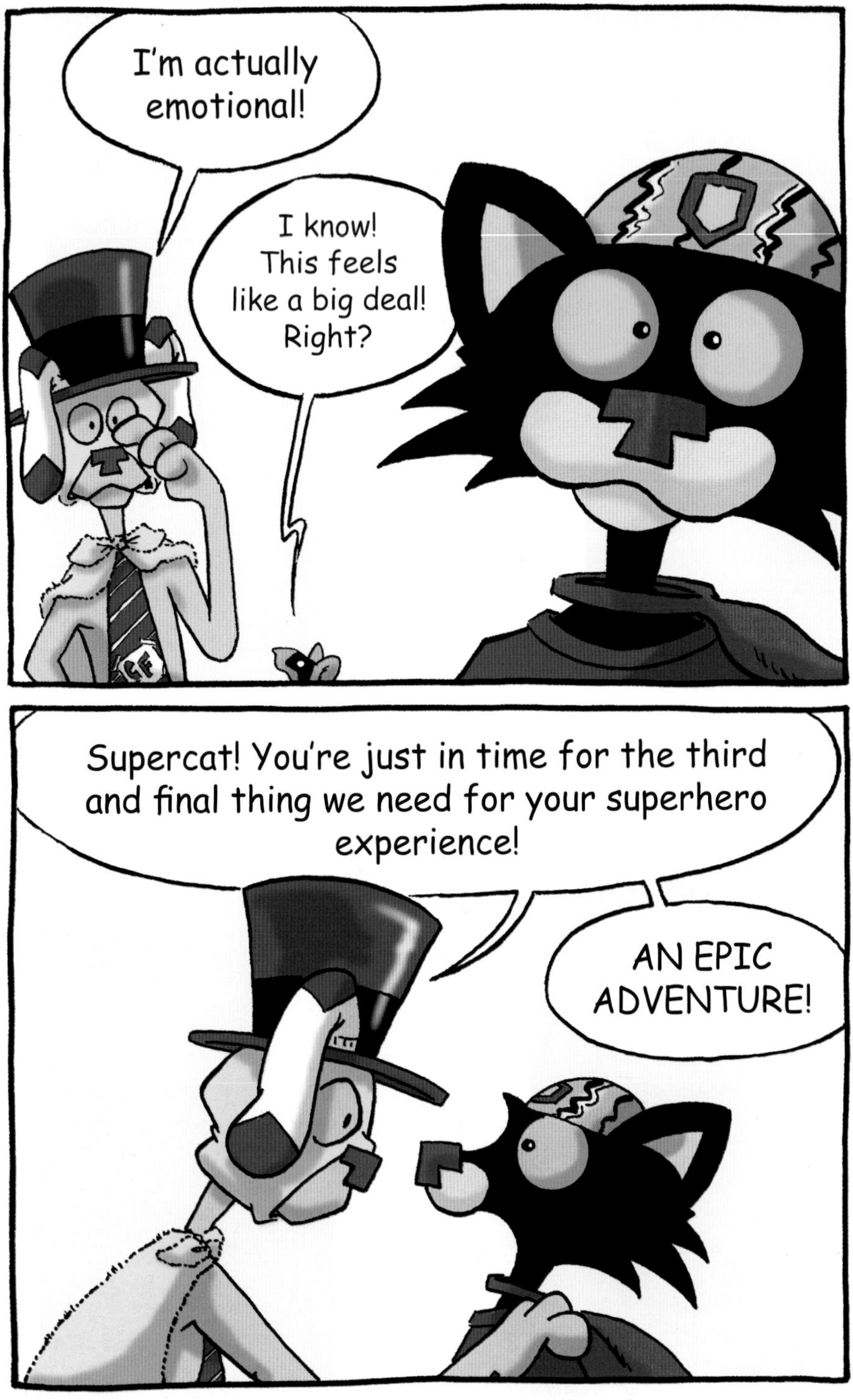
I'm actually emotional!
I know! This feels like a big deal! Right?
Supercat! You're just in time for the third and final thing we need for your superhero experience!
AN EPIC ADVENTURE!

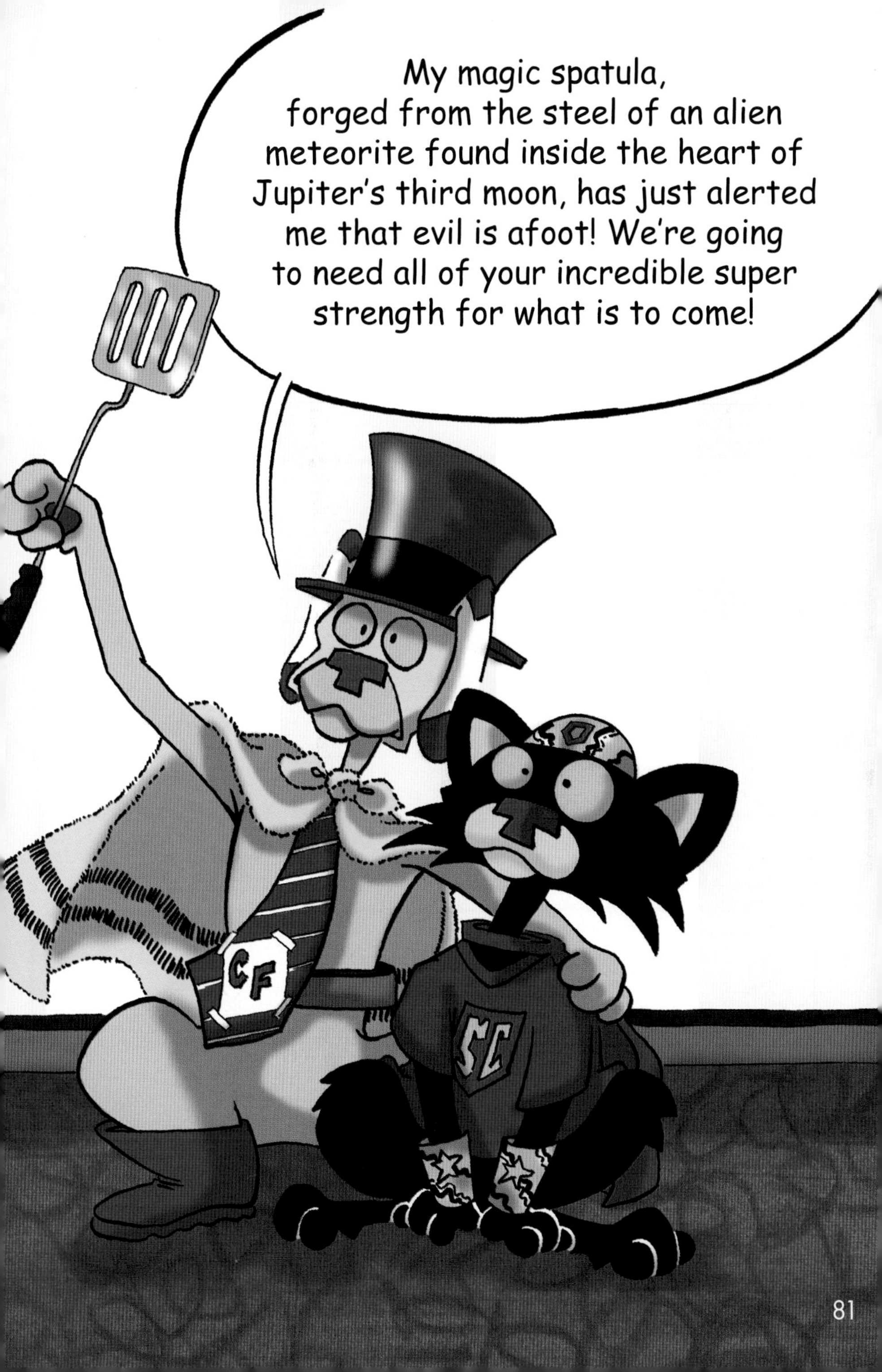
My magic spatula, forged from the steel of an alien meteorite found inside the heart of Jupiter's third moon, has just alerted me that evil is afoot! We're going to need all of your incredible super strength for what is to come!
CF
SC

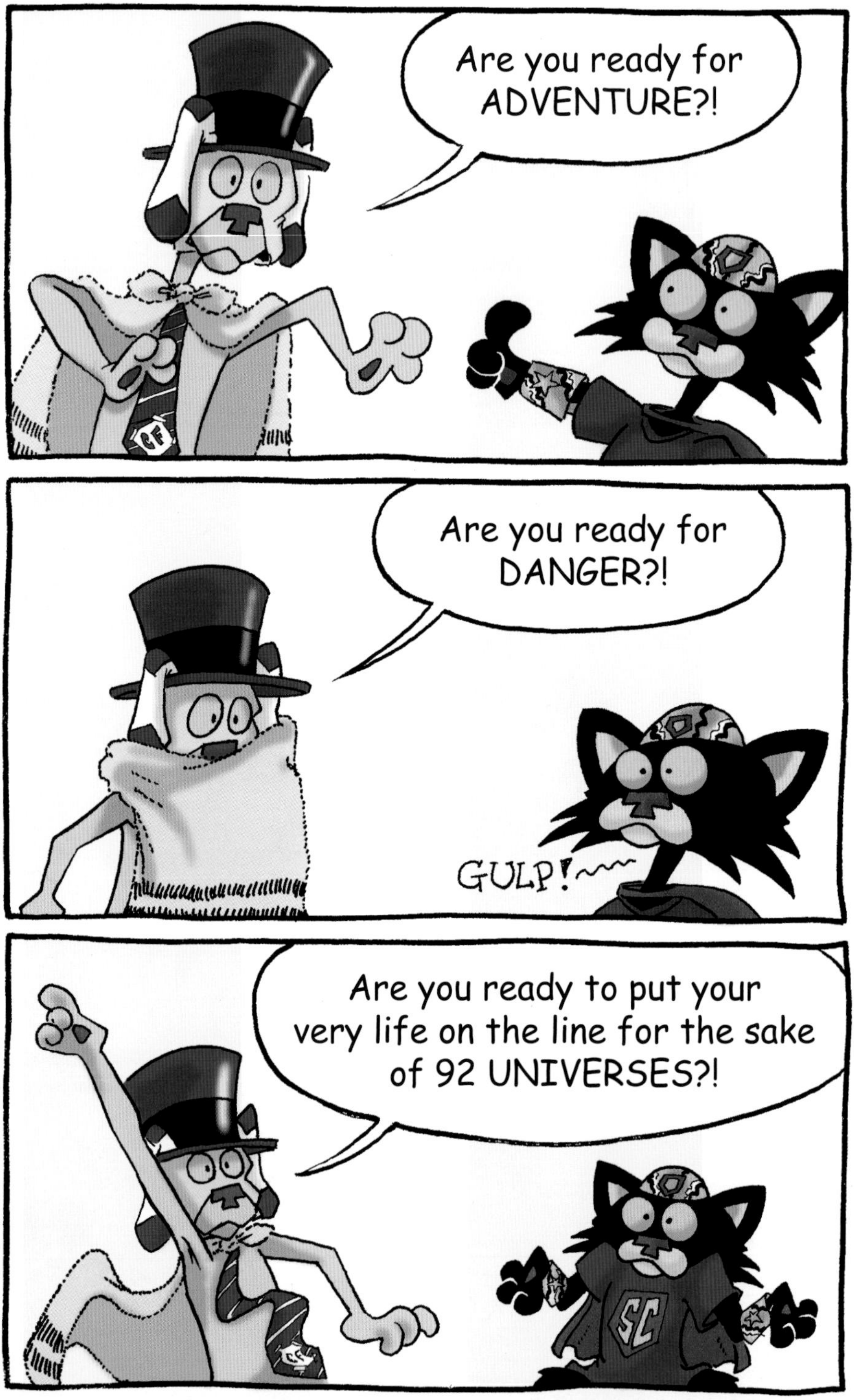
Are you ready for ADVENTURE?!
Are you ready for DANGER?!
GULP!
Are you ready to put your very life on the line for the sake of 92 UNIVERSES?!

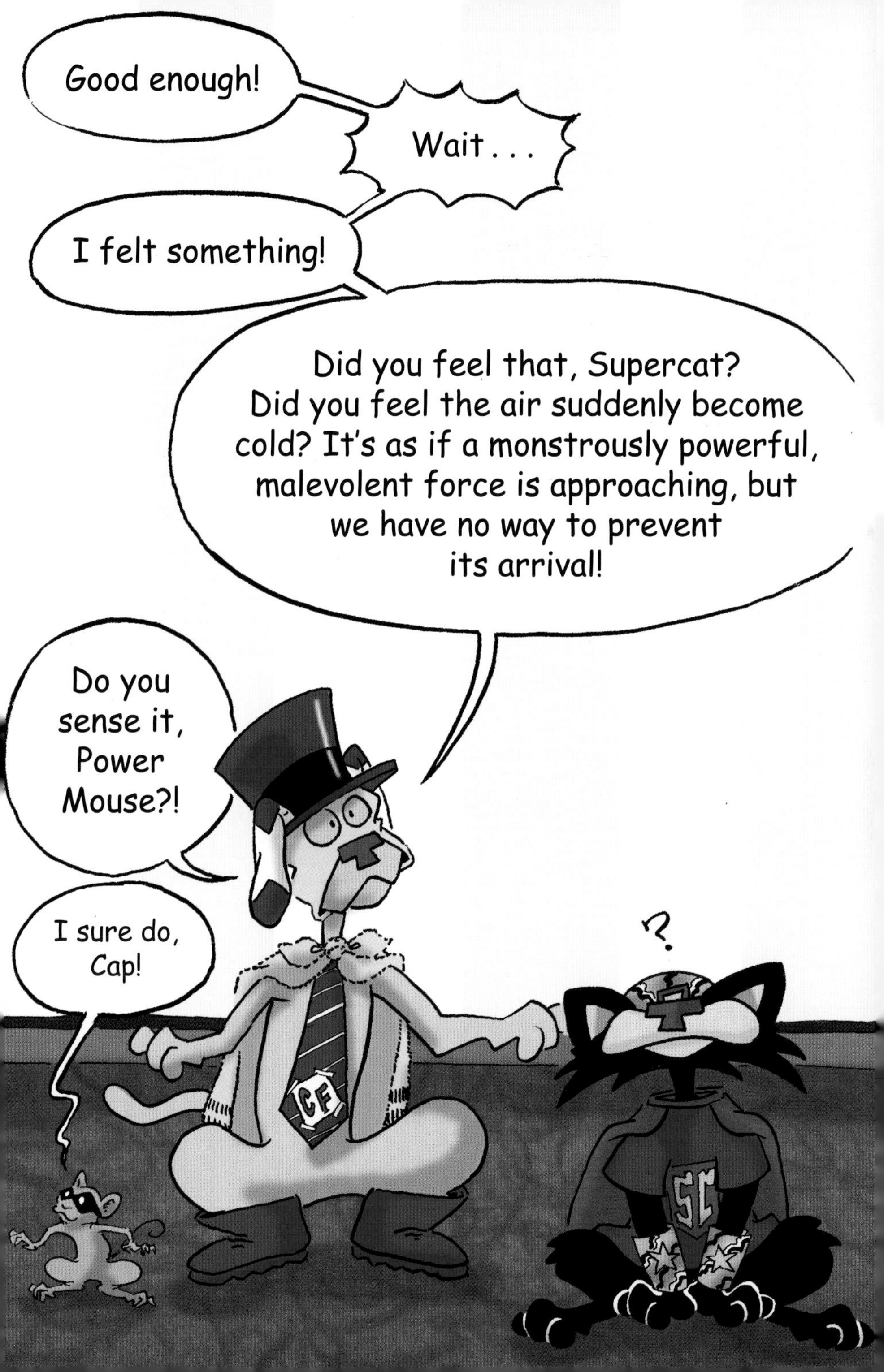
Good enough!
Wait . . .
I felt something!
Did you feel that, Supercat? Did you feel the air suddenly become cold? It's as if a monstrously powerful, malevolent force is approaching, but we have no way to prevent its arrival!
Do you sense it, Power Mouse?!
I sure do, Cap!
?
CF
SC

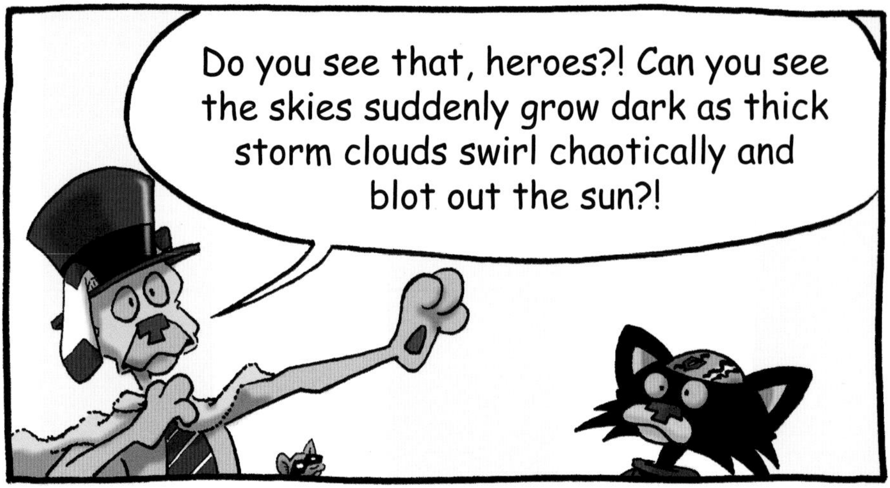
Do you see that, heroes?! Can you see the skies suddenly grow dark as thick storm clouds swirl chaotically and blot out the sun?!

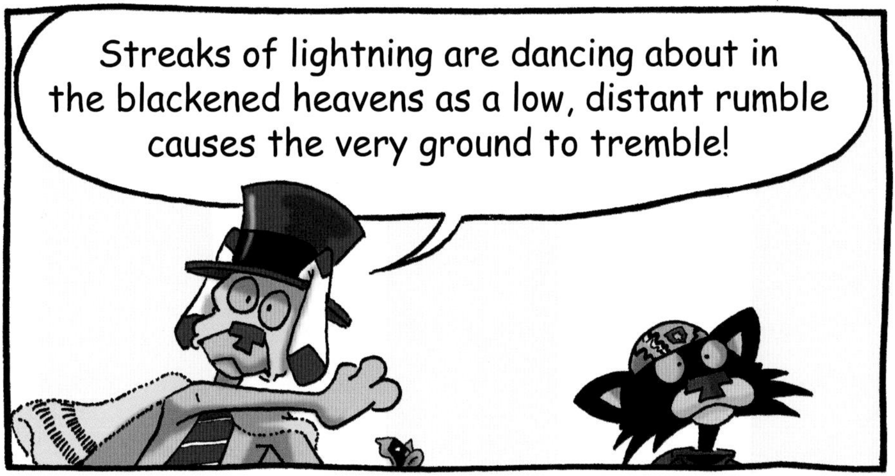
Streaks of lightning are dancing about in the blackened heavens as a low, distant rumble causes the very ground to tremble!

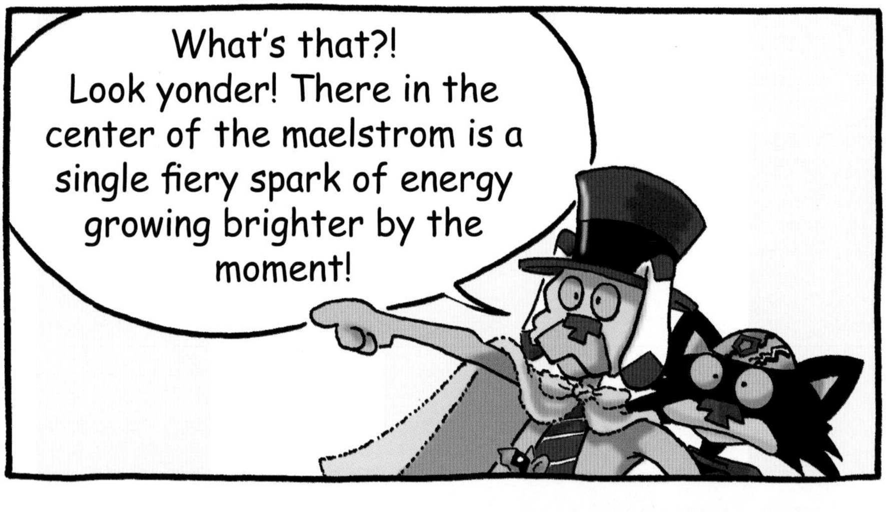
What's that?!
Look yonder! There in the center of the maelstrom is a single fiery spark of energy growing brighter by the moment!

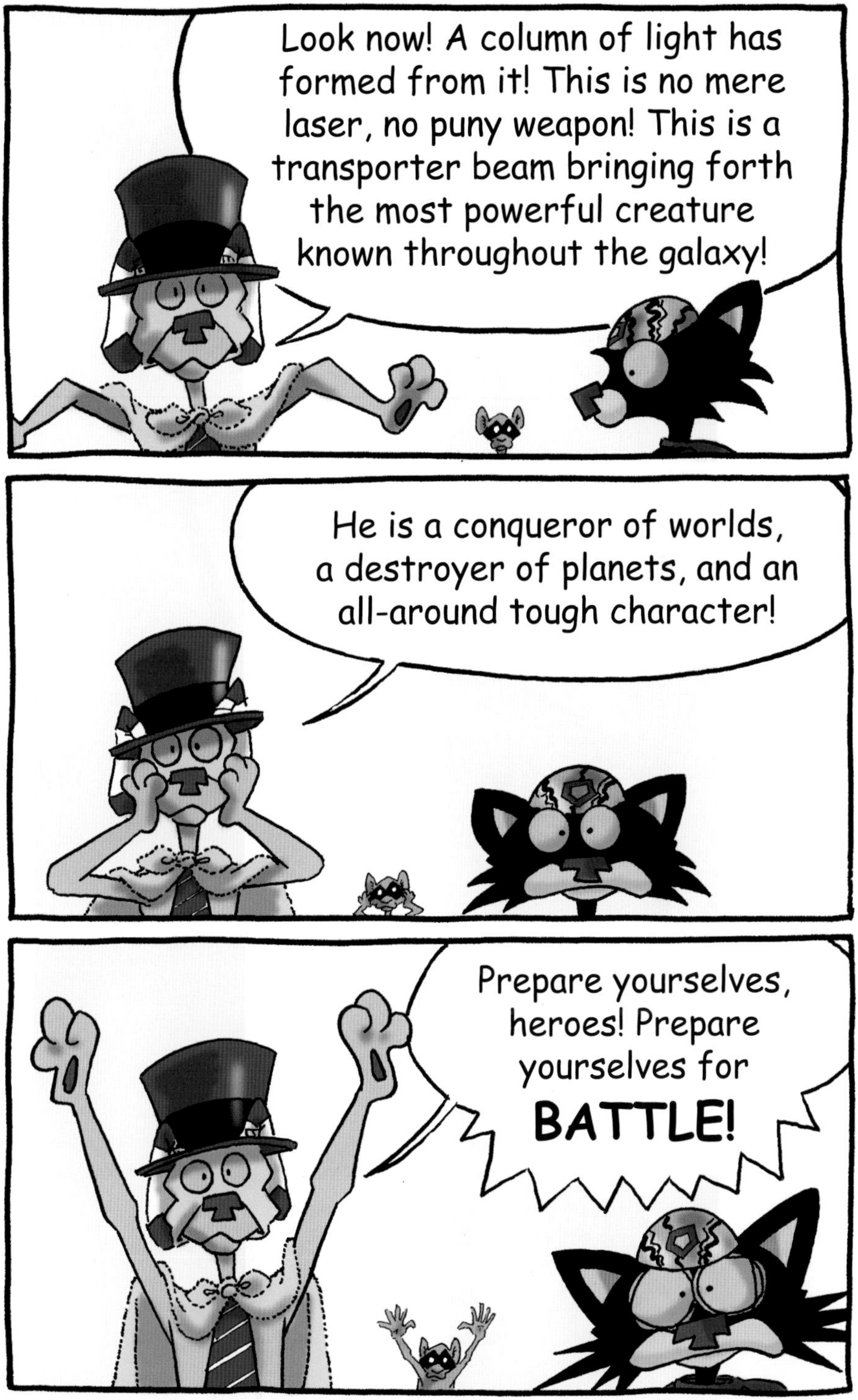
Look now! A column of light has formed from it! This is no mere laser, no puny weapon! This is a transporter beam bringing forth the most powerful creature known throughout the galaxy!
He is a conqueror of worlds, a destroyer of planets, and an all-around tough character!
Prepare yourselves, heroes! Prepare yourselves for BATTLE!

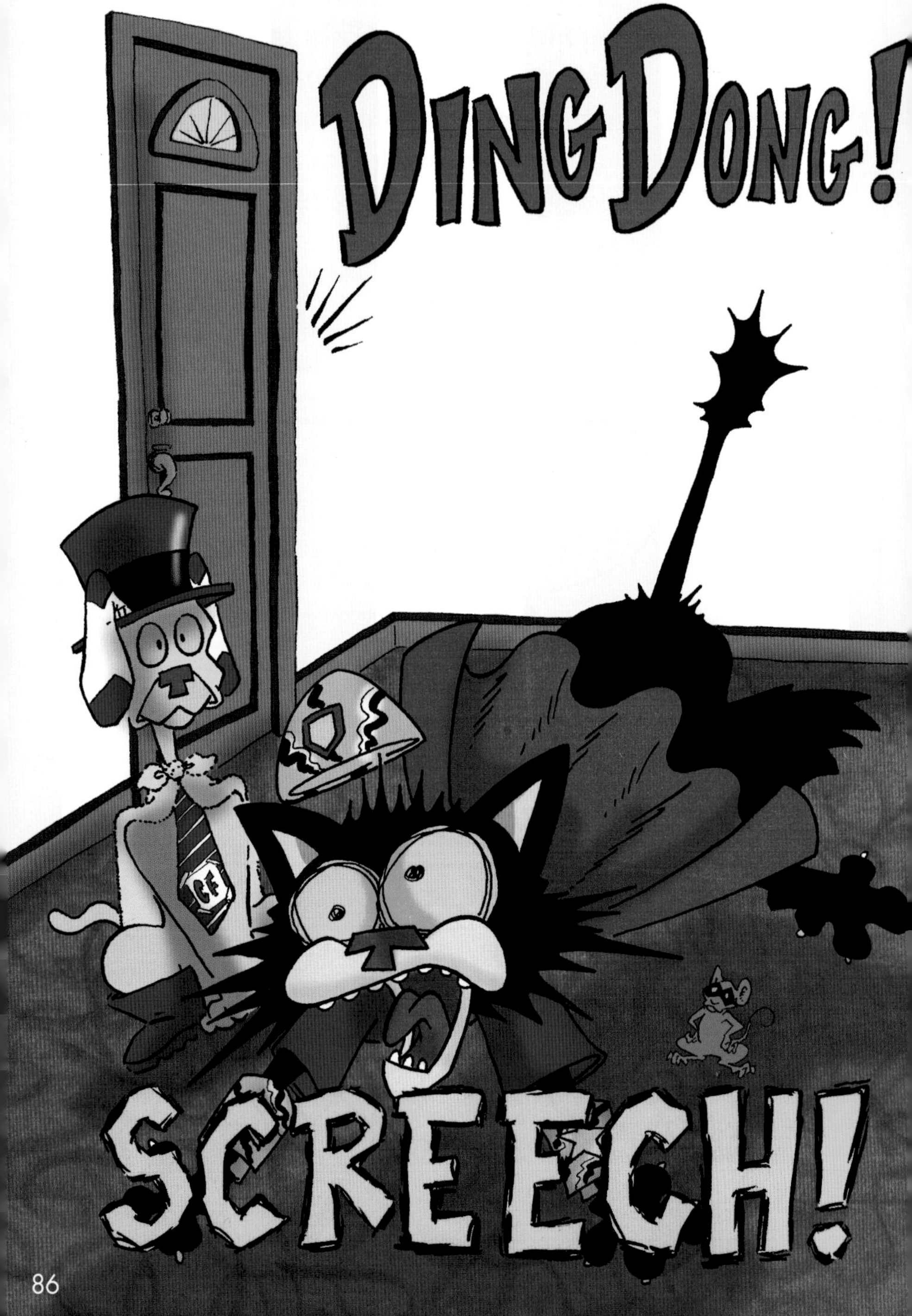
DING DONG!
SCREECH!

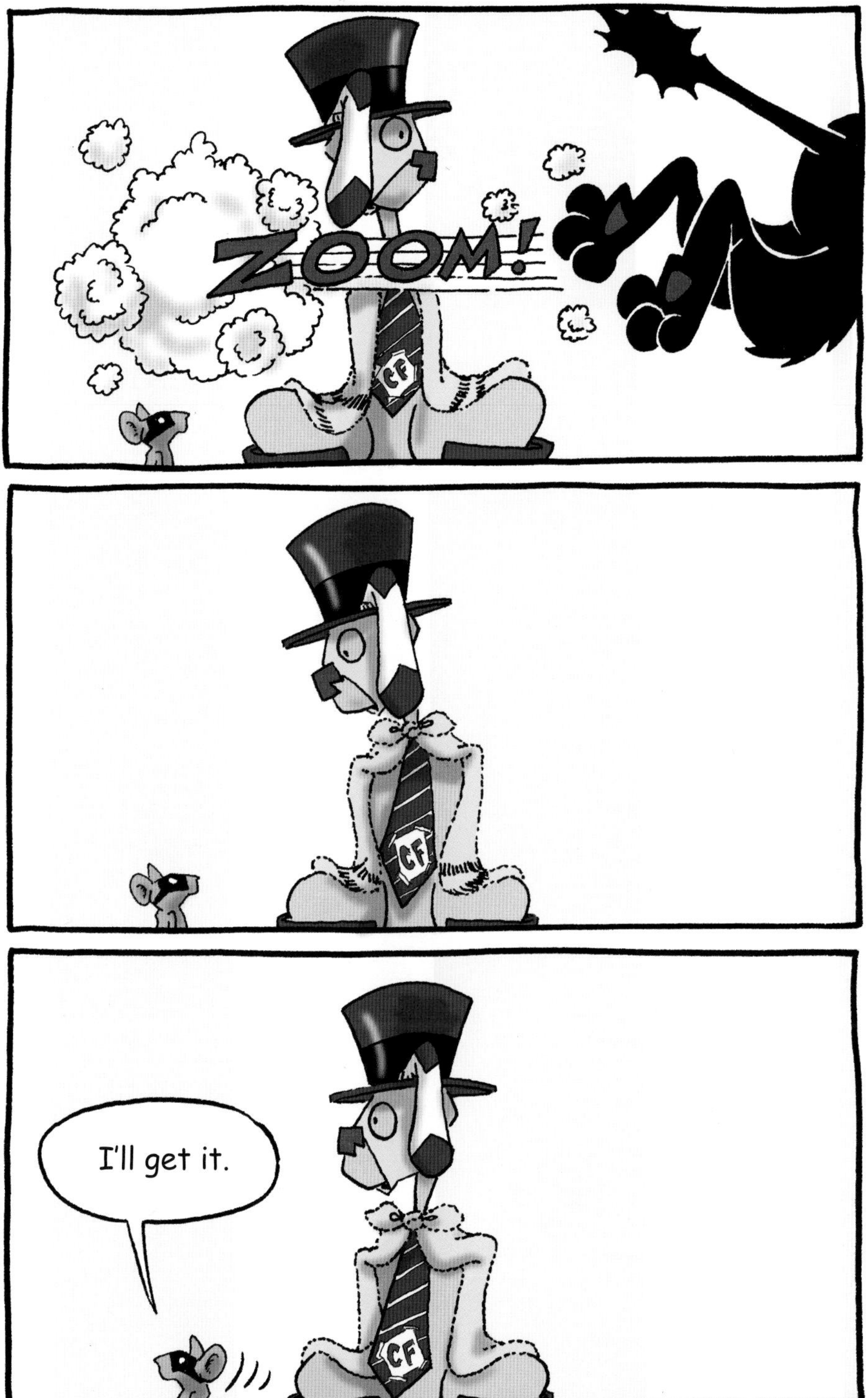
ZOOM!
I'll get it.

•CHAPTER FOUR•

ENTER DR. LAGOMORPH!

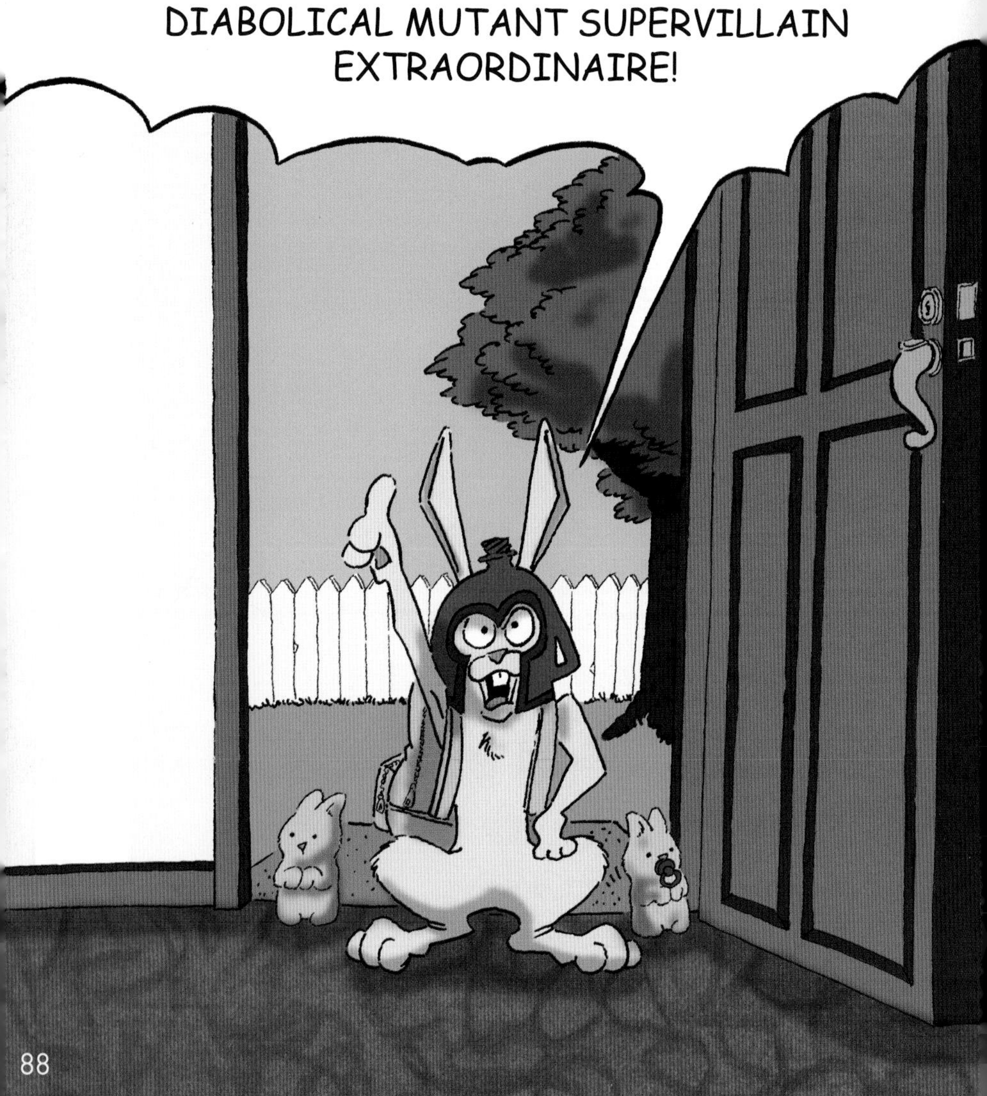
DIABOLICAL MUTANT SUPERVILLAIN EXTRAORDINAIRE!

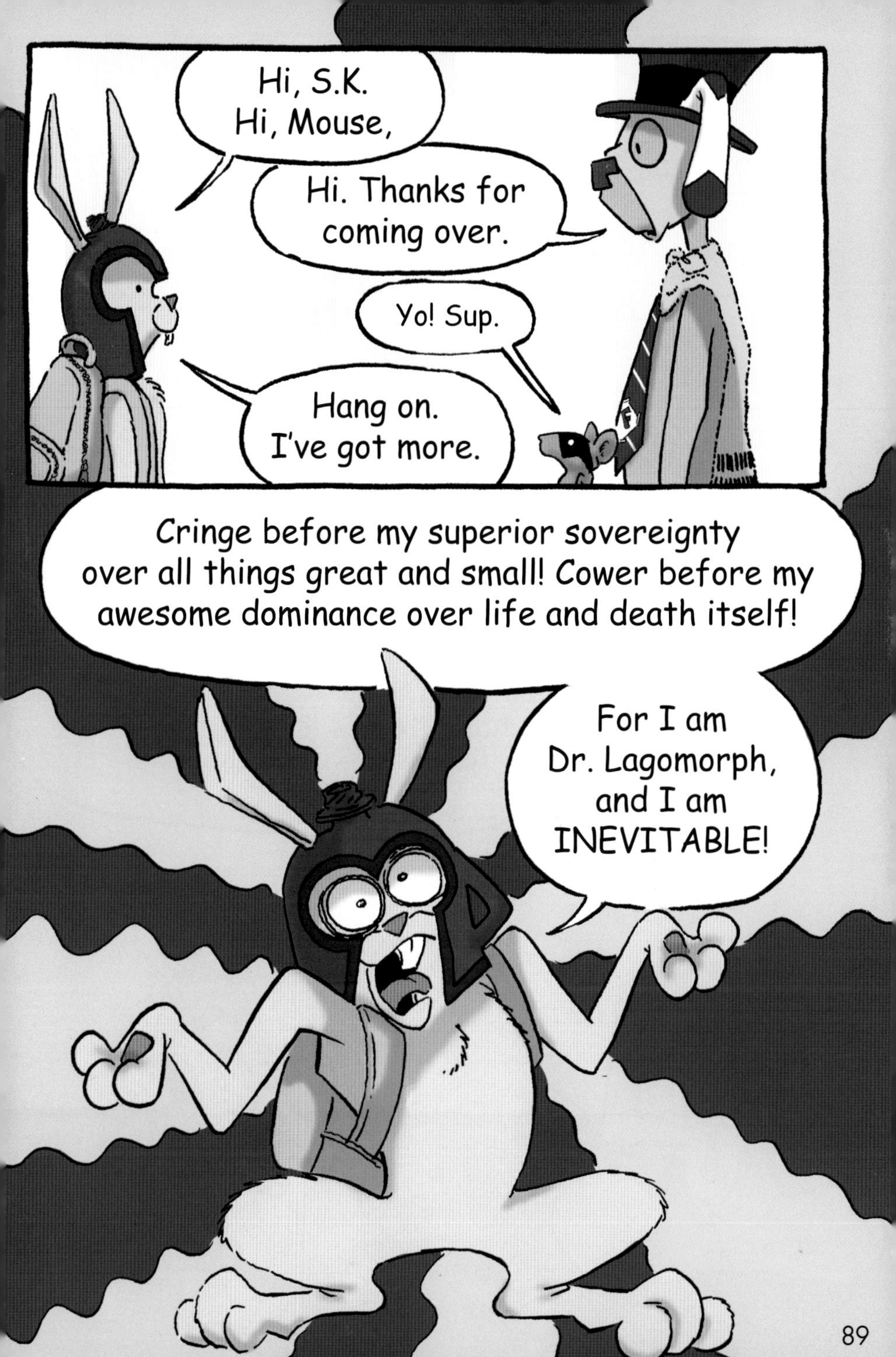

Hi, S.K.
Hi, Mouse,
Hi. Thanks for coming over.
Yo! Sup.
Hang on. I've got more.
Cringe before my superior sovereignty over all things great and small! Cower before my awesome dominance over life and death itself!
For I am Dr. Lagomorph, and I am INEVITABLE!

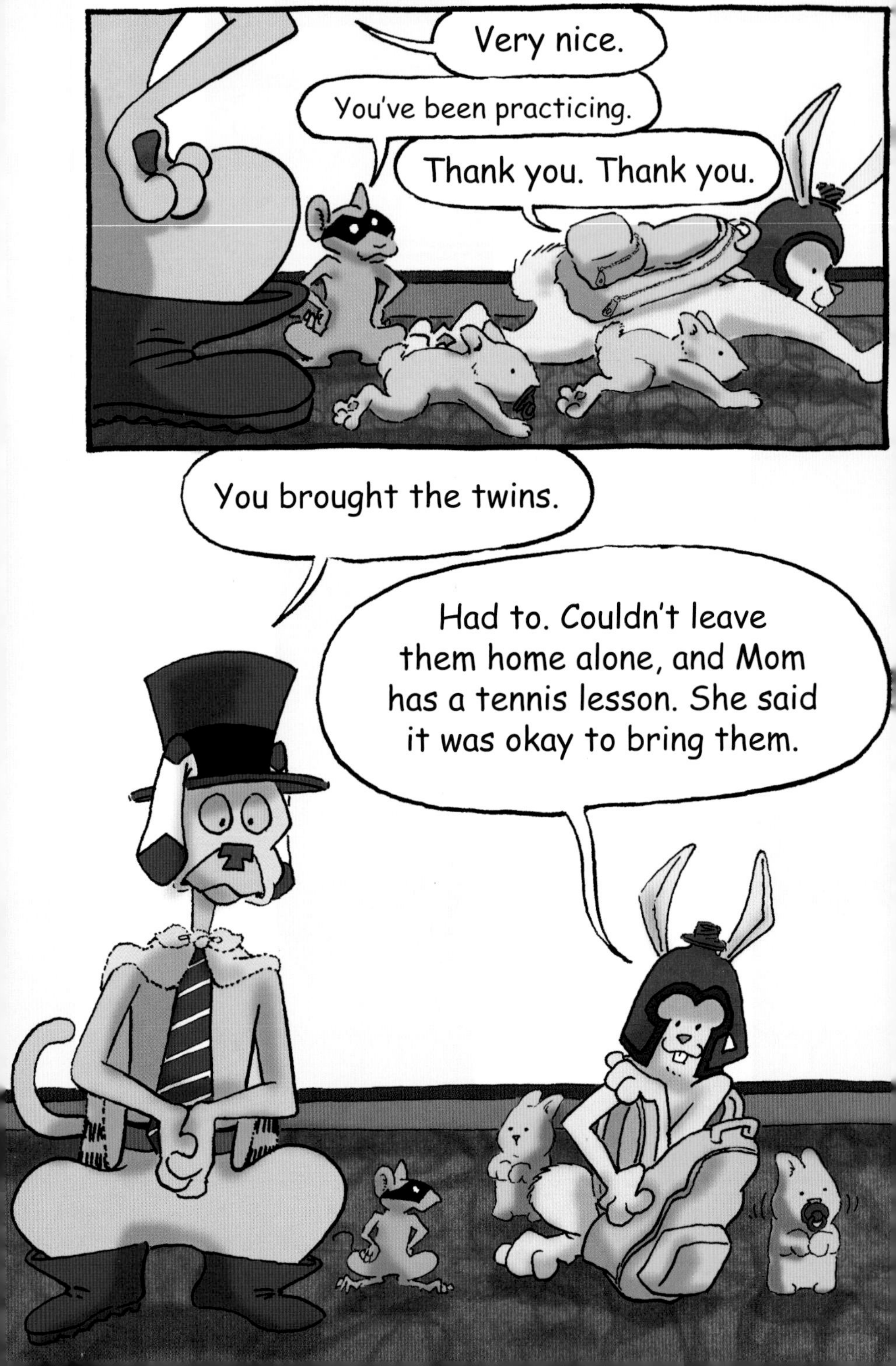
Very nice.
You've been practicing.
Thank you. Thank you.
You brought the twins.
Had to. Couldn't leave them home alone, and Mom has a tennis lesson. She said it was okay to bring them.

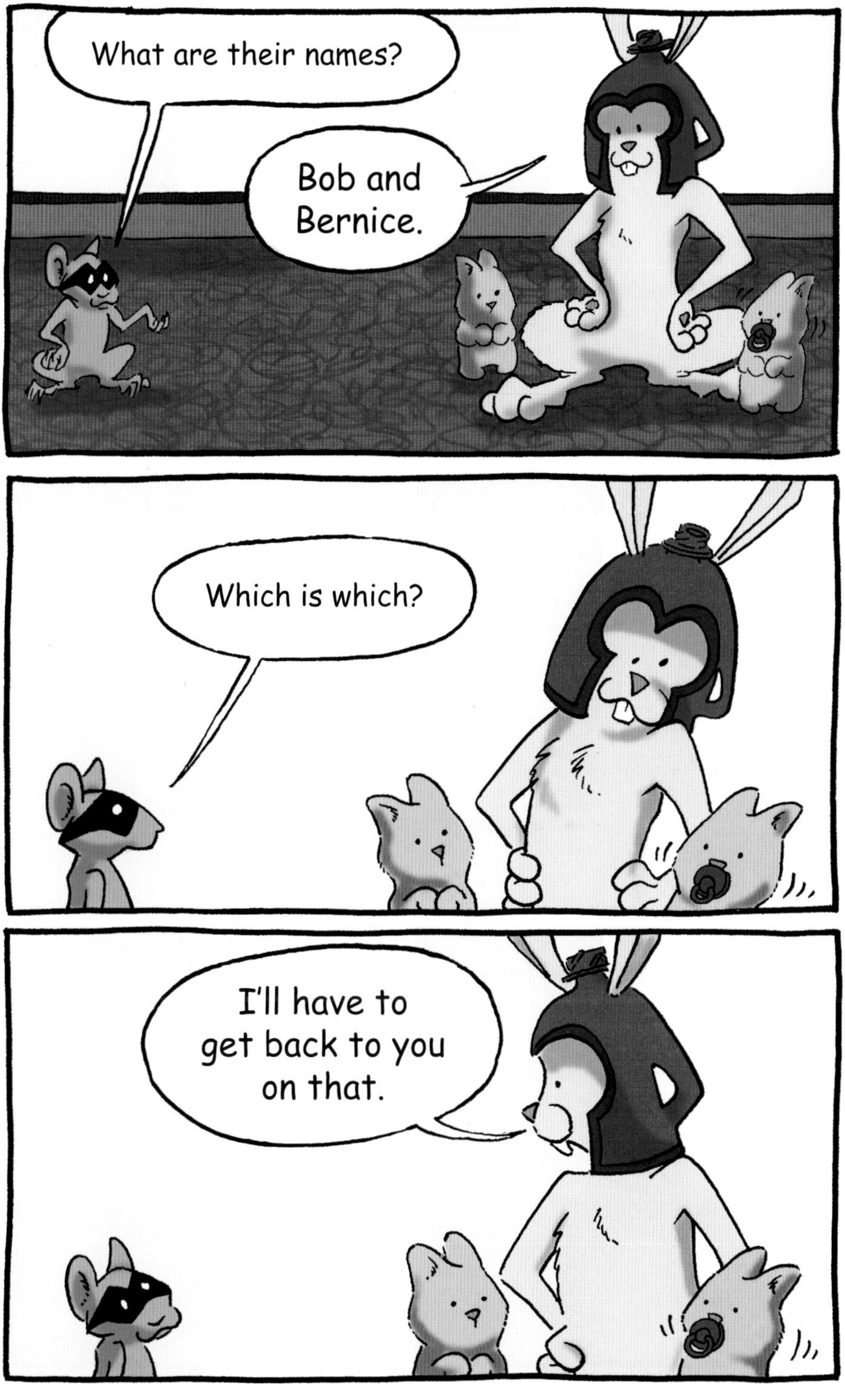
What are their names?
Bob and Bernice.
Which is which?
I'll have to get back to you on that.

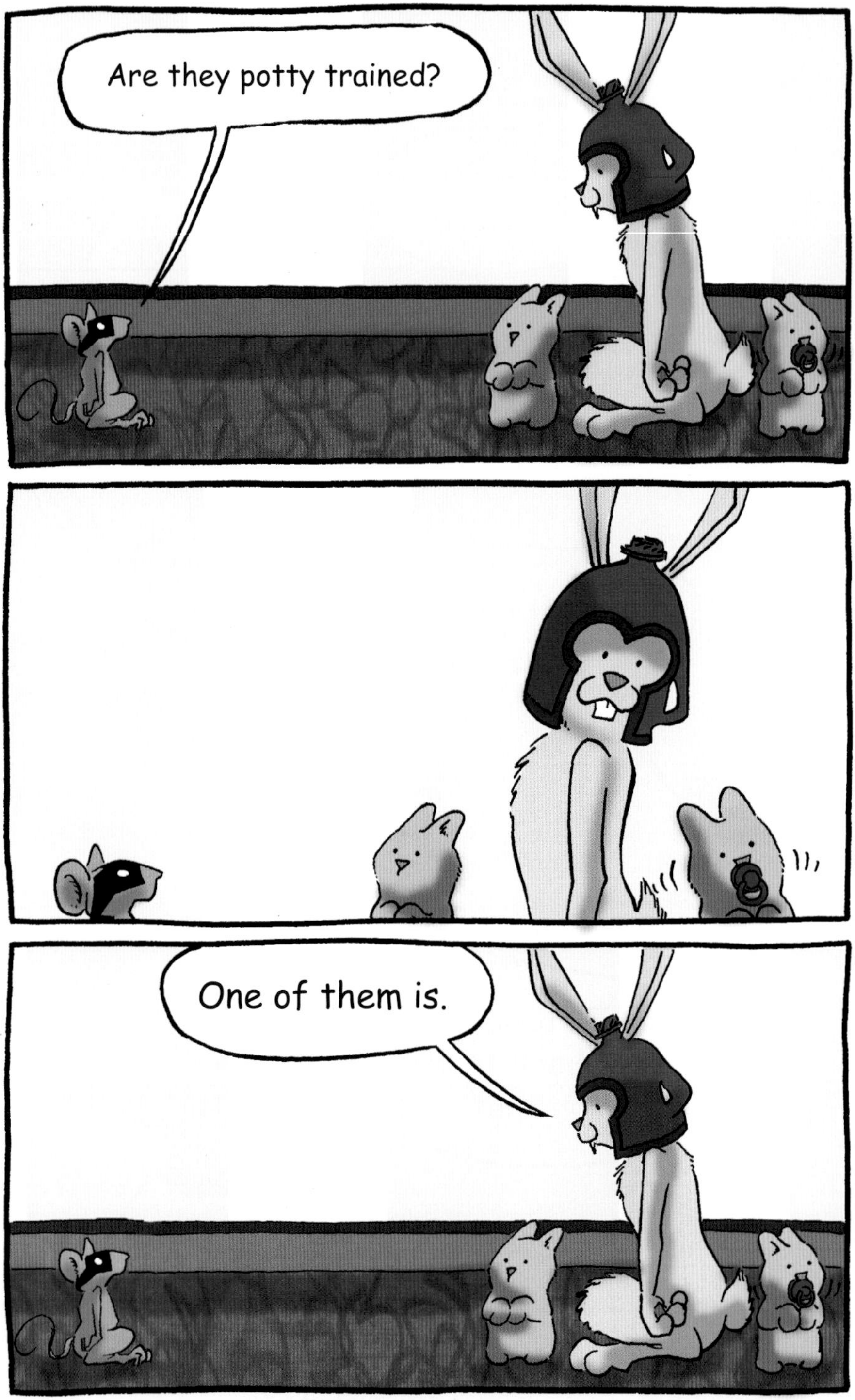
Are they potty trained?
One of them is.

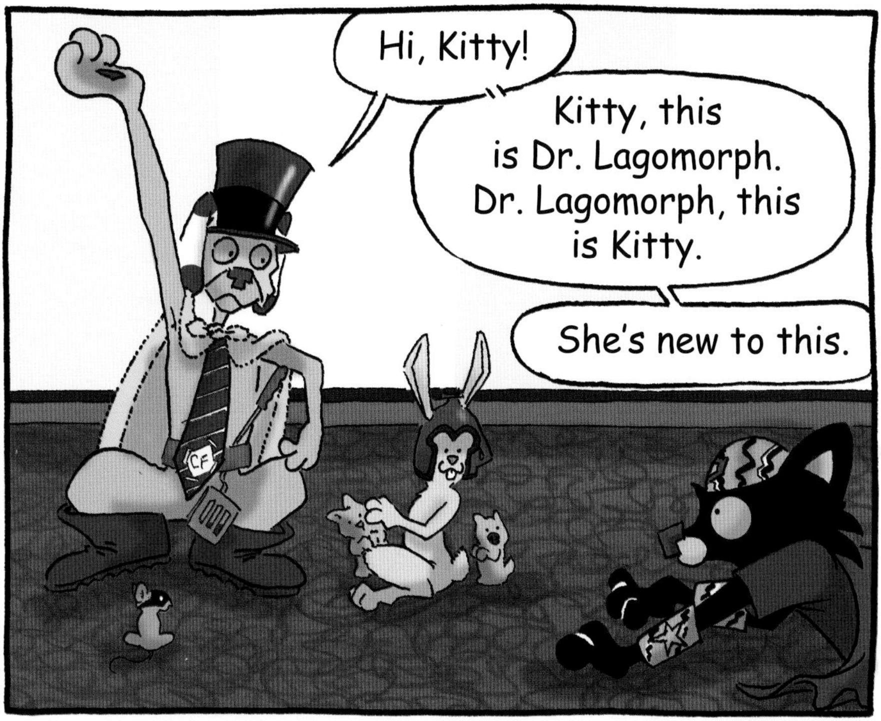
Hi, Kitty!
Kitty, this is Dr. Lagomorph. Dr. Lagomorph, this is Kitty.
She's new to this.

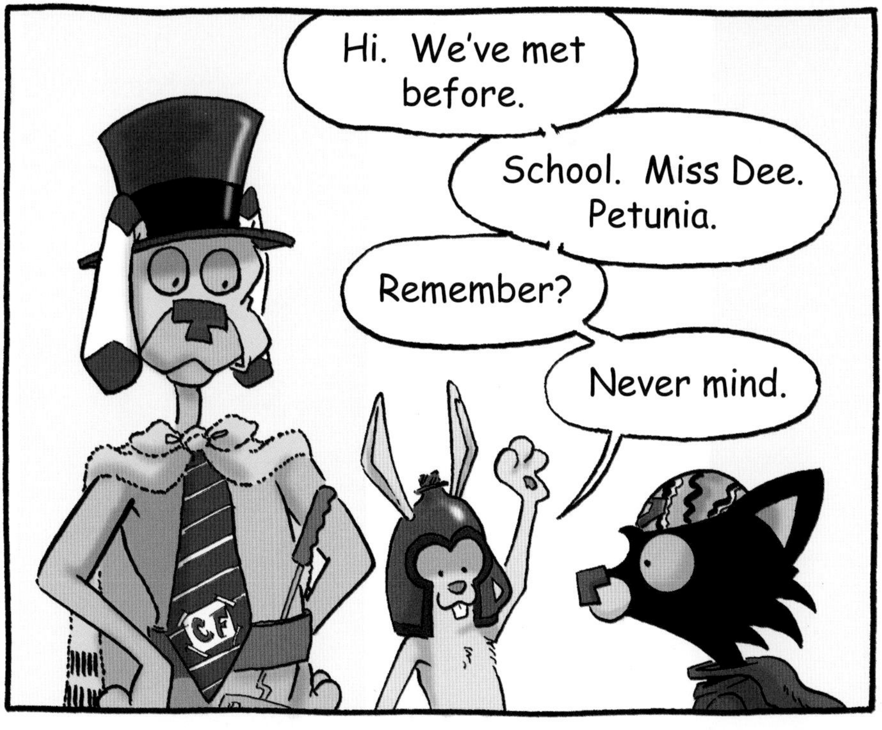
Hi. We've met before.
School. Miss Dee. Petunia.
Remember?
Never mind.

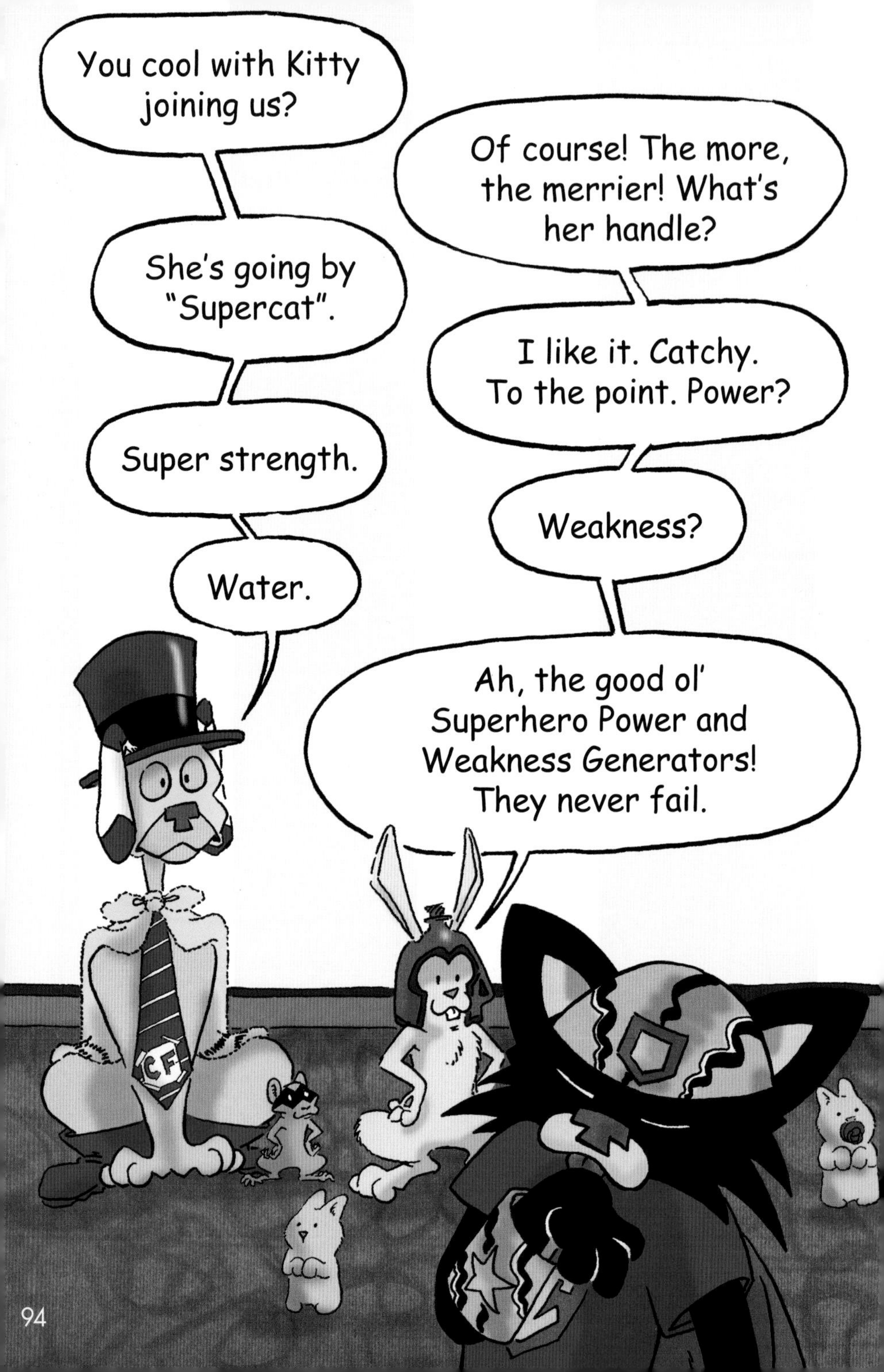
You cool with Kitty joining us?
Of course! The more, the merrier! What's her handle?
She's going by "Supercat".
I like it. Catchy. To the point. Power?
Super strength.
Weakness?
Water.
Ah, the good ol' Superhero Power and Weakness Generators! They never fail.

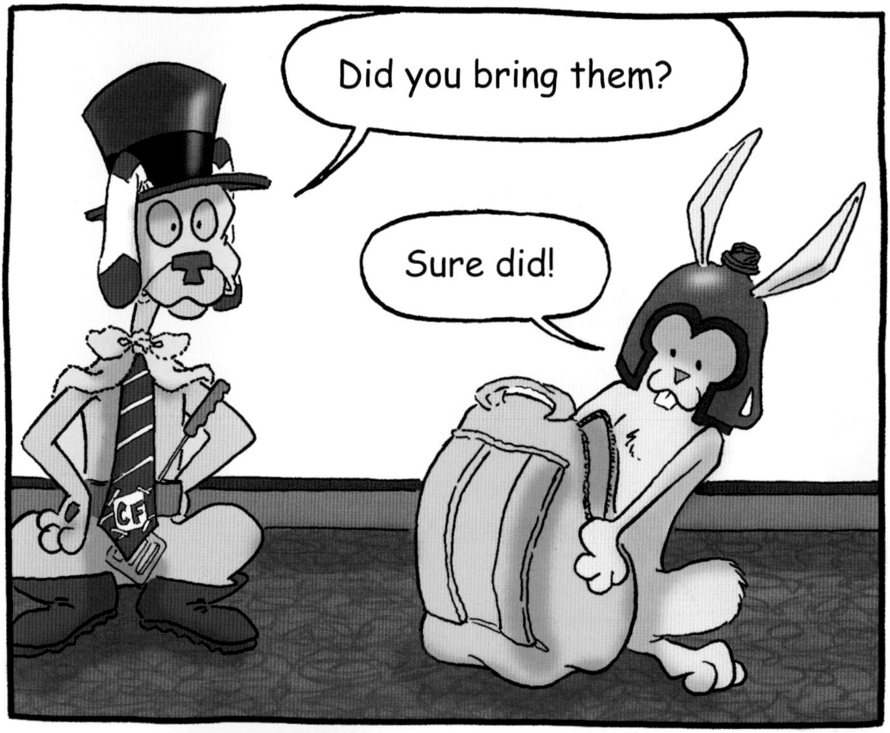
Did you bring them?
Sure did!
CF

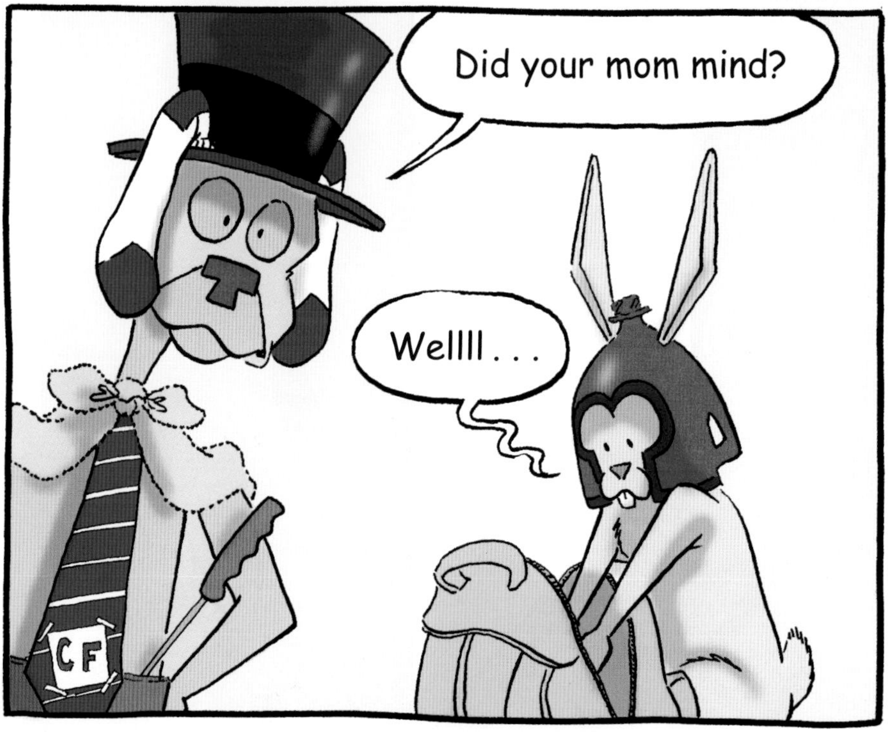
Did your mom mind?
Wellll . . .
CF

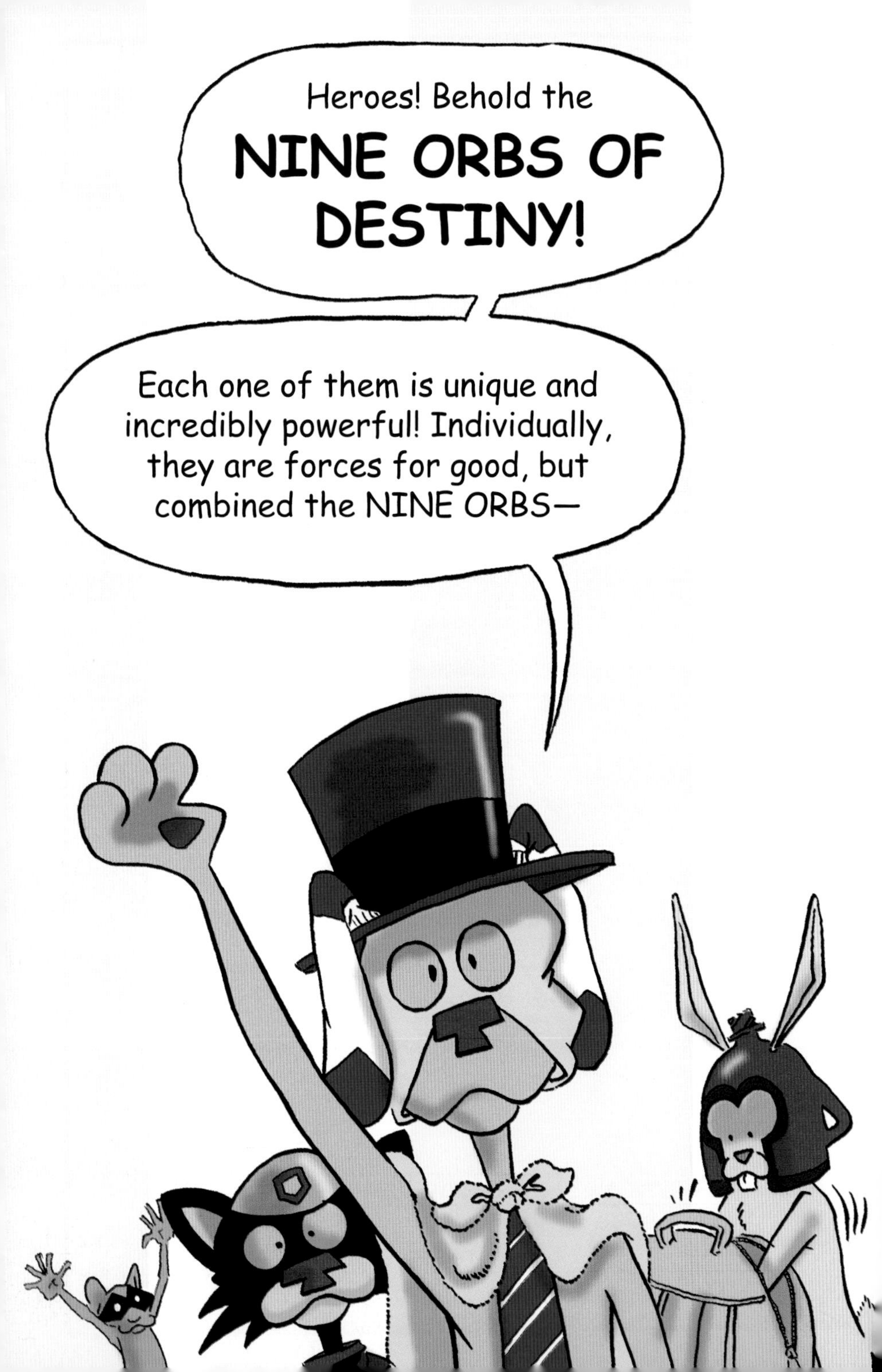
Heroes! Behold the NINE ORBS OF DESTINY!
Each one of them is unique and incredibly powerful! Individually, they are forces for good, but combined the NINE ORBS—

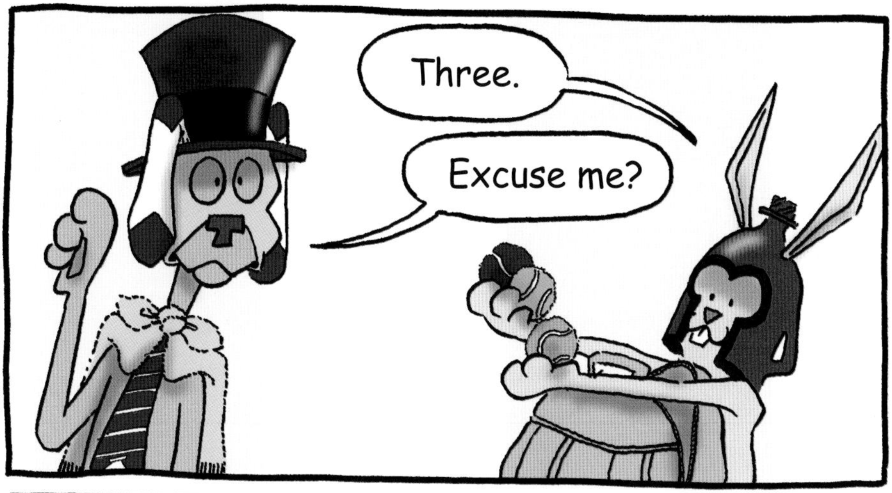
Three.
Excuse me?

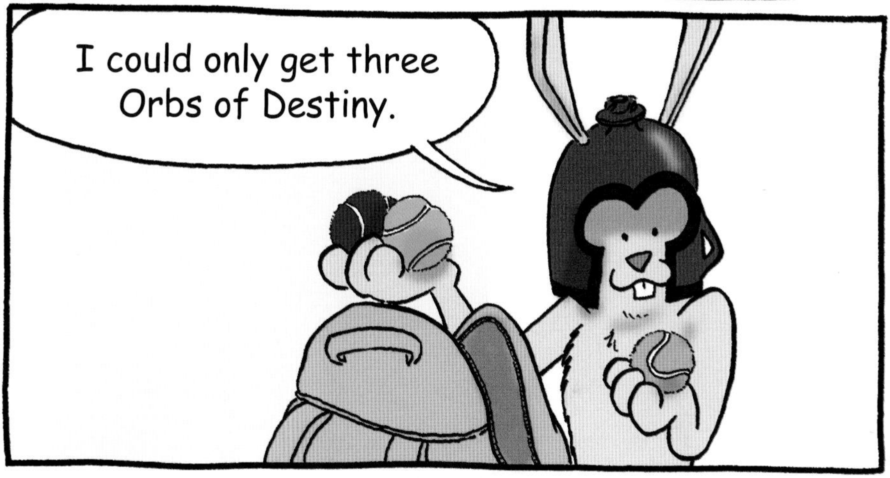
I could only get three Orbs of Destiny.

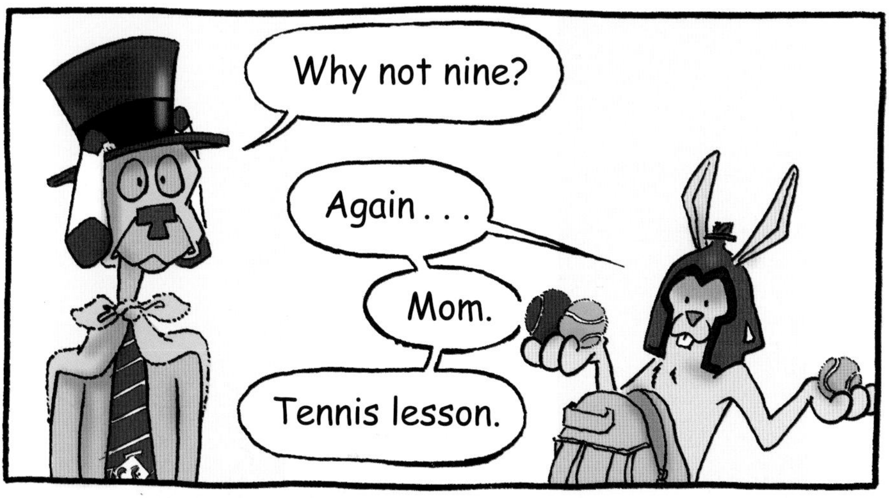
Why not nine?
Again . . .
Mom.
Tennis lesson.

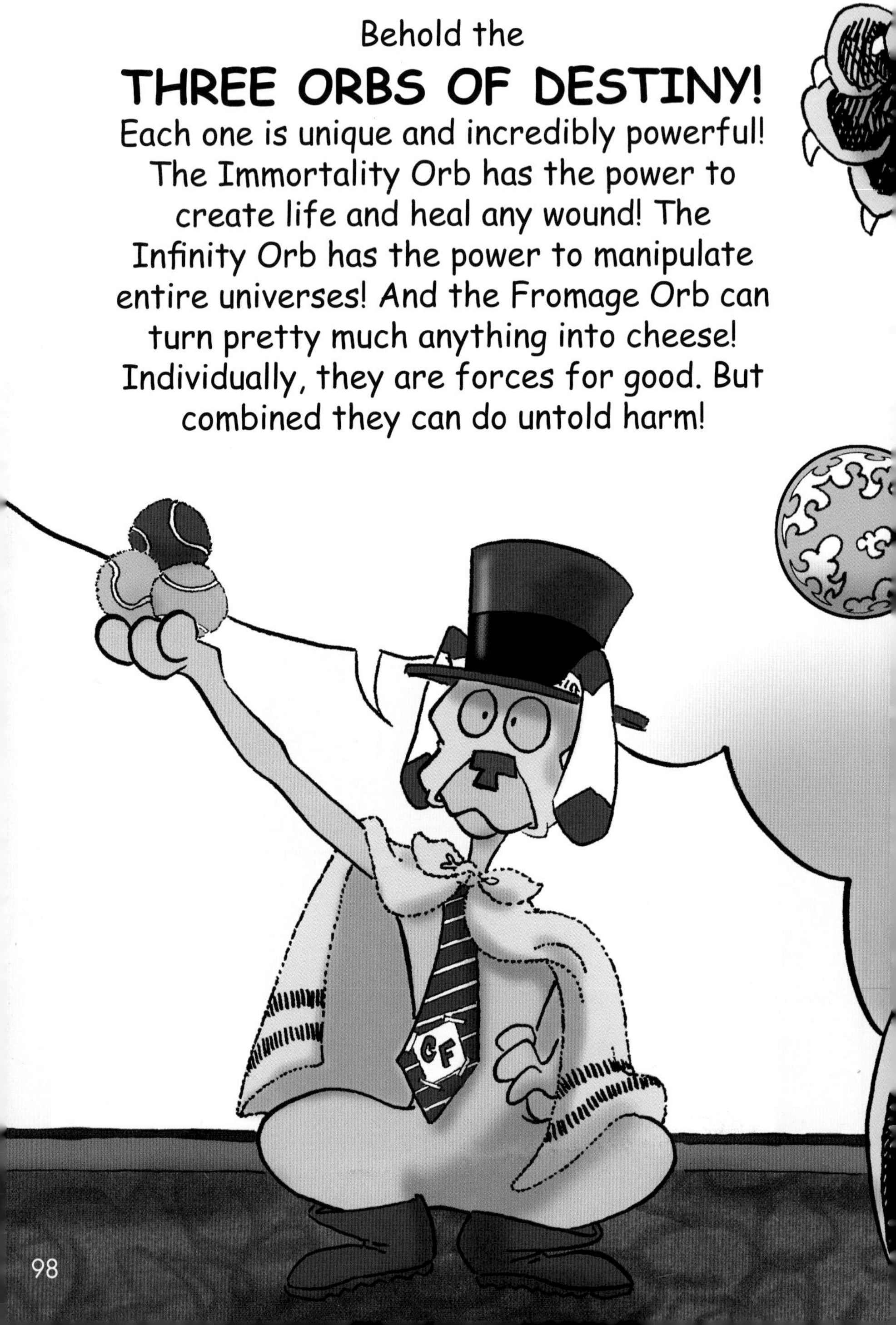
Behold the
THREE ORBS OF DESTINY!
Each one is unique and incredibly powerful! The Immortality Orb has the power to create life and heal any wound! The Infinity Orb has the power to manipulate entire universes! And the Fromage Orb can turn pretty much anything into cheese! Individually, they are forces for good. But combined they can do untold harm!
CF

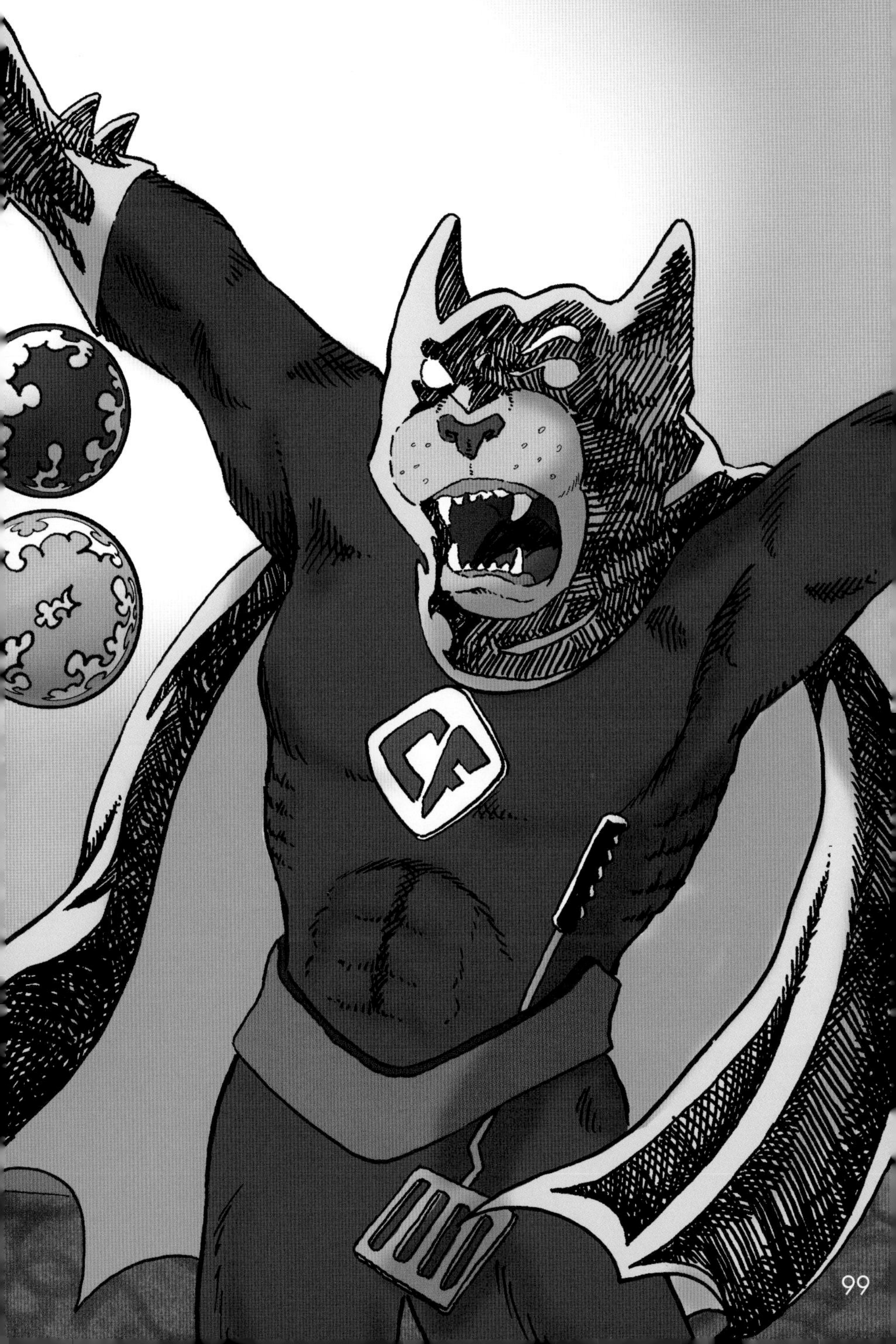

And I, Dr. Lagomorph, have spent centuries scouring the galaxy, searching for these orbs so I could use their seriously cool powers for my own nefarious plans! I have tracked them to this location, and soon they will be MINE! Once they are in my furry little paws, I shall combine their powers and transform 92 UNIVERSES into CHEESE. And I shall become a god!

MWAH-HA-HA-HA-HA!

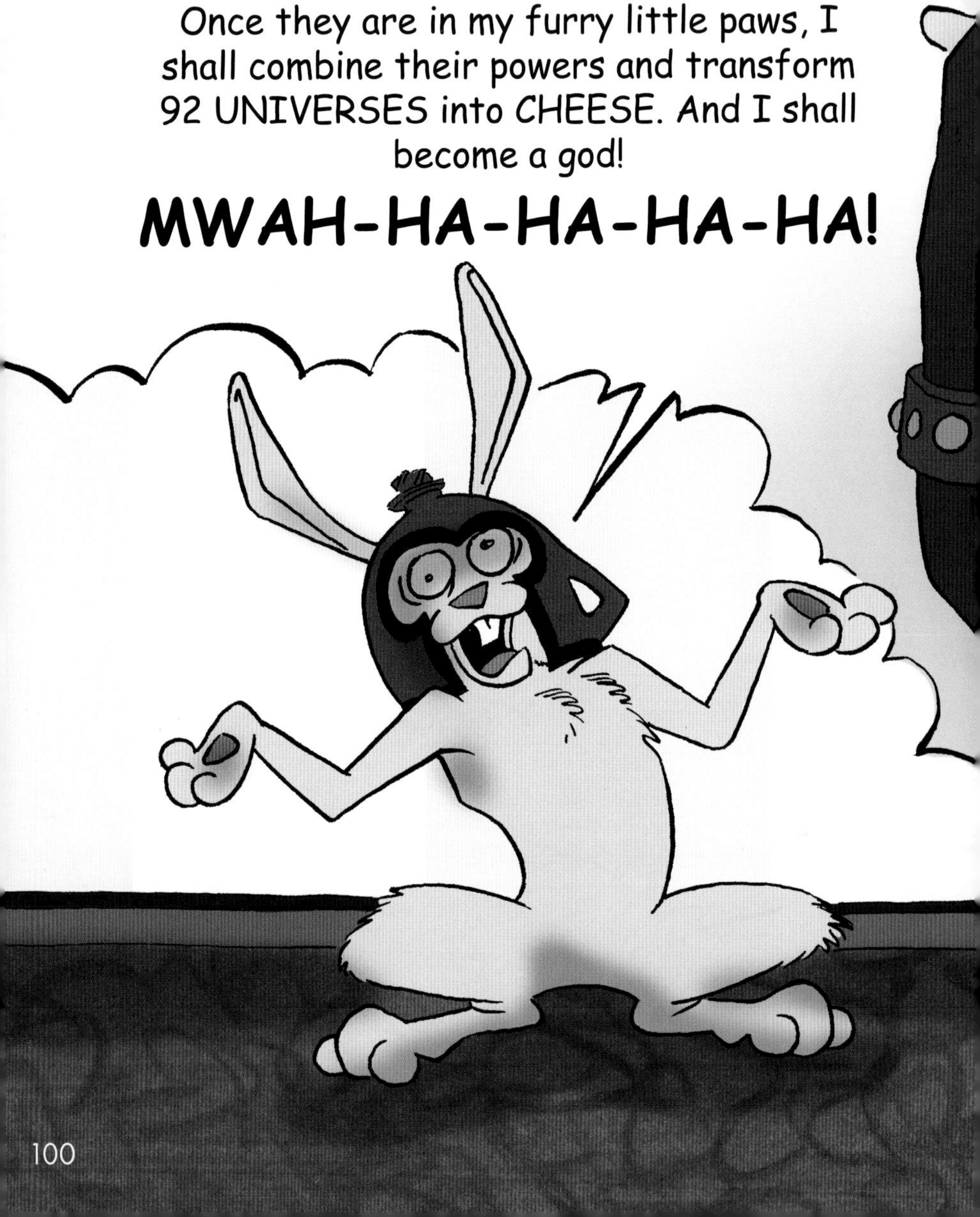

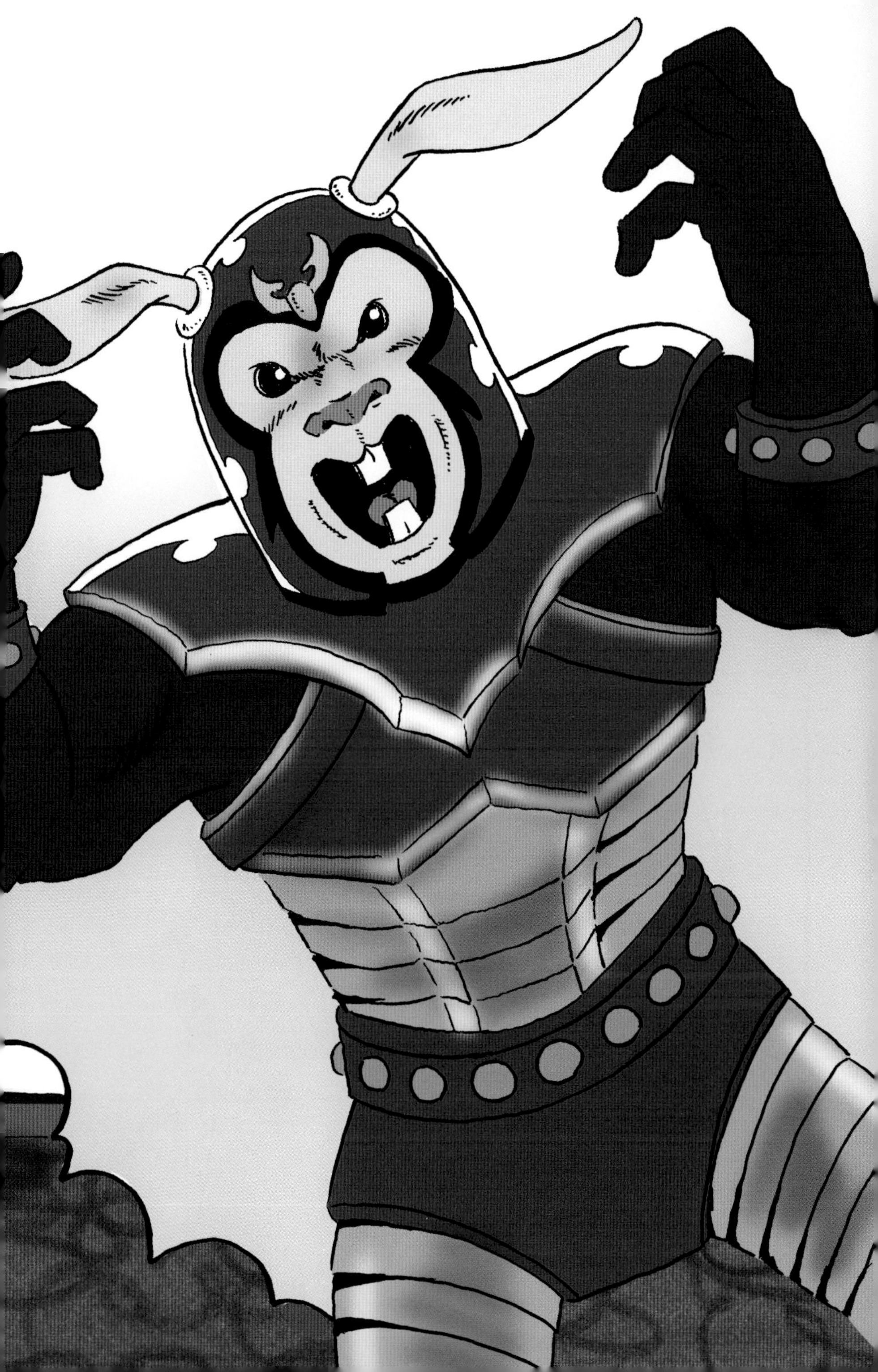

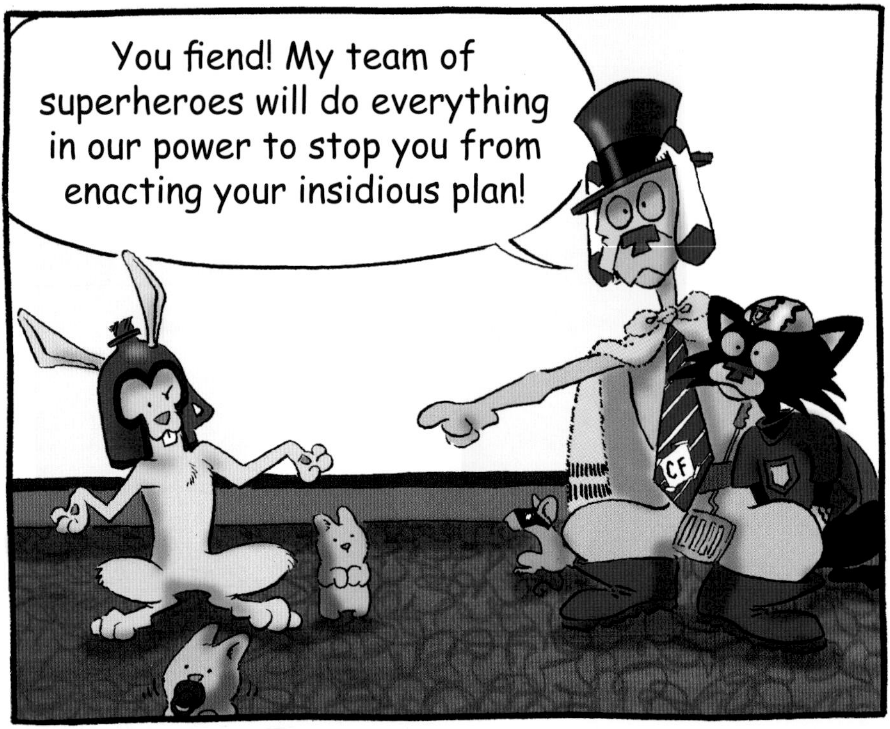
You fiend! My team of superheroes will do everything in our power to stop you from enacting your insidious plan!
CF

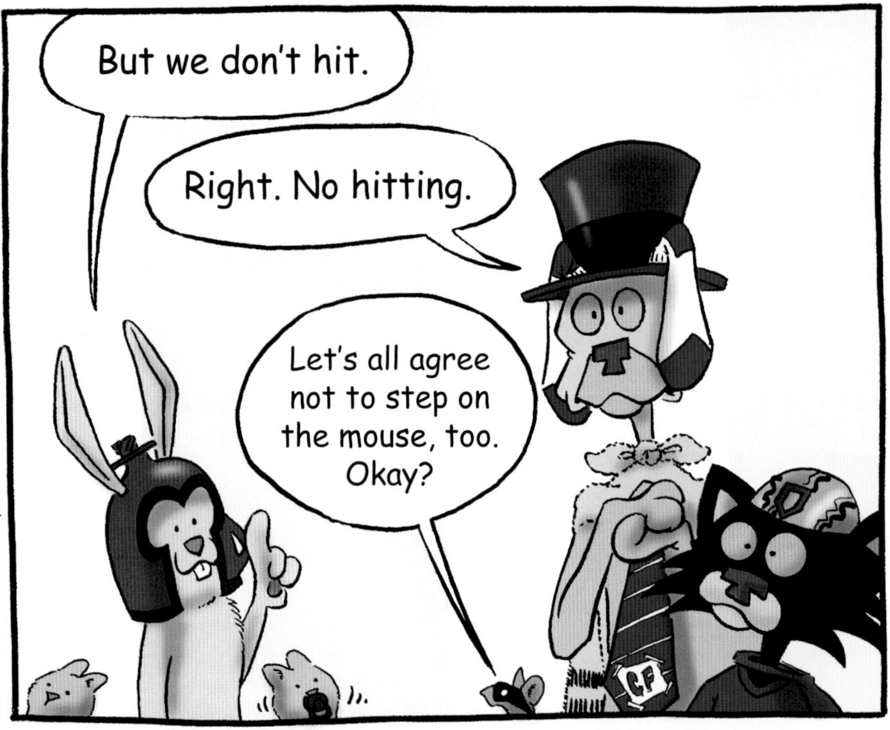
But we don't hit.
Right. No hitting.
Let's all agree not to step on the mouse, too. Okay?
CF

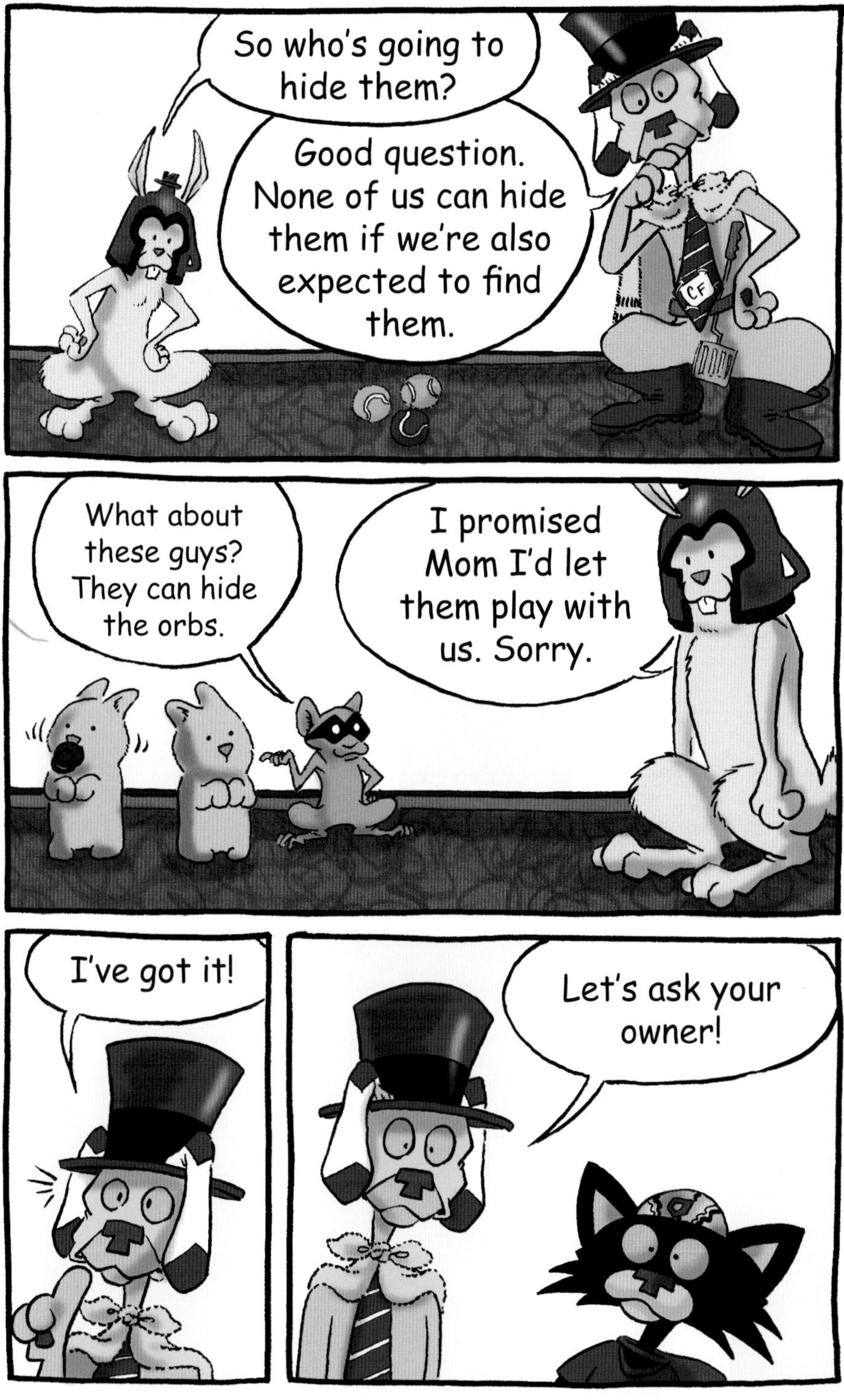
So who's going to hide them?
Good question. None of us can hide them if we're also expected to find them.
What about these guys? They can hide the orbs.
I promised Mom I'd let them play with us. Sorry.
I've got it!
Let's ask your owner!

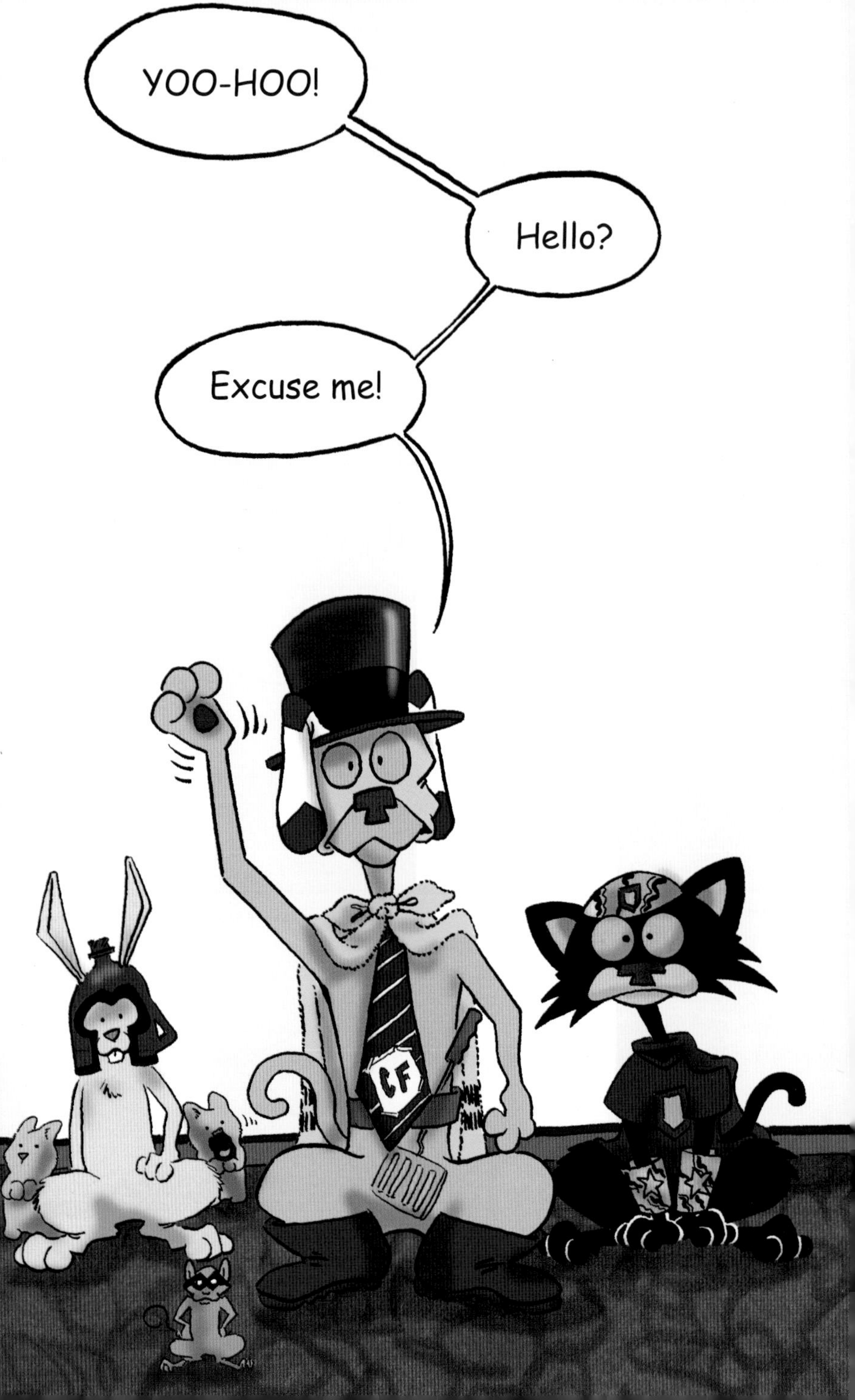
YOO-HOO!
Hello?
Excuse me!
CF

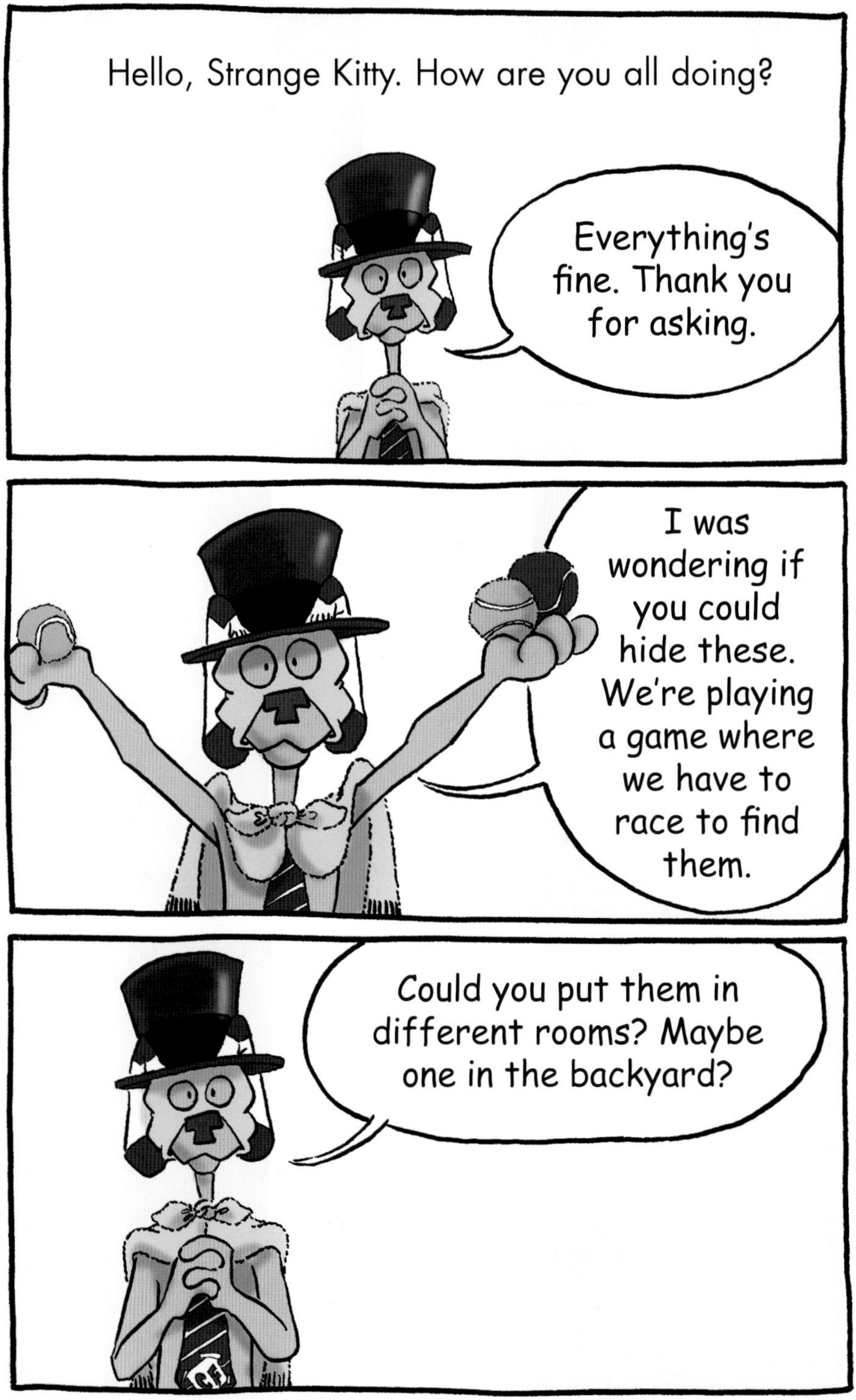
Hello, Strange Kitty. How are you all doing?
Everything's fine. Thank you for asking.
I was wondering if you could hide these. We're playing a game where we have to race to find them.
Could you put them in different rooms? Maybe one in the backyard?

I'm so glad to hear that you guys are doing something creative with your time. Sure! I'll hide them, and I'll let you know when they're ready. Okay?

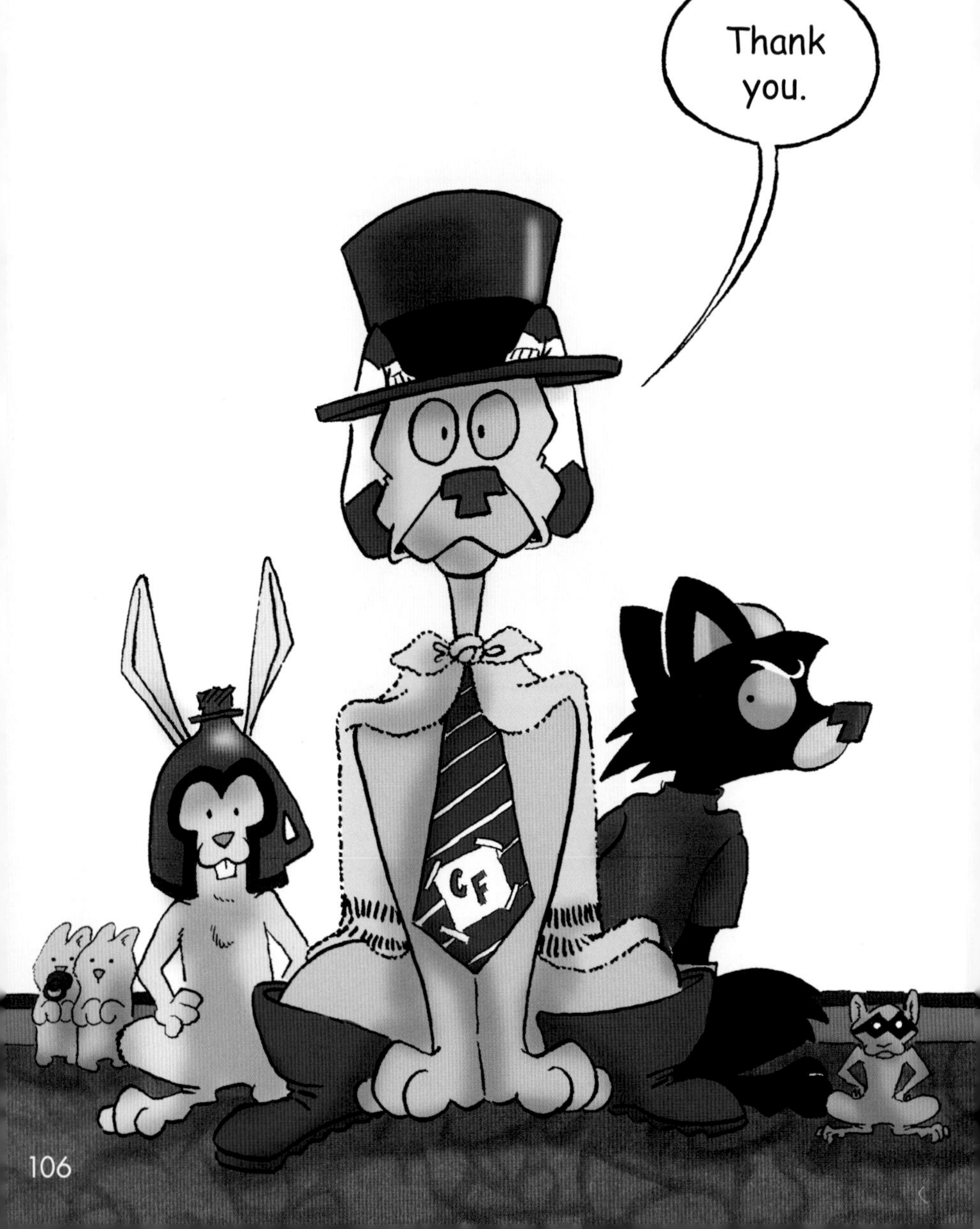
Thank you.

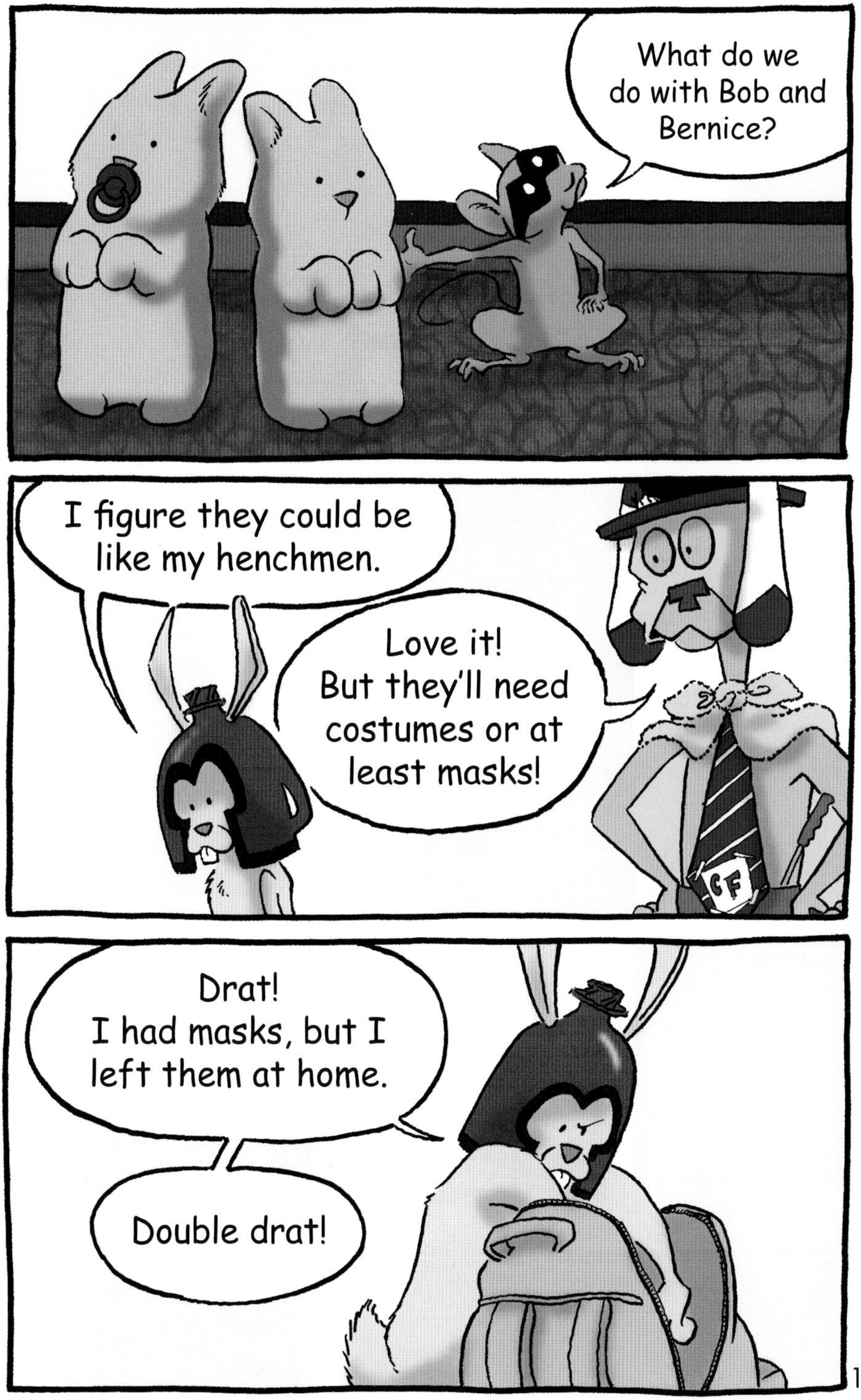
What do we do with Bob and Bernice?
I figure they could be like my henchmen.
Love it! But they'll need costumes or at least masks!
Drat! I had masks, but I left them at home.
Double drat!

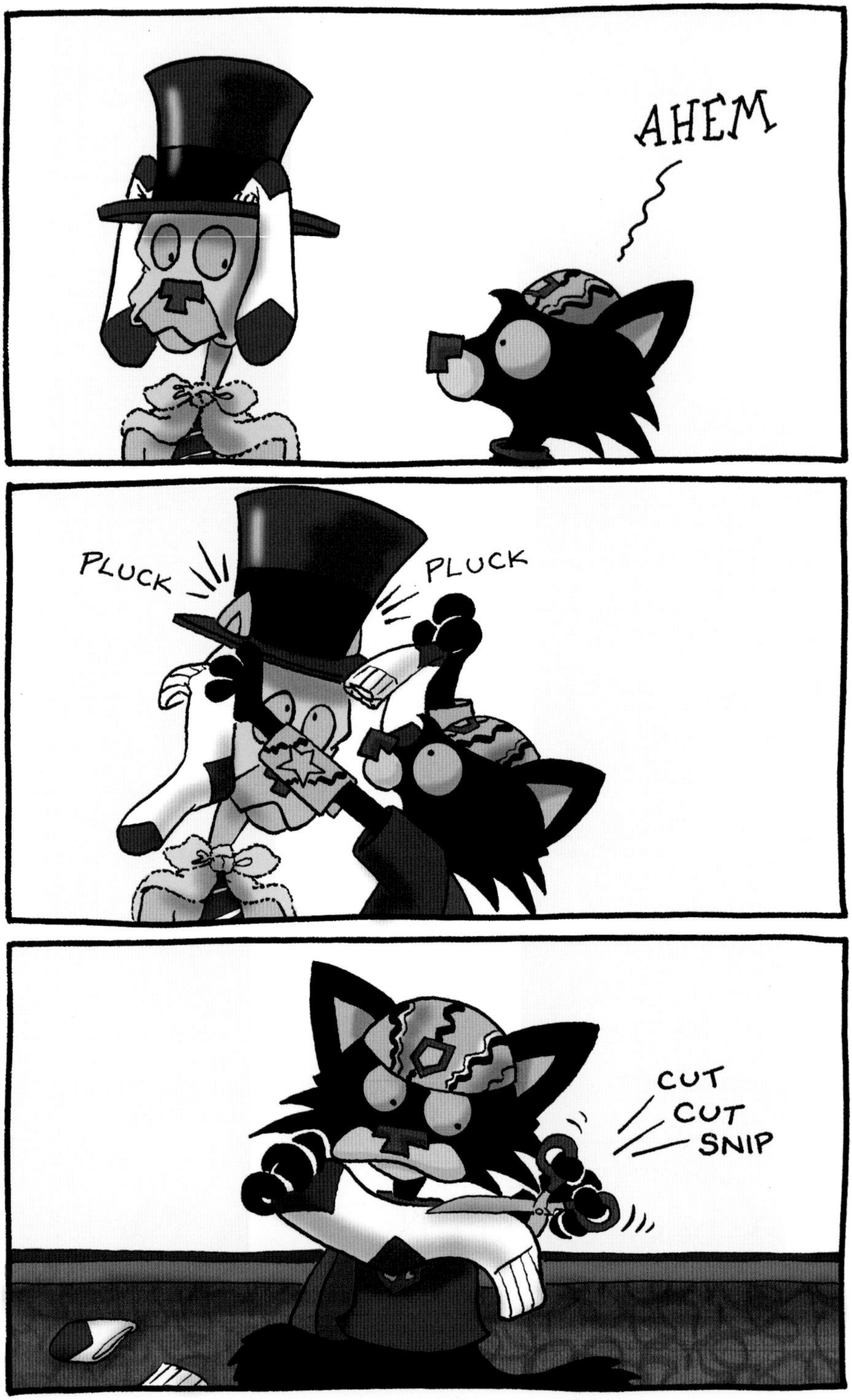
AHEM
PLUCK
PLUCK
CUT
CUT
SNIP

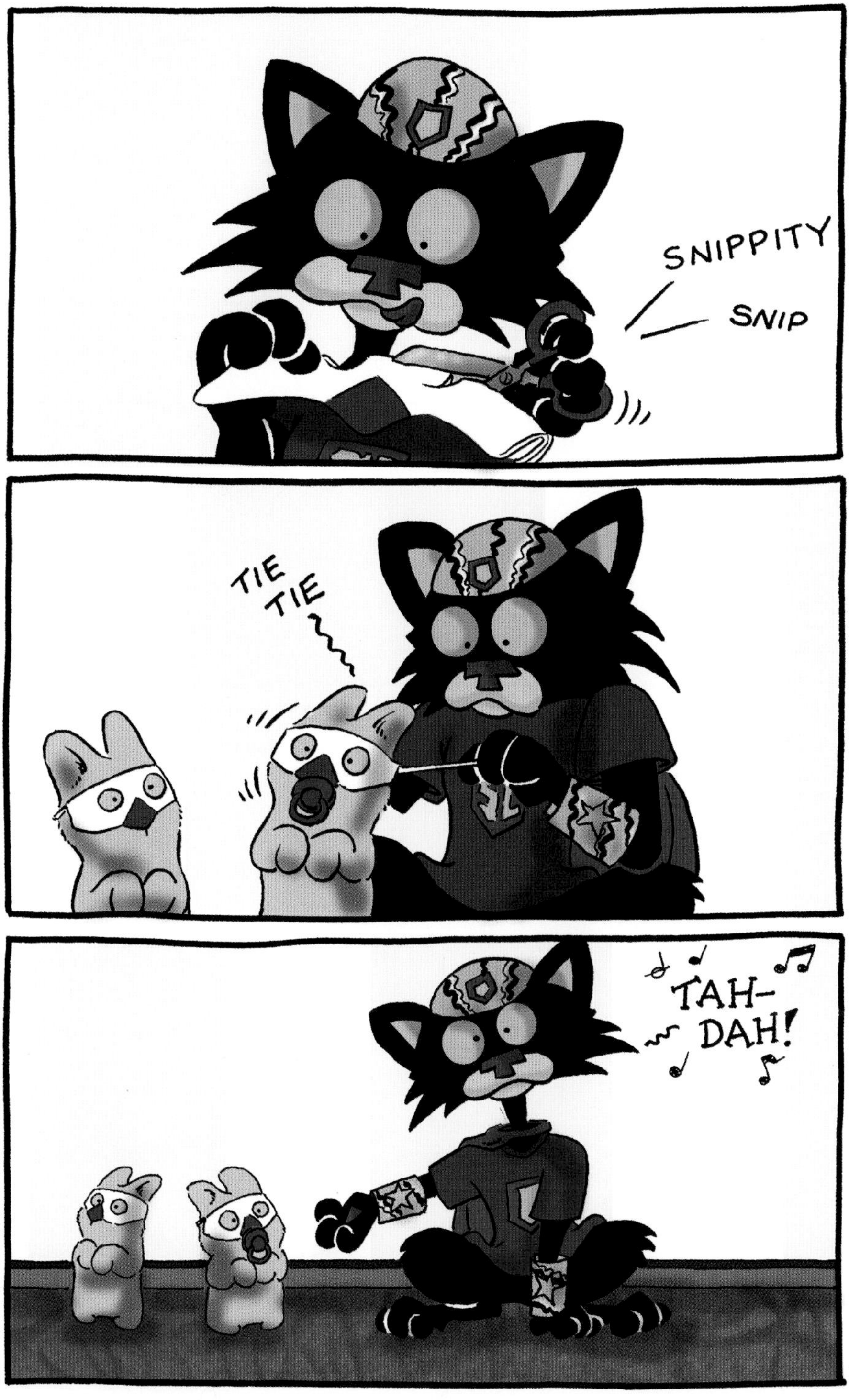
SNIPPITY
SNIP
TIE
TIE
TAH-
DAH!

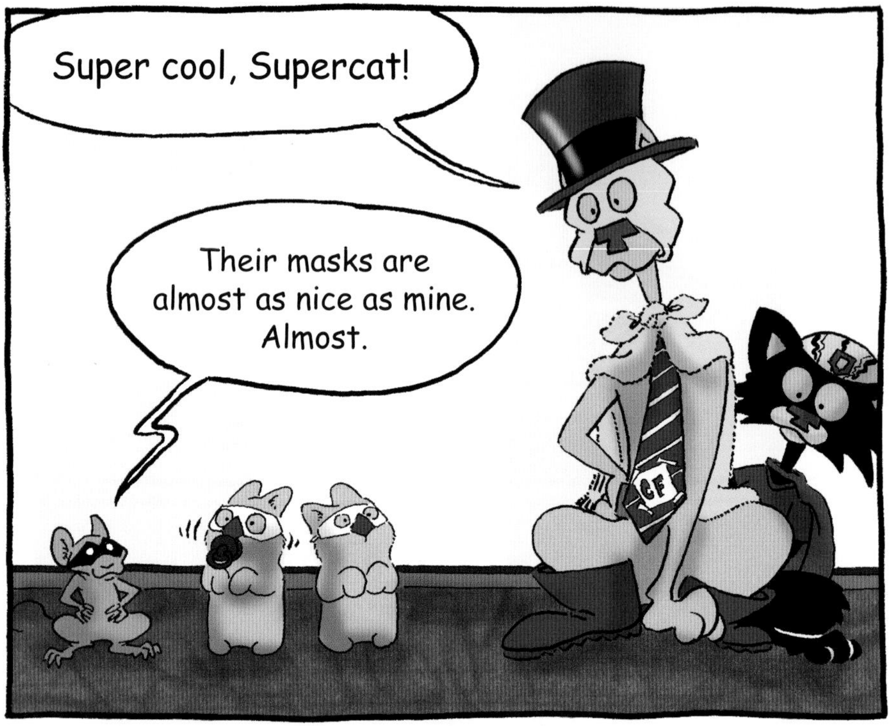
Super cool, Supercat!
Their masks are almost as nice as mine. Almost.

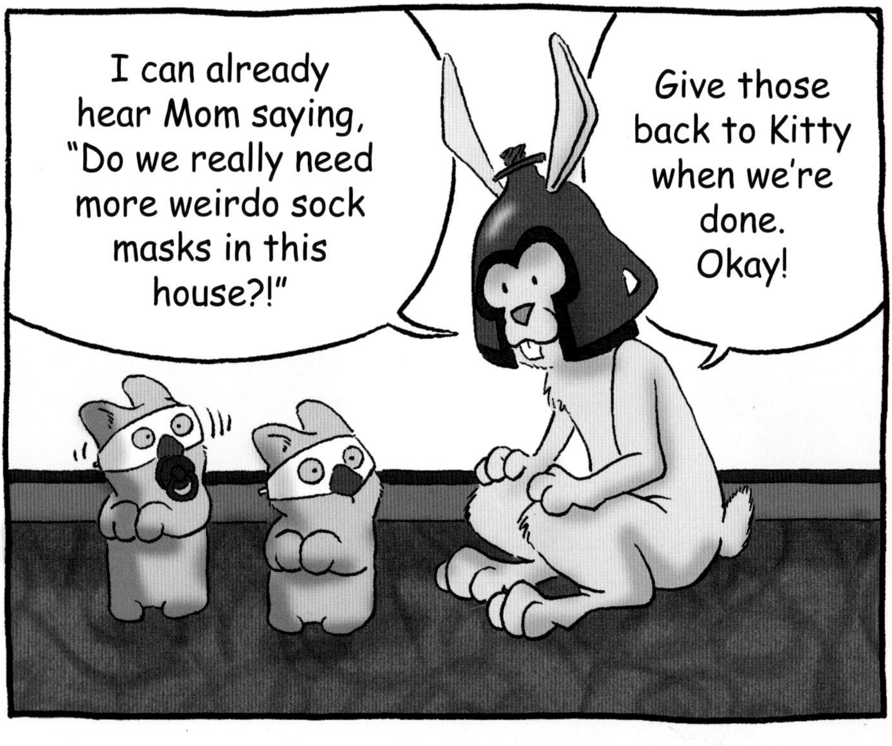
I can already hear Mom saying, "Do we really need more weirdo sock masks in this house?!"
Give those back to Kitty when we're done. Okay!

Okay! I hid them!
One's in the kitchen. One's in the basement. And the last one's in the backyard.

HAVE FUN!

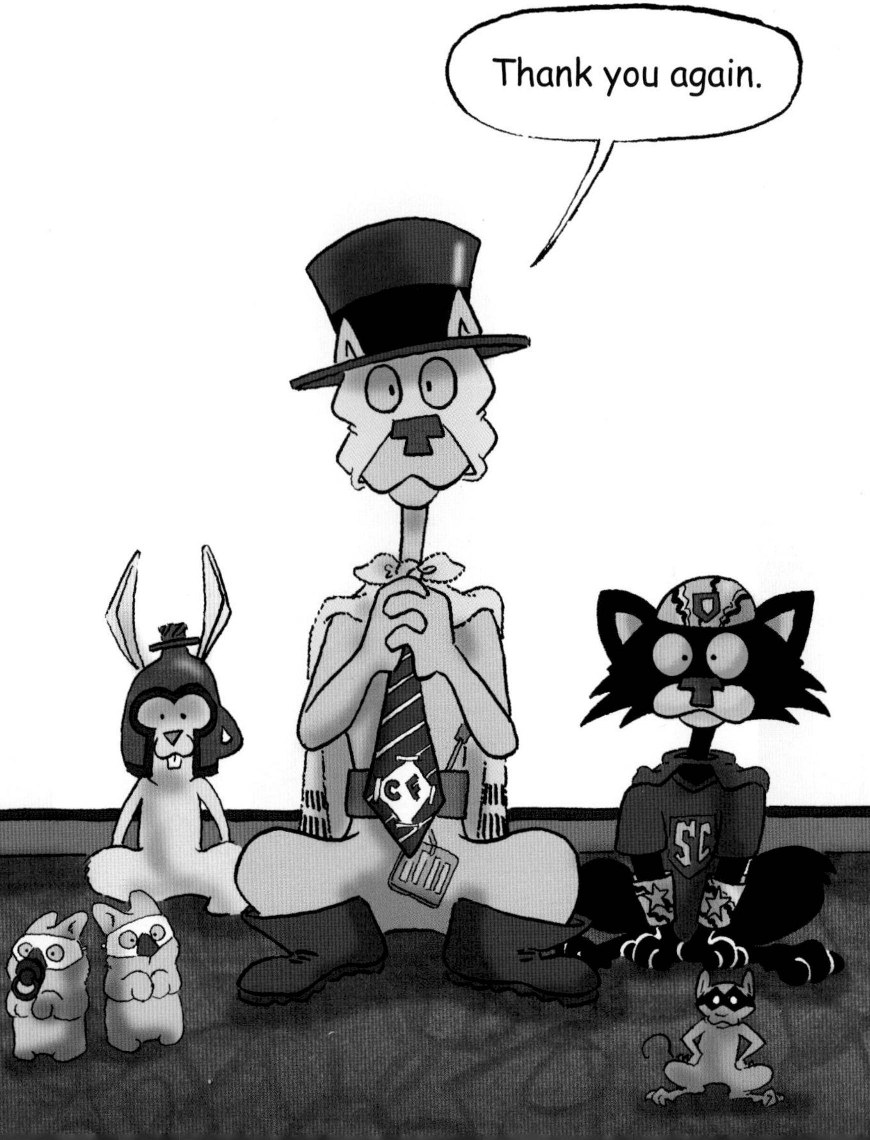
Thank you again.

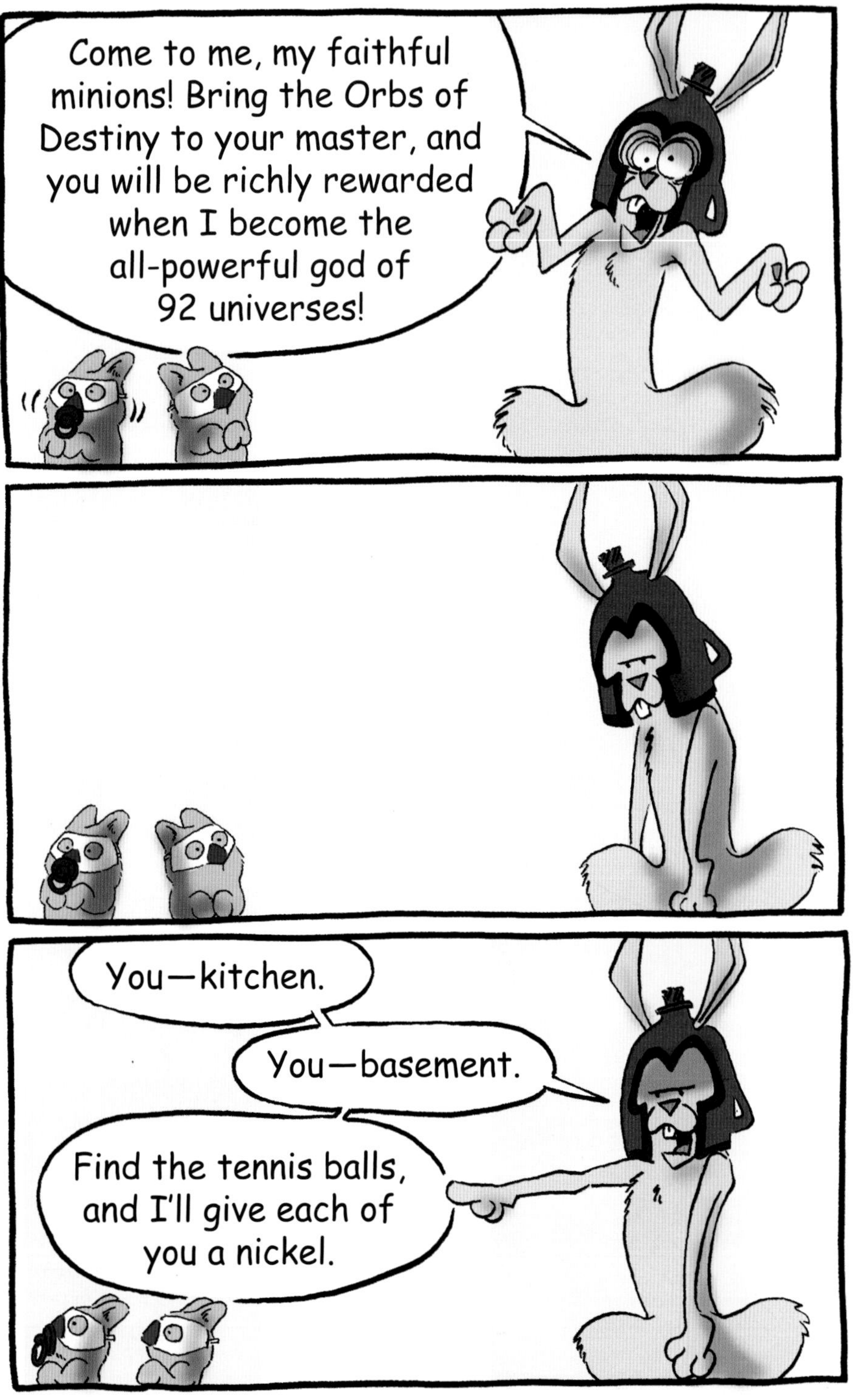
Come to me, my faithful minions! Bring the Orbs of Destiny to your master, and you will be richly rewarded when I become the all-powerful god of 92 universes!
You—kitchen.
You—basement.
Find the tennis balls, and I'll give each of you a nickel.

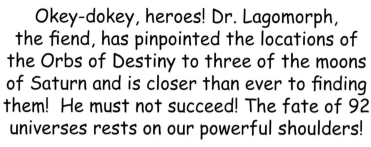

Okey-dokey, heroes! Dr. Lagomorph, the fiend, has pinpointed the locations of the Orbs of Destiny to three of the moons of Saturn and is closer than ever to finding them! He must not succeed! The fate of 92 universes rests on our powerful shoulders!

We need a team battle cry!

How about, "SUPERFRIENDS ASSEMBLE!"?

Hmmm . . . Sounds a bit like gathering the staff for a business meeting.

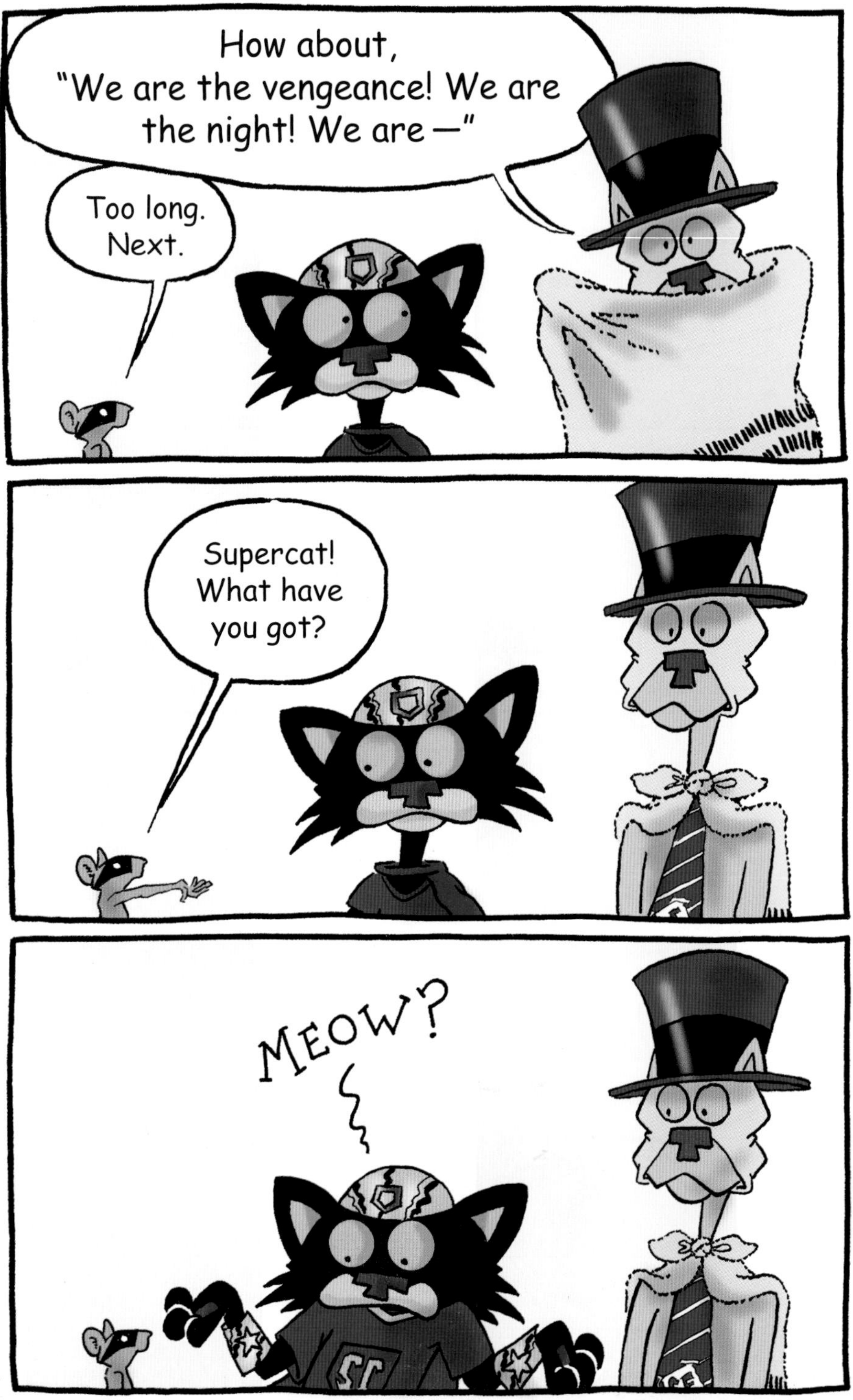
How about, "We are the vengeance! We are the night! We are —"
Too long. Next.
Supercat! What have you got?
MEOW?

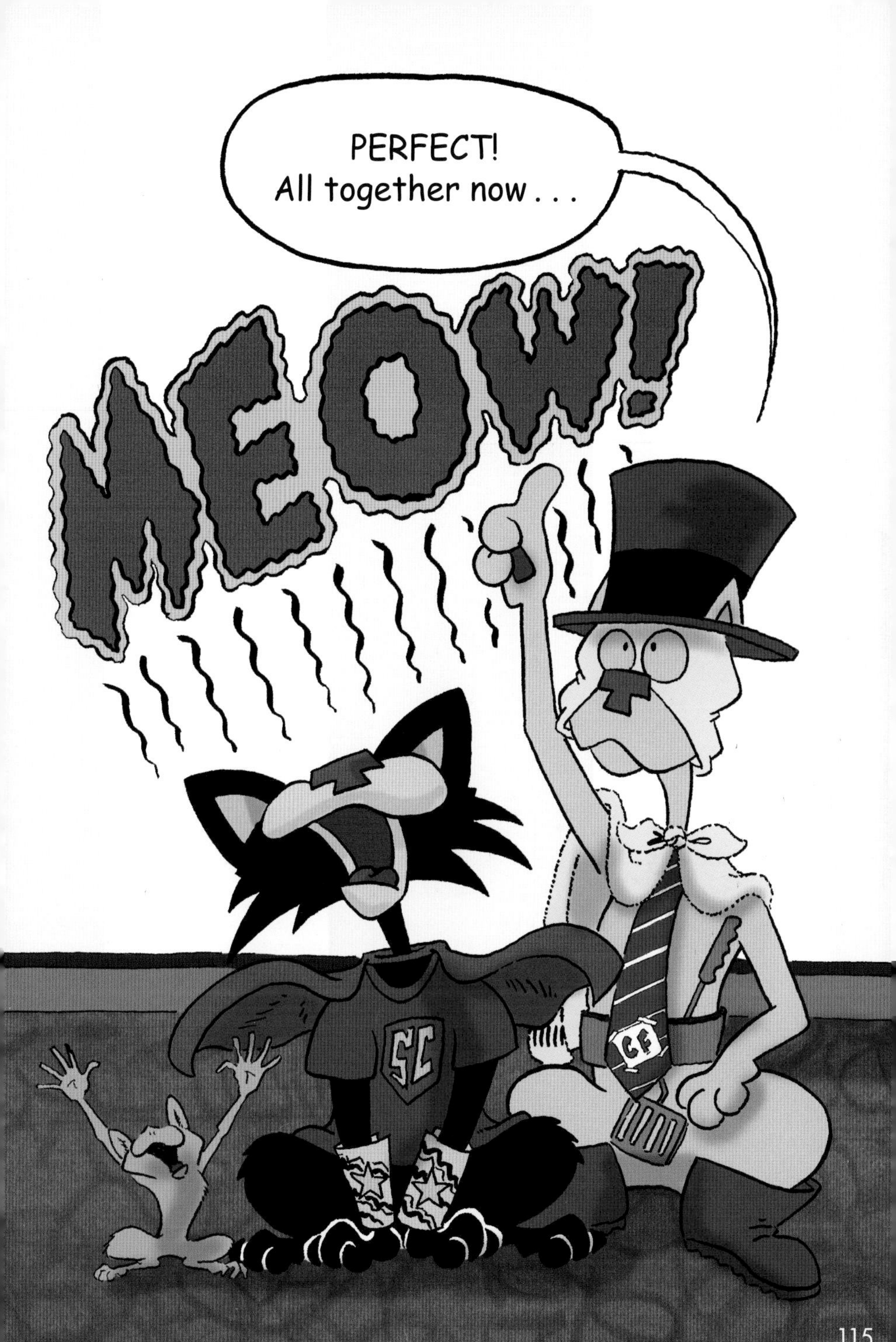
PERFECT!
All together now . . .
MEOW!
SC
CF

• CHAPTER FIVE •

CAPTAIN FANTASTICAT VS. BOB (POSSIBLY BERNICE)

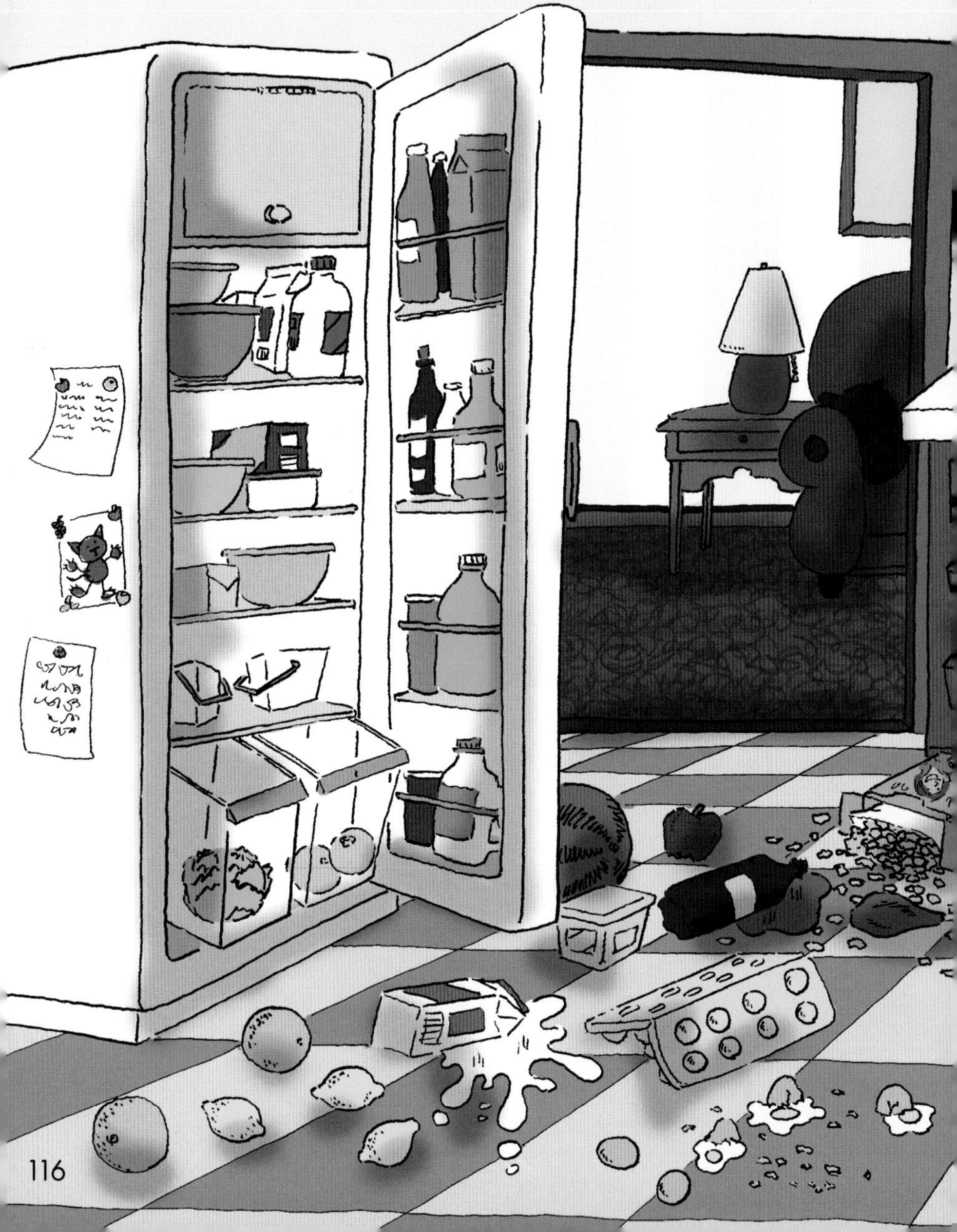

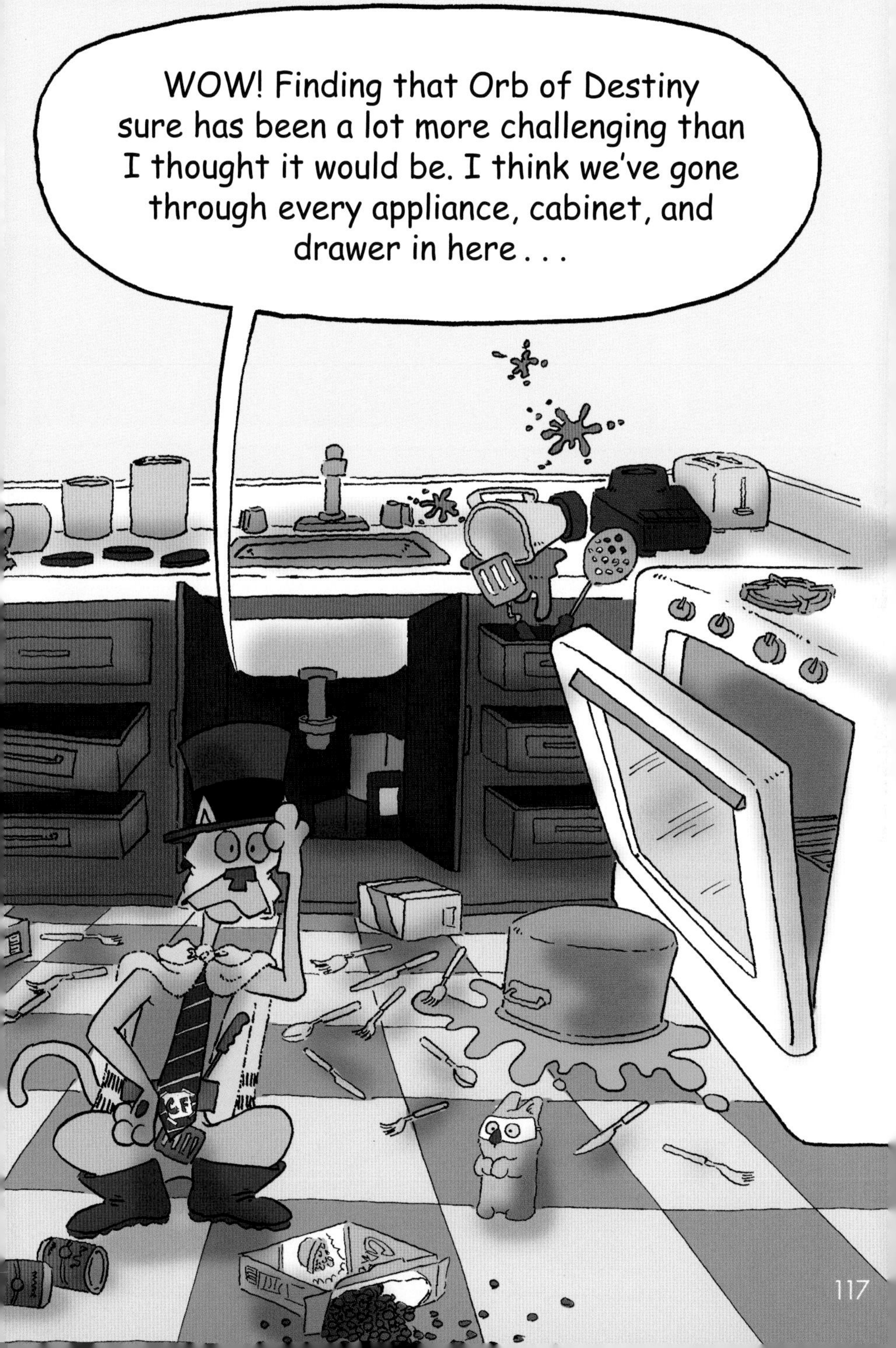
WOW! Finding that Orb of Destiny sure has been a lot more challenging than I thought it would be. I think we've gone through every appliance, cabinet, and drawer in here . . .

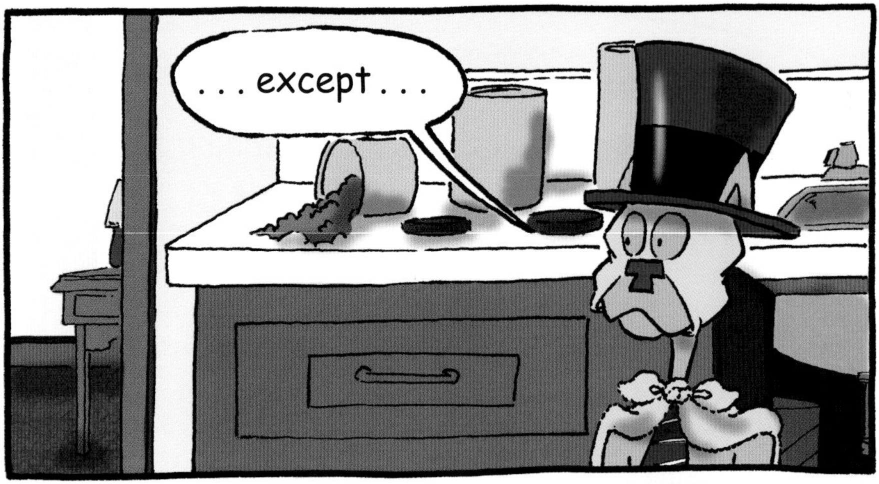
. . . except . . .

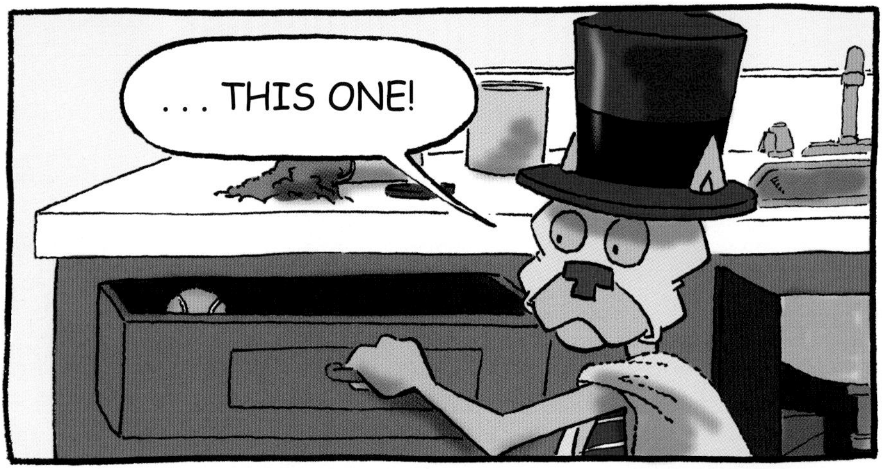
. . . THIS ONE!

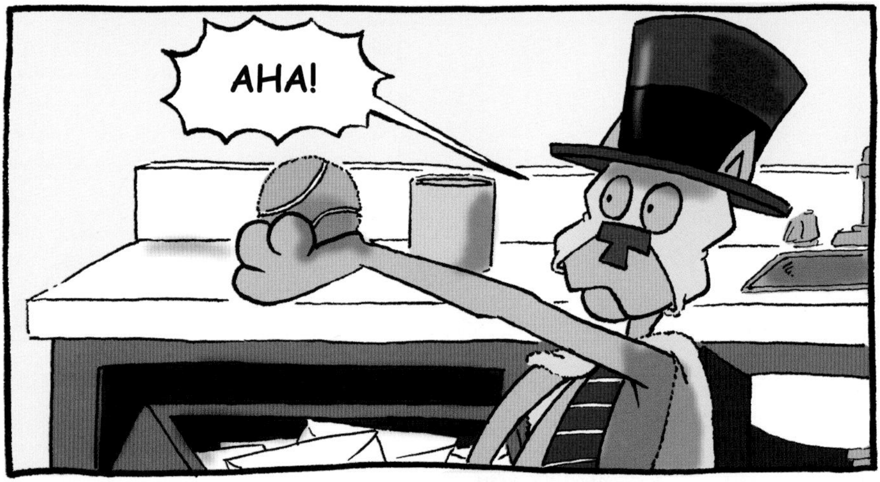
AHA!

JUSTICE HAS TRIUMPHED!

The heroes now have one of the three Orbs of Destiny! Dr. Lagomorph's fiendish plan to turn 92 universes into cheese is useless without all three Orbs!

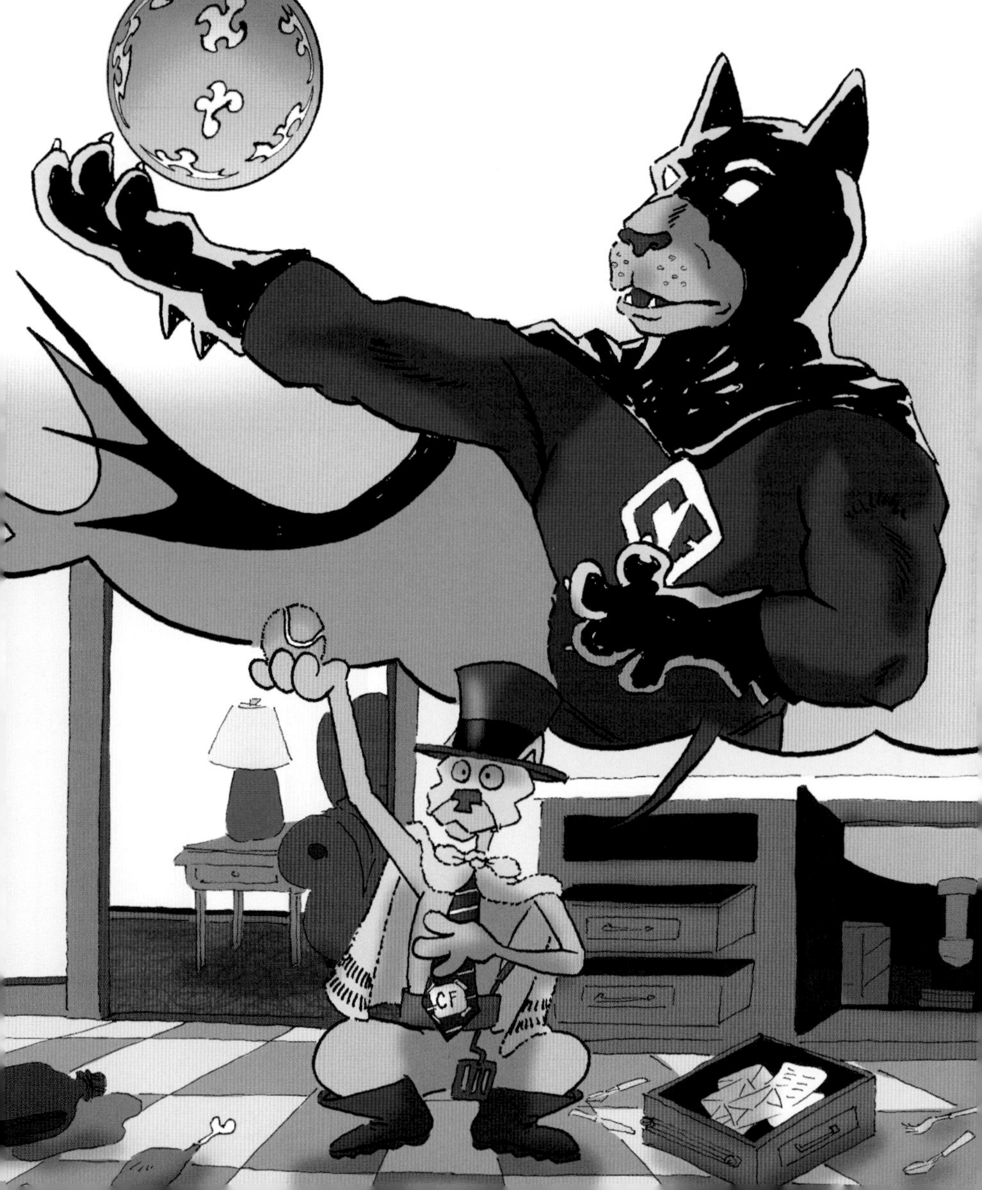
CF

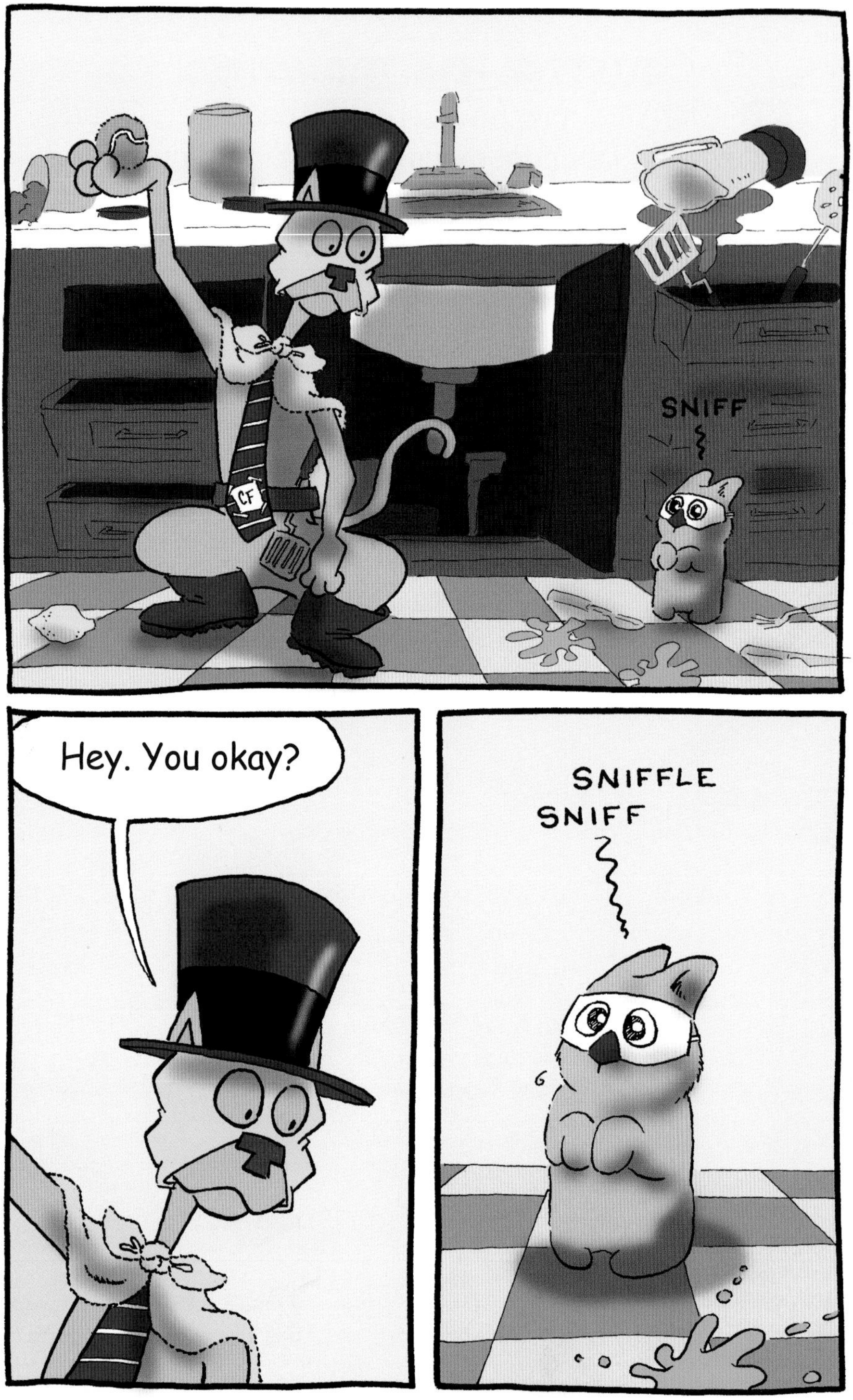
SNIFF
Hey. You okay?
SNIFFLE
SNIFF

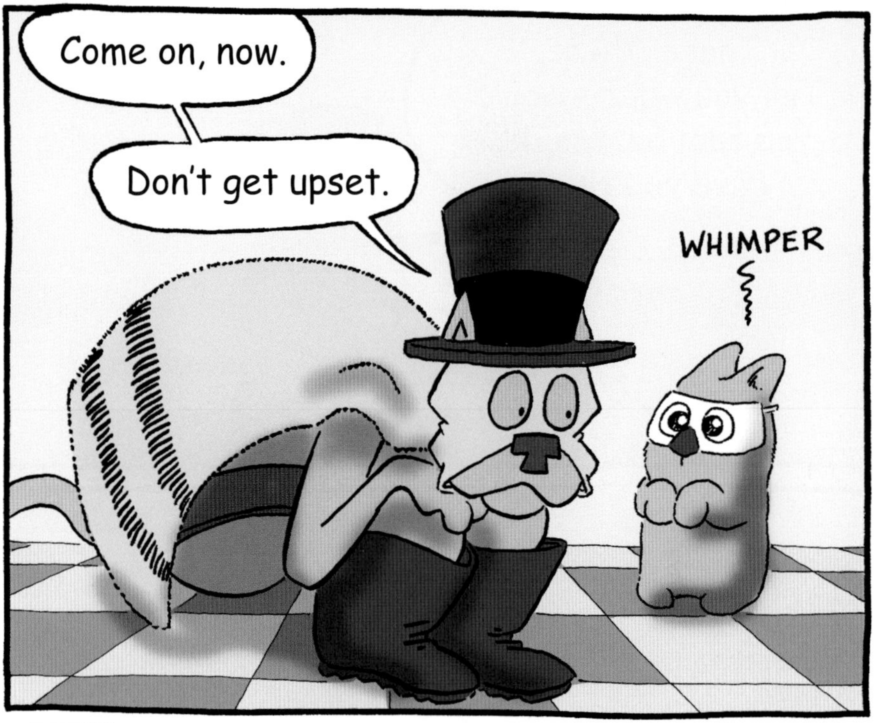
Come on, now.
Don't get upset.
WHIMPER

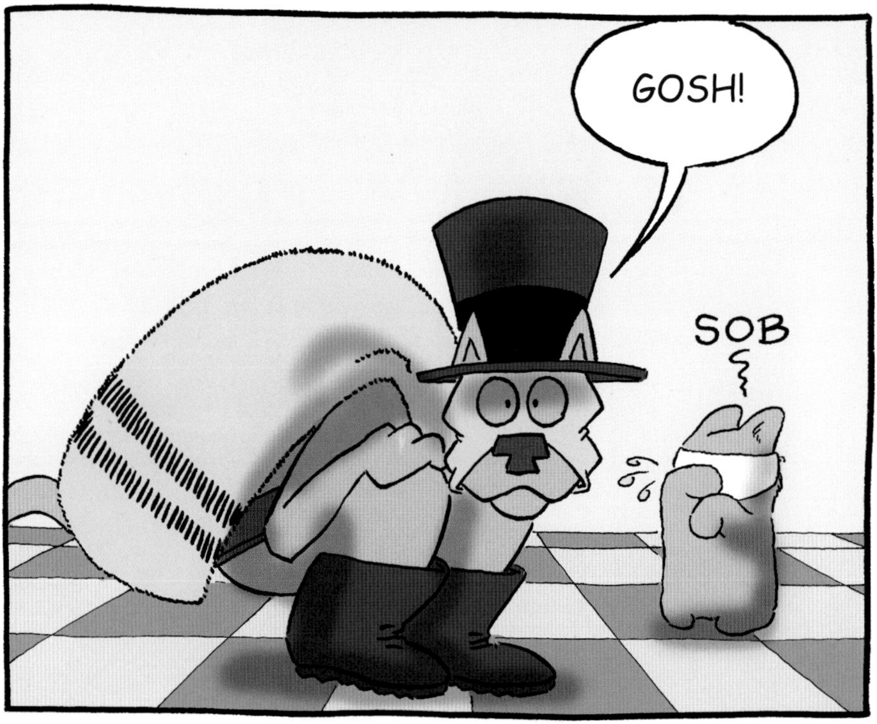
GOSH!
SOB

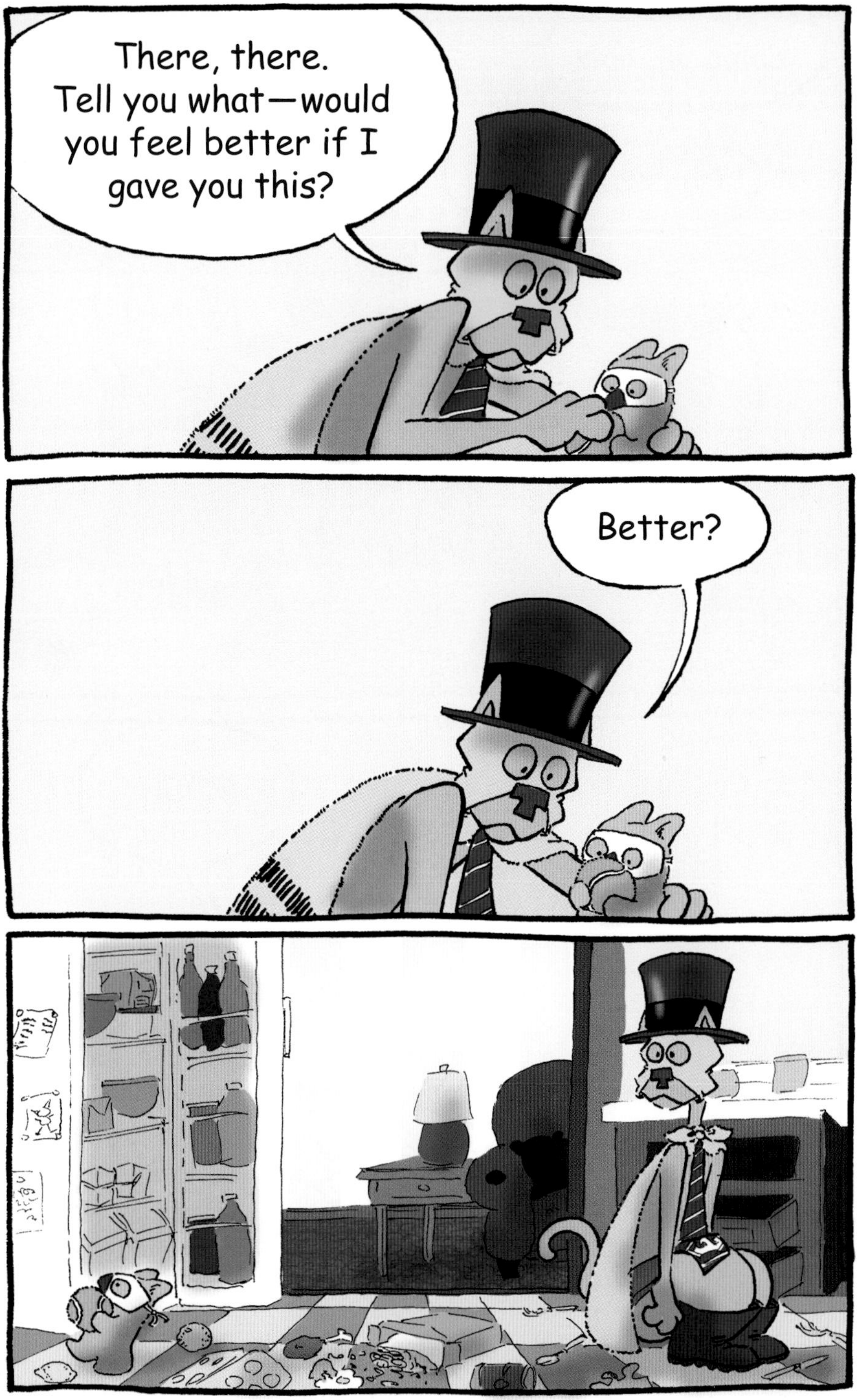
There, there.
Tell you what—would you feel better if I gave you this?
Better?

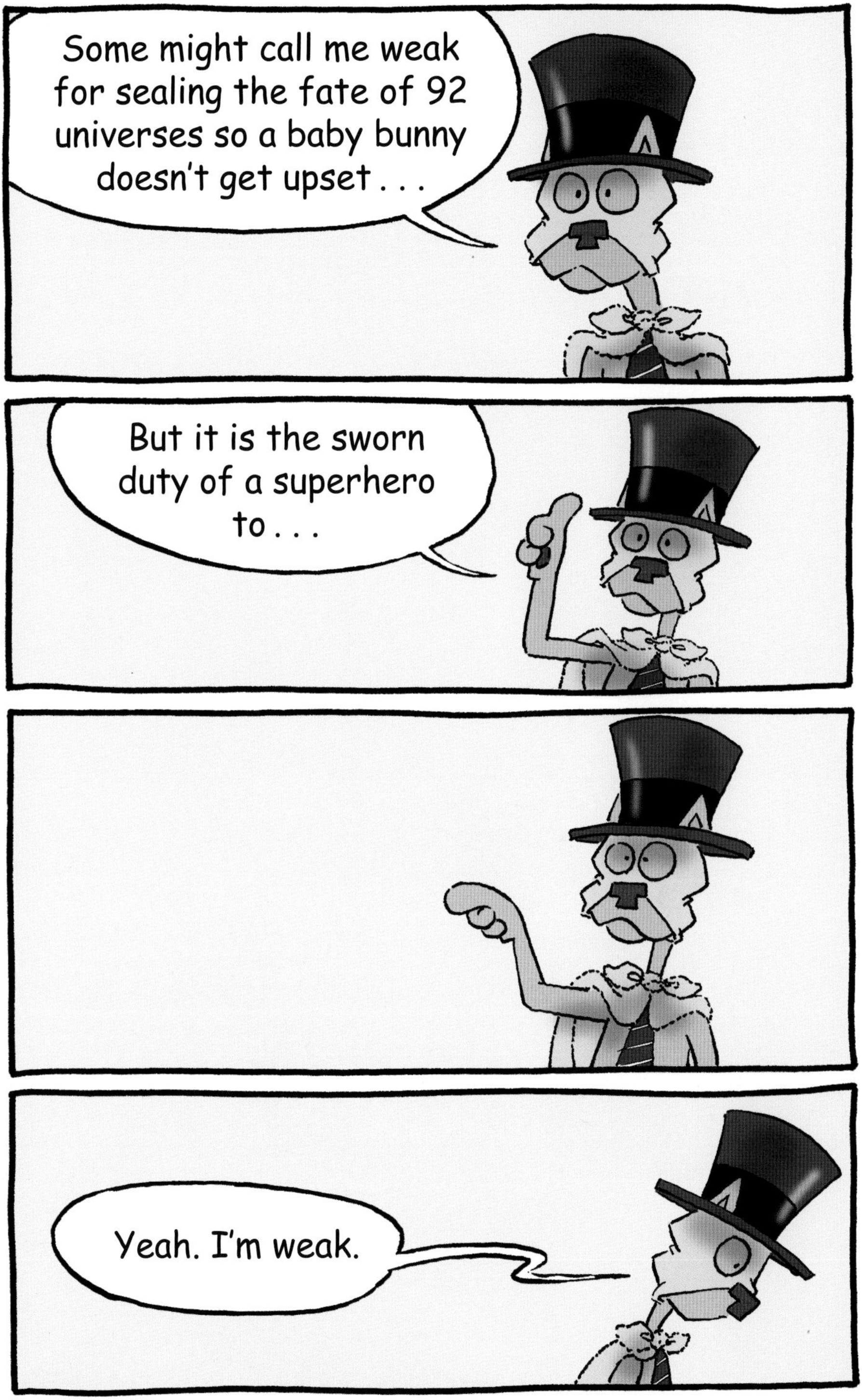
Some might call me weak for sealing the fate of 92 universes so a baby bunny doesn't get upset . . .
But it is the sworn duty of a superhero to . . .
Yeah. I'm weak.

•CHAPTER SIX•

POWER MOUSE VS. BERNICE (POSSIBLY BOB)

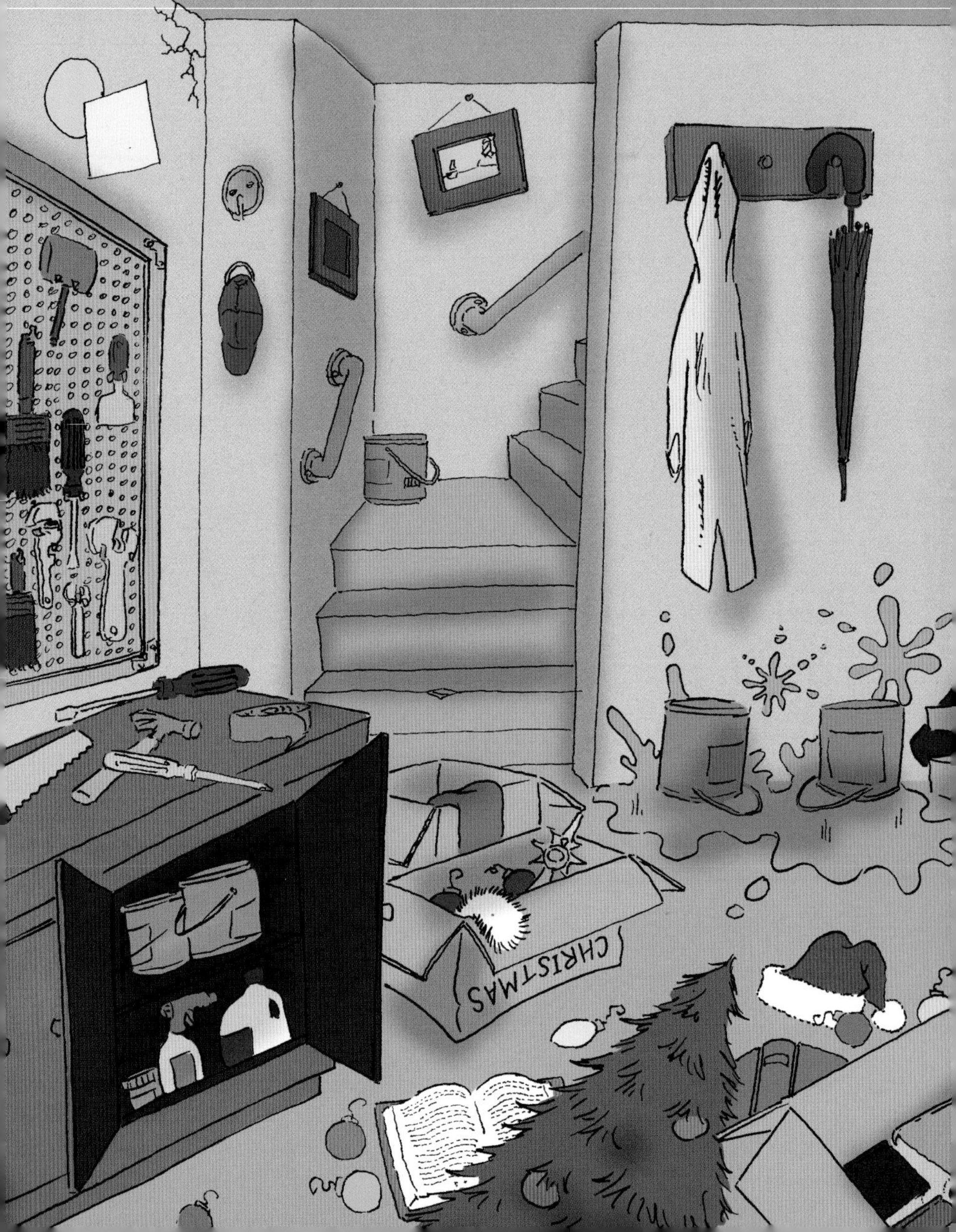
CHRISTMAS

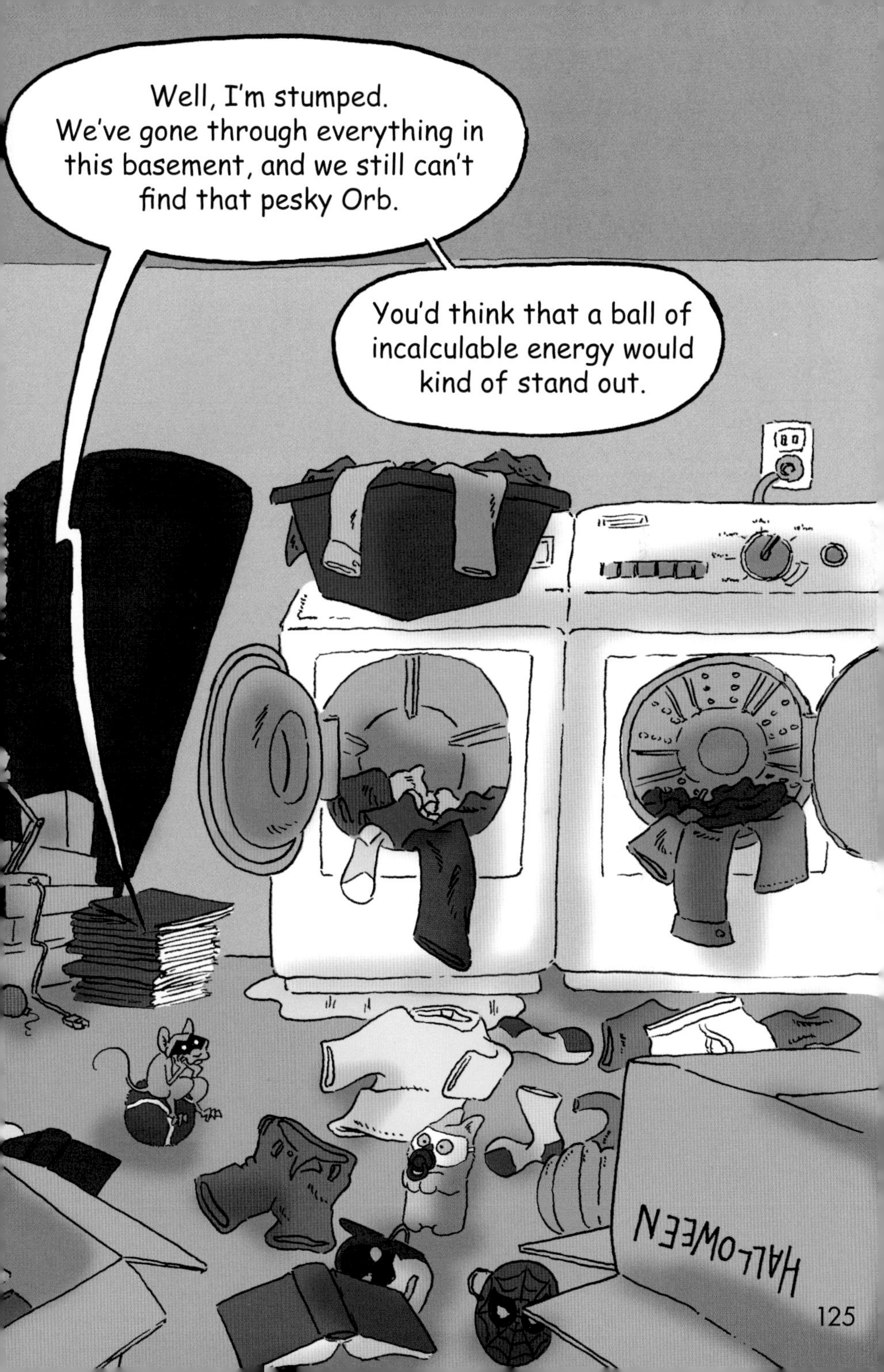
Well, I'm stumped. We've gone through everything in this basement, and we still can't find that pesky Orb.
You'd think that a ball of incalculable energy would kind of stand out.
HALLOWEEN

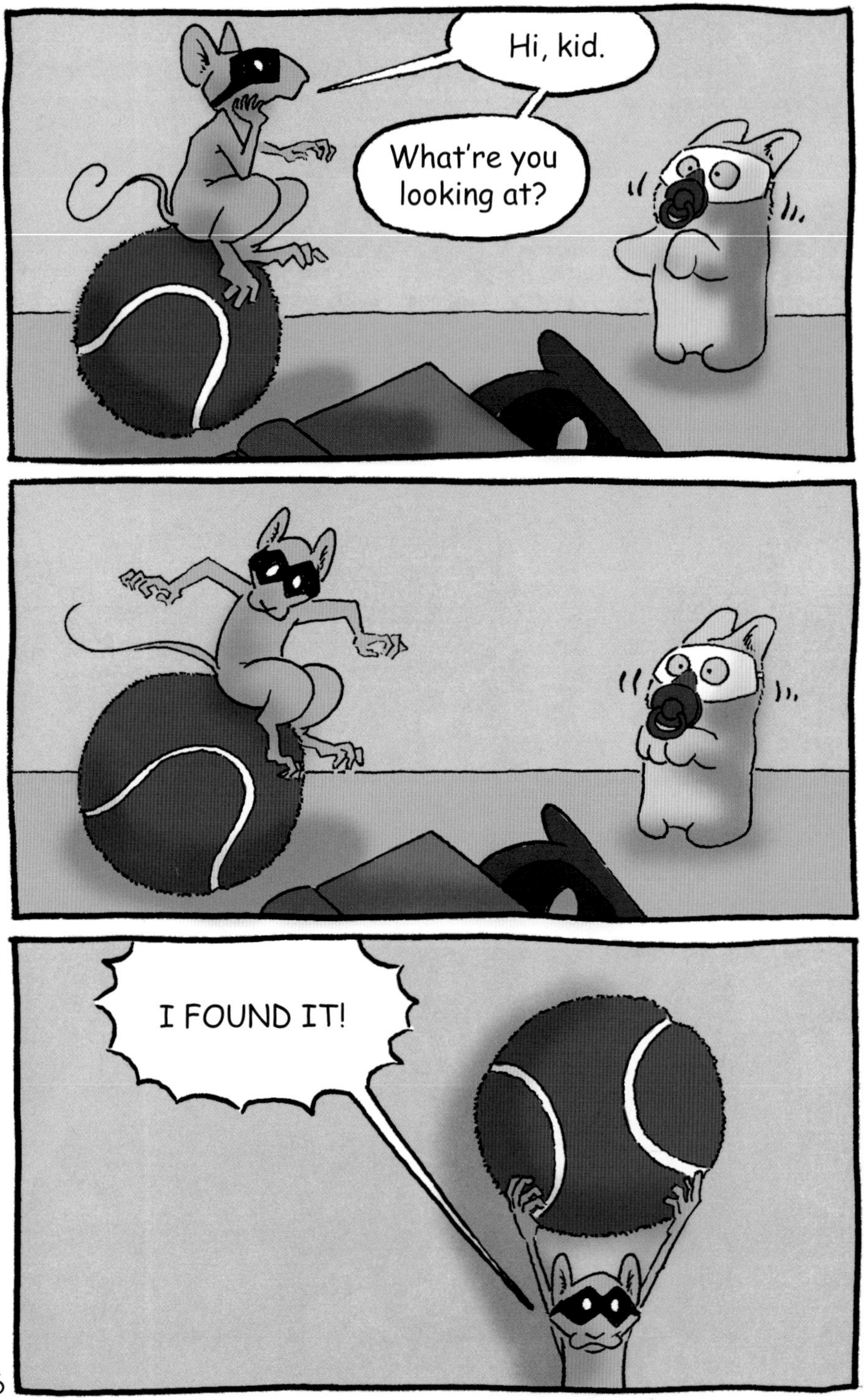
Hi, kid.
What're you looking at?
I FOUND IT!

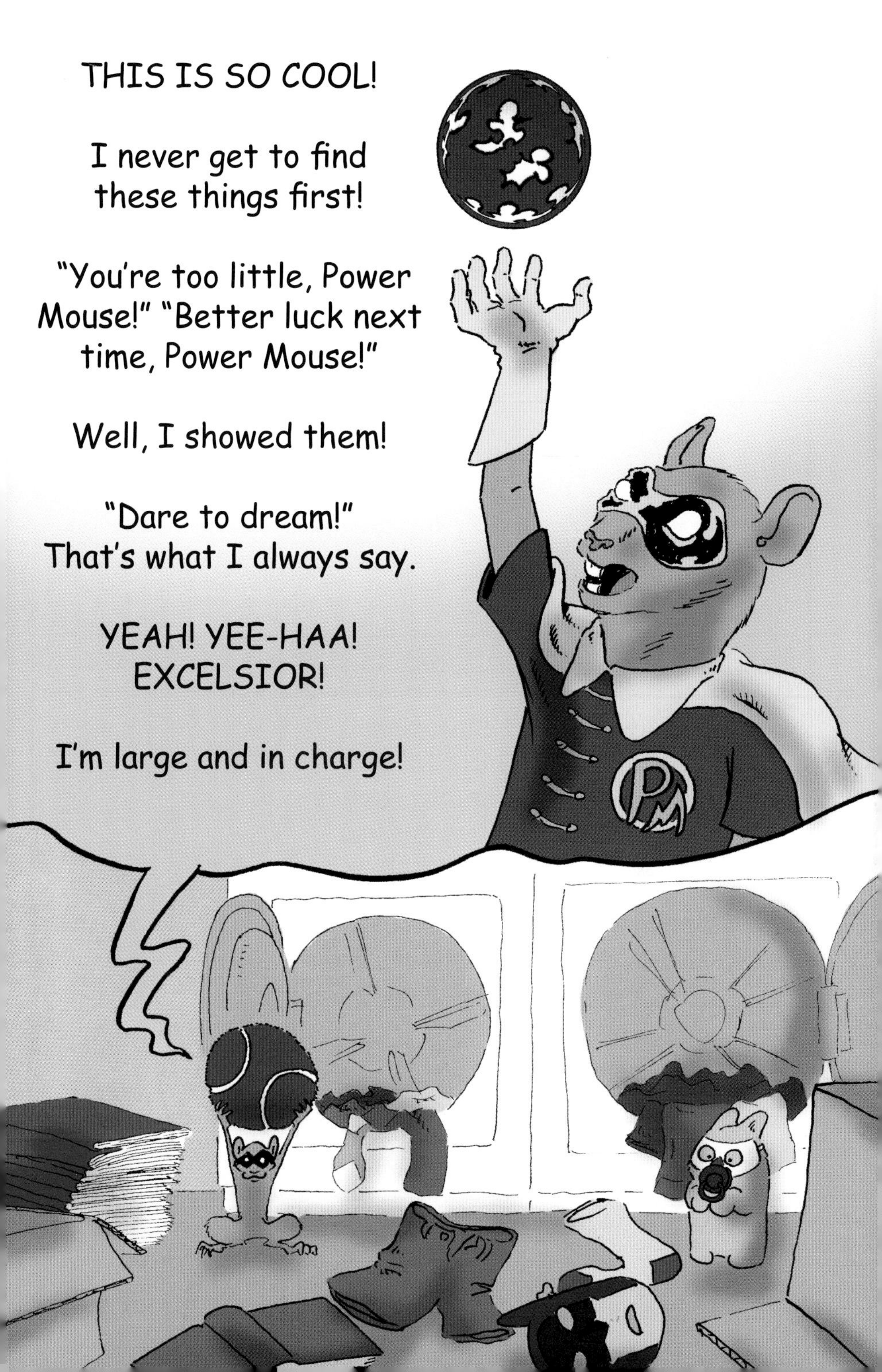
THIS IS SO COOL!
I never get to find these things first!
"You're too little, Power Mouse!" "Better luck next time, Power Mouse!"
Well, I showed them!
"Dare to dream!" That's what I always say.
YEAH! YEE-HAA! EXCELSIOR!
I'm large and in charge!

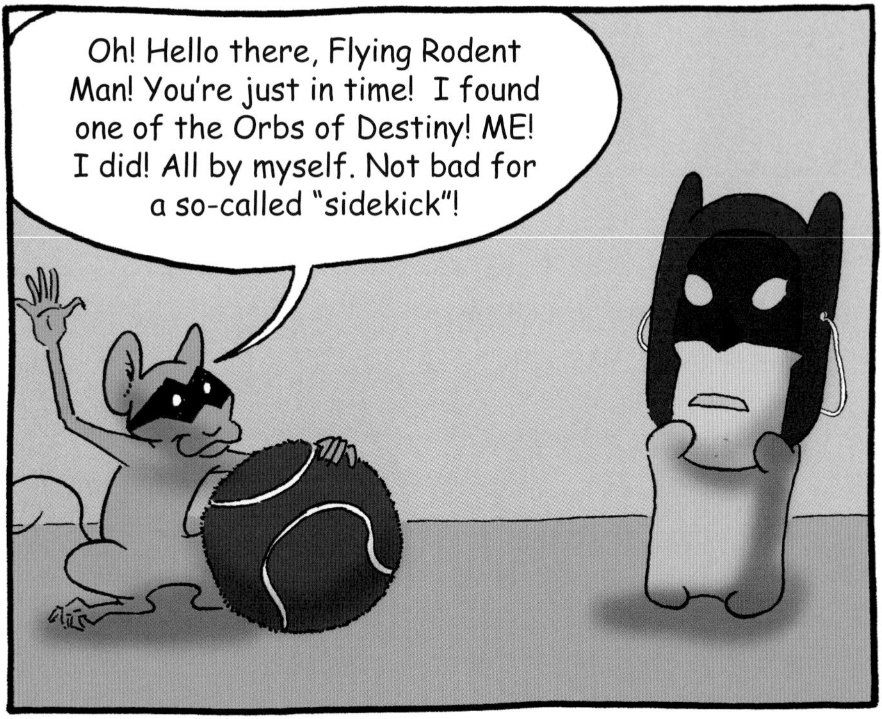
Oh! Hello there, Flying Rodent Man! You're just in time! I found one of the Orbs of Destiny! ME! I did! All by myself. Not bad for a so-called "sidekick"!

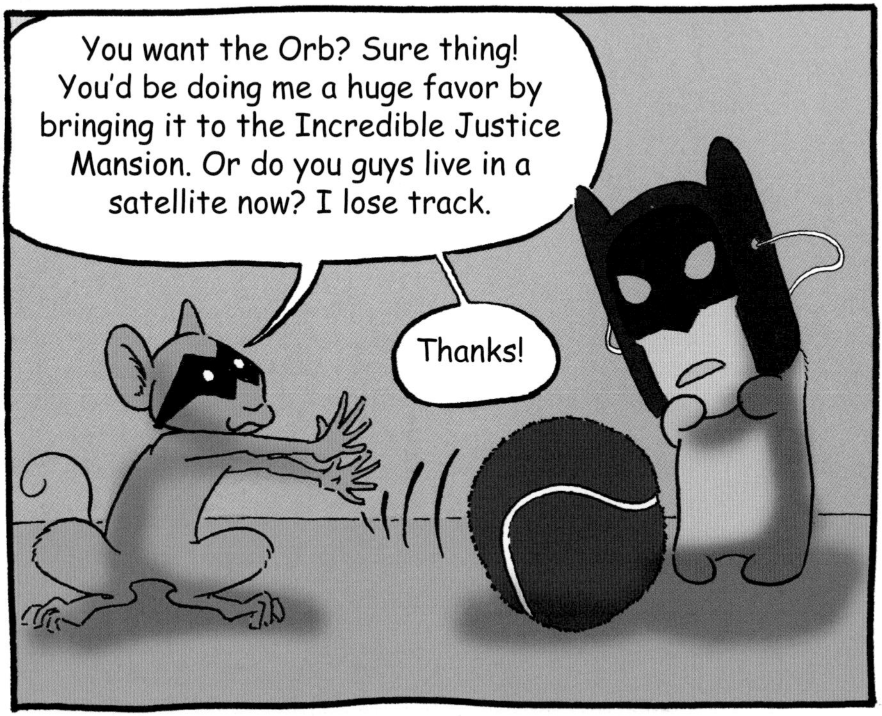
You want the Orb? Sure thing! You'd be doing me a huge favor by bringing it to the Incredible Justice Mansion. Or do you guys live in a satellite now? I lose track.
Thanks!

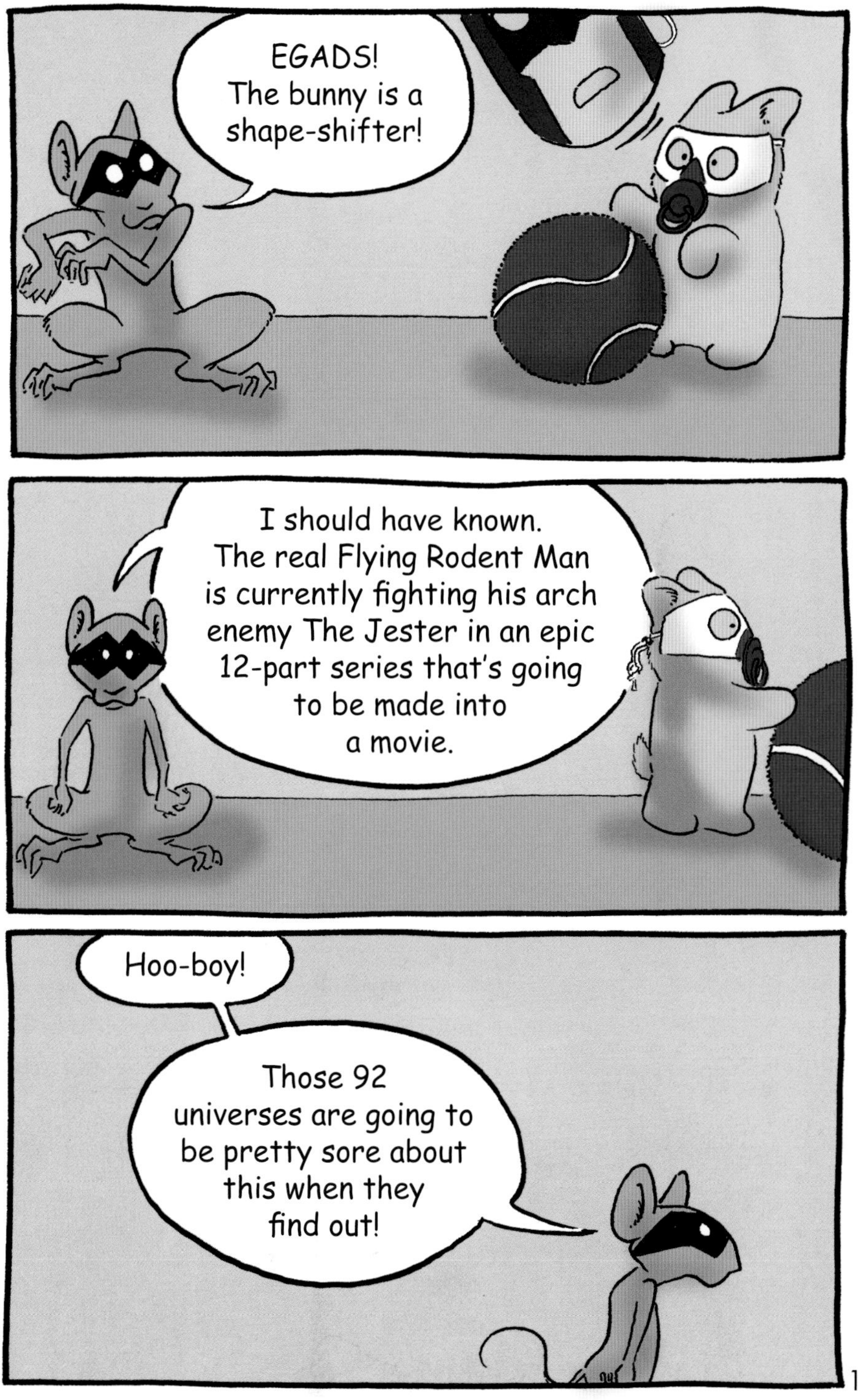
EGADS! The bunny is a shape-shifter!
I should have known. The real Flying Rodent Man is currently fighting his arch enemy The Jester in an epic 12-part series that's going to be made into a movie.
Hoo-boy!
Those 92 universes are going to be pretty sore about this when they find out!

•CHAPTER SEVEN•

SUPERCAT VS. DR. LAGOMORPH

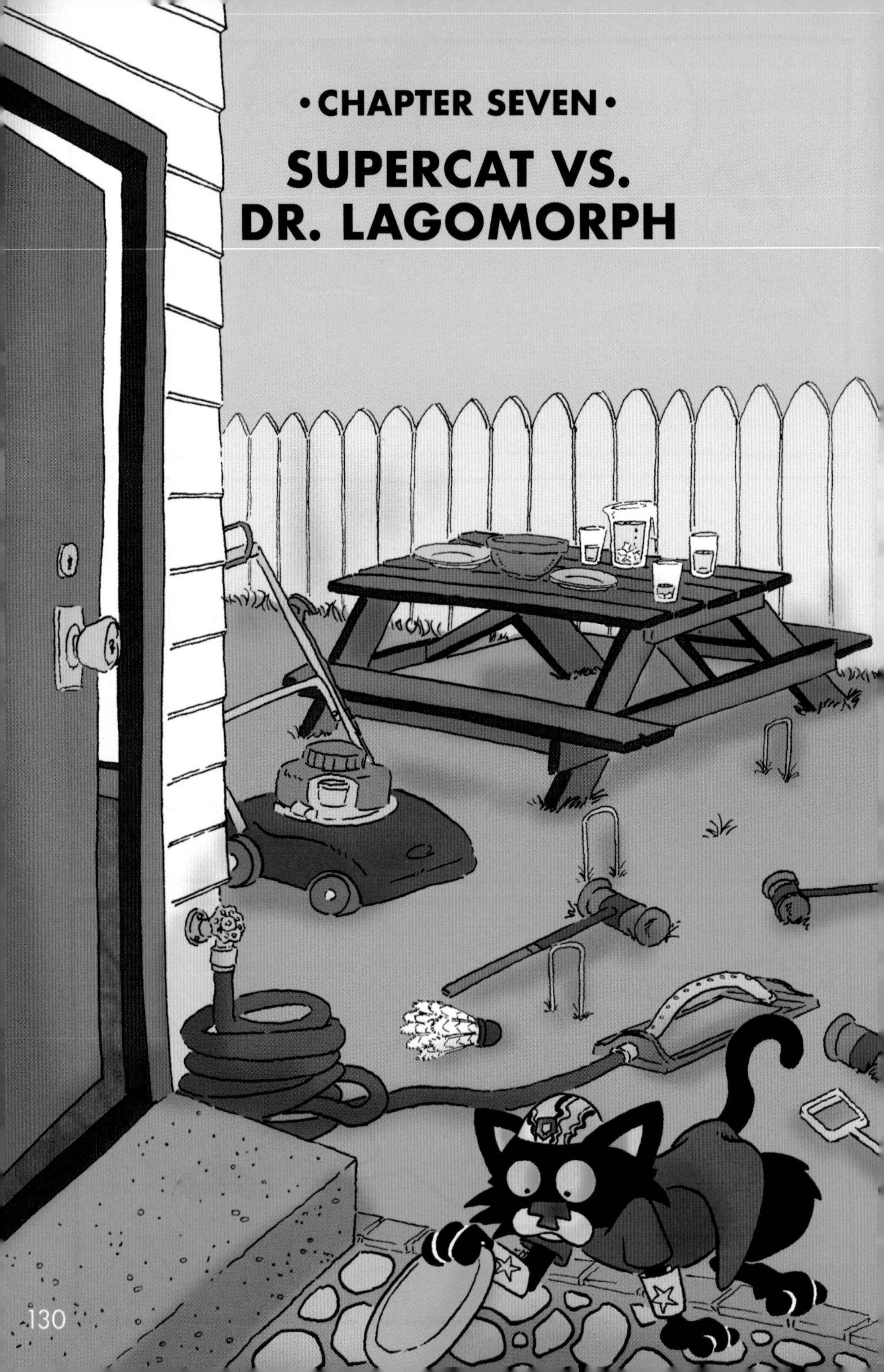

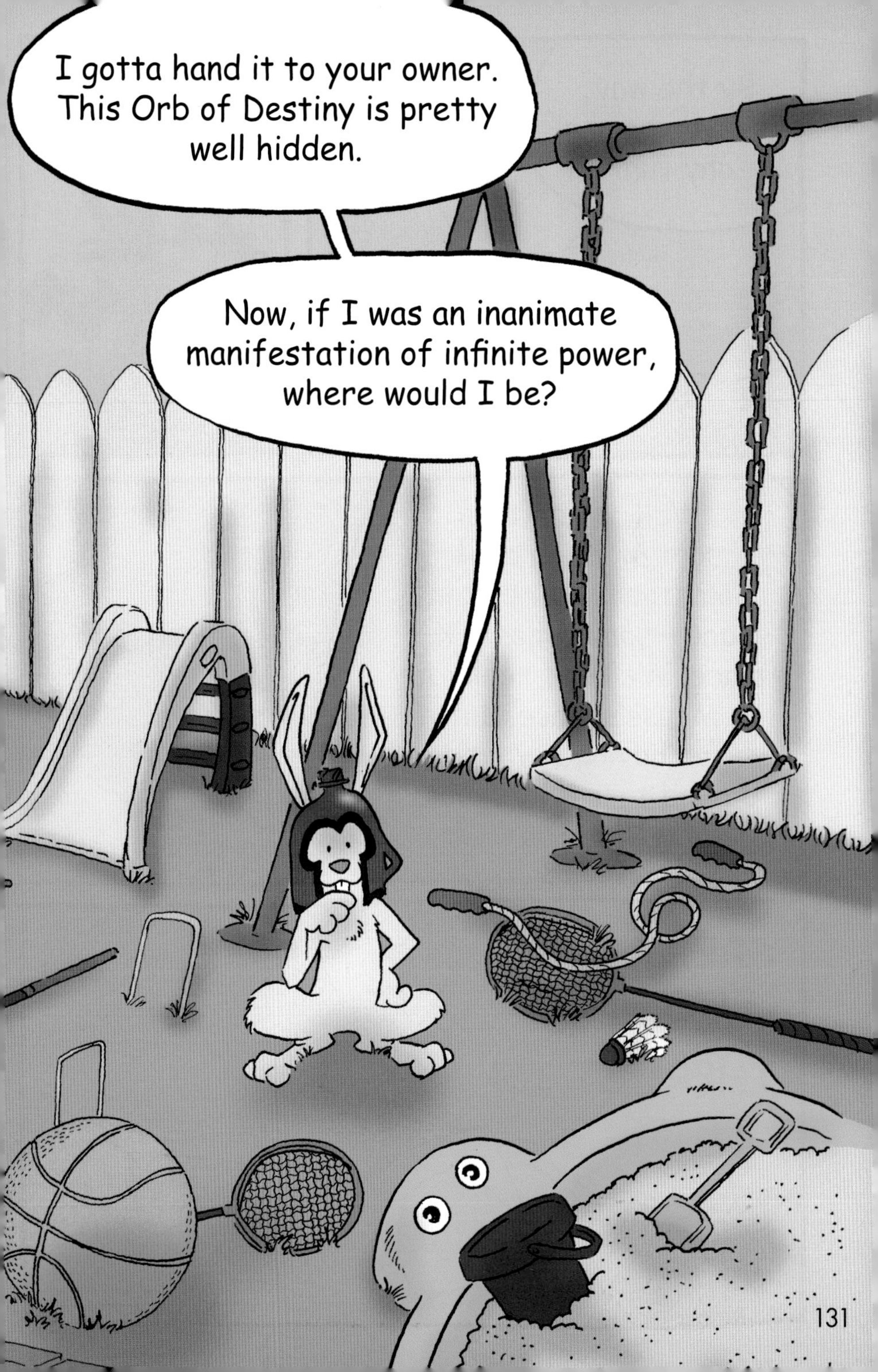
I gotta hand it to your owner. This Orb of Destiny is pretty well hidden.
Now, if I was an inanimate manifestation of infinite power, where would I be?

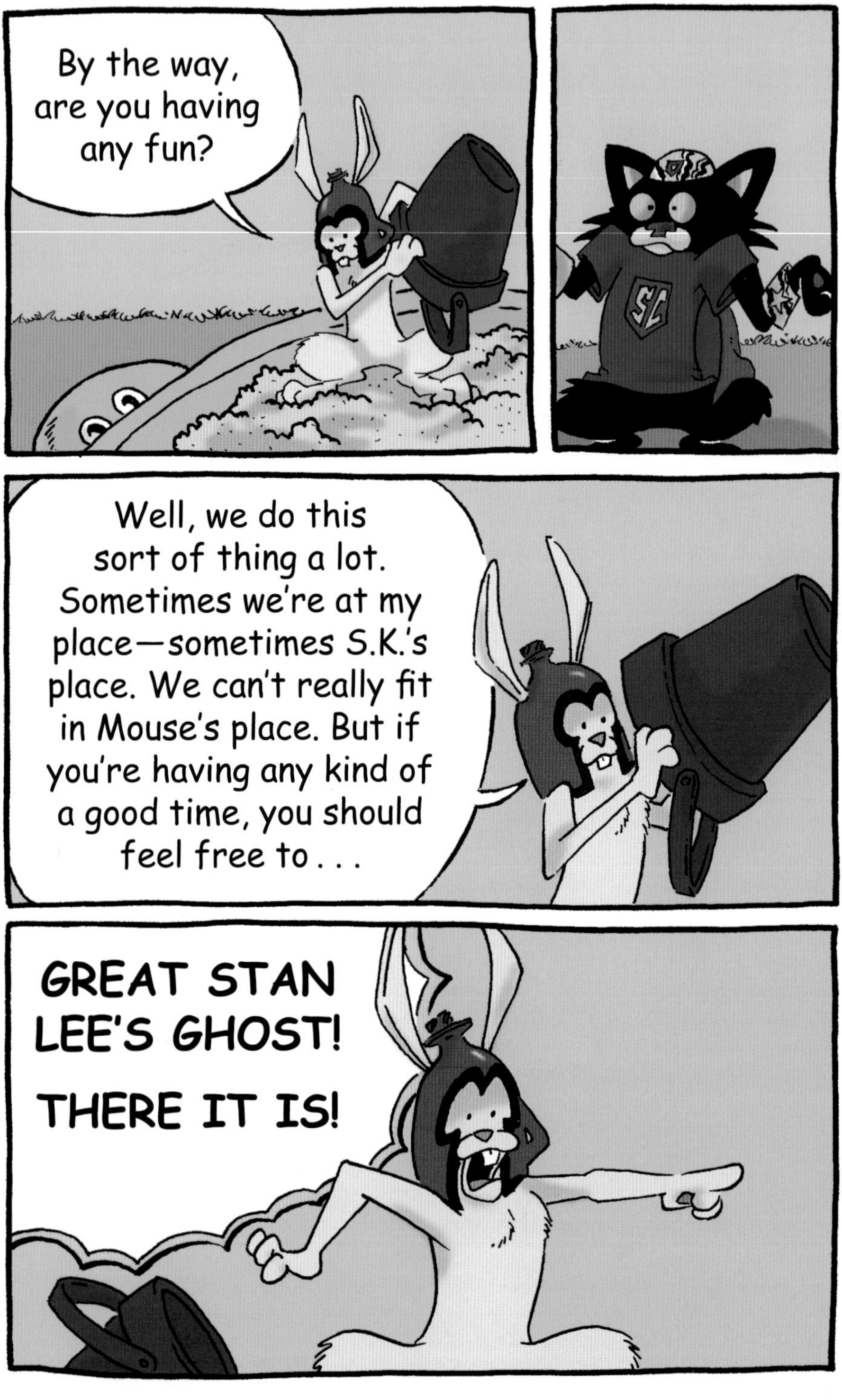
By the way, are you having any fun?
Well, we do this sort of thing a lot. Sometimes we're at my place—sometimes S.K.'s place. We can't really fit in Mouse's place. But if you're having any kind of a good time, you should feel free to . . .
GREAT STAN LEE'S GHOST!
THERE IT IS!

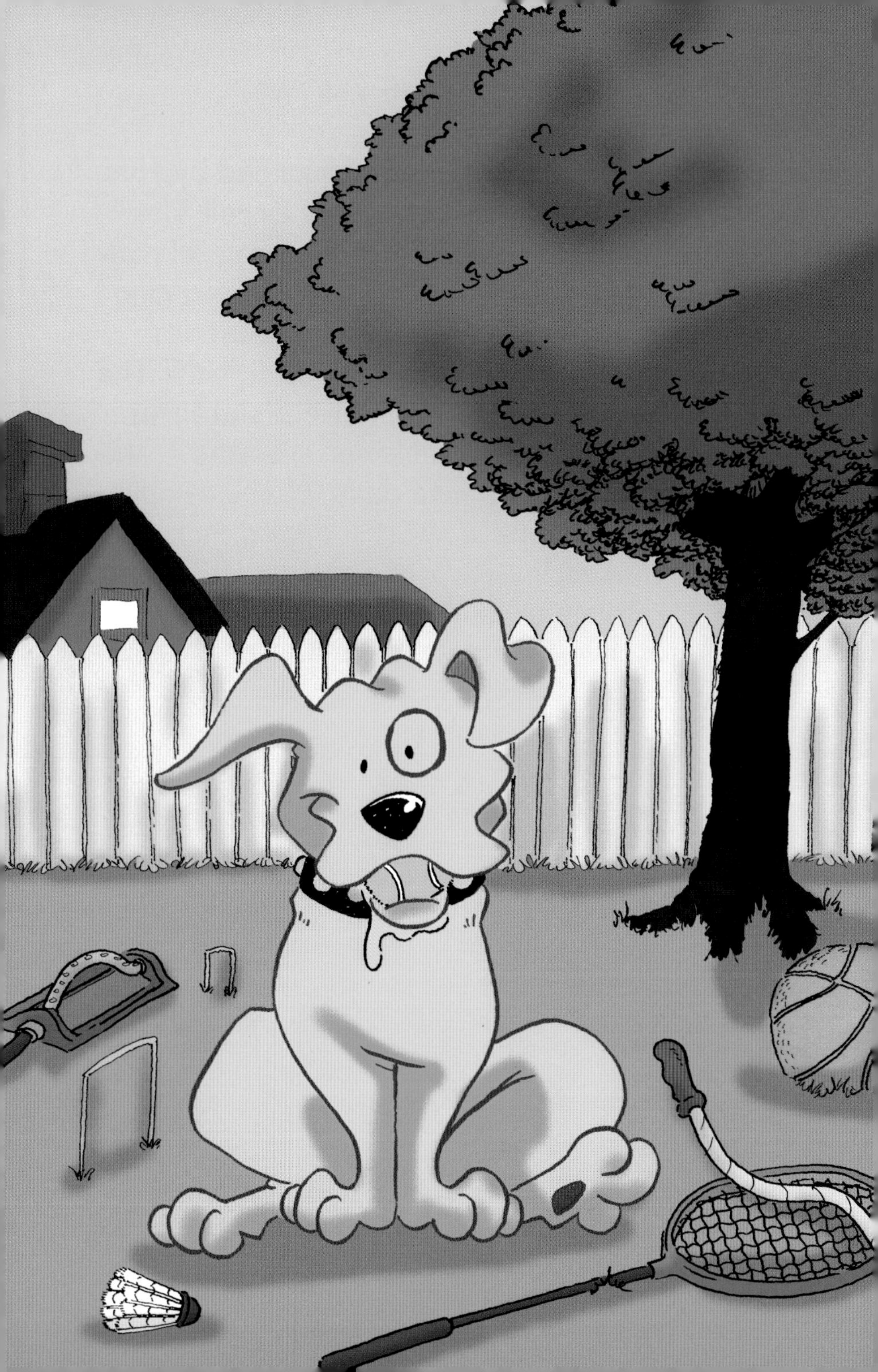

I SHOULD HAVE KNOWN!

The Orb of Destiny is being guarded by the Moist Slobberbeast of Planet Drool! The first of us to pry it from his all-powerful maw will possess it. But beware! Its ear-piercing howl can crack cities... wait... countries... no, wait... THE ENTIRE WORLD in half! The deadly lasers from its eyes have disintegrated entire planets... wait... solar systems... no, wait... GALAXIES into dust! If you remove its head, two more... wait... eight more... no, wait... A HUNDRED AND NINETEEN more will grow back in its place! Many brave souls have perished trying to...

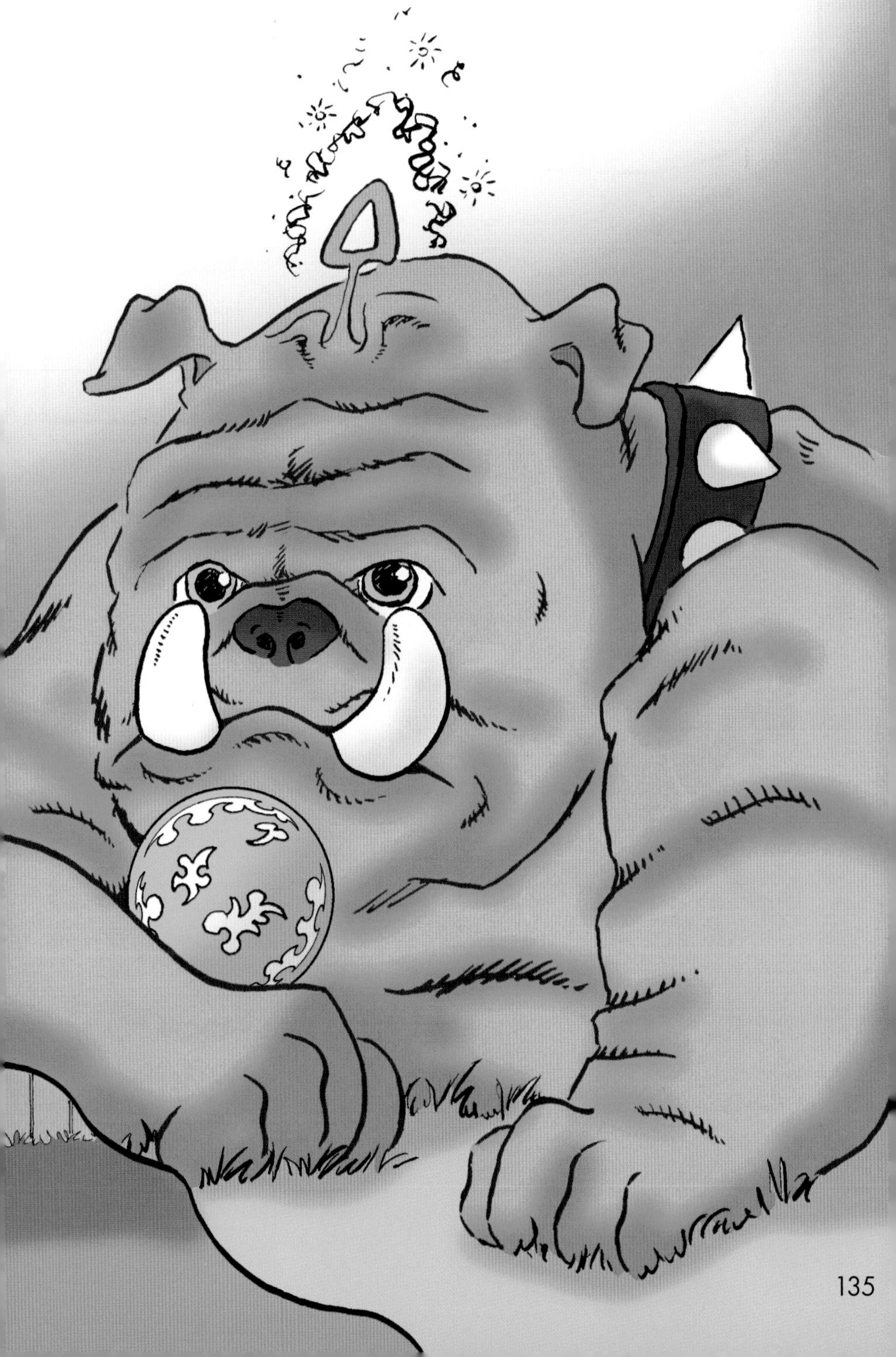

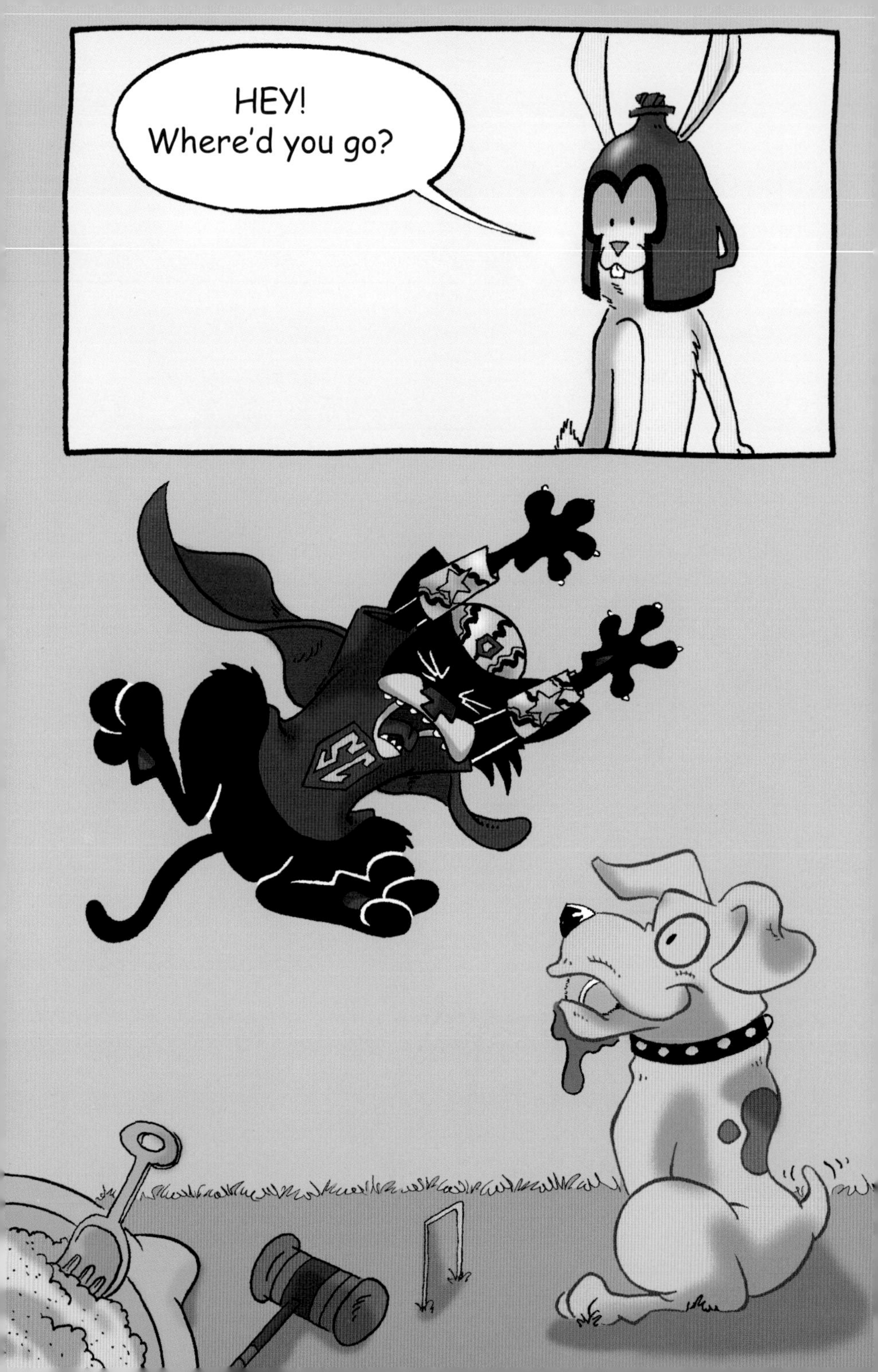
HEY! Where'd you go?

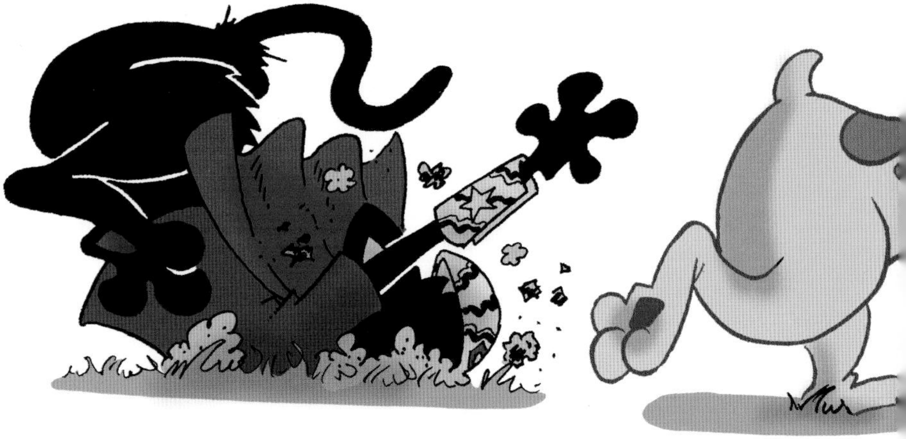

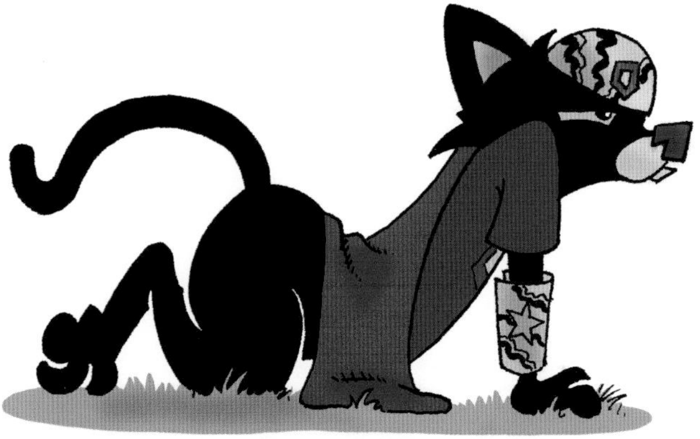

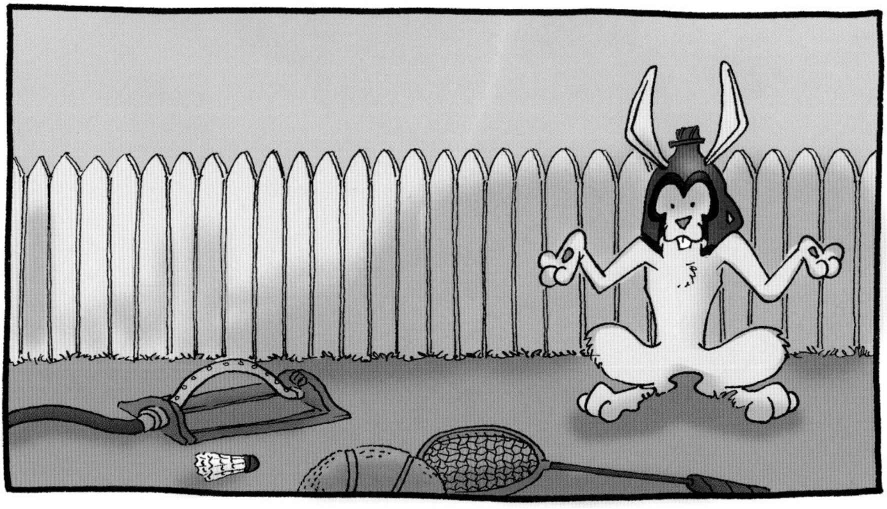

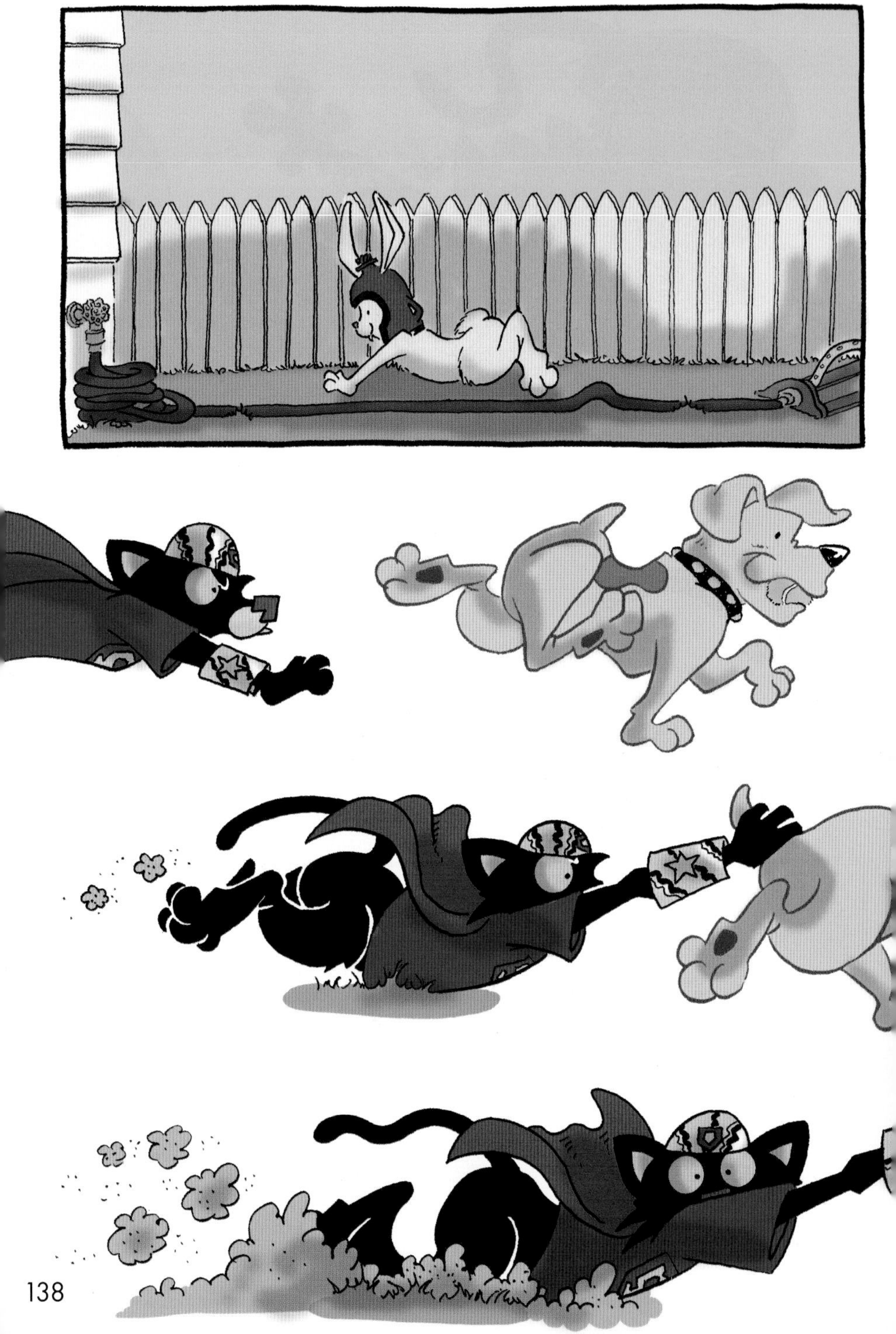

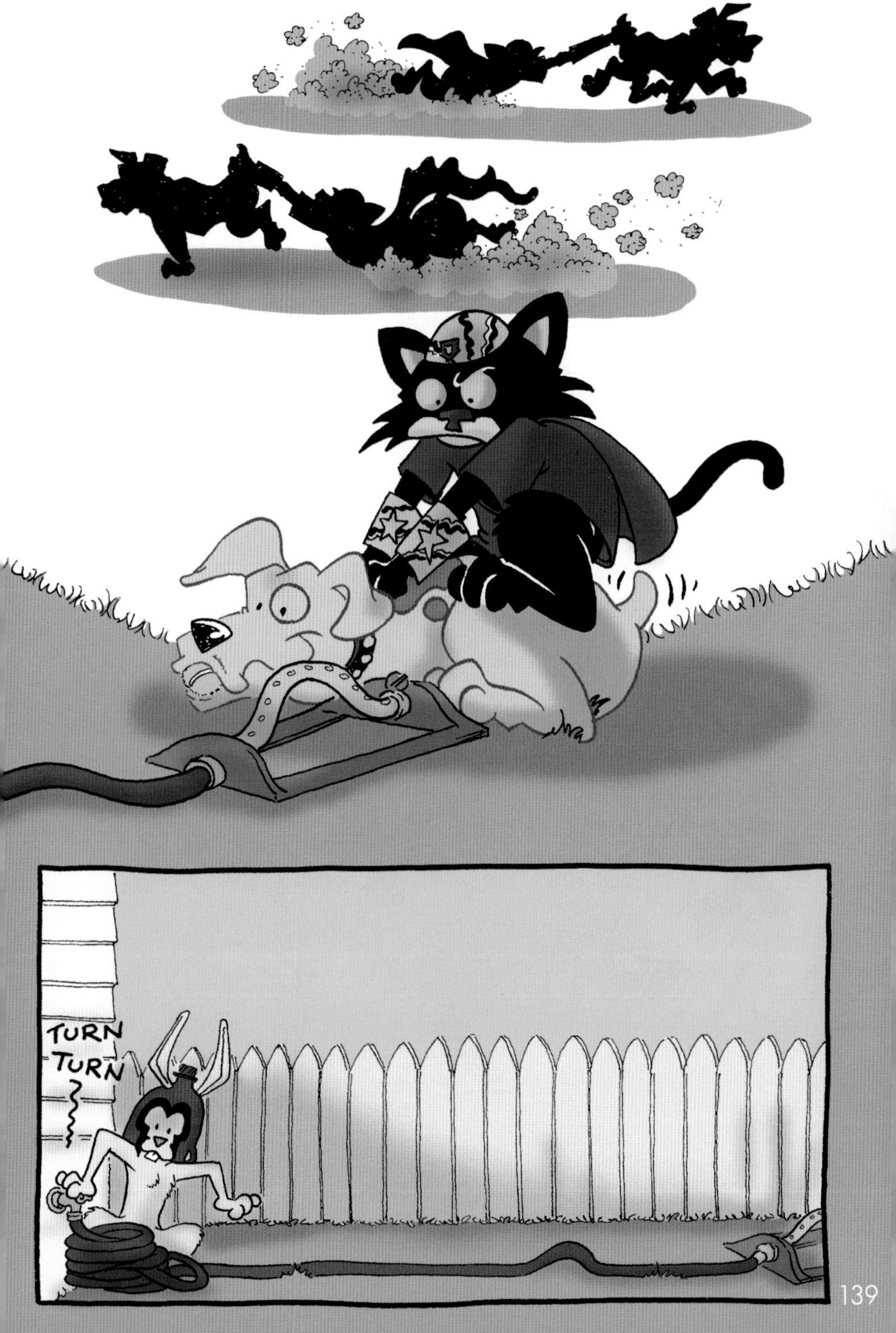
TURN
TURN

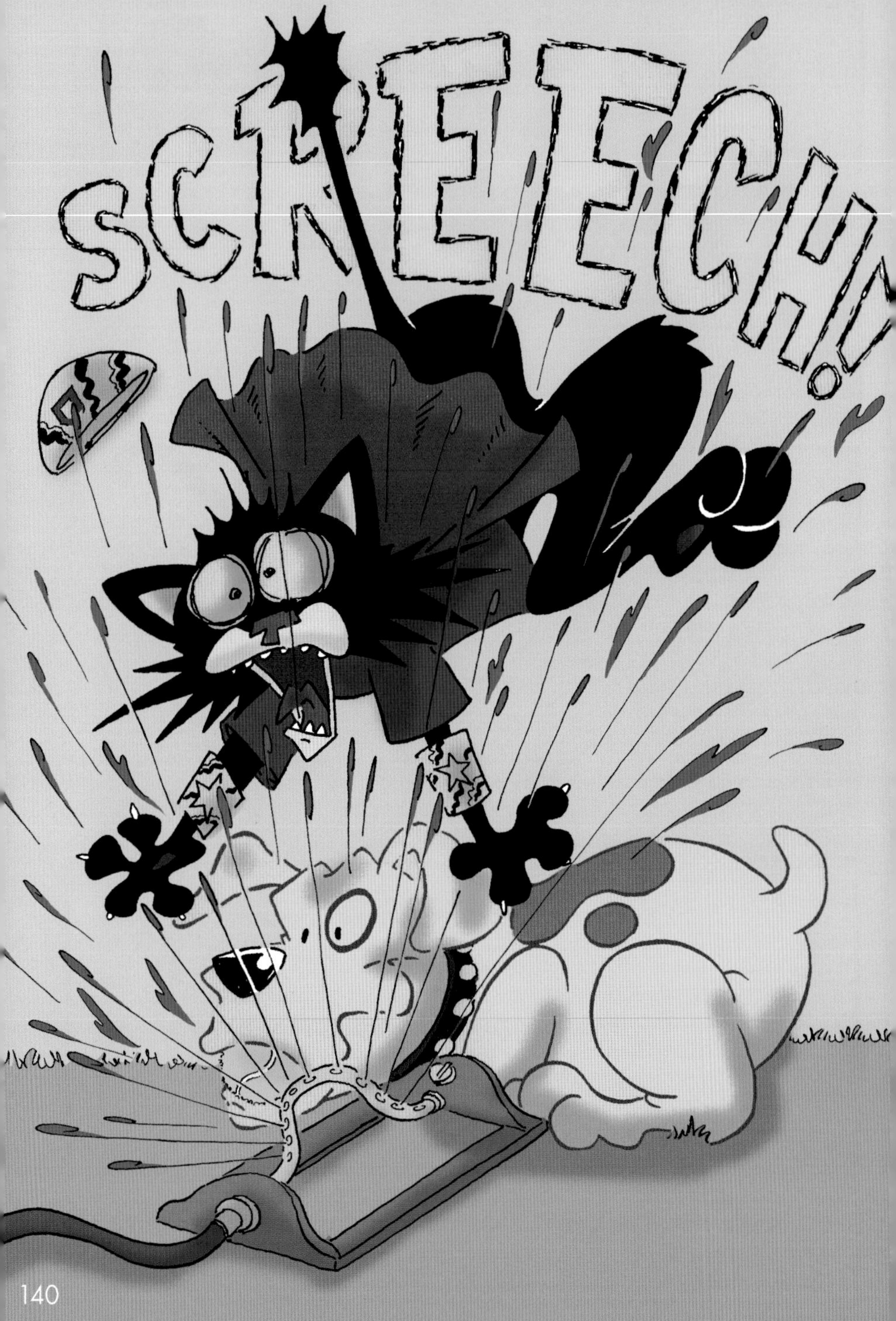
SCREECH!

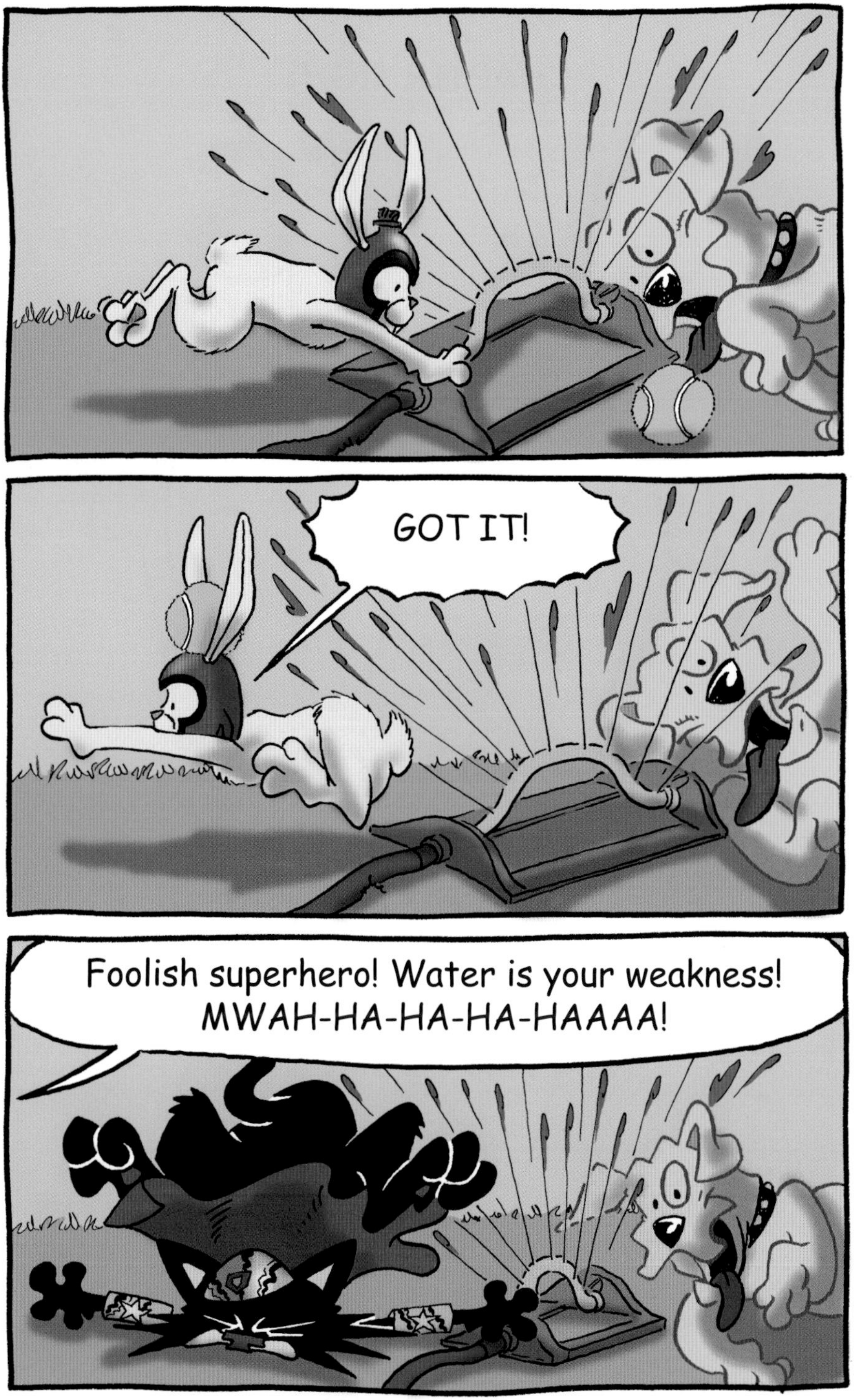
GOT IT!
Foolish superhero! Water is your weakness! MWAH-HA-HA-HA-HAAAA!

• CHAPTER EIGHT •

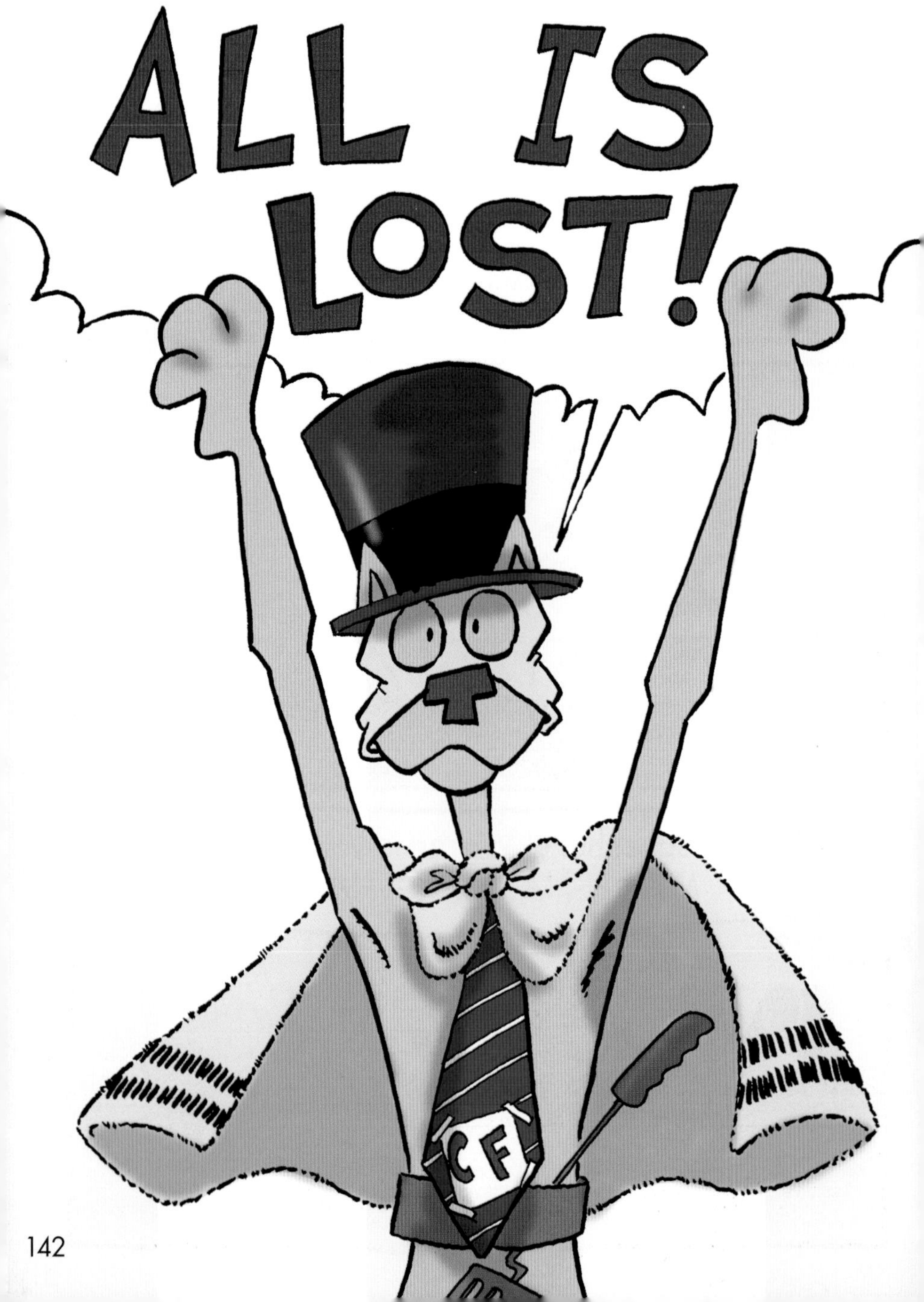
ALL IS LOST!

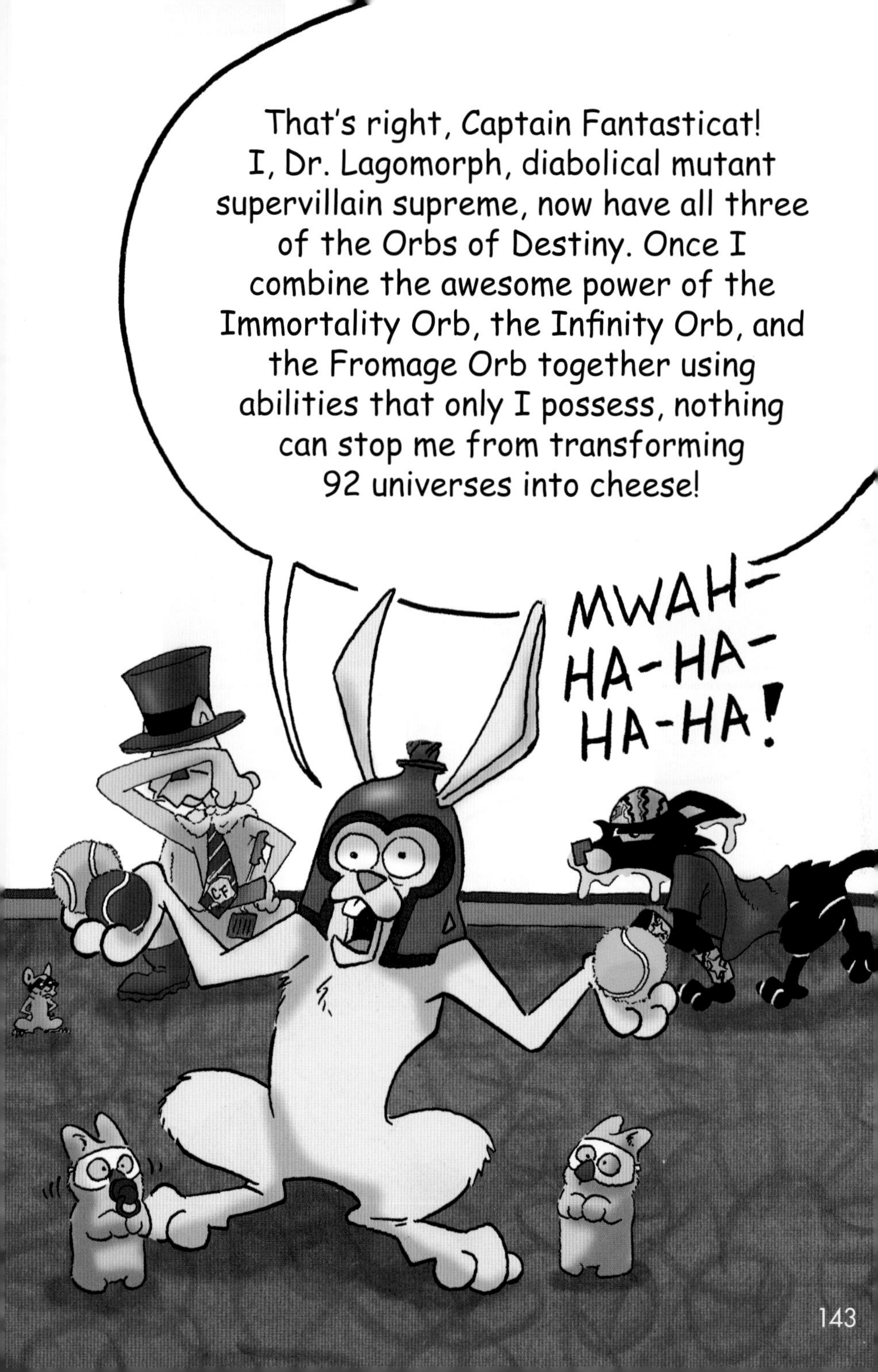
That's right, Captain Fantasticat! I, Dr. Lagomorph, diabolical mutant supervillain supreme, now have all three of the Orbs of Destiny. Once I combine the awesome power of the Immortality Orb, the Infinity Orb, and the Fromage Orb together using abilities that only I possess, nothing can stop me from transforming 92 universes into cheese!
MWAH-HA-HA-HA-HA!
CF

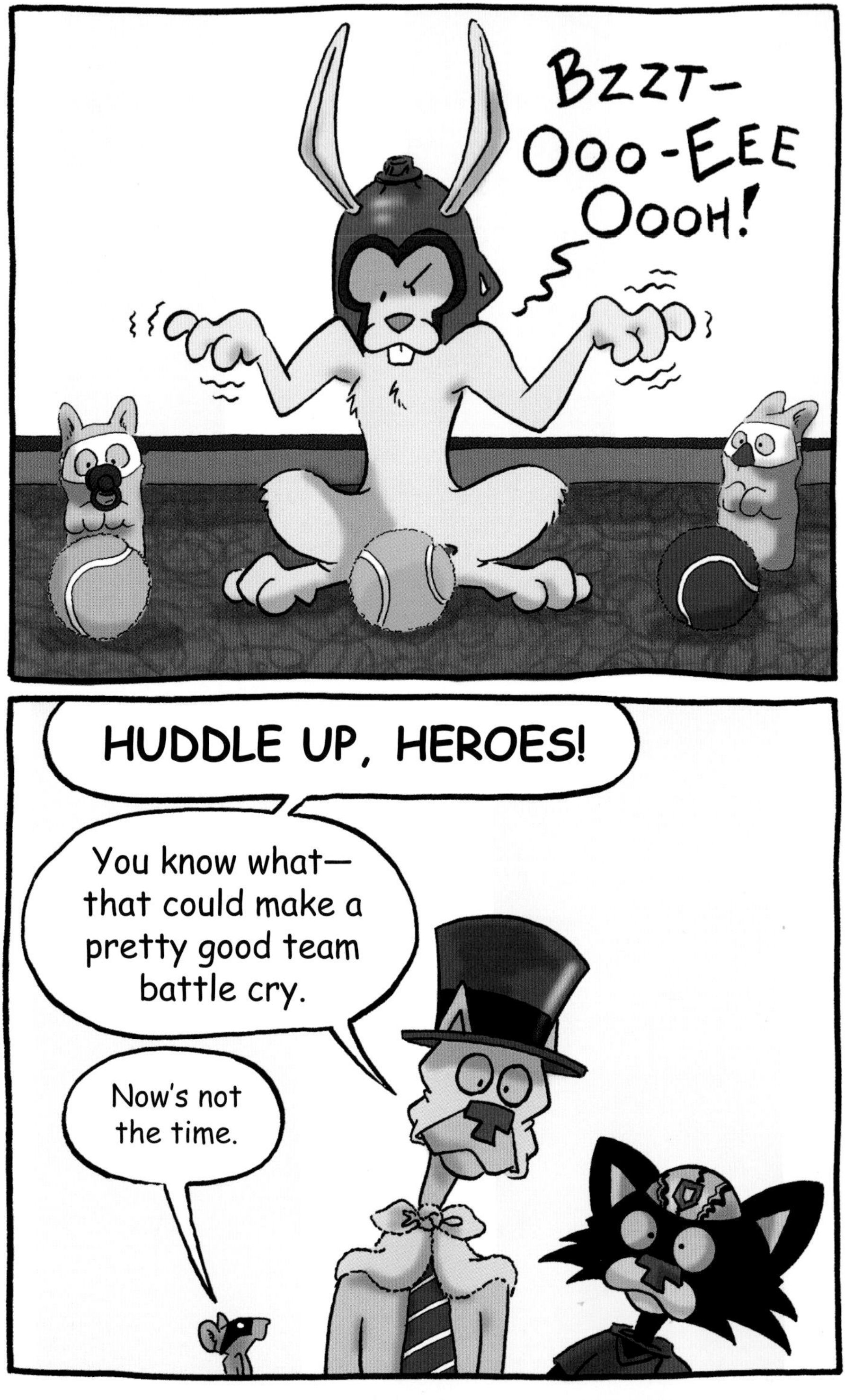
BZZT—OOO-EEE OOOH!
HUDDLE UP, HEROES!
You know what—that could make a pretty good team battle cry.
Now's not the time.

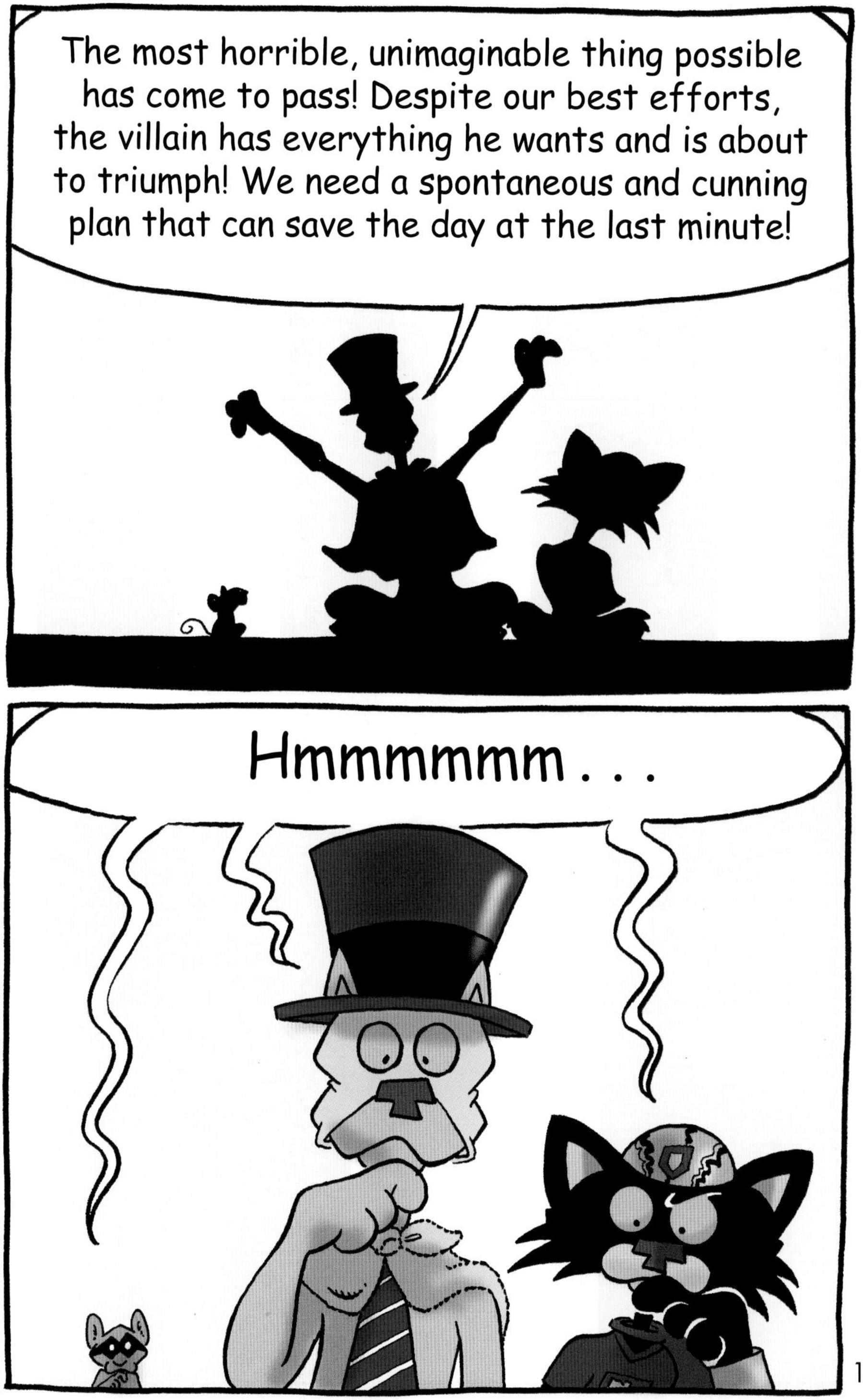
The most horrible, unimaginable thing possible has come to pass! Despite our best efforts, the villain has everything he wants and is about to triumph! We need a spontaneous and cunning plan that can save the day at the last minute!
Hmmmmmm . . .

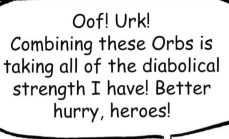

Oof! Urk!
Combining these Orbs is taking all of the diabolical strength I have! Better hurry, heroes!

BZZT-Ooo   EEE-OooH!

I've got it!

We'll turn back time and grab the Orbs before the villains find them!

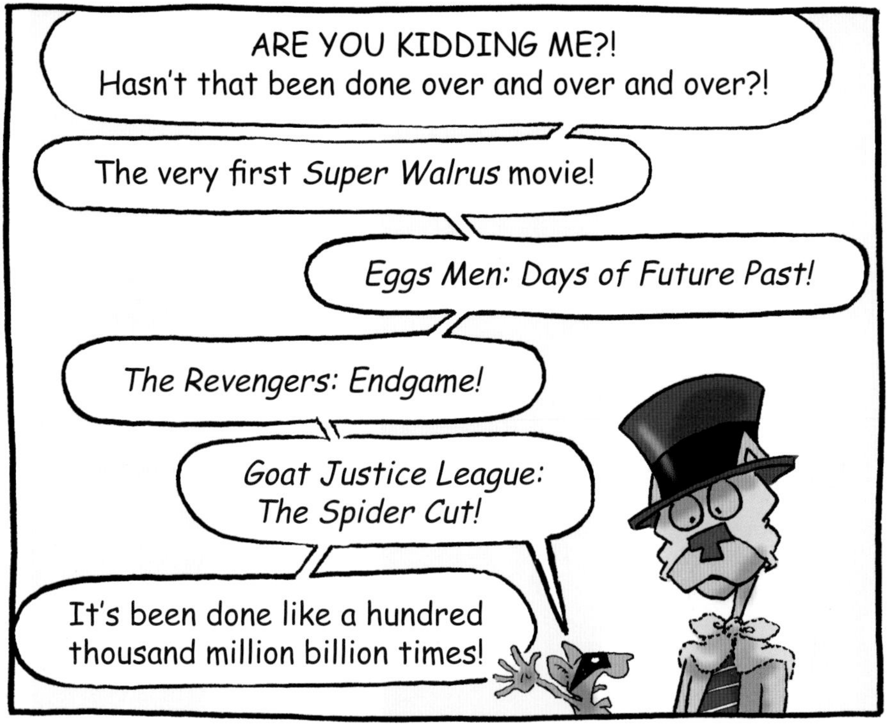
ARE YOU KIDDING ME?!
Hasn't that been done over and over and over?!
The very first Super Walrus movie!
Eggs Men: Days of Future Past!
The Revengers: Endgame!
Goat Justice League: The Spider Cut!
It's been done like a hundred thousand million billion times!
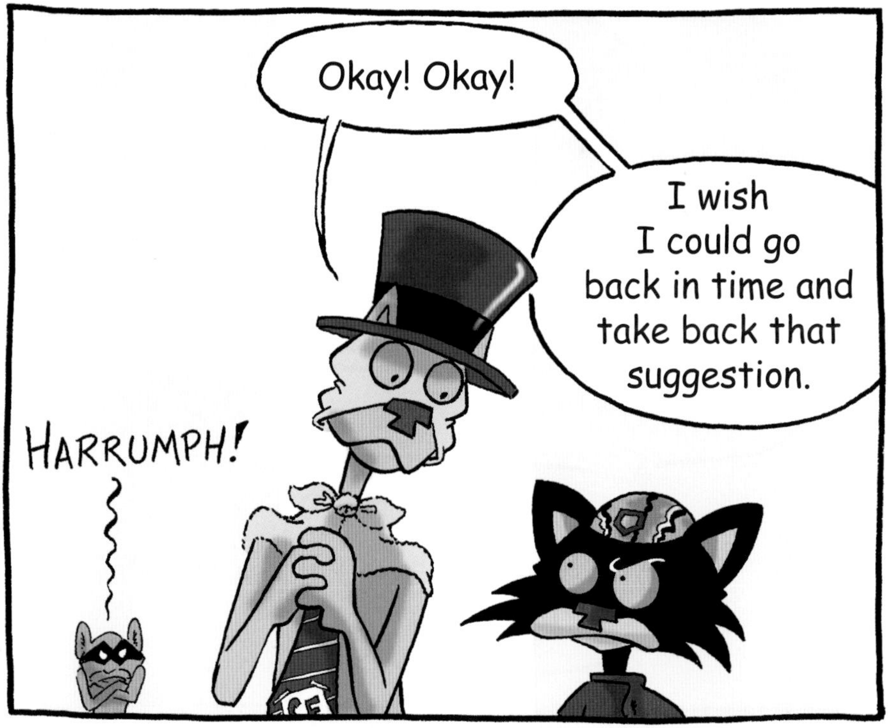
Okay! Okay!
I wish I could go back in time and take back that suggestion.
HARRUMPH!

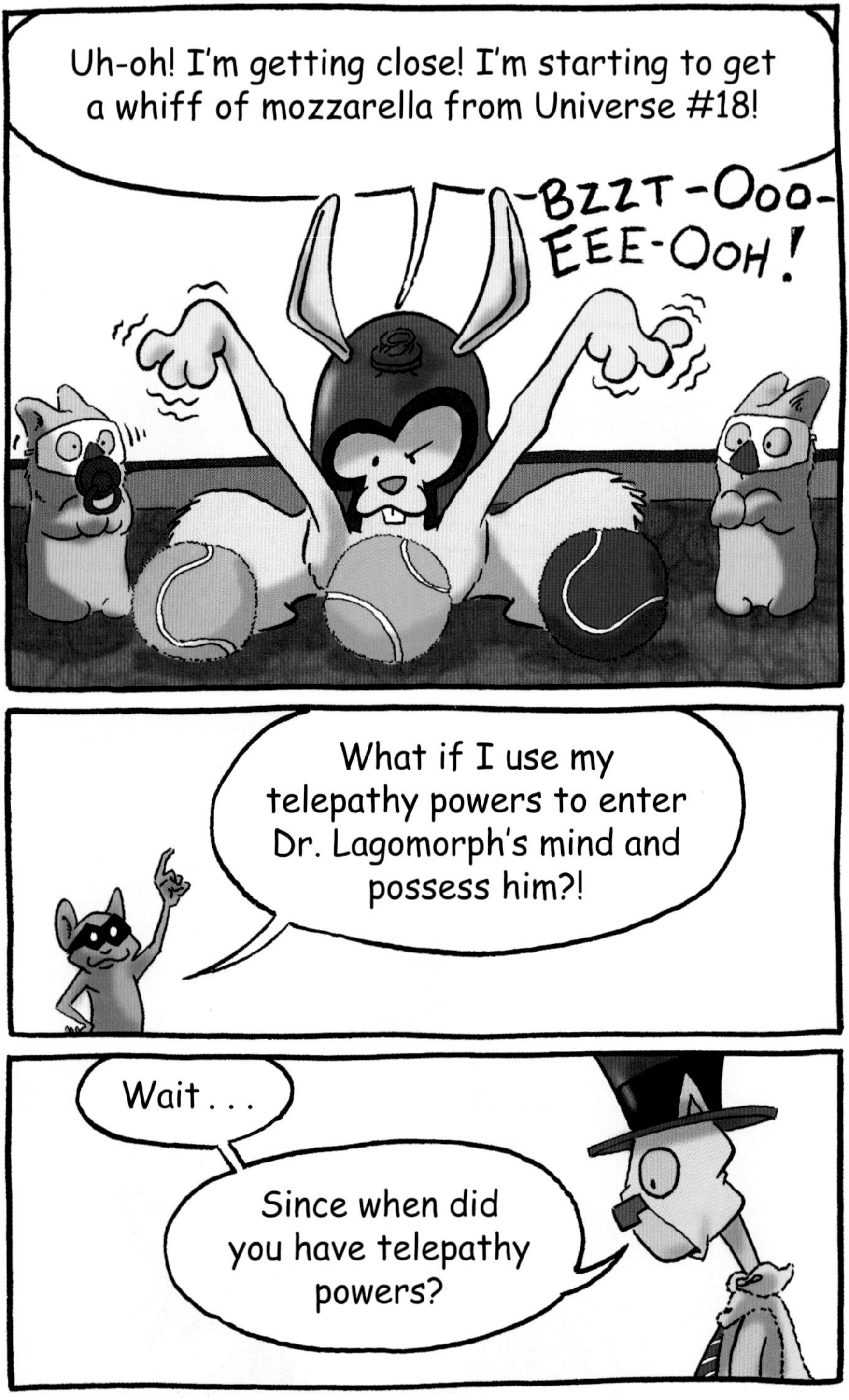
Uh-oh! I'm getting close! I'm starting to get a whiff of mozzarella from Universe #18!
-BZZT-OOO-EEE-OOH!
What if I use my telepathy powers to enter Dr. Lagomorph's mind and possess him?!
Wait . . .
Since when did you have telepathy powers?

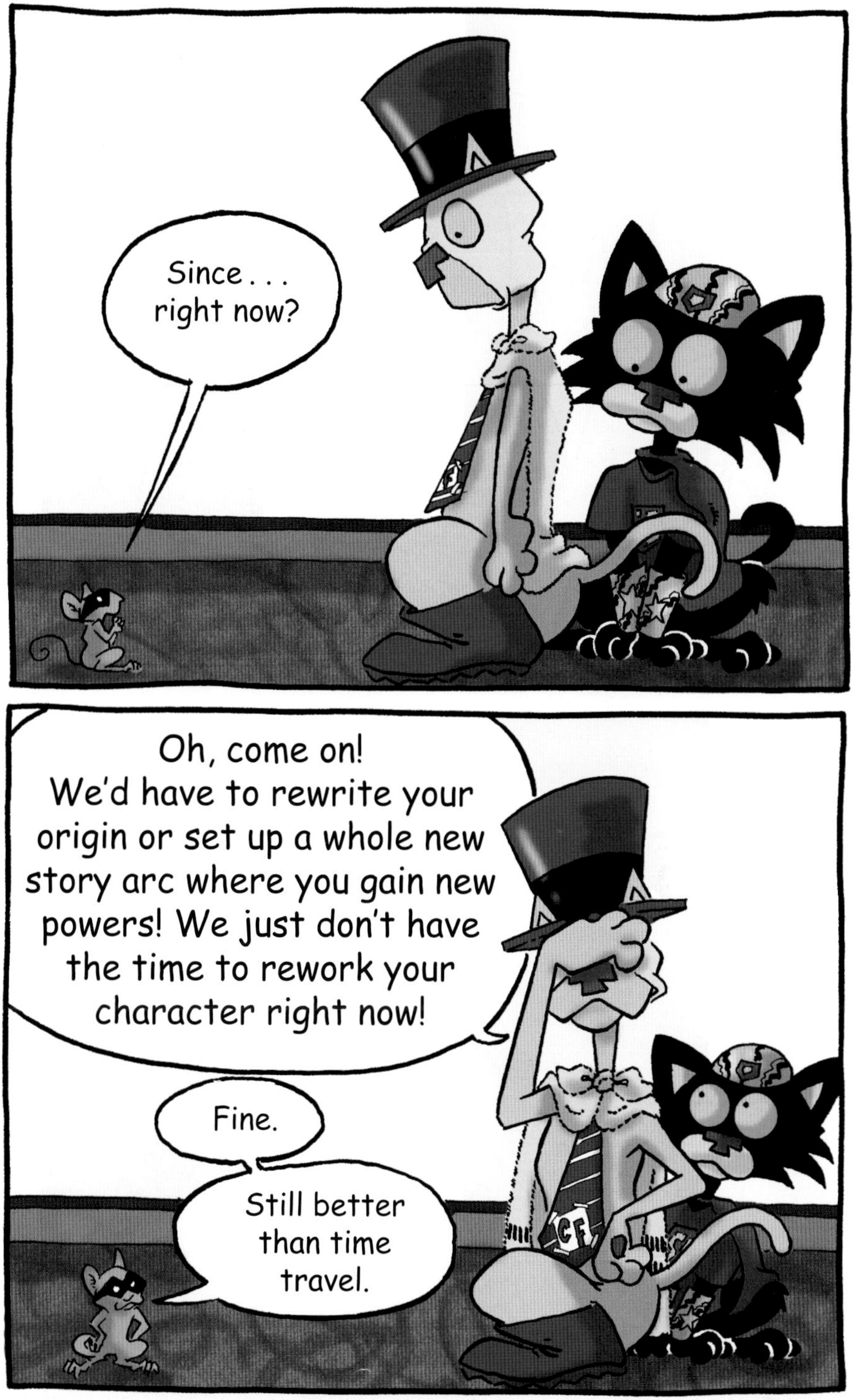
Since . . . right now?
Oh, come on! We'd have to rewrite your origin or set up a whole new story arc where you gain new powers! We just don't have the time to rework your character right now!
Fine.
Still better than time travel.

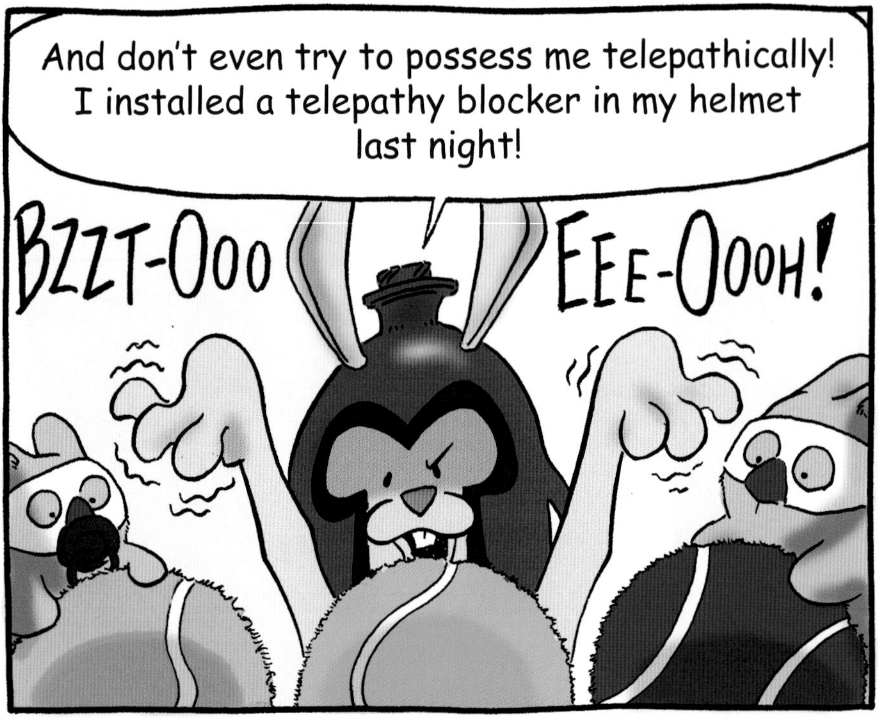
And don't even try to possess me telepathically! I installed a telepathy blocker in my helmet last night!
BZZT-OOO
EEE-OOOH!

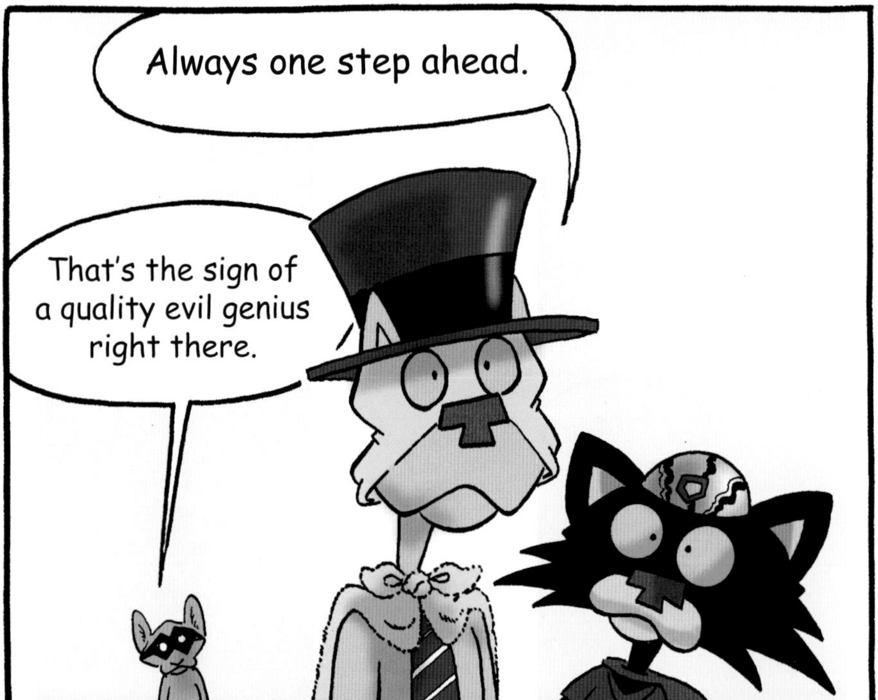
Always one step ahead.
That's the sign of a quality evil genius right there.

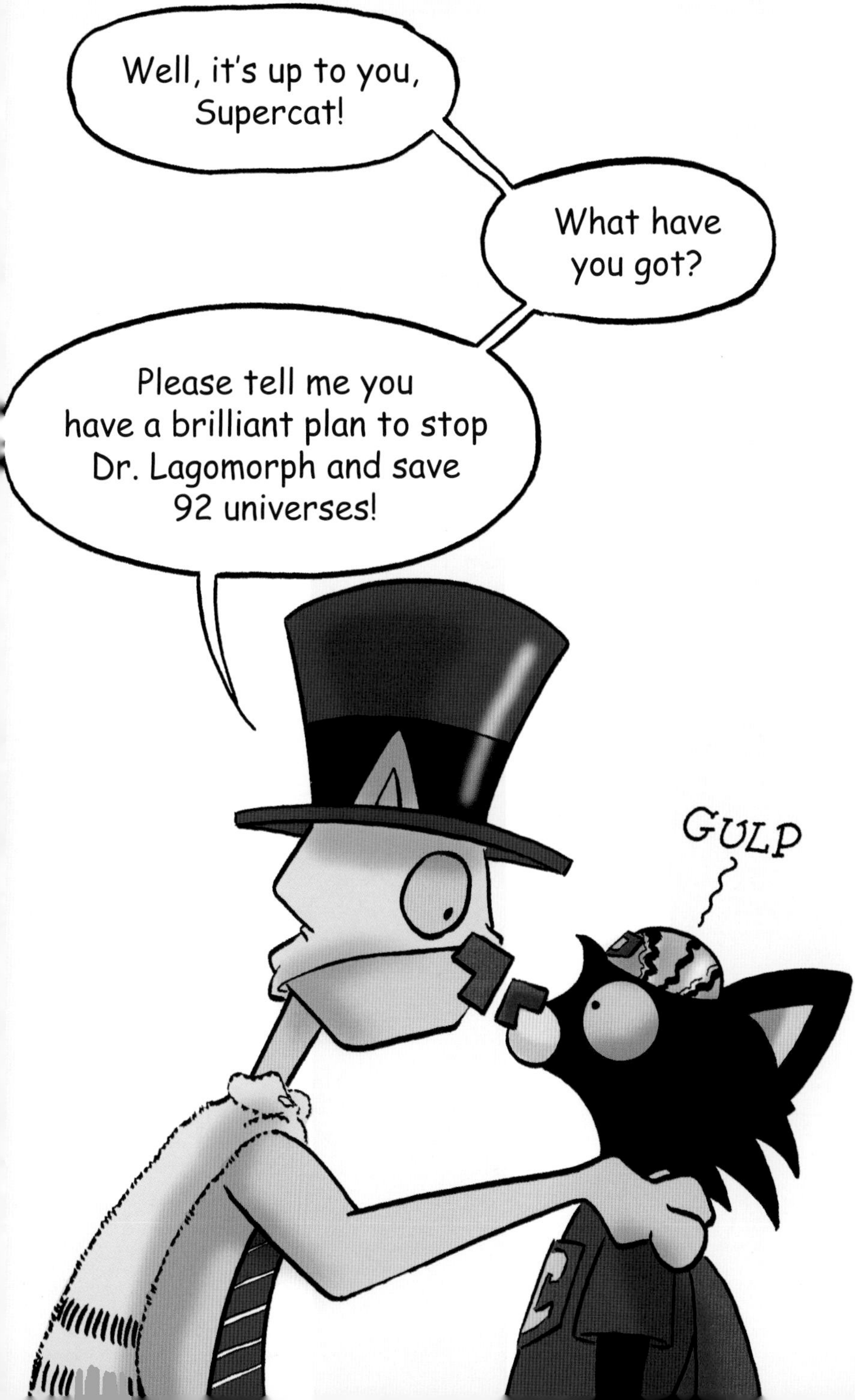
Well, it's up to you, Supercat!
What have you got?
Please tell me you have a brilliant plan to stop Dr. Lagomorph and save 92 universes!
GULP

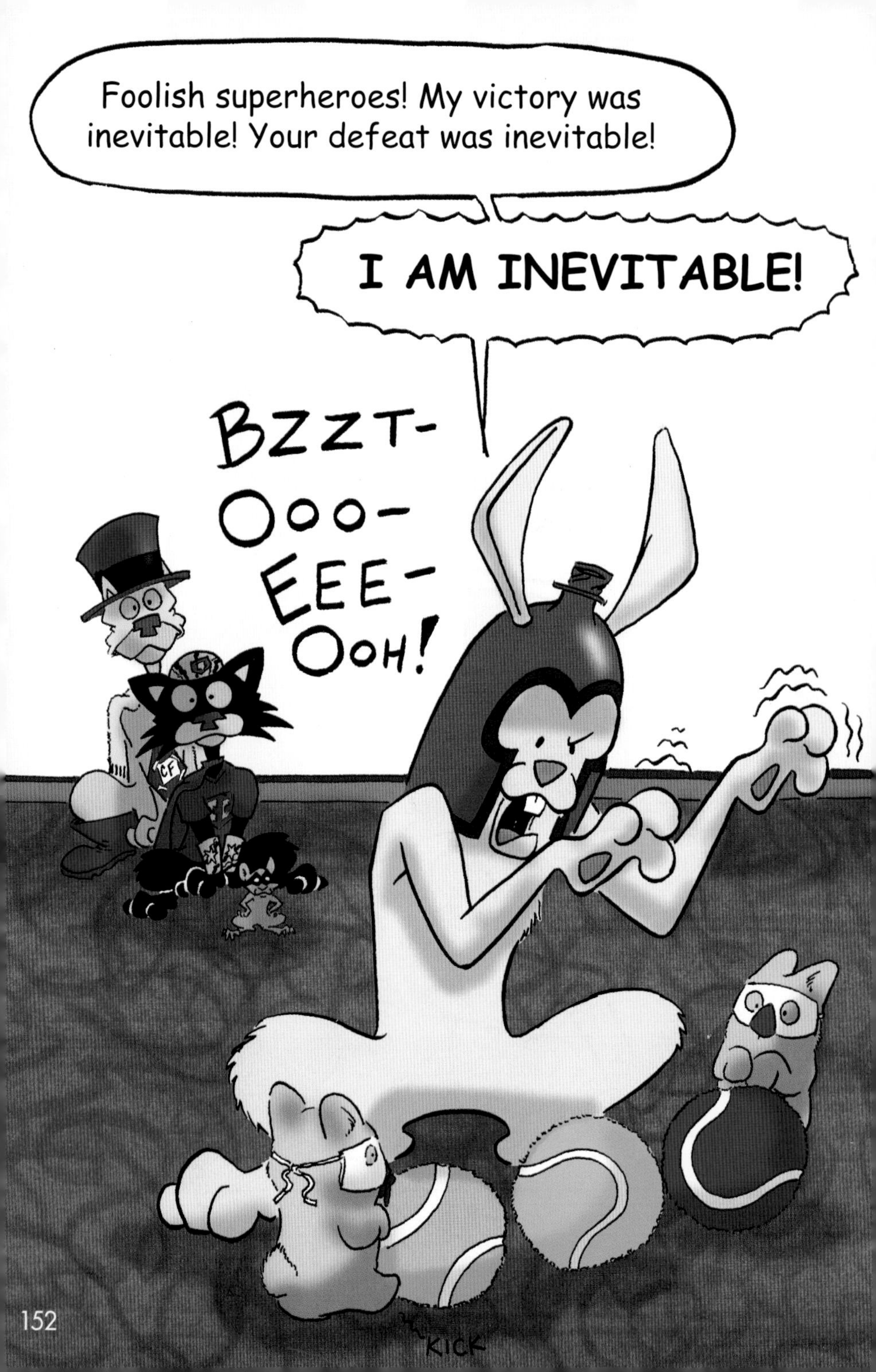

Foolish superheroes! My victory was inevitable! Your defeat was inevitable!
I AM INEVITABLE!
BZZT-OOO-EEE-OOH!
KICK

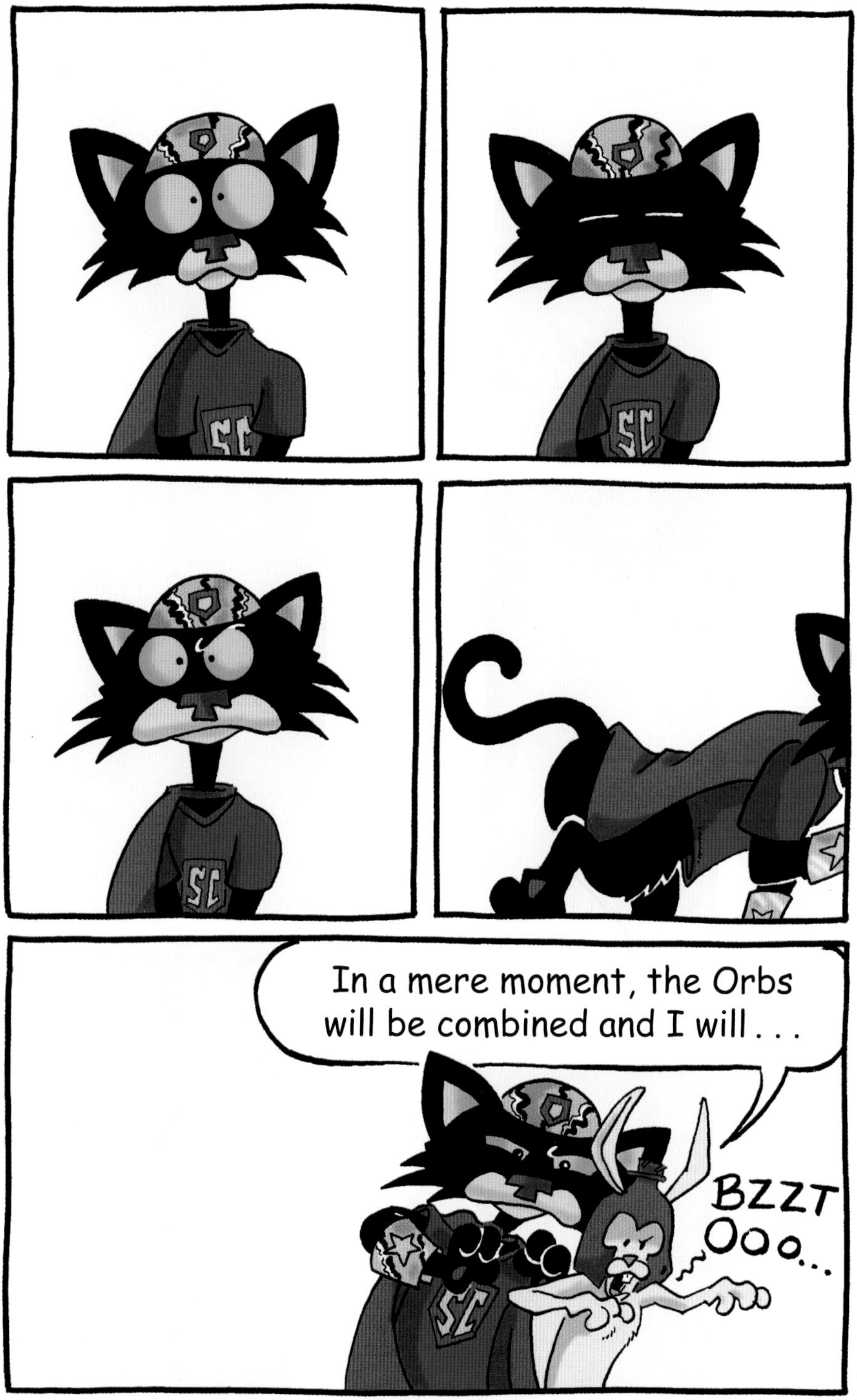
In a mere moment, the Orbs will be combined and I will . . .
BZZT
Ooo...

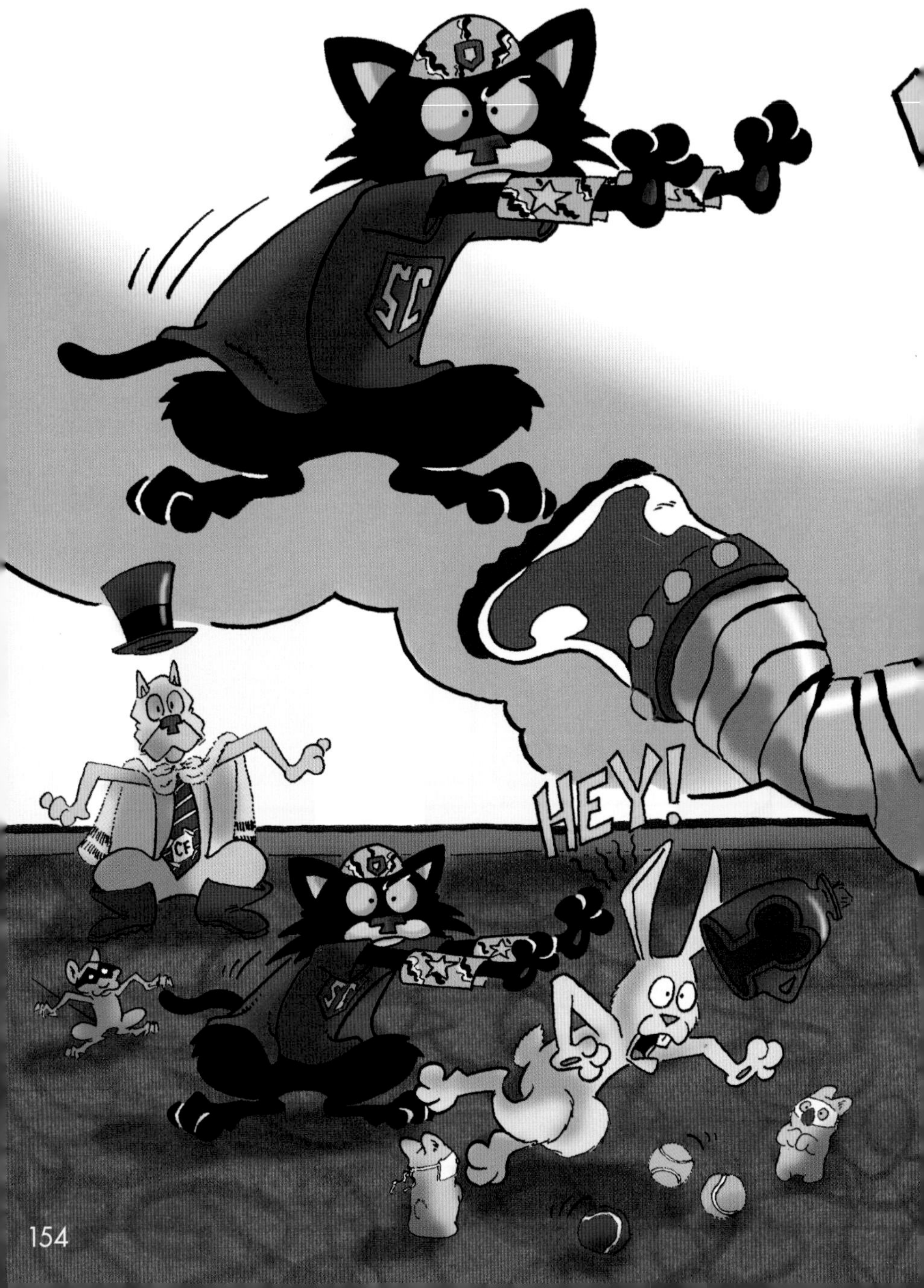
HEY!

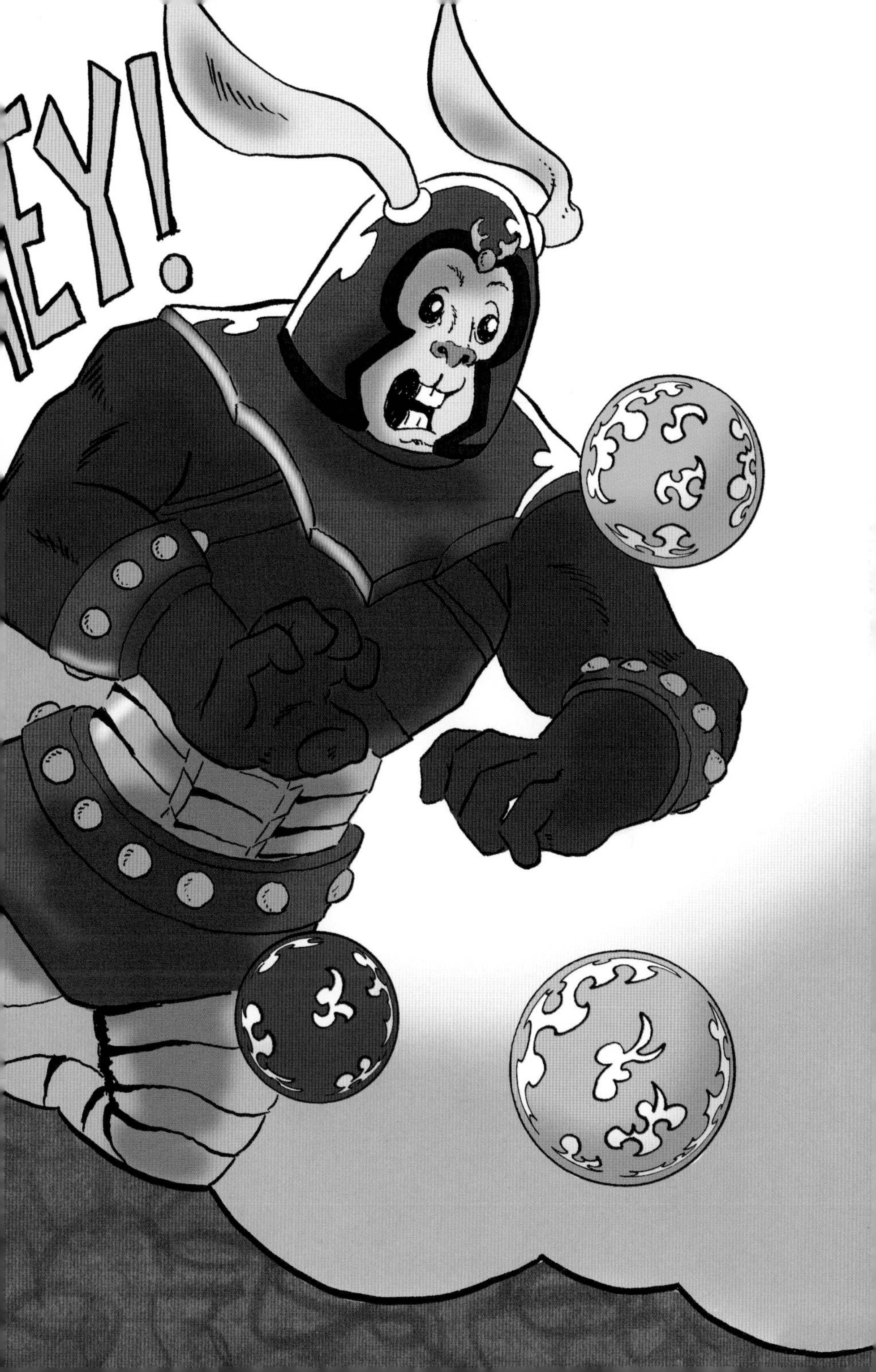
EY!

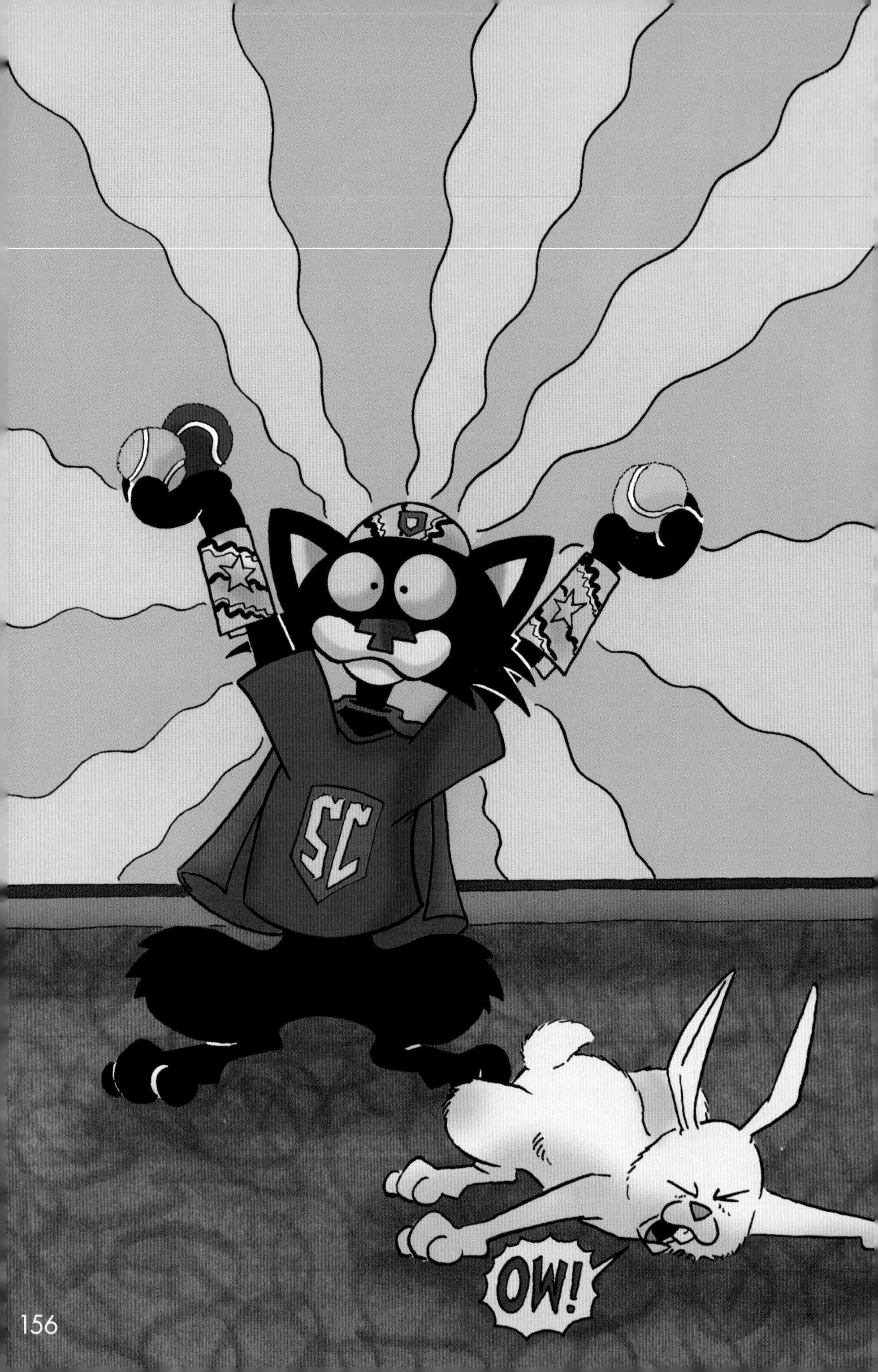
SC
OW!

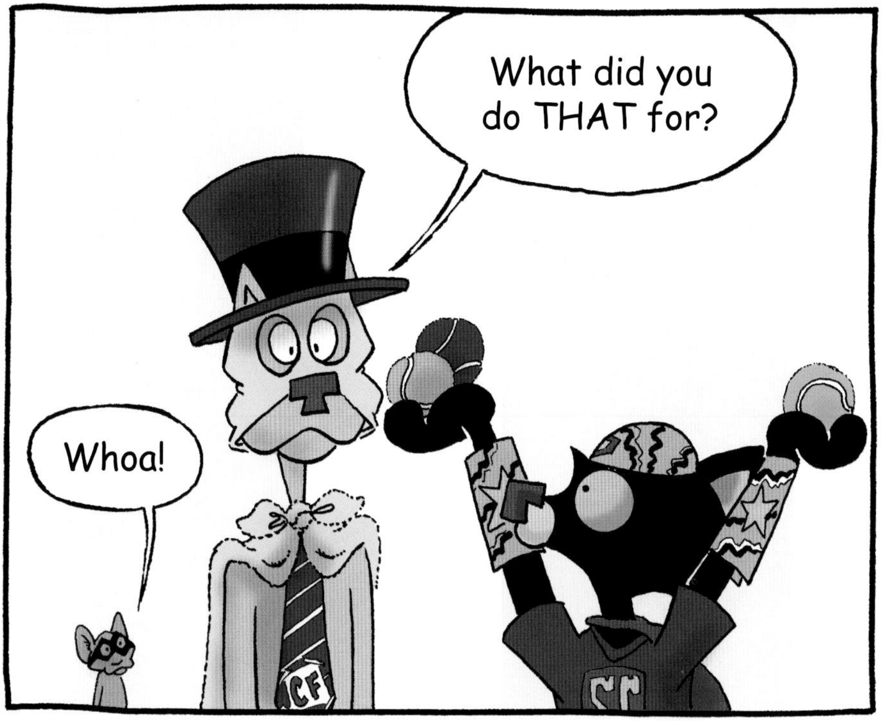
What did you do THAT for?
Whoa!

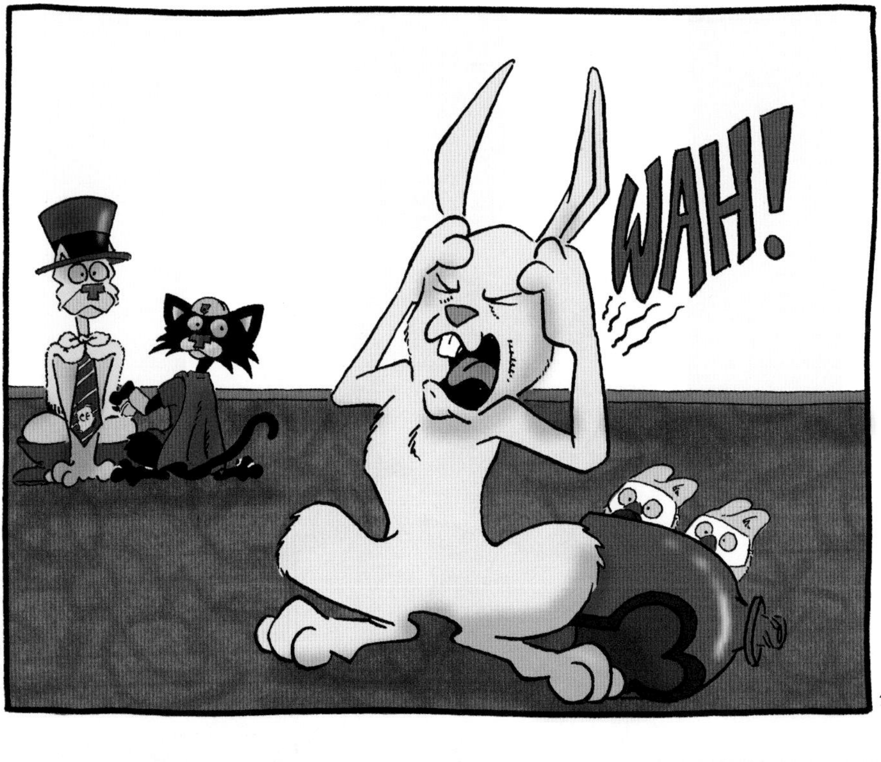
WAH!

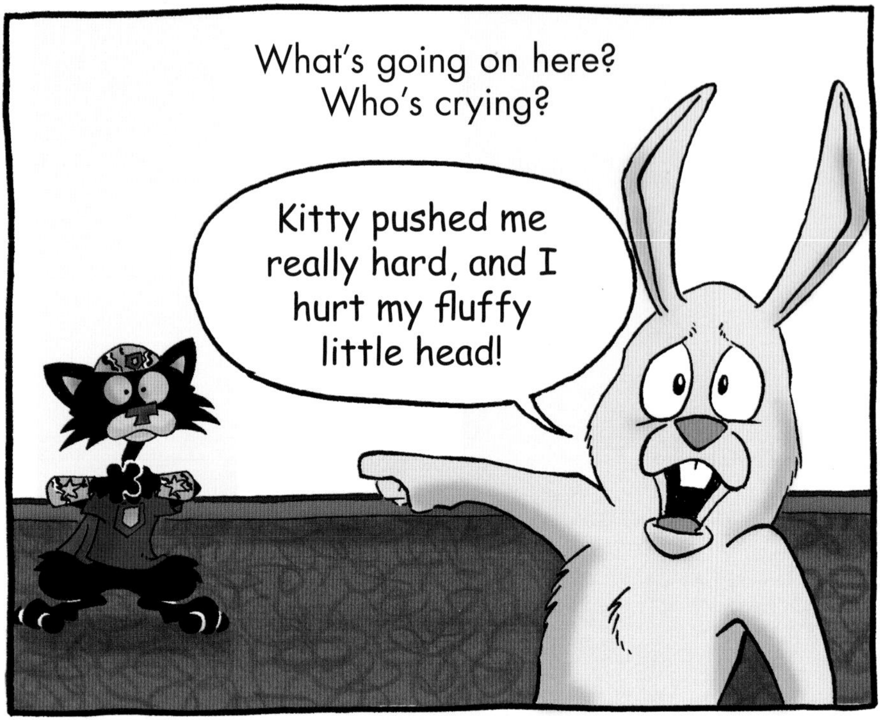
What's going on here?
Who's crying?
Kitty pushed me really hard, and I hurt my fluffy little head!

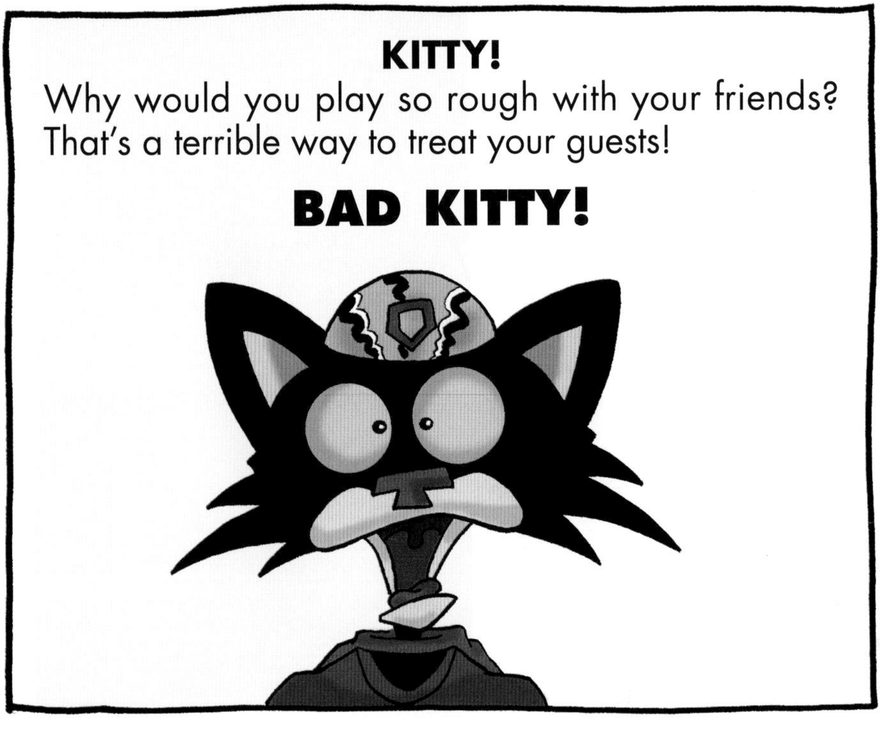
KITTY!
Why would you play so rough with your friends?
That's a terrible way to treat your guests!
BAD KITTY!

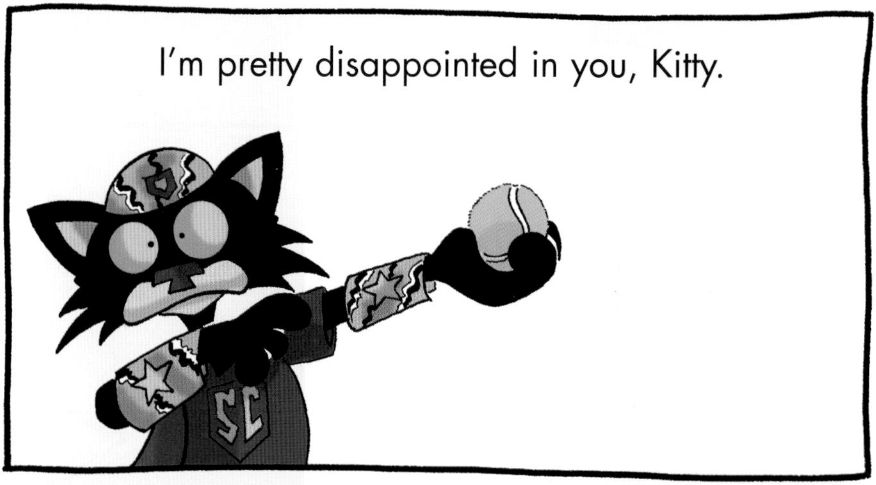
I'm pretty disappointed in you, Kitty.

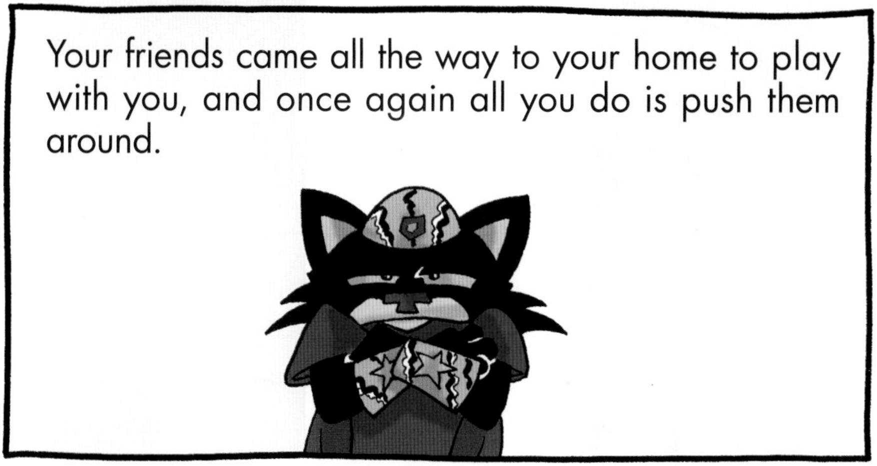
Your friends came all the way to your home to play with you, and once again all you do is push them around.

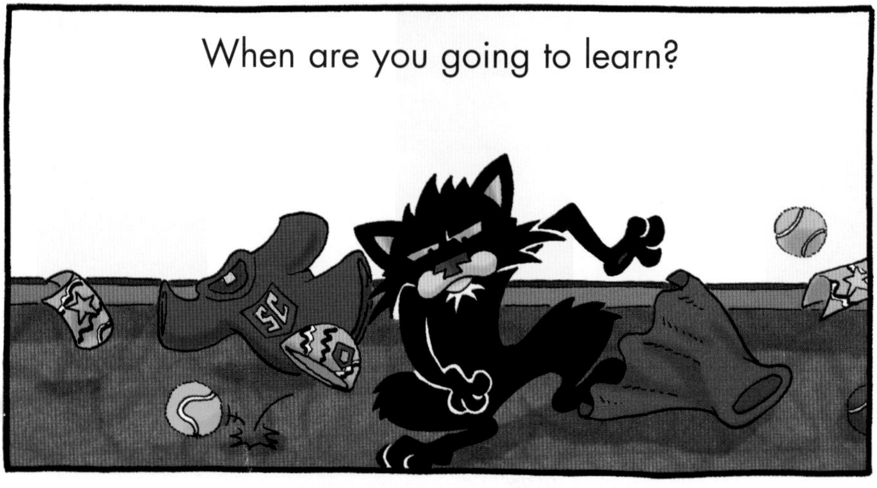
When are you going to learn?

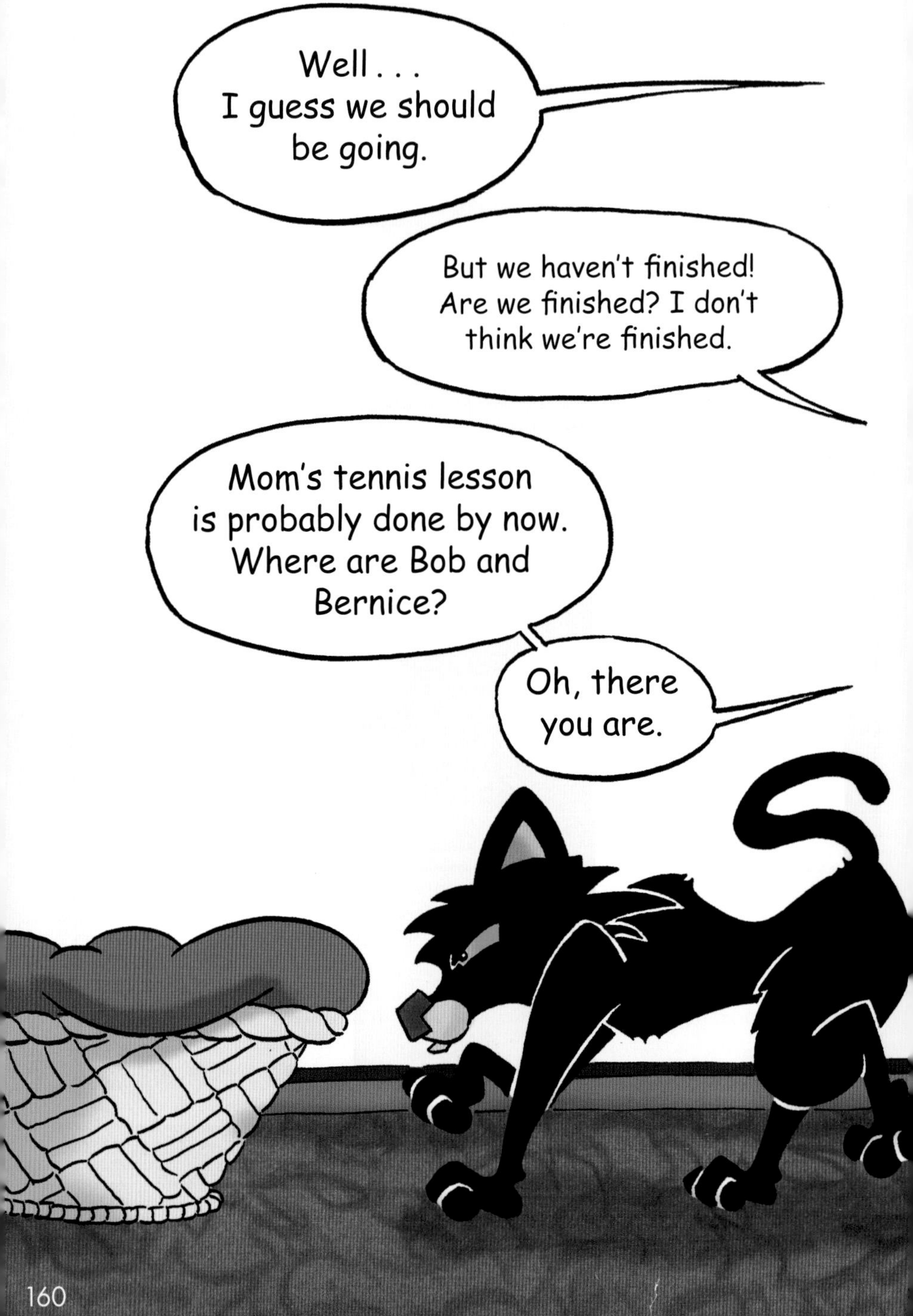
Well . . .
I guess we should
be going.
But we haven't finished!
Are we finished? I don't
think we're finished.
Mom's tennis lesson
is probably done by now.
Where are Bob and
Bernice?
Oh, there
you are.

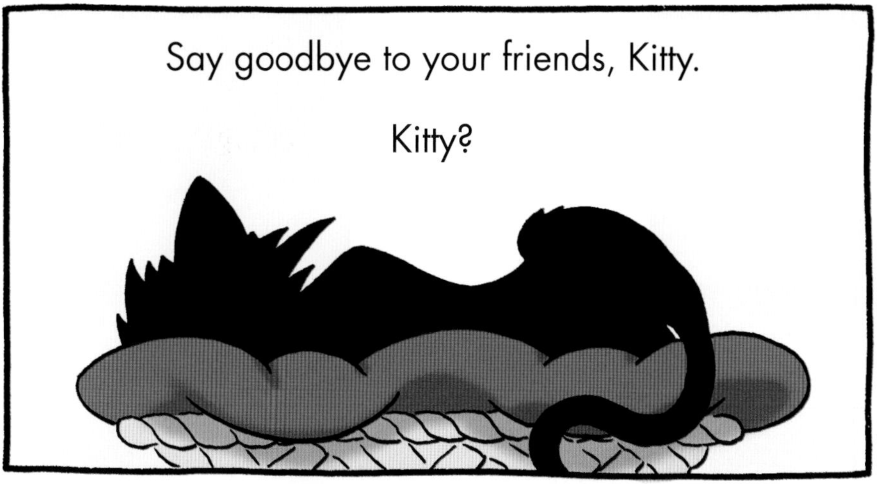
Say goodbye to your friends, Kitty.
Kitty?

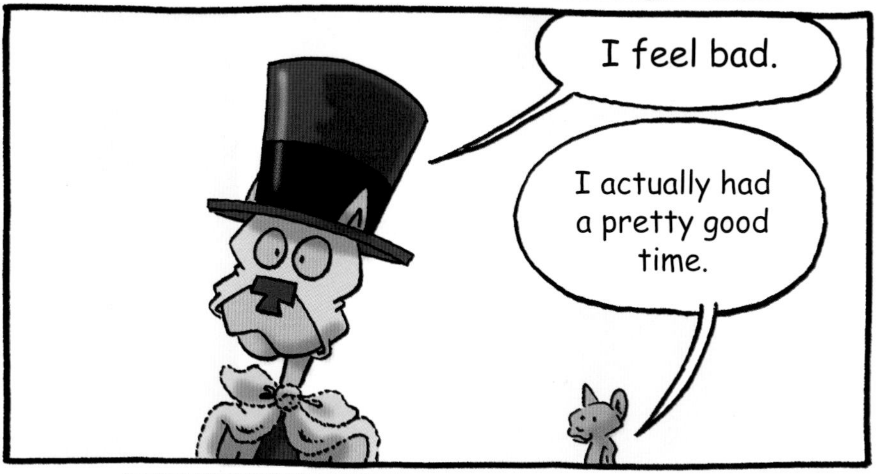
I feel bad.
I actually had a pretty good time.

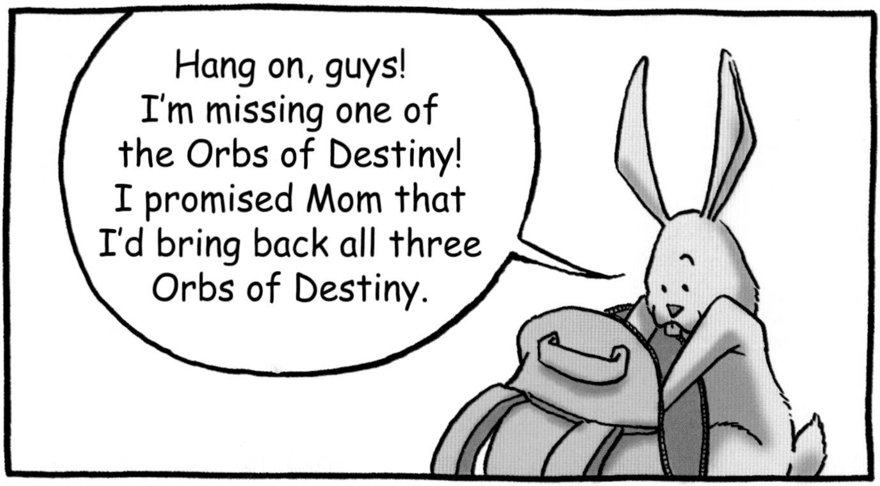
Hang on, guys! I'm missing one of the Orbs of Destiny! I promised Mom that I'd bring back all three Orbs of Destiny.

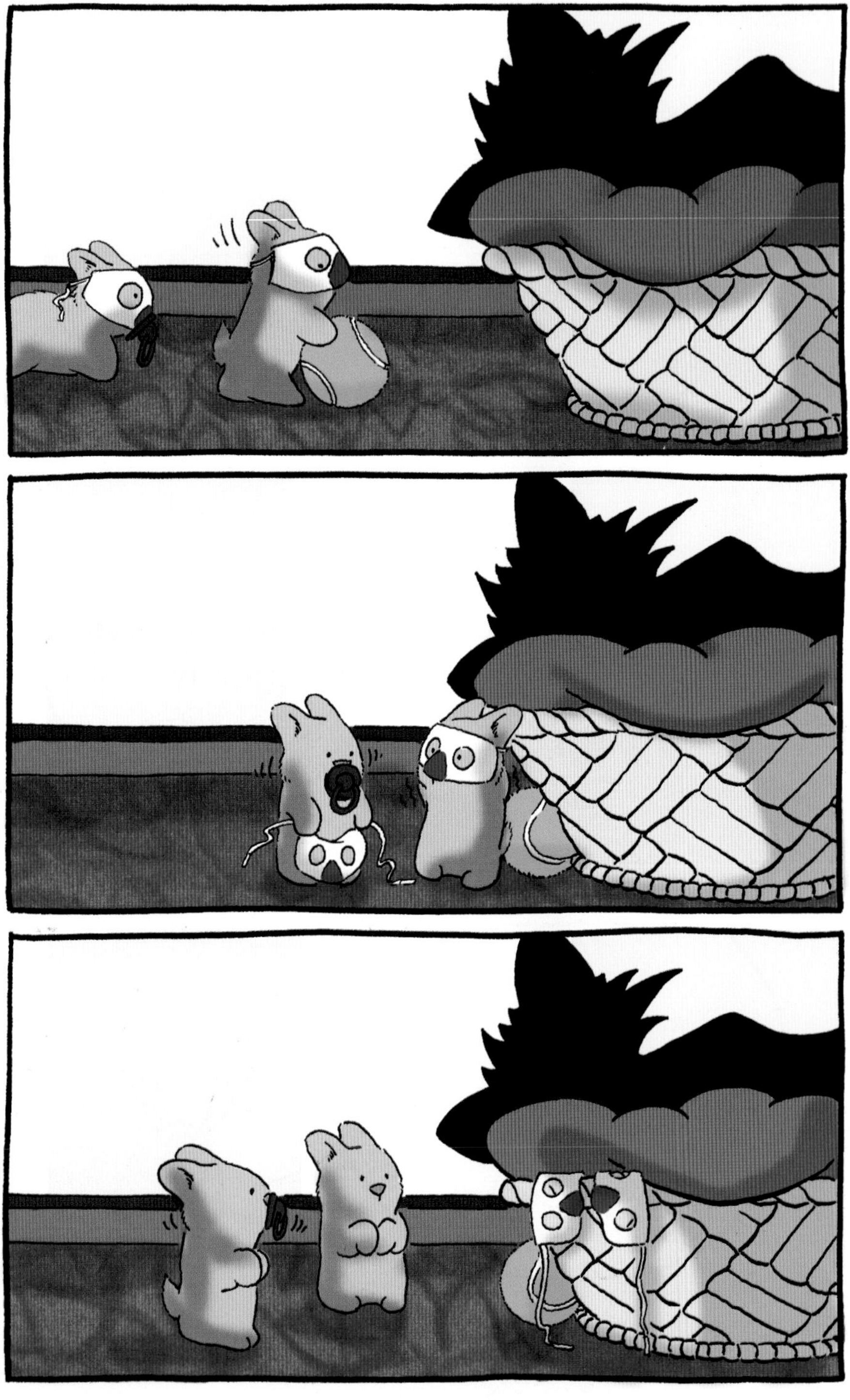

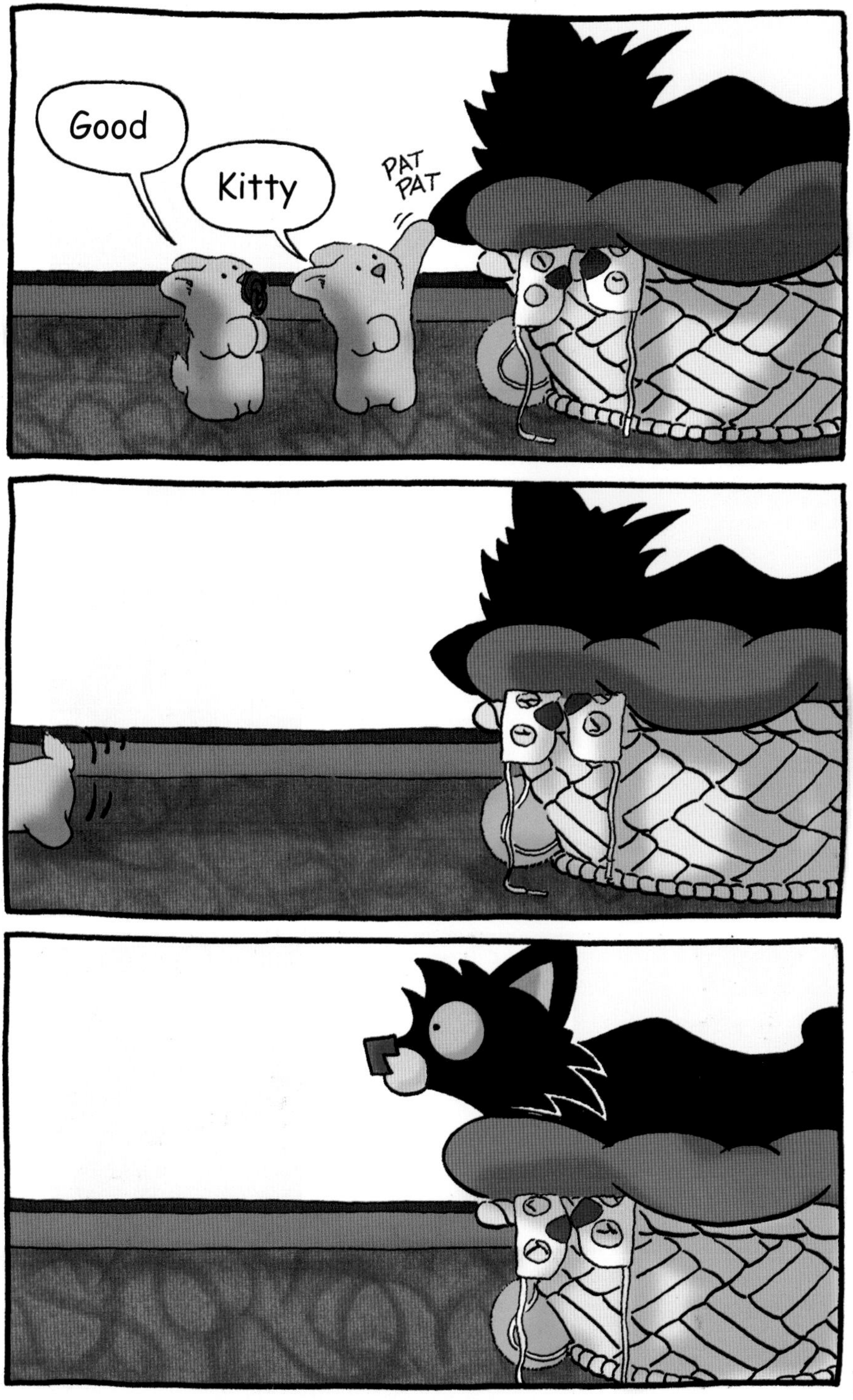
Good
Kitty
PAT PAT

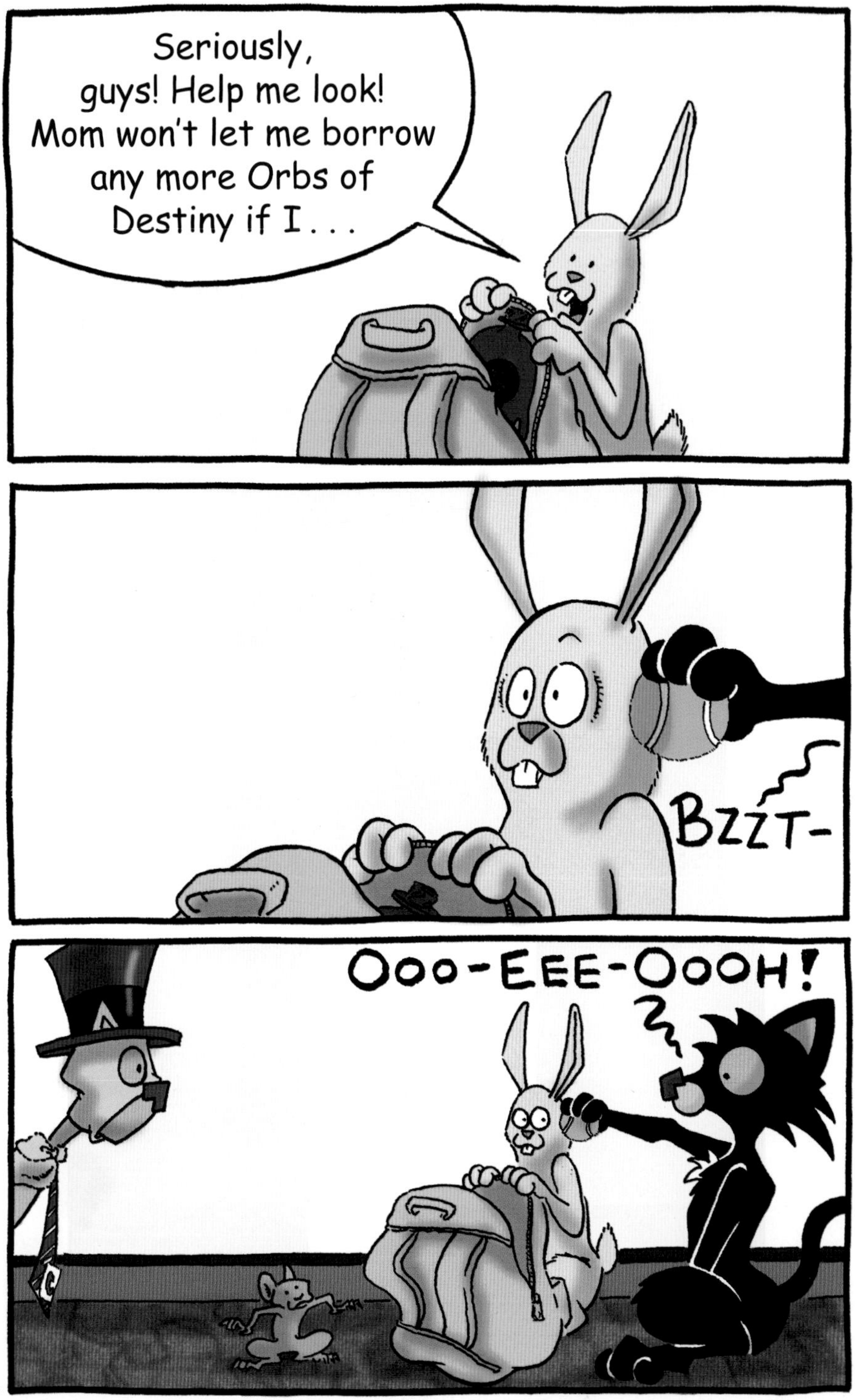
Seriously, guys! Help me look! Mom won't let me borrow any more Orbs of Destiny if I . . .
BZZT-
OOO-EEE-OOOH!

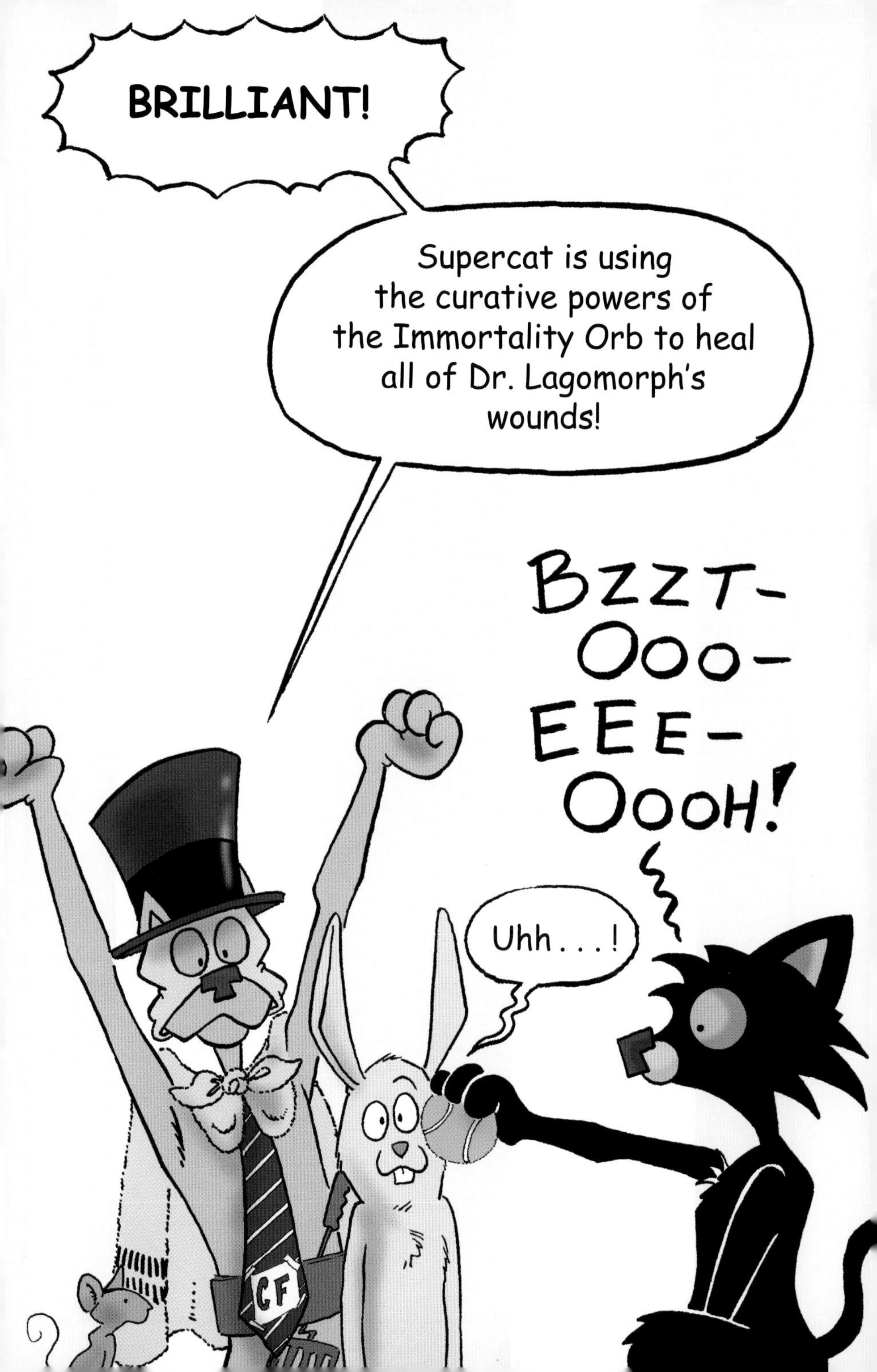
BRILLIANT!
Supercat is using the curative powers of the Immortality Orb to heal all of Dr. Lagomorph's wounds!
BZZT-OOO-EEE-OOOH!
Uhh. . . !
CF

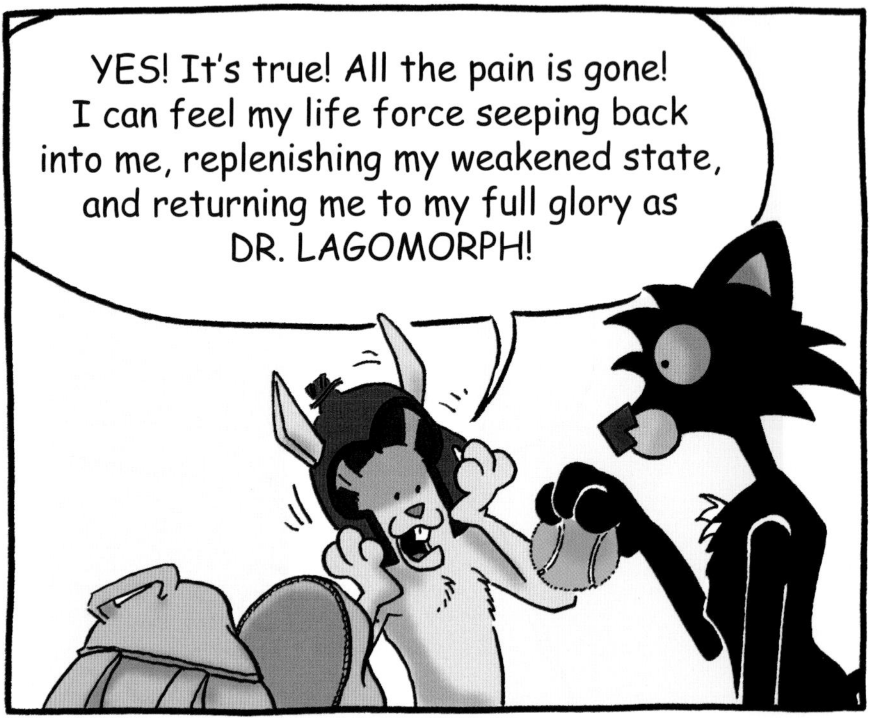
YES! It's true! All the pain is gone! I can feel my life force seeping back into me, replenishing my weakened state, and returning me to my full glory as DR. LAGOMORPH!

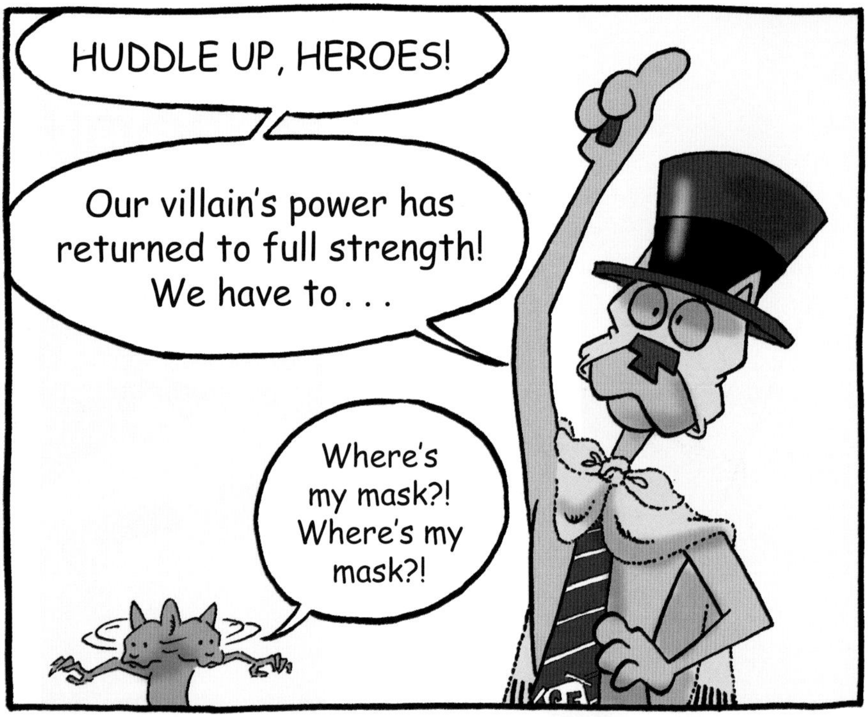
HUDDLE UP, HEROES!
Our villain's power has returned to full strength! We have to . . .
Where's my mask?! Where's my mask?!

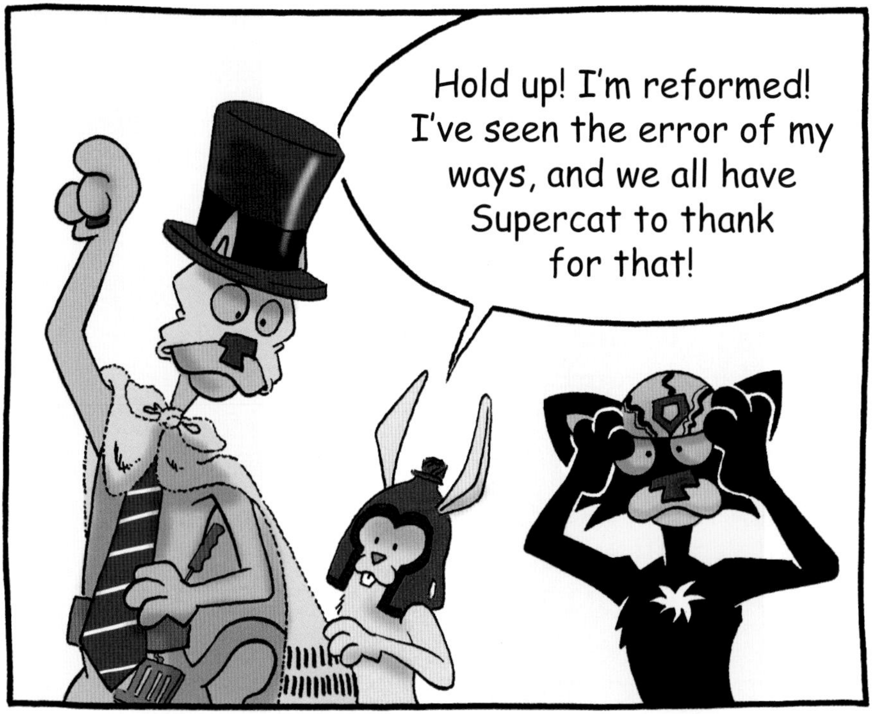
Hold up! I'm reformed! I've seen the error of my ways, and we all have Supercat to thank for that!

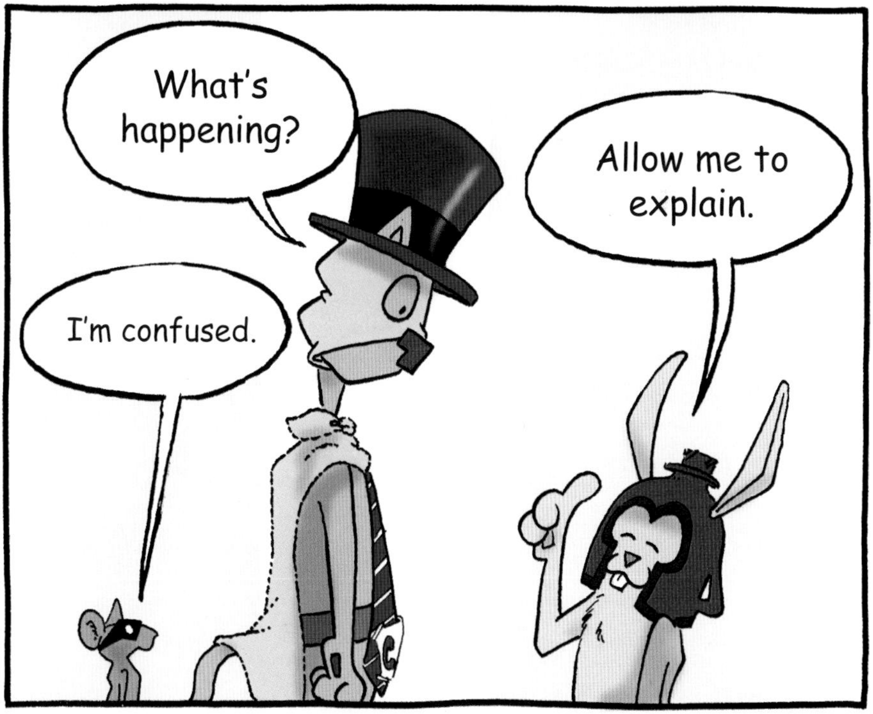
What's happening?
I'm confused.
Allow me to explain.

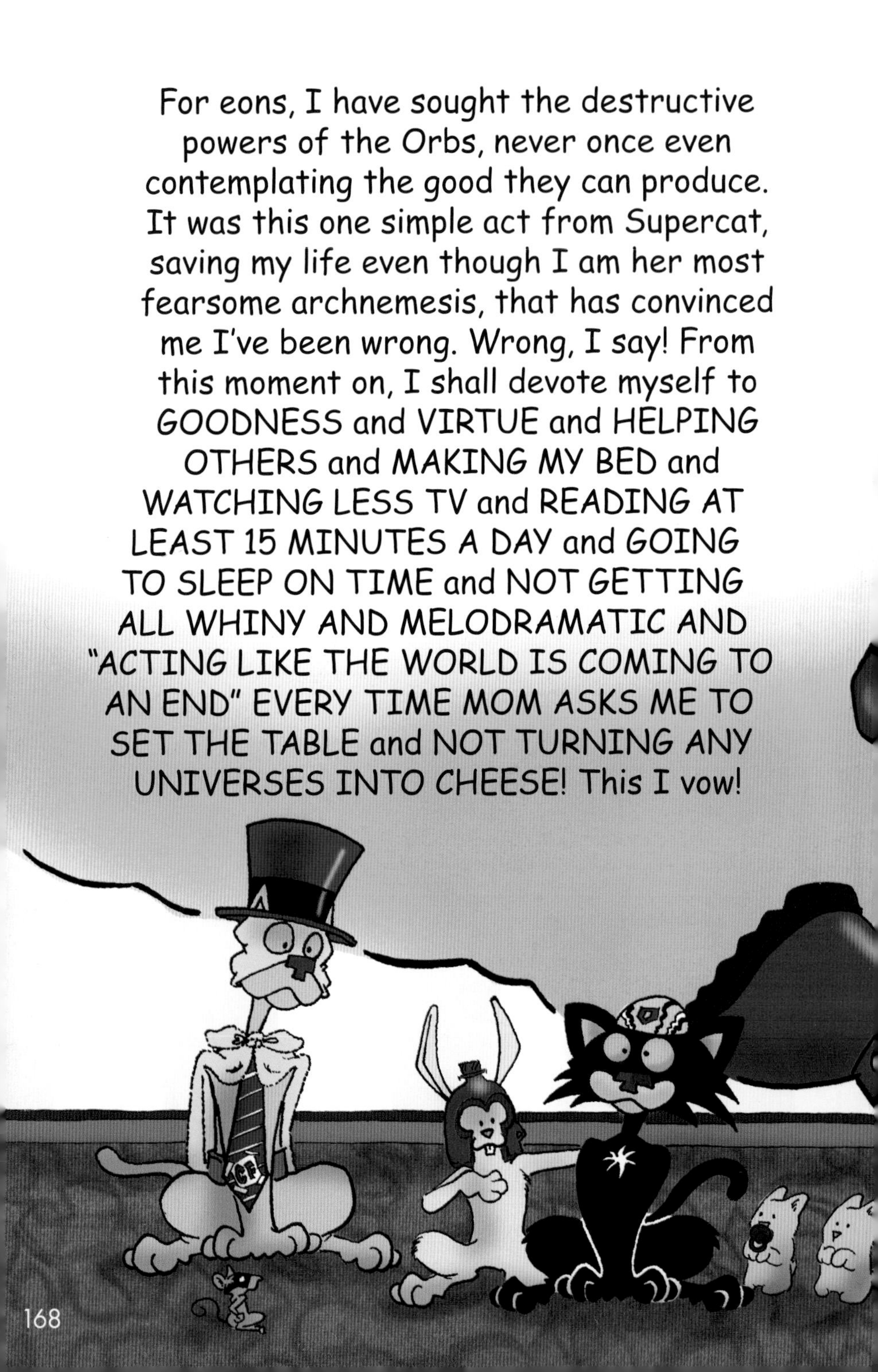
For eons, I have sought the destructive powers of the Orbs, never once even contemplating the good they can produce. It was this one simple act from Supercat, saving my life even though I am her most fearsome archnemesis, that has convinced me I've been wrong. Wrong, I say! From this moment on, I shall devote myself to GOODNESS and VIRTUE and HELPING OTHERS and MAKING MY BED and WATCHING LESS TV and READING AT LEAST 15 MINUTES A DAY and GOING TO SLEEP ON TIME and NOT GETTING ALL WHINY AND MELODRAMATIC AND "ACTING LIKE THE WORLD IS COMING TO AN END" EVERY TIME MOM ASKS ME TO SET THE TABLE and NOT TURNING ANY UNIVERSES INTO CHEESE! This I vow!

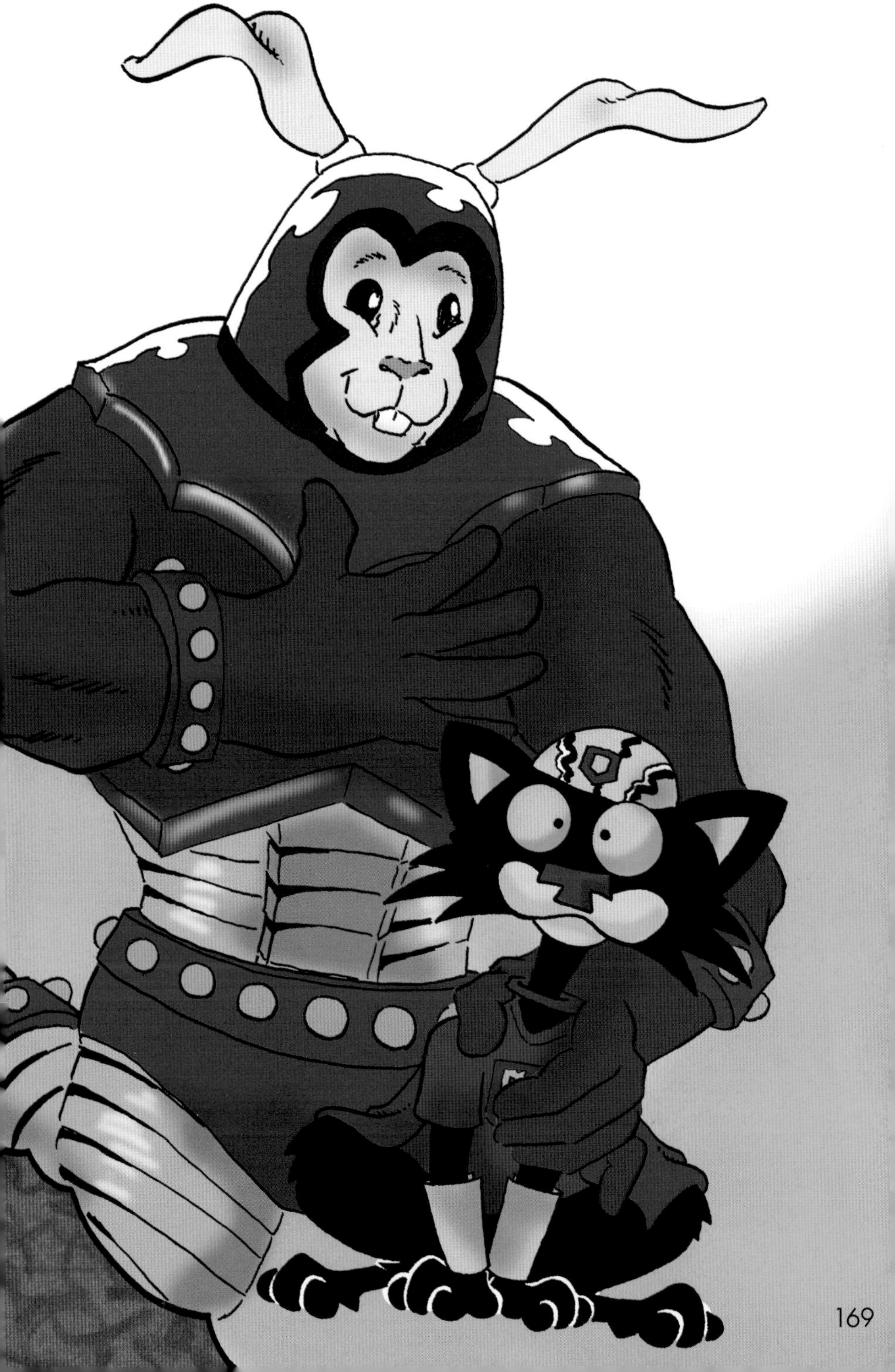

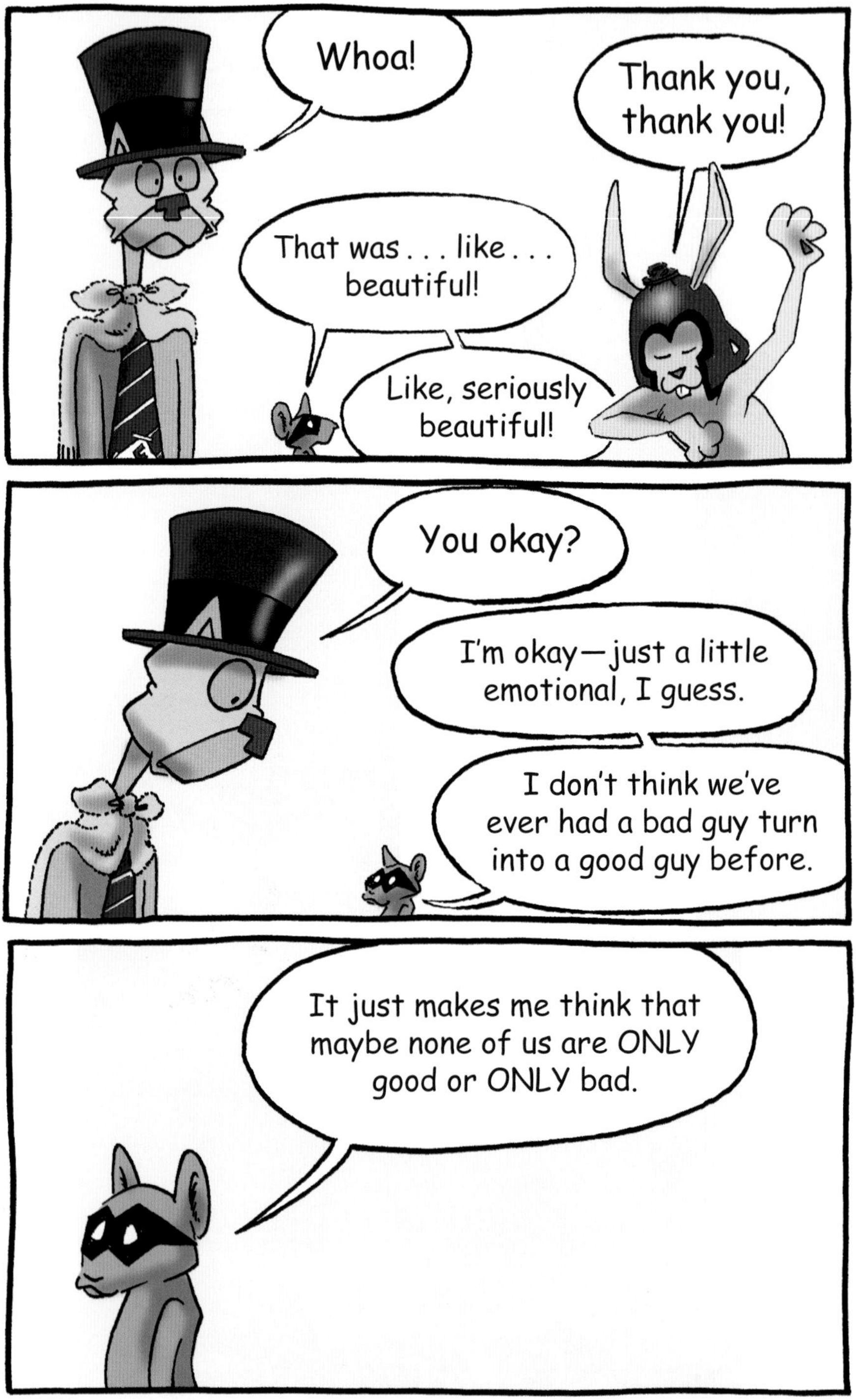
Whoa!
Thank you, thank you!
That was . . . like . . . beautiful!
Like, seriously beautiful!
You okay?
I'm okay—just a little emotional, I *guess*.
I don't think we've ever had a bad guy turn into a good guy before.
It just makes me think that maybe none of us are ONLY good or ONLY bad.

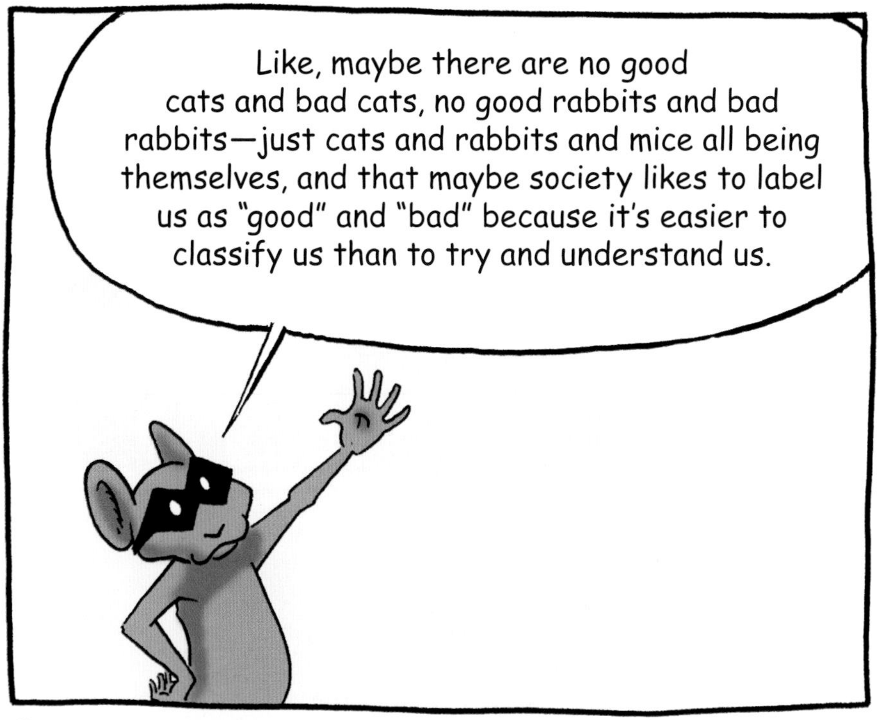
Like, maybe there are no good cats and bad cats, no good rabbits and bad rabbits—just cats and rabbits and mice all being themselves, and that maybe society likes to label us as "good" and "bad" because it's easier to classify us than to try and understand us.

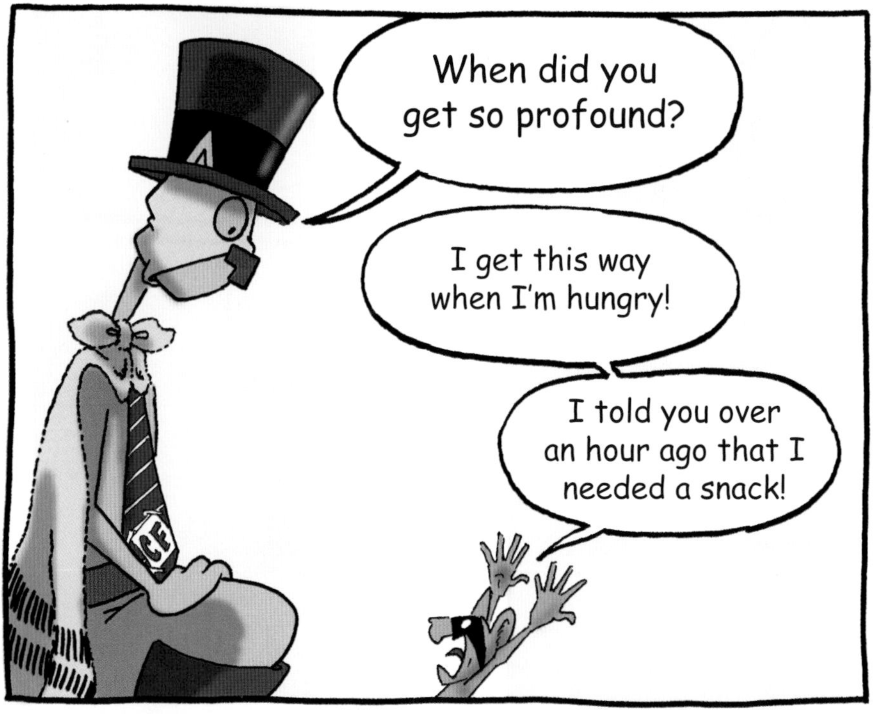
When did you get so profound?
I get this way when I'm hungry!
I told you over an hour ago that I needed a snack!

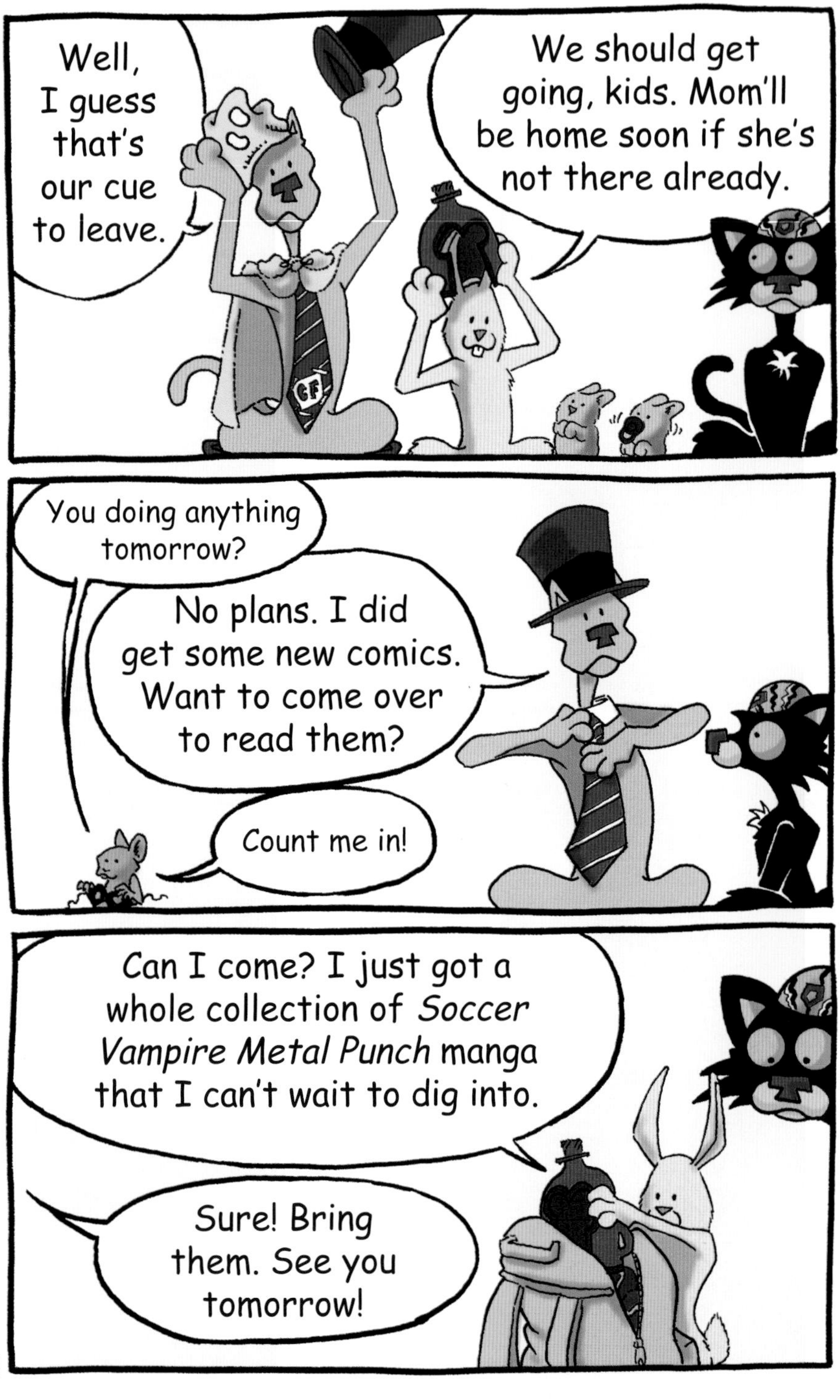
Well, I guess that's our cue to leave.
We should get going, kids. Mom'll be home soon if she's not there already.
You doing anything tomorrow?
No plans. I did get some new comics. Want to come over to read them?
Count me in!
Can I come? I just got a whole collection of *Soccer Vampire Metal Punch* manga that I can't wait to dig into.
Sure! Bring them. See you tomorrow!

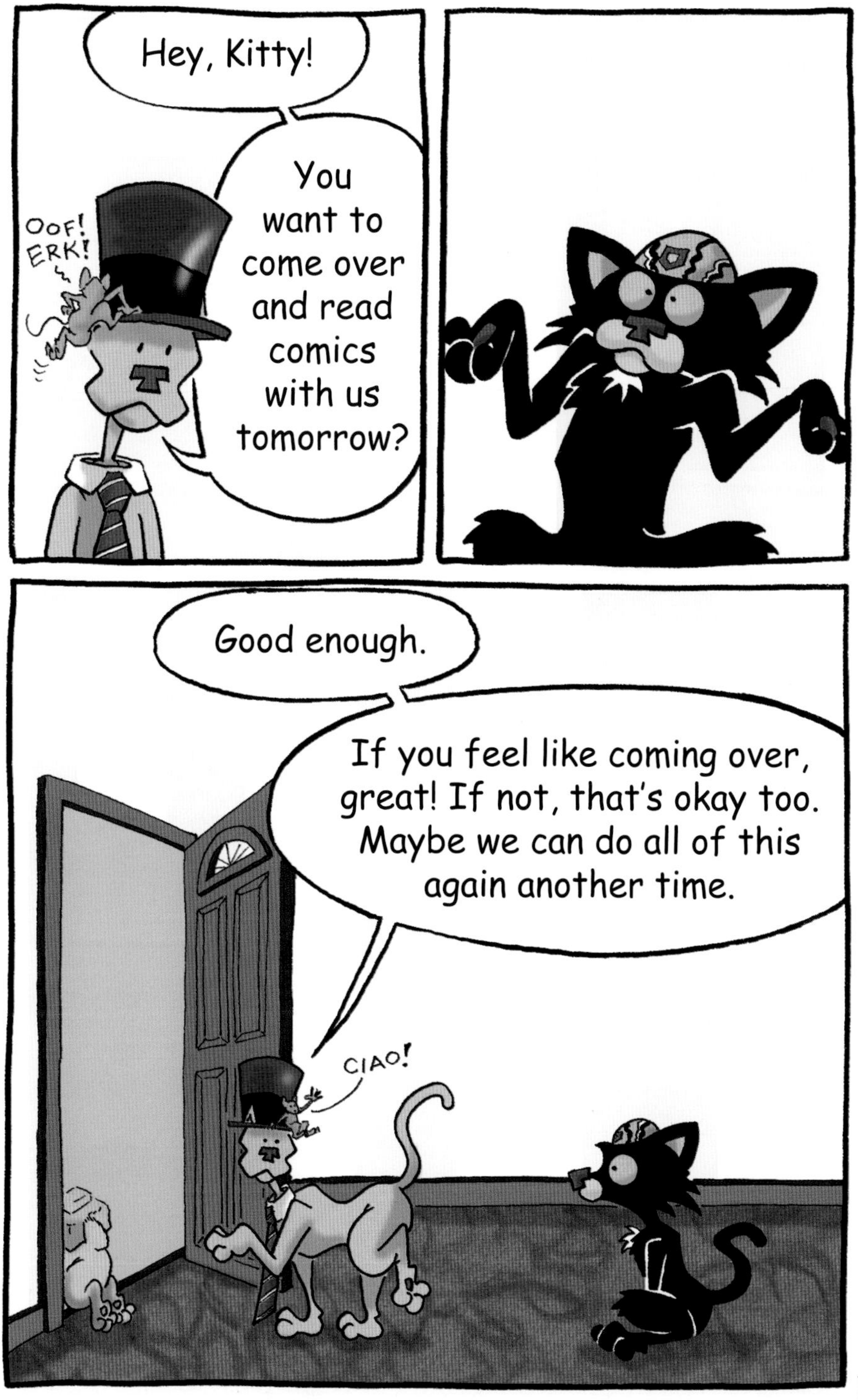
Hey, Kitty!
You want to come over and read comics with us tomorrow?
OOF! ERK!
Good enough.
If you feel like coming over, great! If not, that's okay too. Maybe we can do all of this again another time.
CIAO!

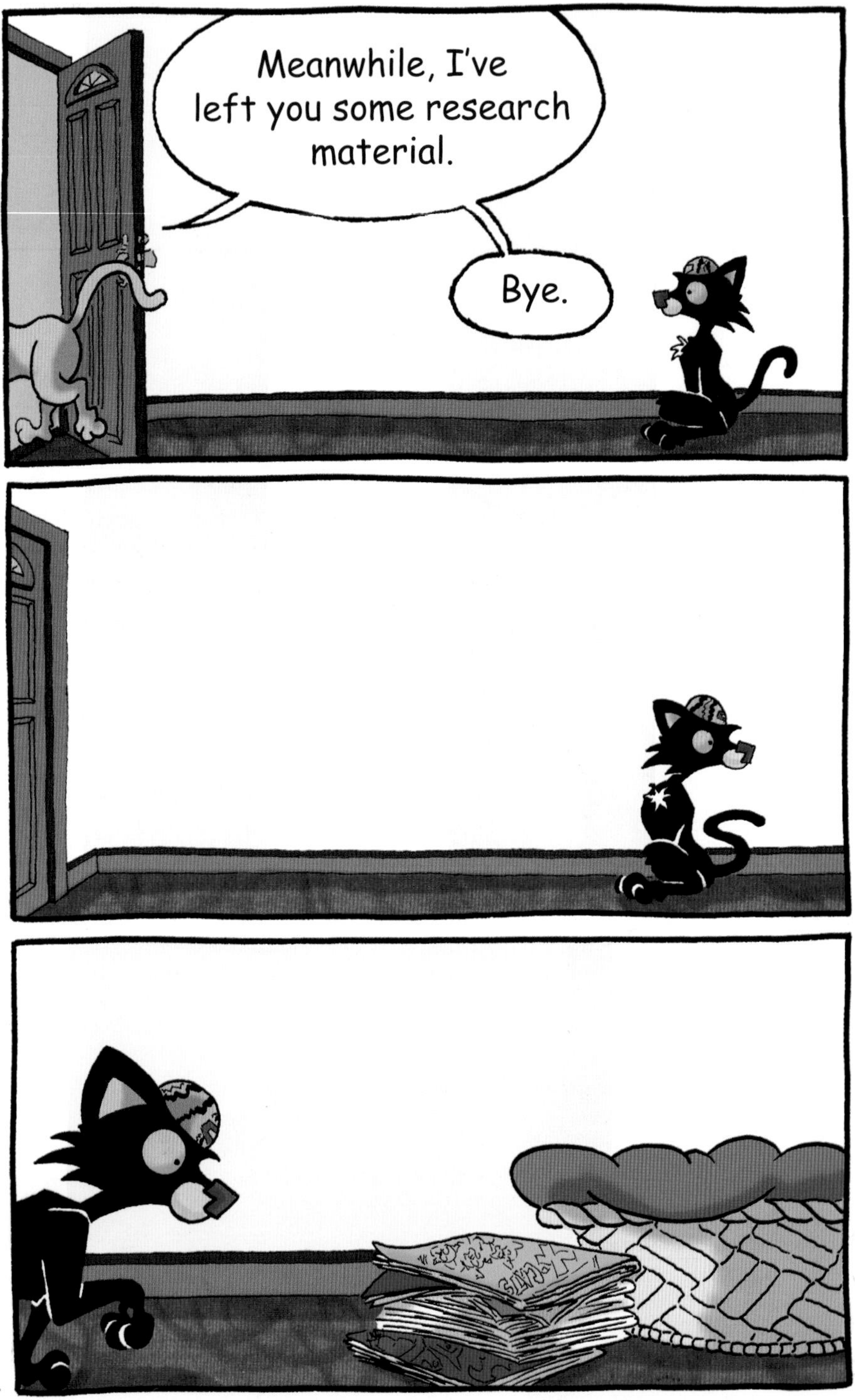
Meanwhile, I've left you some research material.
Bye.

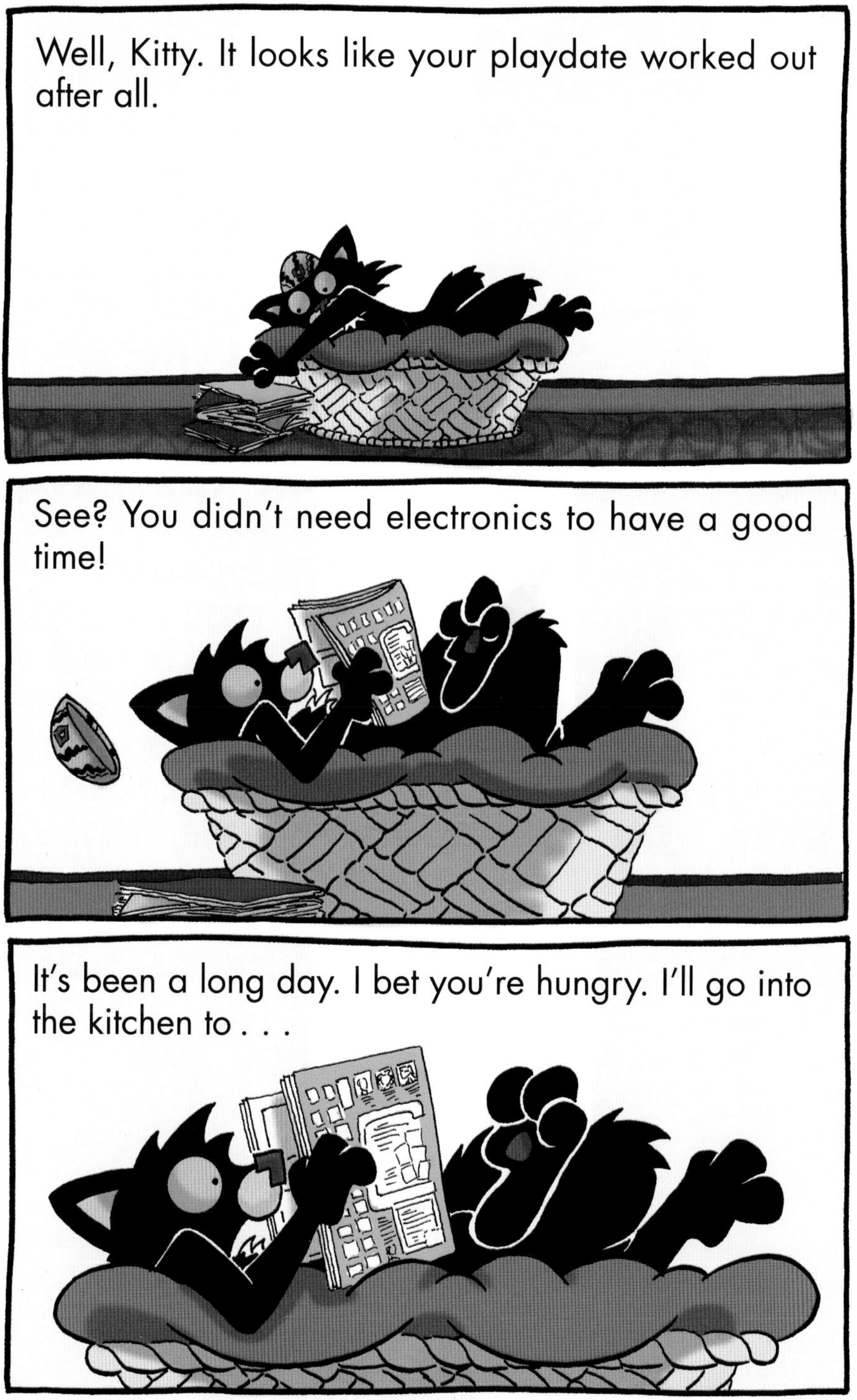
Well, Kitty. It looks like your playdate worked out after all.
See? You didn't need electronics to have a good time!
It's been a long day. I bet you're hungry. I'll go into the kitchen to . . .

HOLY SALAMI!

KITTY! WHY IS EVERYTHING IN THE KITCHEN PULLED OUT OF THE DRAWERS AND CABINETS AND ALL OVER THE FLOOR?! WHAT ELSE DID YOU AND YOUR FRIENDS. . . HOLY SALAMI! WHY DOES THE BASEMENT LOOK LIKE A CATEGORY 1 MILLION HURRICANE BLEW THROUGH HERE?! DO I EVEN WANT TO KNOW WHAT YOU DID IN THE BACK YARD?! HOLY SALAMI! WHO LEFT THE HOSE RUNNING AND FLOODED EVERYTHING?! WHY DOES THIS WHOLE HOUSE LOOK LIKE A SHIPWRECK AFTER I SPENT THE ENTIRE MORNING CLEANING IT?! AND WHY ARE THERE RABBIT DROPPINGS ALL OVER THE PLACE?! I'M GLAD YOU HAD A GOOD TIME, KITTY, BUT LOOK AT THIS PLACE! JUST LOOK AT THIS PLACE! YOU'VE GOT ANOTHER THING COMING IF YOU THINK THAT I'M GOING TO CLEAN THIS ALL UP BY MYSELF. KITTY! HAVE YOU HEARD A SINGLE WORD THAT I'VE SAID? KITTY! DON'T IGNORE ME! ARE YOU